VENGEANCE

OF THE **FORGOTTEN**

GODDESS

Rebekah Sinclair

Rebekah Sinclair

WARNING: This book contains content that may be triggering.

- Mentions and depicts mental health trauma responses such as anxiety, PTSD, and panic attack disorder.
- Depicts non-consensual sexual content and sexual assault such as non-consensual oral sex.
- Mentions and depicts graphic violence leading to death.
- Mentions and depicts child endangerment, abuse and death.
- Contains explicit language, sexual content, physical violence, abduction, and death.

To: Every Forgotten Goddess

When you remembered who you were...
...and the game changed.

Enjoy listening to Vengeance Of The Forgotten Goddess playlist on Spotify!

A song has been added for each chapter to represent the tones or themes of the chapter.

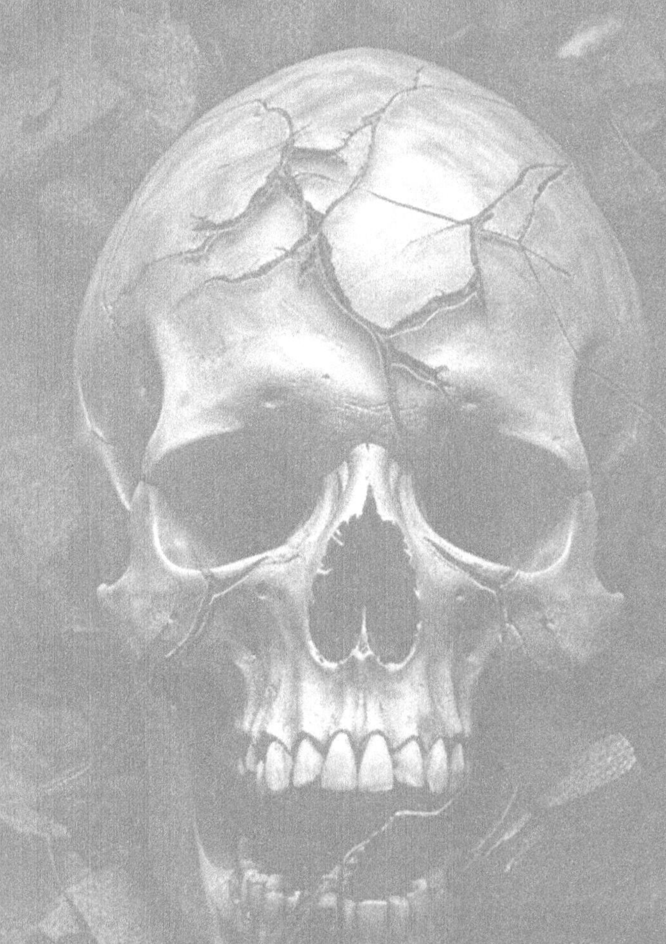

ACT I

THE PROCESSION OF THE SIREN

I *wonder if dying feels like flying.* What a ridiculous notion. It seems like lifetimes ago that a naive part of me stood in a bookstore, daydreaming about winged beasts of ancient mythology, and fantasizing about death.

I've died a thousand times, but it never felt like this.

Death is a sweet embrace, like a silk scarf slipping from your grasp and drifting away on an ocean breeze. Or like finally letting go at the end of the night and fading off to sleep. This is pain, raw and fracturing.

I knew going to Tartarus was dangerous. I knew Ares would be watching, waiting for me to return, likely hoping I would find the power he has craved since first meeting me. I knew we would lose lives.

But I never—never once—questioned who would be here waiting for me when I stepped off the crimson desert dunes of Tartarus, returning to Gaea. My powers sense every life standing on the golden sands of the Sahara, yet I look for her.

"Where is Callie?" My throat tightens as I scan the battle-worn crowd. "Hermes..."

"Rhea," Hermes covers his mouth, choking on his sorrow. Tears well in his navy eyes. "It was the wards."

No.

No, please, goddess of mercy, don't let this be true.

But my soul knows the reality my mind rejects. My heart splinters, and a piece of it falls into the dark abyss, never to be repaired. And this is what living feels like. Pieces of yourself break away with pain and loss until death's sweet caress offers final salvation. The souls of Achilles and Calypso are no longer tethered to this realm.

I close my eyes, trying to shut the world away, willing this moment to move backward. I want to feel the warmth of her yellow aura brush against my skin. But there is nothing.

She was supposed to be here when I got back.

I was going to tell her everything that happened on Tartarus. We were going to eat popcorn and laugh about the filthy Harpy King that she would have slaughtered the second his clawed feet touched the crimson sand. She would have listened closely as I told her of the Dune Sea and the pegasus. Callie would have shed a tear for the trials of the cyclopes and the loss of Nocturna.

"Bring me back a souvenir," she said to me with a smile and a wink. I didn't even answer her.

My hand instinctively covers the pocket holding the two medallions of red dandelions. I was going to make a necklace from them so we could each wear one.

Another piece of my heart crumbles into nothing.

I should have said something. I should have said goodbye.

Dropping to my knees, I hit the hot sand with a thud. The wind mourns the loss of its temptress. The billowing sorrow swirls in the currents, lifting my hair with it.

My breaths are shallow as my tears plop onto the sand.

Thoughts have stopped running through my mind, leaving it as empty as my body is numb.

I sense Hermes kneel next to me. His hand lingers, a slight tremble in his fingertips before he places it on my shoulder with a squeeze. I hold onto him with both hands, praying to every star that burns in the night sky that I'm dreaming. That Hermes is here to wake me up and pull me from this nightmare.

I've scoured every face on the battlefield, and the last tether of my desperation turns me around. It feels as if I'm not in control of my movements. Like someone else is animating me and shifting me around the Sahara sands.

The ancient library looms at the edges of my vision, and the flicker of a burning flame makes my stomach drop. Maybe that is Achilles, and I am wrong. I watch with wide eyes, holding my breath as bodies walk down the slope from Alexandria's large doors to the sand below.

I stare at the woman leading the procession.

Daphne.

Hermes' mother is alive.

Around me, immortals chatter and breathe heavily after the exhaustive fight they just survived. My mind is nothing more than a hollow pit of longing, and the noise around me is muted, muffled as if I'm submerged underwater.

The world zeroes in on the long-lost woman who meant so much to me, carrying a book in her arms. If she is still alive, Callie can be too. Maybe if I convince myself of the lie, it will come true.

Daphne looks exactly as I recall her from my memories. Long, wavy hair the color of raven's wings blows to the side as she walks with stoic purpose. Her deep purple stola billows and catches around her sandaled feet with each step. The book she carries is thick, clutched close to her chest like a treasure. The ivory leather binding and gold-capped corners remind me of Callie.

Walking in step behind Daphne, two long rows of Librarians emerge from the ancient building for the first time in millennia. Tall and imposing, these beings move with a graceful, almost imperceptible motion as they glide down the ramp. The thick brown robes they wear barely register the faint breeze.

The Librarians resemble towering trees, their skin the color of aged driftwood. Their oblong heads are smooth and featureless, save for deep black void eyes. Without noses or mouths, their faces remain mysterious and unreadable.

The two directly behind Daphne carry torches. One torch still blazes with an orange flame dancing in the breeze. The other torch seems to have been extinguished long ago, waiting for its companion to finally be snuffed out.

The symbolism of the torches is not lost on me, and my eyes begin to burn. Clutching my throat as it tightens, I blink quickly, forcing myself to take a labored breath.

Reaching the base of the ramp, Daphne stops, and the procession behind her does as well. I watch a lone tear roll down her cheek, and for some reason, it breaks the last of my denial. A deep crevasse opens down the center of my heart.

She holds her chin high and takes a deep breath before speaking. "Immortals of Gaea,"

I cover my mouth at the sound of her voice, a familiar stranger I've not heard in so long, echoing across the desert. Hermes' grip on my shoulder tightens as he takes a sharp breath, as if waiting to see if the vision of his mother is real or a cruel mirage.

"We must all bear witness, for the procession of the siren." Daphne holds the book flat before her. A third Librarian behind her moves from their position. "The twin Titans of Hesperides perished before renaming their apprentice. But the magic and might of the Titans are bestowed by the realms, as is the honor of apprentice."

Daphne's warm eyes roam over the gathering, pausing on Hermes and me. The heartbreak in the crinkle of her eyes and the furrow in her brow is barely perceptible but present all the same.

"Though never named, Calypso commanded the winds with honor and valor. It is with her death that we honor the apprentice of Hesperides, the Temptress of the Four Winds, and bid her and her mate a happy rest within the Void of Souls."

Daphne bows her head, her chin quivering as she struggles to hold back her sorrow. The Librarian pulls a long golden key from their robes and inserts it. Turning the key, a loud click reverberates across the atmosphere, adding a heavy finality to this new reality.

The story of Calypso has been told, and the book of her life closes forever.

"No." I beg, as if speaking my plea will make any difference.

The Librarian returns to their position in the procession. The two torchbearers raise their torches. The single lit flame sways eagerly in the breeze, unaware that the soul it represents is no longer alive.

The cold, blackened torch embodies the spirit of Patroclus. The second–Achilles. The mates of the Temptress, honored as they walked beside her in life. The flame of Achilles, who also walked beside her in death, is ready to be extinguished to rest with his mates."

Zephyr steps forward first, followed by a dozen Wind Sirens who stand shoulder-to-shoulder. The mournful currents swell low to the ground. With the rise of their arms, the Sirens call upon their element, and it obeys their request with reluctant obedience.

In a spiral around the bodies of the Librarians, the wind snuffs out the remaining torch. The embers of the eternal flame that burned alongside the book of Calypso rise into the skies.

I follow the glowing cinders until I lose them in the sunlight. Blinking, tears fall down my cheeks.

When I look back, the procession of Librarians is returning up the ramp, but Daphne lingers at the bottom, meeting my stare. The book is no longer in her hands and is being returned to the great library.

"What happened?" I can only muster a weak whisper, but it feels like it carries across the desert for miles like a scream. Still kneeling on the sand, I place my hands on the grit of the Sahara and squeeze two fistfuls as hard as I can. I want to feel it.

I want to feel anything but this numbing emptiness within me.

Just as I witnessed the echo of New York's destruction, I call upon the stolen essence of Sensory within me. The residue of the battle's emotions drowns me.

"Don't go back there, sweet girl." Daphne speaks into my mind, offering me a warning.

"I have to."

I have to know. I need to know how it happened and if she

was in pain. A sob breaks from my throat, and I stifle it with my hand. What if she suffered? I can't stand the idea of her hurting, lying on the sand and bleeding out.

Finding my footing, my legs move of their own accord to the bloody battlefield behind us.

My powers flare around me, and the echo of the fight under the eclipse plays out at my command.

A large dome seals off half the army that fought here moments ago. I watch as the ghostly memory of Hermes assaults Ares and his dark legion of warriors. Viewing the battle through the Sensory lens, I see the tormented God of War and prisoners forced to be his army.

The pain of their captivity ripples off them like heat waves distorting the atmosphere. I close my eyes to make the vision go away. Hermes couldn't see the lie. He had no idea who he was really fighting.

He has no idea.

As I pull on the fluid streams of the battle's emotions, I hear the clashing weapons and the discharge of elemental powers. I hear her as she fights, somewhere in this replaying vision of the past.

Turning swiftly, my hair swirls with my movements, and I brush it out of my face as I search for them. All around me, the echoes of the fight rage on, just as it did during the eclipse when I was traversing Tartarus. I see the sky darken as the moon passes before the sun. Powers swell as immortals clash and rage around me.

Then I find her. A gasp escapes me.

Her long hair, held in a tight ponytail on top of her head, swings with her powerful movements. Callie's face is firm and resolute as she battles with Achilles close by her side. Their movements seem almost tied together, fighting as one to protect and defend each other.

The eclipse fades away, and the last sliver of moon bids goodbye to the bright sun. Hermes and Callie pause, knowing my fate was sealed behind the wards.

The whisper of Hermes' resolve wraps around me as he prepares to die. So sure, in his path, he doesn't hear the dragon's blast against the wards. From Tartarus, the Titan essence of his power joins me in a relentless assault against the closed portal, fighting with desperation to open it again.

The residue of our battering still lingers high above us as I observe the echoes of the fight. *"Gods, please, someone help me."* My prayer from Tartarus resounds through the atmosphere, bouncing off everything and slamming into me. *What if I cause this?*

Could Callie hear me and thought she needed to answer my plea with her life?

A swell of frosted green wafts within the dark clouds, and my mouth gapes open as I stare at it. Seeing with the eyes of Death, the silhouette of Patroclus stands within the storm.

Long dead from the Battle of Troy, he is now pure energy and light. Yet, I see him all the same. Even knowing this is just a memory, I raise my hand. I reach out as if I could touch him, as if he were still here to answer me.

Something happens, drawing the attention of Callie and Achilles to the sky.

Everything slows down as I watch her death unfold around me, unable to stop or change the outcome racing toward me. Recognition burns brightly in their eyes, and the mates decide what they must do. They say goodbye to Hermes, and I feel his heart shatter just as mine is now.

I sense the war within him as he contemplates dropping the dome and releasing the Shades and Dark Mages upon the others or holding back Ares' forces. Protectiveness flares within him, and he holds back Ares' forces within his cage of light.

Clutching my chest, I grab at my shirt, trying to loosen it and give myself more air, but it's pointless. All the wind of the realm died with Calypso, and I'm suffocating without her.

As the dragon and I pound on the wards from Tartarus, Callie and Achilles ascend into the clouds. They hold their bond within their embrace, and I watch as the light of Patroclus encases them. Blazing with Achilles' fire and eroded away by Calypso's winds, the mates enter the Void in an explosion of power that dismantles the wards.

Like a glass ceiling shattering, I watch the particles of sunlight and fire burst and rain down to earth. Holding out my hand, I sense the power that was used to erect them so long ago. It's the same power that was used to destroy them today: the unbreakable power of a mating bond.

Collapsing again, I rest my head against the hot sand and cry. Coughing and sputtering, I inhale the grit of the desert and choke on it.

"I need to get out of here." I claw at the collar of my shirt and grab a fistful of sand with the other. I can't spend another second in the graveyard from the eclipse's battle. Not knowing where I'm going, the swirl of my portal opens, and I run away from the suffocation of the desert.

The wind whispers through the wildflowers, carrying a scent that should be sweet, but it tastes of grief on my tongue. I collapse onto the soft ground, the vibrant blooms bending beneath my weight. My hands tremble as I press them into the dirt, grounding myself, trying to catalog the trials of Tartarus against the heavy weight of grief that collapsed on me as I returned to Gaea.

My breaths come in ragged sobs, each one tearing through me with the ferocity of the battles that took place. But it's not my own near death that haunts me; it's the loss of Calypso. She sacrificed everything to ensure my escape. Her laughter, bright and unyielding, echoes in my mind—a joyful sound that will forever be silenced.

I curl up, pulling my knees to my chest, allowing the tears to flow unchecked. I knew the risks when I left; we all knew the risks. But knowing did not prepare me for the reality her absence would bring. And with her went Achilles, their destinies entwined even in death. The thought of them, forever gone from this world, is a weight too heavy to bear, and I collapse under it.

The sky above me darkens, clouds rolling in as though even

the heavens mourn their sacrifice. A gentle hand touches my shoulder, and I flinch, unprepared for the contact. But when I look up, it's Hermes who kneels beside me, his eyes a mirror of my pain.

"Rhea," he whispers, his voice thick with emotion. The usual lighthearted twinkle in his gaze is extinguished, replaced by a deep well of sorrow. Hermes' presence is a comfort, yet a new wave of agony washes over me because Calypso was not only my best friend but his sister. And Achilles—his friend, as steadfast as the stars—are both lost to us now.

My cries and sobs flow across the realm, unhindered. Hermes sits beside me, and our bodies mold together. Not saying another word, he weeps with me, his arms firmly holding me. For hours, we share this grief, a bond of loss that no words could adequately describe. So, we say nothing.

Guilt gnaws at my heart, a relentless beast. My mind flows, replaying every moment of the past few days before the eclipse, recalling the hundreds of pages of texts and archives we scoured trying to pull out a detail of something that was missed. I search through every second I was away on Tartarus and berate myself for all the time I wasted. If only I had gotten through the Dune Sea quicker or been wary of the Danaids when I met them in the desert.

I could have bypassed the night spent with them, blindly falling into their false sense of hospitality. I would have never crossed paths with the Harpy King and been thrown in his dungeon. He would have never followed my trail to the cave of the dragon. I close my eyes as another death stacks up on the misery that is already consuming me. Nocturna would have survived. I would have never been suspended by hooks from the ceiling as the eclipse faded away.

So many moments wasted. Each one a ghost of regret that will haunt me. Each memory a dagger that twists deeper into my soul. My tears slow. Hermes reaches out, his fingers interlacing with mine, squeezing gently like a lifeline amidst our shared sorrow. I don't remember taking the keepsake dandelions from my pocket until I realize I'm squeezing something within my palm. Opening my hand, I just stare at them. A flood of memories collide with me, and fresh tears flow down my face. Hermes turns me, holding me tighter, and I lose myself in the sorrow all over again.

After a while, Hermes begins telling me stories of him and Callie as children. I lay my head against his chest as we watch the wildflowers swaying gently in the breeze, their vibrant colors a stark contrast to the gray clouds above. A lone white dove flies overhead, its wings cutting through the darkening sky. It is as if nature itself mourns with us, each rustling leaf and chirping bird a eulogy for our fallen friends. Perhaps it's a parting gift from the selfless Temptress, a reminder that she remains a part of this world through the beauty she's left behind.

I recognize this field from the earliest memories of this lifetime. Before the accident, a carefree girl resided within this body, dancing with her mother in fields of dandelions. A little brother, just a wobbly toddler, would chase after the seeds as they floated away. Those days were filled with laughter and love, nothing like the all-consuming grief that fills this field of wildflowers today.

Every thought I have is like a magnet pulling me back to memories of Calypso. Fresh waves of tears flow down my face with each tug. Thinking of the seeds billowing in the winds makes me think of Pat and Callie, dancing in the clouds. Then Achilles and Callie, burning to ash.

"I don't know how to move forward," I confess, my voice a mere whisper against the rustling leaves of the tall oak giving us shade. "She did this for me, Hermes. *They* did this for me, for us. And now she's...they are just... gone."

"I know," he says, his voice breaking. "Calypso was brave, stronger than most gods dare to be." Hermes kisses the top of my head as his warm hand rubs down the length of my arm. "Pat and Achilles too, an unstoppable trio."

In their deaths, they will become legends. But legends are cold comfort to a grieving heart. How do we honor their legacy? How do we live up to the courage they showed in their final moments? It seems impossible. Sitting up, I hold the two medallions in my palm and look at them. Blurry through my teary vision, I blink, and the tears drop onto my palms. All these powers within my hands and I can do nothing to bring them back. No healing water to stitch them back together. No life to restore them and the most useless of all my abilities, death.

The thing that my hunter seeks the most is the power that I understand the least. The power I wish I could use to rethread the broken strands of fate that stole my chosen sister from me.

"She loved fiercely, and everyone she loved lived in her heart, Rhea." Hermes shifts himself, bracketing me with his long legs and pulling me against him. I feel the beat of his heart against my back as I lean against him. "Just like they will live in ours. We will carry them with us, forever. Callie will live on in your memories, through the love she gave so freely."

The current swells around me, like a gentle caress on my

cheek, and I close my eyes to absorb it within me, feeling my friend in the wind's touch.

"We will honor her, and Achilles and Patroclus," Hermes continues, his resolve firming and chasing away the tears that make his voice crack with sorrow. "We will carry their stories, and we'll fight with their courage. And we will protect what they died for." Hermes takes my chin and gently turns me toward him. "Starting with you, Rhea. Always, you." His words wrap around me like a shield as his lips meet mine. It's a fleeting semblance of peace in the turmoil of my emotions.

Together, we sit in silence, two gods bound by loss, finding comfort in the presence of one another. The field of flowers, a silent witness to our pain. The blooms defiantly urge us to remember not just how they died, but how vibrantly they lived.

I take a shaky breath, my gaze falling on the dandelions still clutched in my palm. "She loved these flowers," I say, my voice a whisper.

Hermes stands and extends his hand to me. "Come on," he says gently. "Let's gather more flowers."

I take his hand, allowing him to pull me to my feet. Together, we walk through the field, picking wildflowers. Each bloom is a memory of our fallen friends, a silent tribute to their sacrifice. The simple act brings a measure of peace, a shared activity that binds us in our grief.

As we work, Hermes begins to speak again. "Did I ever tell you about the time Callie blew an entire fleet of ships across the Gulf of Corinth because she was mad at me?"

I laugh, the sound bittersweet. "No."

They got into an argument, though Hermes couldn't recall what started it. Callie got so angry with him; a tempest grew off the shore as she argued with him. "Callie blew the entire fleet of Delphi across the Gulf of Corinth, then refused to bring the ships back into dock." Hermes chuckles sadly at the memory.

With a bouquet of beautiful flowers gathered in my hands, I turn the glass orbs to fine sand, the cases holding the flowers crumble away with a simple thought. Adding the two crimson buds to the center, I give them over to the winds.

Placing a kiss on the ends of my fingers, I blow my farewell into the realm. The rush of air steals the delicate seeds from the cluster of flowers. The wild and unpredictable element of the Temptress carries the seeds and petals away. I watch it until they disappear beyond the tree line.

"Perhaps one day, we'll come back here and see a field of crimson flowers." Daphne's voice surprises Hermes and me, and we turn quickly.

She stands within the tall grass, looking very much at home in this glen of the woods. Her solemn smile falters when she looks at us. Opening her arms, she allows her tears to parade down her face as she rushes to us.

"Mother," Hermes is breathless as the woman he thought died centuries ago embraces us.

Daphne hugs us both, releasing the worry that we would never see each other again as she holds us. "My loves," she pulls back, placing a hand on each of our cheeks as her eyes bounce between us. "You fought so bravely. I'm so proud of you both."

"Daphne," My words are cut off with the guilt I feel at receiving her praises. We let Callie and Achilles die. The goddess that Daphne revered as her own daughter perished to save me and yet, she embraces me.

"Mother, how is this possible?" Hermes covers Daphne's hand with his own, his large form swallowing hers. Daphne was the nursemaid of my last life. She died protecting me and shortly after, my life as Juliet ended.

"The Fates gave you a very clever mate, my son." Daphne's warm eyes lift some of the chill from the approaching cool night. As the sun dips closer to the horizon and casts a golden glow across the meadow, the fireflies begin to twinkle around us. As if warning the creatures of the daytime that night approaches, the glow of their small bodies are like lanterns glimmering in the last light of day.

"You stumbled upon a truth, sweet girl. A truth that cost our lives. You paid the highest price, you pushed me into the shields protecting the great library, then you took your own life. And I have watched every day since, waiting for this moment."

"I thought you were poisoned, like me."

"There have been so many lies woven into the very fabric of this realm, it's time to uncover them." Daphne stands and straightens her deep ambrosia stola, holding her hand to me. "Your journey is far from over and you can be sure your hunter is not taking time to rest. There is much to prepare, and we must get started right away."

"*He doesn't know yet.*" I speak to only Daphne, "*And I don't know how to tell him.*"

"*He is ready to know the truth.*" She answers. "*They all are.*"

My long-awaited return to the Library of Alexandria has been the focus of so many lifetimes. The truths of the past locked within are more valuable than the sum of the realm's treasures. Yet, taking those first steps inside seem impossible. As if delaying that moment can delay my future, my destiny. Callie would never let me give up so easily. She would endlessly climb any obstacle, helping to pull me over when my faith is low, and my resolve is wavering.

So, I stand up. I take a breath. I will let my sorrow fuel my strength as I fight to protect the sanctity of their sacrifice. Their belief that we could keep going and make it to the end, victorious. They believed it with every fiber of their hearts and so I will believe it too.

My silver portals swirl, delivering us to the stone pathway that leads to the monolith of onyx stone. Climbing the tall steps is nearly a burden for my short stature, but Daphne walks alongside me with all the grace and poise of a deadly hunter. As we reach the top, the massive door opens, flanked on each side by a tall Librarian.

I feel exposed under the stare of their void eyes, unable to blink without eyelids, their gaze carries on for eternity. They bow in reverence as we pass, and we return the gesture.

The scent of aged parchment and forgotten magic permeates every inch of the sanctuary that has slumbered for eons.

All around me, towering shelves laden with ancient tomes stretch toward the shadowy peak of the massive pyramid, their secrets cloaked in the dim, mystical light filtering through floating orbs of yellow light. It feels as though the very air is thick with the silent watchfulness of the Librarians, and I tread carefully, profoundly aware that I am walking through a slumbering world of knowledge that has awaited my return.

This is a sanctuary of the ancients, and now, it's mine to explore.

s if the great Library has held its breath for eons, Alexandria seems to lift a curtain, revealing the grandeur of the ancient structure for my mate.** Beside me, Rhea's breath catches in awe, her eyes wide as we step across the threshold that countless others have sought but never traversed. The air inside is cool and still, untouched by time or decay, preserved by Rhea's intricate spells.

We walk deeper into the heart of the library, our steps echoing on the ancient stones. Every surface is covered with scrolls and books, their spines embossed with gold and ancient scripts. The wisdom of ages waits silently for us, a treasure trove of the world's forgotten knowledge.

The walls, made of polished black onyx, shimmer with a subtle, almost ethereal luster, their dark surfaces reflecting faint, ghostly light. Each step we take causes the light to dance, creating an otherworldly glow that highlights the intricate carvings and ancient hieroglyphs etched into the stone. The scent of aged parchment and ink lingers in the cool, still air, adding to the sense of stepping back through time.

The central chamber of the pyramid is vast, far larger than any traditional structure, extending upwards to a pointed apex where a single source of light casts a gentle glow over the area. This light not only illuminates but seems to animate the hieroglyphs and intricate carvings that decorate the walls, telling stories of forgotten times and divine interventions of the gods in a realm of mortals.

Twelve alcoves showcase the carving of the twelve Titans. Behind each arched doorway is the rich history of every realm. Knowledge shared across the eons and beyond the horizons.

Statues of deities and scholars act as sentient guards. Their jeweled eyes, imbued with precious stones, catch the light, creating the illusion that they are alive, overseeing the seekers of knowledge.

The mosaic floor of dark and light stones depicts the constellations as seen from the Earth, turning the ground into a map of the heavens. It's much like the ceiling of the library I created for Rhea. She breaks her trance and shares a pointed look. With a squeeze of my hand, I feel the same sentiment resonate down our bond as she recognizes the similarities.

Rhea and I sense the powerful aura of a great being, lurking just within the dark shadows to our right. The shadows recede, and the figure emerges, not quite human, not quite spectral. The Chief Custodian of the Librarians—the sworn guardian of this sacred place.

In contrast to the other Librarians, whose skin resembles the grayish tone of aged driftwood, this being's skin boasts a rich mahogany hue, polished to a subtle gleam that catches the light with every movement. His height exceeds that of the others, making him tower even more impressively among the tall shelves and vast spaces of the library.

"Welcome, Hermes, Messenger of the Gods, and Rhea, Goddess of the Twelve Realms," the tall guardian hums, his voice rustling like leaves in the wind. "We have awaited your return to these halls of wisdom."

Rhea steps forward, her presence commanding yet respectful, but I can sense the turmoil within her. Her thoughts are a whirlwind, each step a battle between confidence and doubt. *How do we know who we can trust?* She smiles brightly, a mask to hide her uncertainty. "Thoth," she says, her voice steady despite the storm inside.

As Thoth bows, the air seems to hum with ancient power. His presence, both imposing and reassuring, fills the vast space. "You remember," he replies, a hint of amusement in his tone. I feel a swell of recognition too, the name echoing with memories of ancient legends and the hieroglyphs that decorate the walls around us.

"Outside, truth has withered under the weight of lies and time," Rhea's voice resonates through the chamber, carrying both frustration and hope. "But here, the true history of Gaea lies preserved. We need that truth to understand the shadow that hunts me."

Thoth nods, each motion imbued with deliberate grace. "Your hunter is as ancient as these scrolls," he says, his gaze intense. "Come, let me show you where your destinies first crossed."

We follow the Librarians through labyrinthine aisles, deeper into the library. The air grows denser with the musk of leather and parchment, each breath a page from history. Rhea walks in front of me, listening with rapt attention as Thoth tells her of the library's layout.

I still can't wrap my mind around the sight of my mother beside me. Memories of her kindness and strength flood back, mingling with the pain of her loss. I recall the nights spent staring at the stars, wondering if she was watching over me from the Void, and the countless times I wished for her guidance... and my father's.

"I can't believe you're alive." My voice is barely above a whisper, a mix of disbelief and hope tightening my throat.

"Yes, my son," she replies, her smile both gentle and sad. "It's been so long."

I feel a surge of anger and confusion. "I thought you were gone forever. I mourned you."

She takes my hand in hers, her touch familiar yet surreal after so many years. "I'm sorry. There were forces at play that neither of us could have withstood if the truth had been known."

"I could have helped you. We could have faced it together." The thought of all those lonely years, believing her dead, fills me with a fresh wave of sorrow and frustration.

"I know, son," she says, tears glistening in her eyes. "Every day apart from you has been agony. The hunter who chases Rhea sought to remove her allies. We are hunted, just as she is."

Her words strike a chord deep within me. I feel the anger and confusion mixing, but a sense of understanding is easing into my emotions. "Why now? Why is all this happening now?"

She looks at Rhea with a mix of pride and sorrow that only a mother can have. "Because now she is ready. The danger has grown, and the time has come for us to stand together. You and Rhea, you need to know the full truth to face what's coming."

I squeeze her hand tightly, feeling a swell of conflicting emotions swirling within me. When we thought she died, it was just Callie and me. Our father passed so long ago and then my mother. We were orphans, in the middle of this eternal war.

Callie and I got through it together, but knowing my

mother was here all along tarnishes what my sister and I survived together. My mother's eyes reflect understanding. Of course, they do—she's a Sensor. She watched every emotion we've had these past four hundred years, and then I realize the emotion she has likely been living with this whole time: help-lessness.

She's been locked in a protective bubble, helpless to watch her children in pain and unable to comfort them. She's watched our struggles without being able to encourage us, and worst of all, she's watched us being hunted, knowing she can do nothing to protect us.

"I know it will take time, but I hope you can find it in your heart to forgive me."

As we walk deeper into the heart of the library, past the towering shelves and the watchful eyes of ancient statues, I feel a sense of resolve settling over me. "I already have, Mother," I say softly. "It's just... a lot to take in. But I can't tell you what it means to know you are okay."

We stop walking, and I hug her. A touch filled with centuries of longing and love. "We will face this together, son."

Thoth leads us to a secluded chamber, where the walls are lined with murals depicting the celestial dance of gods and Titans.

Here, the Librarians gesture to a mural older and more intricate than the rest. It shows a figure cloaked in darkness, with eyes like emeralds, reaching out towards a goddess who radiates starlight. The goddess stands defiant, a mirror image of Rhea when she dismounted from the back of my dragon and walked toward Ares.

But on today's battlefield, she paused. Something happened when the powerful beam of my Absolute Light powered across the realm. She shifted and no longer was she fixated on Ares, but someone else, hiding among the throngs of our allies.

I didn't sense it then, overwhelmed by the dragon's rage within me, but Rhea closed herself off in an instant. Our bond was blocked, her thoughts were shut off to me as she gathered a thick shield around herself. She realized something incredibly profound, but she's not shared it yet. Each moment it seems as if she becomes more tense as I feel her holding back.

"This is the one who seeks your power," the eldest Librarian says, pointing to the dark figure. "The hunter who pursues the ancient power over death itself, yearns to devour this formidable force from you, Rhea."

"Some of the answers you seek lie within these walls," another Librarian responds. "Learn from the past, for it will arm you for the battle to come. We will guide you, for your fight is part of a larger cycle, one that affects us all."

Beside me, Rhea's resolve hardens, her determination as palpable as the ancient magic that surrounds us. This library, a fortress of forgotten truths, will become our sanctuary, our war room. The battle ahead looms large, but so too does our readiness to meet it.

With a deep and steadying breath, Rhea's gaze seems to dive into me from the intensity of her honey eyes. Her caress across our bond is reassuring and almost apologetic, as if she knows her next words are going to shock me.

No matter what, I trust you. I pass my encouragement into her mind. I feel her hesitation, prolonging the revelation of a truth she has learned. It's as if she wants to protect me a moment longer, and it only makes me love her more. As if anything could ever amount to the agony of losing her, a pain I've walked with far too many times.

My mother stands on the other side of me, and Rhea looks to her with a nod. It seems the two most important ladies of my life are sharing a secret. One I'll soon be welcomed to know as well.

I still can't believe my mother is alive, hidden away within the ancient library. The levels of complexity to this ageless game of cat and mouse continue to overwhelm us with surprises with each step forward we take.

Rhea faces Thoth again. The air around him thrums with a quiet power, a testament to his centuries of guardianship over the sacred texts and artifacts. Yet the formidable leader of the Librarians stands with stoic patience, waiting for my mate to voice the thoughts running through her mind.

"My hunter has worn many masks over the eons, but today, the truth slipped out," Rhea's voice trembles slightly. "Perhaps for the first time since first setting foot upon this realm." She turns to Thoth, urgency sharpening her words. "We need to know everything from the beginning."

"This is the beginning of the end," I murmur, the echo of our past conversations hanging in the air. So many eons we have fought this battle, but the entire time, we were fighting a lie. My heart plummets, and I close my eyes as her words soak into me. Have we been chasing a phantom?

Rhea squeezes my hand, her grip grounding me. Her touch is my anchor in this sea of uncertainty. "And to get to the end, we must return to the beginning." Her eyes meet mine, a mixture of resolve and apology.

"We'll cross all twelve realms if we must, little goddess. Whoever your hunter is, they won't live beyond this lifetime."

Regret for the words she hasn't even spoken yet floods us, and I put my arm around her, remaining steadfast by her side. Everything will change when she speaks the name of her hunter, the great deceiver, and she knows it. But more so, she knows it's going to hurt me.

She takes a deep breath, preparing for the revelation that will undoubtedly shake us all. "Take us back to the age when my hunter was known by another name. Take me back to when Atlas was called Loki."

Formerly known as: Atlas

As I step through the shadowed archway into the Labyrinth, the cool, damp air of the true Underworld greets me like an old friend.** My footsteps echo off the ancient stone walls, a rhythmic sound that matches the drumming of anticipation in my chest. With each step, obsidian waves of my Titan aura resonate within the ancient monolith, waking up the dark creatures that lurk inside.

Today, the game changed; today, they made a move out of turn.

I fling open the doors to the Labyrinth's vestibule, and a shockwave of my anger billows to every dark crevasse and reaches every shadow. They want to change the rules of the game? Fine. So will I.

But first, I allow my rage to consume me.

"Gods dammit, Calypso." My voice echoes across the smooth stone around me. Pounding my fist through the granite wall, my Earthen powers repair it without a thought. "You were not supposed to sacrifice yourself."

All these weeks, I have planned and worked to coerce

Hermes to end his life, only to be thwarted in the final moment by Calypso. My own daughter.

"It was to be your brother that gave up his life today, not you," I yell into the abyss, spit flying from my mouth and dripping my chin.

For millennia, I've worn countless faces, but none so ingeniously as Atlas—the weak-minded mage with a moral compass too heavy for his own good. How deliciously ironic, the immortals thinking me harmless, a mere footnote in the grand tome of immortality. But as the shadows of the Labyrinth envelop me, I shed the facade like a second skin, reveling in the freedom of my true nature.

And now Rhea knows too.

The mask slipped, and the briefest glimpse of my reality shone through on the battlefield today. The fear in her eyes—gods–it was exquisite. A flavor I've longed to enjoy for so long. She thinks she understands the depth of my deception, the breadth of my power, and the darkness of my ambition. But what she knows is merely the surface of my intentions.

As I descend deeper into the heart of my dark abyss, the whispers of the captive immortals reach my ears, their voices a cacophony of despair and madness as they flee from me. Here, in this forsaken place, I am no mere trickster or illusionist; I am a ruler, a god among shadows, commanding a legion of broken divinities.

Tonight, the final act of my grand masquerade will commence. Rhea, with her precious power over Death, will be the jewel in my crown. To consume her power is not merely to gain control over Death—it is to reshape the very foundations of immortality, to redefine the essence of power and dominion.

Finally, I will possess the supremacy of the twelve Titans,

and never will another immortal amount to the vastness of my power. All will bow to my control and kiss the foot of my throne as I sit at the helm of the twelve realms.

I descend the spiral staircase, receding further beneath the realm's surface. Dozens of pits hold my captives, those I pull up when I have use for them. And tonight, I need my old mate.

In my private chamber, I pause before my ancient mirror, a relic as old as the Labyrinth itself. My reflection sneers back at me, the corners of my lips twitching upwards into a smirk. The simple shift of Lumos around my eyes fades away. No longer brown but green like brilliant emeralds look back at me.

I recall my mates when they loved the color of my eyes, bright like spring grass that turned brown with their betrayal.

"It's nearly time, sweet puppet." I call out over my shoulder, a promise to myself as much as a proclamation of the inevitable.

Ares, a huddled mass in the corner, whimpers hearing my voice. The fear that trickles off his weak aura intoxicates me as he floods our chamber with his fright.

It calms me, stifling some of the rage at today's failure and I release a relaxing breath.

I remove the armored wrist guards suffocating my arms and toss them to the stone ground at my feet. Turning to face Ares, I don one of my favorite masks for the screams it elicits from him, the dead and rotting face of Apollo.

"All my careful plans, gone in an instant. Poof." I snap my fingers and he winces.

Starving and bound eternally in the Thaumium collar, the former glory of the God of War is the mirage that I allow everyone to see. All that look upon him see the towering and strong form he used to possess, caped in a crimson cloak with the gold ram's armor, his enemies would quiver when he stepped upon the battlefield.

Now, it is he who trembles at the sight of me.

Well, not me exactly. He has enough consciousness to recognize it is me, I've always made sure of that. But he's not looked upon my face in centuries.

With the rotting image of Apollo tormenting his mind, I creep close to Ares, sharing the same breath as he takes in a long-gargled lung full of air. With his weakened form from eons of starvation, he can't even muster the strength to scream. "You're almost as delicious as Rhea will be."

Nothing was as intoxicating as the sounds of her pain when I tortured her, breaking her limbs and searing her flesh through the disguise of my puppet. Not only did I feast on her pain, but Ares' as well.

Yes, it was Ares' hands that grabbed her arms, snapping them in two. But it was me, pulling the strings of his mind, feeding him the words to recite.

I forced him to hurt her, and I forced him to watch it. His regret and hate for me were as palpable as her sorrow, and together, they were a delicious meal. But Ares is a feast I've consumed thousands of times, and I'm starving for a new banquet.

I grasp his chin and force a kiss upon his withered lips. I consume his wails as he feels the rotting flesh of Apollo embrace him. His limbs shake and fear locks him in place when I force my tongue into his mouth.

Pulling back, I stroke the brittle hair Ares has managed to keep in his state of degradation. "Sweet puppet. Do you recall how excited I was only a few weeks ago?"

I think back to the day Rhea was captured from Once

Upon a Spine by Lupo's imbecilic twin grunts. I couldn't wait to tell him the goddess was finally ready to restart our game.

Shifted into the tiny form of my spy, I was a mere fly, dancing on the knuckles of the greatest goddess the realms have ever delivered. Rhea even looked at me, focusing on the body of the little fly as she regained consciousness in Lupo's cells.

The last time I had looked upon her was the day of the car crash. The day when our new game began.

"Do you recall how many souls we sent to the Void in our search, puppet?" I force Ares to turn around. His face is a slobbering mess, and his mumbling grows as I pull the thread of his mind that lowers him to his knees before me. "Are you hungry, puppet? It's been so long since I fed you."

I stroke a finger gently down Ares' face. A small moment of tenderness that he so rarely receives. His sorrow is making my erection build, and I crave a release.

"So many women burned at the stake to force her ascension." I remove my belt and add it around Ares' neck with his Thaumium collar. "The Salem Village will carry the scar of our hunt forever, I believe."

Leaving him there on his knees, I step back to the armchair in the shadowed corner of our chambers. With a heavy sigh, I drop into the brown leather chair and hold out my booted foot.

The God of War crawls to me as spit hangs from his mouth. My belt clanks with each pitiful shuffle. He'll crawl to me and unlace my boots because I will it. Then he'll pour me three fingers of bourbon.

Calypso was not supposed to be with Rhea in that alley, but I knew her presence would only help to bring out the goddess faster.

Lupo never required coercion to embrace his depravity. Neither did Moros or Ariyana. Servants of Darkness, so greedy for power. And power is just what I gave them.

I allowed Lupo to strengthen Calypso, just as I had allowed the princes of Troy to strengthen her many times before. Each time the caged bird was captured and then freed; she grew stronger.

But she moved out of turn today; a chess piece that took the wrong square.

She's done this before. Robbing me of Patroclus' power on the battlefield of Troy. It was only a matter of time before I would collect Achilles' power, but Calypso needed to be strong enough to lose both her mates and survive their deaths. She wouldn't have understood at first, but I would have made her, then the Siren that should have been my daughter would admire me for what I will bring to the realms.

With both boots removed, Ares kisses my feet before I send him scooting off for my drink. His old, weathered tunic is barely more than thin threads at this point. If I had more use for him, I might have thought to get him new coverings. But it's nearly time for us to part, so there is little use in wasting the effort or the clothing.

With a mere thought, the shadows bow to my whim and carry The Book of the Dead to me. Rubbing my hand over the human leather cover, I open it to the pages I've all but memorized over the years: rituals for binding souls, casting phantom chains around the formless ethereal light that resides within all lifeforms.

"You know, puppet, you and Apollo really should have questioned my fascination with the mortal soul much deeper." I flip through the pages of the ancient text, rubbing my fingers over the dark ink that stains the thick parchment before closing the thick book with a loud thump. "But that is all in the past, right? Moving forward is all we can do."

I pull on the phantom chain that links Ares to my total control.

"We certainly wouldn't want to dwell on your betrayal, would we?" I stroke a finger down his withered cheek as I take the tumbler of bourbon from him. "Do you remember, puppet?" I whisper before taking a long pull. "Do you remember what it felt like to shatter our bond? To weaken me?" With a deep sigh, the liquor warms me and pulls the strain in my muscles as I recall that day on the Grecian shore.

"It was my first time casting such a dark spell. I was almost nervous." A chuckle rises from my throat. "Ah, but that rush when my power gripped yours. The only thing better is drinking the essence of a Titan."

I close my eyes, tilting my head back as I recall the sensation of it. My body warms as I think about that first time. Nothing has ever compared to that first taste of the Titans' powers coursing within me.

"Come make me feel better, puppet." Drool escapes Ares' mouth as he soundlessly wails at my command. But he's powerless against the tethers I have around him. He could fight with everything he has left in him and still, he will obey me; just like they all will soon.

Resting my head back on the chair, I unbutton my fighting leathers and cast myself back into the memory of that amazing day. A million emotions rushed through me, each one more exciting than the next as the power trickled down my throat.

I was a slave to it from that moment on.

Ares' mouth around me pulls a satisfied moan from my

throat as I relive every second of it. Memories of the power coursing through me erupt as my pleasure crescendos. Ares takes every drop and when I open my eyes, I'm more sated than before.

Dragging my finger through Ares' slobber, I wipe it on the remnants of his torn and dirtied tunic. "Thank you, puppet. I'll be able to enjoy breaking what is left of your mind much better now."

Finishing my bourbon, I relish the burn of it as I work to calm myself.

Calypso is not the first to betray me. No, far from it.

My mates betrayed me, and I've punished them appropriately over the ages. Tearing them apart and using them to torment the people they once cared about.

Returning to my position in front of the mirror, Ares follows and remains kneeling in front of me. "You know how naughty you were to go against me. Every punishment you have been given; you have earned. You know that, don't you?" I take hold of the belt strapped around his neck and pull.

The mirage I force him to see shifts from the rotting flesh of Apollo to the children of my mates, the objects that stole Apollo and Ares' attention from me.

Hermes first. His healthy form rotting away to nothing. That will soon be his fate once I consume the power of his mate. "He's going to join the starving legions of the Labyrinth soon, puppet. Forever wallowing in the misery of knowing he never had a chance of saving her."

Ares still loves him and the pride he still carries for Hermes taints the taste of fear I'm lapping up. "Why do you anger me, lover?" My grip around his throat tightens as I shift to my next façade, Flint. "Have you come to love your torment?" I sneer as

I force the recent visions of Flint's death into his muddled mind.

"I loved fueling the flames of Flint and Hermes' feud. Your two sons, hating each other until one consumed the other." I make him see Flint's crushed body. I make him taste the decay and feel the gritty ashes of Flint's withering body blow against him.

What is left of Ares' crumbling heart breaks again with the images I control. "If only I had let you be the father you wanted to be, do you think he would have been a different son for you? Do you think Terra would have been a good daughter?"

Ares' children only ever felt my disdain for them, never their father's affection or pride.

A tear escapes down Ares' face and I lick the path it followed before I stifle his emotions once more. "Why do you tease me, puppet?" I rub my cock growing hard again in my leather pants. "You know how I love it when you weep."

The images in his mind cycle through the torturous visions of the children he loves. Hermes withering away, Flint decaying into nothing on the winds, Terra rotting away within her own stone vortex. Ares' grief washes over me and I take in a deep breath, savoring it. "You didn't even conceive them willingly, old Flame, so don't look at me like that."

After Flint was such a disappointment, I wanted stronger immortals to be bred for my army. I made Ares and Demeter conceive a child and Terra was strong, but I realized the Elementals' powers are too unpredictable.

So, Demeter poisoned the waters of Gaea so the Elementals could not replenish their bloodlines, and I turned to the Shifters. Their strength is much more predictable, so their children have been raised to feed the front lines of my battalions.

And the goddess of night has no idea the legions I have waiting for her.

Just imagining her death on the battlefield is making my blood surge. My hands are tingling to wring her neck as I feast on the Titans' essence within her.

I force Ares to stand before me, his back against my front. "How much shall I make you resist me today, puppet?" I unzip my pants and free my erection. The torment of my emaciated mate and recollection of my ages-long deceit is working me into quite a state of arousal. "This will be our last time together, so I think we should make it a really good one. Don't you agree?" I yank the leather belt around his neck, immobilizing him against me.

Ares' mind is little more than mush at this point, but he still tries to pull away from me. What a fighter my puppet is. I don't know why I've let him keep this small bit of consciousness after all these ages.

"Who am I kidding? We both know why I keep you like this." My mirage settles back into the rotting flesh of Apollo and Ares opens his mouth to wail. I fist my dick and shove him against the mirror with a grunt. "Because you're such a bad puppet, and you deserve this, don't you?"

Hours have passed above the surface of Gaea, but the Labyrinth remains the same. My neck cracks when I stretch it from side to side as I step into my cavern deep beneath the immortal prison. Behind me, the hungry shadows of darkness wrap around Ares' lifeless body, pulling it into the obscurity. Soon, there will be no evidence he ever existed here.

Gathering my cloak around me, the fabric darker than the void between stars, I prepare to leave the safety of my secret lair. Patting the door with fondness, I let the rock consume the entrance, devouring any trace of my essence.

My heart beats a tempo of impending victory, each throb a step closer to the ultimate power needed to complete my collection.

"Rhea, dear Rhea, you have played your part with such unwitting grace. I cannot help but admire your strength, your resilience. But the game is mine to win; it always has been."

The Labyrinth falls silent behind me, as if holding its breath, awaiting the culmination of centuries of deception. I feel the heavy gaze of eyes upon me and pause at the base of the tall spiral stairs that will take me back to the entrance of the Labyrinth.

Without turning to face the darkness, I call out my instructions over my shoulder, knowing the beasts within the obscurity will obey me. "Summon as many as you can from Elysium. I promise them a rich feast. And ready the Labyrinth. You'll soon have visitors."

My boots pound on each metal step as I ascend the tall stairs to the atrium of the prison. Each step settling my resolve deeper and deeper within me. In only a few days' time, the curtain will rise, and the final act will begin. When my expert performance is done, I will take my bow and stand as the Titan of the twelve realms.

A very, very long time ago

My portal of fire extinguishes into a plume of smoke as I look behind me, scanning the horizon in all directions to make sure I was not followed. Seeing an empty expanse of land, I tip my face to the blaze of the Tartarus sun and take in several ragged breaths.

Letting the sun recharge my resolve and wiping the sweat from my brow, I send a wave of heat and a panicked message to my family. *"Apollo,"* I don't waste time composing myself. There is no time to mince pretenses now when I only have seconds to act. *"We have to evacuate this realm."*

Placing a careful shield against the third prong of our fated connection, I feel the concern tighten across our tether as Apollo hears my call. The wave of my heat reaches him, and he realizes I've arrived in the realm.

My heart beats as if it will pound out of my chest, finally being close enough to Apollo to feel his aura. I need to see him with my own eyes. I need to feel him in my arms, or I may not be able to take my next breath. *Gods, he doesn't know yet.*

Sensing his location from the surge of my element, I open a

new portal to him. He's in the Glen of the Gorgons, and the majestic horses whinny at the flash of my fire.

As soon as the flames of my portal sizzle into nothing, my eyes find him in an instant. Three long strides and he's in my arms. My grasp is firm on the back of his neck, and my hand is tight on his gods-damned armor that is preventing me from touching his body.

As hot as the fires of Vulcan, our kiss ignites the bond within us. I've been starving for the touch of my mate for nearly a year fighting the war of the Titans. *The war of lies.*

Breaking our first embrace in too long, I touch my forehead to his and release a tense breath. With our eyes locked on each other, I know I have only moments before war arrives in Tartarus.

"Gods, I've missed you." Apollo is as breathless as I am.

Pulling away, his rich blue eyes scan me, taking in the damage to my armor and the soot and sweat that covers my exposed skin. I bring him back to me for another chaste kiss. "Look into my memories." I whisper against his lips as my tongue invades his mouth.

The kiss is quick, as his light moves through my mind. It's warm and soothing, and I've longed to feel his power brush against me each day we've been parted. I refrain from releasing the groan of pleasure that wants to escape me as a tidal wave of sorrow courses through me. I shut my eyes, knowing what he is about to see.

Apollo pulls back with a gasp, his eyes wide in shock. "No."

"Vulcan is gone, and Prometheus has been consumed. I saw–" My throat tightens against the words as my heart is still breaking with the destruction I just witnessed. "I saw him."

Tears well in my eyes as I recall the look in his stare as he consumed the power of my Titan.

My home realm is gone, and our mate is a monster.

Gone was the evergreen forest of compassion that used to live in the eyes of our other mate. The only thing there now is a black void of desolation and a craving to consume.

"Loki." Apollo gasps and then stumbles.

I nod my head, my heart breaking as I watch the pain in Apollo's eyes. "Our mate; our mate is the god-killer. All this time, it was him all along." I can't believe the words I'm saying.

The wind swells gently around us, delivering an oppressively warm rush of air. The hairs on my body rise in warning as a rush of chills cascades down me. He could already be here for all we know.

"How," Apollo looks to the crimson grass as he blinks his tears away quickly. "How did you escape?"

"Through the realm portal inside Volcano Pyroclastos." Taking Apollo's hand in mine, we hold onto each other tightly. I rub my thumb across the top of his hand and turn his gaze back to mine. "Apollo, where are the children?"

Fear reddens his cheeks, and I feel his distress squeeze our bond. "Shield yourself, lover. Loki can sense everything that passes through our connection. Where are they?"

"Hermes is off realm."

"Get him back here, Loki is coming."

Apollo forms a bow of sunlight and, with an arrow glowing with his aura, he points his beacon toward the sky. Releasing the string, his arrow travels at great speed until it can no longer be seen.

Leaving the atmosphere of Tartarus, Apollo's power bursts

and races across the heavens. His light will travel quickly across the darkness of space, and Hermes will answer.

"Callie, please tell me you are with Daphne?" Apollo calls to his daughter, and she opens her answer to us both.

"We're at the castle of Hyperion."

"Thank the gods." We both breathe a relieved sigh as my eyes flick through the unfamiliar faces of the warriors of Gorgon.

Where is she?

Finally, I see the tall stature of the Chieftainess Ceto. Her warriors have alerted her to my arrival, and she nods at me once, making haste to collect her daughters and join us.

Clasping wrists, we greet each other quickly, but the sharpness in her eyes tells me she understands my arrival does not come on the cusp of good news. "Does Vulcan still stand?"

Vulcan, the last stronghold before Tartarus and Gaea, the last two realms of refuge from this war. I feel my face drop like a shadow has been cast over me. "No, the Fire Mages and Prometheus have lost. Tartarus is in imminent danger, and I feel there will be no delay in the next attack."

Ceto looks to her daughters, Stheno and Euryale. "Prepare for war." Her long braids, capped with stone beads, begin to point in different directions. I suspect she is giving out orders to her tribespeople and directing them with the tendrils of her power. After a second's pause, she returns her attention to Apollo and me. "I must confess a recent understanding. My mate, Phorcys, has bargained with Chaos. Hyperion will be betrayed."

"It's not Chaos," Apollo interrupts. "We have recent understanding to share as well." I feel Apollo's power reach into the minds of the Gorgons as he shares my memory with them all. "It is our mate, Loki."

"I am sorry." Ceto's condolences carry a much heavier weight than a sympathetic compassion.

She understands what this means for us. Ending the Titan wars means we must kill our mate. And with Loki's death, we likely are fated to die with him. Apollo and I squeeze our hands tighter as the knowing passes between us. If that is what the Fates have destined, then so be it.

No matter the cost.

Gaea will have to be our final stronghold, and my mind is already racing ahead to a plan of protection. We must do what we can to shield the last realm of power from Loki's consumption, and it's there, we're going to have to defeat him.

"We must alert Hyperion and evacuate as many as we can." I tell Ceto, though I know the Chieftainess needs no counsel from me on the ways of war. She is a formidable warrior, and we fought together at Elysium as we tried to save the realm from the Titan's battle.

All these ages, fighting the wrong enemy, when the real adversary was sleeping in our bed. Rage boils within me like a fire under a cauldron.

"We'll be angry later, Ares." Apollo's aura rushes over me and settles my temper in an instant. Like pouring cool water over a flame, my anger turns to smoke with his touch. "Hermes is on the way."

No sooner does my mate finish his sentence than a swirl of blue starlight delivers Hermes to the Gorgons' tribe. We eat up the distance between us and embrace. I swear, each day he grows stronger, looking more like his father.

"Ares," the young god that is as dear to me as a son of my

own has traveled far and fast at the call of his father. "What is the news from Vulcan?"

"All is lost." With my hand on his shoulder, I pass the vision and watch as his expression shifts through a torrent of emotions. "Send your messengers and meet us at the castle. Evacuation is the only hope Tartarus has."

"Callie." Hermes whispers his sister's name as he looks behind him. Across the realm and far beyond the horizon, his sister prepares for our arrival. She is closest to Loki, and this will break her heart.

Hermes' eyes water as realization of our mate's betrayal slices through him like the sharpest of swords. Loki and I both have been like their second fathers, loving them as our own. "We should tell her after."

"We tell her now." Apollo directs. "Send the message." Father and son share a look of determination before Hermes closes his eyes.

His powerful aura swells around him as he gathers his ability. Light, more brilliant than all the stars in the night sky, forms at the base of his feet in a spiral up his body, then shoots out of him in a beam heading straight up.

Bursting into hundreds of blue falcons, the messengers of the Herald will race across the cosmos to all the realms that contain life.

Before Hermes' messengers can exit the atmosphere, the falcons of starlight rupture against an opalescent shield. The ground tremors under our feet, and we brace to keep from falling down. The mighty bellow of the cyclops is a deep bass that thunders against our chests, and we cower, covering our ears with our hands.

Seconds pass until their warning shouts stop, and the ground settles.

Horror washes over Ceto's face as she looks at us with her dark eyes, so brown they are nearly black. "The obsidian clouds of Chaos have been seen on the horizon, and Hyperion calls his warriors to fight."

"It's not Chaos." I correct.

"It's Loki." Apollo finishes.

The castle of Hyperion is swarming with Harpy soldiers, and it's a massacre. The Harpies must have formed an alliance with Loki. Tartarus' inhabitants have been taken by complete surprise and run defenseless as swarms of Harpies claw them to death.

I keep a near constant stream of flames pointing upward as my fires burn as many as I can. Women rush past me, clutching their babes as they run for portals, but they have all been dismantled. "Get to the mountains!" I call out as they rush past me.

At the site of the portals, Apollo is fending off Harpies as Hermes helps the refugees escape. Without those portals functioning, the people of this realm are dead.

"Ares, I need you here." Apollo's strained voice booms in my mind. *"Find them quickly."*

"I'm working on it." I grunt back my response just as Calypso and Daphne rush out of an arched doorway.

Harpies chase them into the open from the confines of a tight tunnel. Callie is helping a wounded woman as Daphne defends against the Harpies. She severs their limbs before slicing their heads off with her longsword. Their bodies remain animated for several seconds as their heads crash to the stone ground and roll away.

"Ares," Callie has been crying. "Is it true? Loki?"

"I saw it myself." I wrap my arm around her and kiss the top of her head. My heart is pained watching the hurt my confirmation inflicts.

Daphne meets me and grasps my forearm. Lifting on the soles of her boots, she places a quick peck on my cheek. "I'm glad to see you are safe."

We move in an instant, Daphne taking the other arm of the wounded Tartarian as my flames burst into a flaming sword. Rushing ahead of them, I take down the Harpies that dare challenge our path.

"Once we breach the door and are outside, I'll teleport us to Apollo and Hermes." There are too many citizens rushing by for my portal of fire to flare around them.

Emerging from the hallway into the throne room, I slide to a halt as dozens of Harpies are swarming the interior. Their attention turns to us, and beady yellow eyes narrow as they change their course, heading directly for us.

"Go!" I shout to Calypso and Daphne. My element flares within me, and my flames rise off my shoulders. Bracing my sword in both hands, I widen my stance and prepare to battle the flock.

"There's too ma–" Callie begins to argue.

"Go, Calypso." I shout back over my shoulder as my vision turns thermal. I'll melt this castle to a river of lava and drown every Harpy here before I let them harm my family.

Twenty Harpies head for us, but Callie is as stubborn as I am. I can't blast them with my inferno and risk harming her.

"Leave!" I bellow my plea as Daphne pulls Calypso along with the wounded they are trying to help.

As I raise my sword and the heat of my fire increases, rippling the atmosphere around me. But before my fire reaches the Harpies, they screech and twist. Their flight paths become erratic as all of them are tortured with immense pain at once.

Their forms lock, and their bodies turn to stone, hurtling toward me like petrified sculptures. Their rage and pain are etched on their fossilized faces. I turn, bracing my back against the birds-turned-rocks that are now hurling toward me.

Calypso blasts a shield of wind as I wrap her and Daphne in my arms. The stone figures disintegrate against her power and turn to sand, falling harmlessly to the ground.

Turning back quickly, I have to look twice, believing I'm looking at a younger version of Ceto, before I realize it's her daughter, Medusa.

"You looked like you could use the help." Medusa nods once at me and takes the arm of the wounded tribes person from Calypso.

"Thank you. We're headed to your mother now." I look across the throne room, taking in the dozens of Harpies that have been locked in stone with Medusa's power.

Some clutch the bannisters or columns above; others have their wings outstretched as if caught before they could take flight. It is as if a single stare turned them to stone at once, and Medusa didn't even bat an eye. Impressive.

Opening my portal of fire, we arrive at the mountainside in an instant.

The people of Tartarus cry and pray to their Titan. Huddled together in the shadows of the mountains, they hope for salvation. Beyond the ridge, Hyperion and his giants battle our mate.

"We got an off-realm portal working." Apollo rushes to us, hugging Callie quickly and checking over Daphne for injuries. He looks to Medusa, and a tense stare passes between them before he nods once at her. "They're over there." Apollo indicates with his head, and Medusa leaves us for her sisters and mother.

"She betrayed them, siding with her father, who made a deal with Loki." Apollo explains quickly. I can't hear the exchange, but Ceto hugs her daughter, and the sisters join in. At least they can make amends before it's too late.

Hermes returns to Tartarus on a wave of light, ready to take another group of refugees to Gaea. With a great tremor, we cower again at the mighty bellow of the cyclops. Their roar is deafening, and the sound carries across the realm.

The ground quakes, and a large shadow is cast over us as Hyperion raises the mountains higher. He is fortifying the shield of earth protecting his people as he battles Loki, the immortal who holds the power of nine Titans within him.

Earth, Water, and Death are the only remaining powers he needs to collect. And may the Fates end all our lives should Loki acquire the essence of Death. Nothing in the cosmos would survive him.

A crack sounds high above us, and a large piece of the mountain makes its ascent toward us. The people scream and ready themselves for the mountain to crush them, but it doesn't.

Ceto and her daughters brace, lifting their arms and grunting under the strain. Using their combined powers to grasp the mountaintop, they have stopped its descent only several yards away from crushing the people below.

Hermes and Apollo rush to the people trapped under the shadow of the large rock. Ceto and her daughters hold the mountain with their might, but it's becoming too much for them. Surging to them with my flames, I carry several tribes people to safety, turning in time to see Hermes race in once more.

The fight beyond the mountains becomes a deafening cacophony of clashing powers, and the ground shakes in a constant tremor.

"We need Oceanus!" Ceto growls against the pressure she is holding above her, keeping the broken mountain from killing us all. Her arms shake, and her daughters tremble. Medusa and Stheno begin screaming against the mass becoming too much for them.

"Hermes!" Apollo calls out. "Alert Oceanus!"

Medusa collapses first, her power expended after taking out the Harpies of the throne room and helping her family hold back the mountain. Hermes grabs her, and in a flash of blue light, they are gone.

Apollo and I turn to a raging solar flare of light and fire as we race people to safety. They run and fall in their own panic as the mountain looms with the promise of death above us.

Ceto and her remaining daughters can't hold the mountain back any longer, and Ceto begs them to leave. "We won't leave you, mother." Stheno calls out as dozens more people remain within the danger of being crushed.

"I love you, daughters." Ceto looks at her daughters with apologetic compassion as earth serpents emerge from the rock and dirt at our feet. Like vines, they wrap around her daughters and as many fleeing citizens as she can manage. "Take care of each other." Ceto issues her last command and flings her daughters to safety.

They collide with the ground, rolling away as Ceto releases the mountain.

Hermes arrives, returned from Gaea, just as the fractured mountain breaks against the ground. Hermes drops to one knee, his breaths ragged from teleporting between realms.

Apollo and I lock eyes from our positions on the ground, both of us shielding wounded Tartarians from the shower of rocks and crumbling boulders. We can't save everyone, and it's time we protect our family. We reach the same understanding as a menacing chuckle rolls down our bond.

Are you trying to run away from me, mates? Loki's sinister voice slithers into our minds.

"He can't keep this up or he's going to burn out." Apollo watches Hermes act as a second off-realm portal, ferrying another group of refugees away from Tartarus. With the staff of light firmly in his grasp, Hermes and his Caduceus disappear in another burst of sapphire starlight.

"I know," I confirm, watching gravely as the Titan clashes with our mate over the mountain range horizon. Closing my eyes, I fortify the shield across our bond, and Apollo does the same.

Oceanus arrives on a rush of white-capped water to help his brother. He and Hyperion use their combined powers to battle Loki. Even with the giants on their side, they are still outmatched. Loki holds the power of nine Titans. He assaults them with light and dark, fire and wind, laughing into the deepest recesses of their minds.

Stheno and Euryale take up the place their mother would have held, commanding their people. They organize groups, ensuring the wounded and families are together and ready for Hermes or the other functioning portal.

"We should help them," Apollo says, breathless as Hermes flashes off-realm again.

"We need to fortify Gaea, Apollo," I reply, my tone grave. "If the last of the Titans fall, there is no one to hold Loki back."

Apollo studies me, then tilts his head. "You have an idea, don't you?"

Taking my mate's hand, I raise it to my mouth and place a tender kiss on his knuckles. "I do." Rubbing Apollo's hand on my cheek, I hold it there and close my eyes. For a fleeting moment, the raging battle behind us is silenced as I bask in his touch.

Hermes arrives again, and before he flashes away, I ask him to take us to Gaea. Apollo and I place our hands on his shoulders. Hermes huffs, resting his hands on his knees, catching his breath.

"How many more trips can you handle, son?" Apollo asks quietly.

Hermes shakes his head, not wanting to limit himself and condemn these people to death. "You can't do this forever, Hermes. You're already nearing the point of burnout," I warn him.

"I have to try until I can't anymore." Standing and taking a deep breath, Hermes' light flares around us. In an instant, the harsh blaze of Tartarus is replaced with the cool interior of Oceanus' palace. Atlantis is the landing site for the refugees of Tartarus, and without waiting, Hermes disappears again.

"Your son is very brave, Apollo," a beautiful woman with long black hair rushes to us. She meets me with a quick nod. "I am Athena, apprentice to Oceanus." As if the earth were quaking, the palace rumbles, and a gentle quiver gives us pause. "We need to get the people out of here," Athena urges. "If Oceanus falls, so will Atlantis."

"I'll tell Hermes," Apollo confirms as Athena returns to

the new arrivals, ushering them away. Medusa helps, as do others who are escorting the shaken and trembling refugees. Once the message is passed to Hermes, we make it outside as well.

The palace of Oceanus looks like a large seashell carved into a magnificent building. With tall spires and large rounded balconies, the palace shimmers against the golden blaze of Gaea's small sun. Apollo turns to me and runs his fingers through my hair. "What is your plan to protect Gaea?"

Looking at my mate, I realize how much time has passed since we began fighting this Titan war. So long ago it started, and I recall the day Apollo returned from the site of Artemis' death. Since that moment, we've traversed realms and hidden from a threat that was masquerading next to us the whole time.

As Apollo and I led the armies of the Titans, our mate was secretly the adversary we were fighting. It's no wonder we could never locate the god-killer, always three steps behind. Loki listened to our plans and did the opposite. At times, he counseled us on different paths while he destroyed new realms.

But amid this deception, Loki inadvertently gave us a key to lock the realm and keep him out forever. Pulling Apollo to me, once again our godsforsaken armor inhibits me from holding him as I want. In frustration, I rip away my chest plate and throw it to the sand along with both arm coverings. As I reach for Apollo's, he laughs and removes his own armor. Before the golden metal hits the ground, he's in my arms. His touch against my skin sears a path up the muscles of my arms as I welcome his tongue in my mouth.

I squint my eyes and squeeze the fabric of his tunic in my fist, pulling him tighter against my body. "Do you remember what he said to us, that one day before the battle of Elysium?"

I watch Apollo's eyes as his memory takes him back to that night. Sitting around a flickering campfire, the next day we were to travel to Elysium, realm of Darkness. Loki was going to aid in the arrival of refugees, but now I understand he was on Elysium, fighting against us to steal the power of Darkness from Erebus.

"Tomorrow, when you face Chaos, remember this: the oldest power does not reside within the Titans," Loki said, stroking Apollo's hand. His head rested against me as we shared the warmth of the fire. *"It's the soul-bond between fated mates. That's our true strength."*

Apollo scoffed, his voice calm, almost melodic against the crackling fire. *"Soul-bond... It sounds more like a fantasy than a strategy, Loki. Do you truly believe our bond will shield us from the wrath of Chaos?"*

"Absolutely. We are a single force, bound by something that even the ancients do not understand." Loki sat up, excited to share his learnings. I chuckled as Apollo slid closer to me. Placing a kiss on his temple, I wrapped my arm around his shoulders, accepting his weight against me. *"Older than the power of Titans, first, there were bonded mates. This bond... it enhances us, empowers us beyond our individual capabilities."*

I watched the fires reflection dance in his green eyes, mesmerized by the movement of my element in the gaze of my mate. *"So, we are to believe in the power of our union as much as we believe in our blades and our elements when we face the might of Death, shrouded by Darkness."*

"Exactly." Loki stood, stretching with his arms raised high above his head. Apollo released a yawn, and I placed a quick kiss on his open mouth. He chuckled as I stole the end of his

drowsy release and pulled me back for a longer kiss. One that lights a fire in my stomach even now as I recall it.

"Believe in us," Loki joined us again on the ground before the warm fire. *"Just as a Titan's strength lies in their immensity, our power lies in our unity. They may break our bodies, but our souls are untouchable when bound together like this."*

As the memory ends I can see the moment Apollo understands. The tension in his brow releases, and sadness darkens his sapphire eyes. Brushing my hand through his blonde hair, I push it back, giving me a better look at his handsome face.

"Our bond."

Nodding my head, I confirm his assumption. "He's gone, Apollo." I keep my voice low and soft, speaking only to my mate among the throngs of refugees flooding the beach. "Loki died the day he decided to slay Artemis and steal the power of a Titan."

Apollo's eyes begin to fill with tears, but I knew the second I watched Loki siphon the power of Fire from Prometheus, there is only a monster living inside the body of our mate now.

"But we can save these people." As I speak, Hermes arrives with another round of survivors, looking near passing out. The color has drained from his face, and his hair is matted against his sweaty forehead. "We can save him before our mate comes to consume the power of Theia that he protects."

Apollo looks at his son for a second before Hermes leaves in another wave of starlight. Turning his navy gaze back to me, resignation washes over him, and I feel immense sadness pour down our bond.

"This is not the path I foresaw for us when we bonded all those ages ago."

I huff a half-hearted laugh, giving him a taciturn smile that

I know doesn't reach my eyes. "I know, my bright burning solace." Cupping his face, I kiss him again.

With our slow embrace, we savor each other, agreeing on what we need to do to save this realm and protect our family. The ground shakes, pulling us apart as the palace of Atlantis grumbles. Dust drifts down as the shaking continues. A fissure opens near one of the spires, and it falls into the sea.

Oceanus must have suffered a great wound. We turn our eyes back to each other.

"The Fates can curse me to an eternity in Elysium when my soul departs my immortal body for what I must do, as long as I know you will forgive me, Apollo." The pleading in my eyes begs him to understand how painful this decision is. Not only in the fact we will remove a part of our souls and the physical torment will be nearly impossible to endure, but that we must betray each other and forfeit the promise of our bond, forged beyond the creation of the realms.

"Ares," Apollo pulls me to him, his voice as warm and resolute as the sun's rays breaking through the dark, "as the sun forever chases the horizon, my love will follow you through this life and into the next. Just as your fire lights up my darkest nights, my sunlight will always seek out your warmth. Even if we must untangle our souls, know that my heart will forever be entwined with yours."

Another earthquake jolts the ground as more of Atlantis breaks into the furious sea. As the palace of the Water Titan reflects the destiny we know awaits Oceanus, the waters of Gaea begin to rage. The sea bucks and grey storm clouds roll on the horizon.

Apollo and I walk to cliffs that overlook the waters, giving us distance from the trembling refugees. Tight within my embrace, I hold his stare, trying not to think about anything else beyond this last moment. I run my powers down the bond that secures us to each other, gentle and warm, I hold the ties of our soul within my element.

Apollo tells Hermes to remain on Gaea and that we'll soon shield the realm against Loki. In a rushed argument, Hermes promises he'll return before the wards are up.

"No matter what happens, my love will blaze for you—unyielding and infinite." With one more kiss, I ignite my inferno as Apollo's light shines like a brilliant solar flare.

We are pulled apart by the intensity of the pain. As we attack our bond, I feel the pain my mate endures, a relentless, scorching heat deep within our core. It is as if our very essence is being consumed by an unyielding burn as intense as the sun's surface. Each pulse of sunlight that Apollo commands echoes through him like waves of painful radiation, stripping away layers of our divine connection.

The furnace of my element adds to the agony, and I sense Loki resisting the ties of our bond that are snapping apart. Gaea quivers in the same moment Loki's rage rushes down our connection. Blasting past our shields, we finally feel the dark poison that has taken over our mate, firming our resolve to destroy the tether of our souls. If anything, this may give the Titans a chance to overtake him.

Apollo and I hold firm to each other, bearing down against the force of the self-inflicted attack on our souls. Atlantis suffers several loud cracks, and various parts of the castle made of shells tumble into the realm's waters. Fire, normally my source of strength and power, turns against me, feeling like molten chains tearing through my form, breaking the bond that ties my soul to my mates with every fiery surge. And through it, we persist. *No matter the cost.*

As we feel the frayed ends of our bonds pulled out of our souls one fiber at a time, we surge our powers up to the skies. Flames chase sunlight as our elements weave an impenetrable shield across the realm. On the other side of our bond, Loki's fury builds and threatens to suffocate us in his anger. We know this will weaken us, but the sacrifice must be made. A tumultuous storm of heat and light builds between us, and in a moment, we'll reach the apex.

Worry strangles me as I fear Hermes will not make it back. I sense him surging back and forth between realms, pushing himself farther than I thought possible. He races against our shield, delivering as many refugees as he can.

"No more, Hermes!" I hear Calypso scream at him somewhere within the building inferno of sunlight encapsulating Apollo and me.

"I have to go back for Medusa!" Hermes yells back.

Our bruising holds on each other are searing our skin as the heat of our powers crescendos. The shield is nearly complete. We strain to look up at the sky, watching our powers join above us. We bellow against the agony of our souls ripping apart. Dueling flashes of starlight flare on the edges of our vision. On one side, a strange silver burst of light heralds the arrival of another with the power of teleportation, just like Hermes. Beyond the haze of pain, I see the blurry image of a woman. Long onyx hair blows in the raging winds of Gaea as the storm clouds build around us.

The familiar and reassuring blue starlight of our son dies down, and with a single action, Apollo and I release the final thread binding our souls. A cataclysmic reaction where fire meets sunlight results in a painful, explosive release of energy. Blasted away, I lose my hold on Apollo, and we tumble toward the cliff's edge. Digging my fingers into the sandy rocks, I slide to a halt just before we tumble over the edge. Grasping for my mate, we lock forearms, and I pull him against me.

With ragged breaths, I look into Apollo's eyes, relieved to feel my love for him, still raging as hot as the fires of Vulcan. Part of me worried our love would perish in the destruction of our soul bond, but through it all, our love remains. Our bodies are smoldering with sunlight and smoke, the residue of our destruction as our powers subside. Looking to the beach below, I see Hermes, our poor son, exhausted and trembling, nearly unable to stand as he kneels on the beach.

But it's the figure next to him that holds my gaze. Another immortal, with eyes the color of an evergreen forest, looks back at me. With charred clothes, smoking and casting a glow of sunlight, Medusa carries the evidence of our bond's separation, just as Apollo and I do.

Beyond her, another Medusa stands with Athena, surveying the beach of refugees. As I flick my eyes back to the strange figure that holds my stare, chills cascade down my body, chasing away the heat and burn of our powers. Within seconds, the facade of Medusa melts away, and I gaze in horror into the furious eyes of Loki.

"My gods, what have we done?"

"**T**hat was the last independent thought Ares had, while still in control of his mind,**"** Thoth says as he closes the book of Ares and places it on the table. On a nearby shelf, the book of Apollo is closed, locked just like Callie's. Just like so many others.

"Loki visited the library shortly after arriving." Thoth pulls out a scroll and unravels it. Penned in simple script is a short message: "The game is still on."

"It was after leaving this that he asked we refer to him in our transcriptions as Atlas." Thoth continues as my mind reels from the exploration back in time.

Atlas. The name reverberates through my thoughts like a sinister echo. My hunter, the master of deceit, the orchestrator of unimaginable pain, cloaked himself in the guise of an ally, a mentor. He has woven his malice into the very fabric of our existence, manipulating us like mere pawns in his infernal game.

Ares, once Loki's mate, a proud and noble warrior, reduced to a puppet, his every action dictated by Loki's twisted will. The weight of it all crashes down upon me, and I feel the ground beneath my feet give way to an abyss of betrayal and sorrow.

How could I have been so blind? Loki's influence, his corruption, reached farther and deeper than any of us could have anticipated. The enormity of his betrayal is suffocating, a darkness that consumes every corner of my mind.

He didn't just take Ares' free will; he shattered the very essence of what it means to be a god, to have autonomy and agency. He used his relationship with Callie and Hermes to disguise himself deeper, all the while only waiting for the day he could cut them down. Every war incited, every life lost, every bond broken, have all been a part of his elaborate scheme.

"The game is still on." The audacity of his message ignites a fire within me, a burning resolve to end this. People put their immortal lives on the line for him as he laughed behind their backs, playing a game none of us knew we were a part of. Yet, a fear lingers. If he could twist Ares, the embodiment of war and strength, into his tool, fool all of these immortals with his carefully worn mask, erase the memories of lifetimes, what hope do we have against such a force?

But as I look at my mate, the torch of my determination blazes brightly.

The immortal Ares saw arrive on the beach through a portal of silver starlight was me. That was the first time I arrived at Gaea. I came, looking for Hermes. I wanted to fight with him, to be here to protect him.

Hermes thought he brought Medusa back again. Confused about how she ended up back in Tartarus, she was the first refugee he delivered to Gaea. He had nearly pushed his power to the point of burning out. Collapsing with exhaustion, he wasn't thinking clearly and brought one more survivor back with him.

The wards closed off the realm as Hermes and I each arrived at the Grecian beach at the same time.

But it wasn't Medusa he carried back; it was Loki, shifted into the form of the Gorgon. With the stolen power of Fenrir, Loki became the greatest shapeshifter to exist. Like Lucas, he can transform into any beast. Like Kai, he can transform into any person.

I bow my head in shame as I realize Medusa was never a traitor.

She didn't haunt my nightmares or work against us. She is a victim of Loki's deception from the beginning. Using her form and taking advantage of Hermes' exhaustion, he made the first move of his game.

And the rest of us unknowingly stood like pawns on his game board.

Seshat, Thoth's mate and partner in running Alexandria, speaks softly as we absorb the truths we've just seen. "When Loki stepped foot on that beach, he came for retribution against his mates. But the fate of this realm changed in an instant, the moment he found a new target. You, fair goddess."

"Everything else served to bring us closer to his web," Hermes adds.

He's been very quiet, reliving the betrayal of his second father. Rationalizing the notion that every action Ares took over the eons of this great battle was against his will. Every war incited, every innocent slaughtered, went against the nature of Ares.

A God of War, yes. But Ares was a defender and protector of those who could not fight for themselves. It was Loki's manipulation that kept Apollo and Ares apart, even after sacri-ficing their bond to secure Gaea.

Hermes grasps the sides of the black stone table and stares at the book of Ares.

A single tear wells in Hermes' eye and falls when he blinks. "Does he know what is happening to him?" Hermes sniffs, blinking several times and turning to Thoth. "Is Ares aware that Loki controls his mind?"

Thoth doesn't answer but bows his head in reverence.

Oh, my gods, he does.

Stifling a gasp, I cover my mouth with one hand and grasp Hermes' wrist with the other. Moving my hand under his, I weave my fingers between his and pull his arm against my body.

His feelings are thundering within him, and he's trying hard to shield me from sensing the depth of his sorrow through our bond, but I push forward, wrapping my essence around him as I wrap my arms around him.

Seshat gestures her hand toward the book of Ares. Her arm, like the branch of a tree, ends in an oblong hand with four long digits. "The Great Deceiver enjoys the torment it causes. Yes, Loki ensures Ares is aware of all that happens."

Before Seshat can explain further, an ambient wind hums low in the Library. Dozens of whispered phrases travel on the current that sweeps through the expanse, rustling the rolls of parchment. The book of Ares is illuminated in a gentle white light that thrums softly. A rush of the gossiping wind causes the pages of the book to flip to the end, showcasing blank parchment.

"What is happening?" Hermes asks as we both look around at the ethereal event taking place.

The gust surges faster, and the whispers grow louder as the currents race through the shelves and tomes. I strain my ears trying to decipher what the Wind is saying, but it's too hurried. Like a hundred secrets being told at once. Some of the murmurs are sharp, others seem to be pleading. Thoth and Seshat step back next to Daphne, standing side by side and observing.

Hermes and I watch with earnest as we see the pages fill quickly with an account of something. Daphne stands from her seat in the corner and watches along with us. Her eyes move quickly to Thoth and Seshat before shock registers on her face. Placing her hands over her stomach, she sucks in a deep breath. "By the goddess," she exclaims.

"Can someone tell us what is happening?" I ask, my eyes blowing wide as I try to keep up with the fast-moving text being inked on the parchment by the magic of this great building. The whispers of the wind soften, and the book's glow dims.

Daphne looks upward, stifling the tears that fall from the corners of her eyes despite her efforts. "The God of War is finally at rest." She places her hand on Hermes, the compassion in her eyes softening as her son looks back at her. "Ares' suffering has come to an end, and his soul can finally join your fathers."

Ares has died.

Seshat closes the book and turns to Thoth. From within his robe, he retrieves a lock. Another Librarian comes from the darkness and pulls the burning torch from its fixture on the shelf.

There is no procession for the God of War. No memorial in tribute to his life or recognition of his death. As Thoth moves toward the book, readying the lock to seal the story of Ares forever, Hermes stops him.

"No." Hermes sniffles again, though there are no tears. "He was the Apprentice of Prometheus, and he deserves the honor." Holding his hand out, Hermes pleads silently for the burning torch.

Holding it in his hands, the flames dance upon his face and cast long shadows. Placing my hands on each side of the flame, I conjure a wind and, with the stolen power of the twin Titans of Hesperides, I extinguish the fire.

I track the tear that falls down Hermes' cheek, and it brings sorrow to my own eyes. Turning behind him, Hermes places the extinguished torch in its holder.

Holding my hands out to Seshat, I nod. Understanding my request, she places the book of Ares in my grasp. Hermes turns the lock over in his hands several times before raising the metal to his mouth.

Placing a kiss on the lock, he holds it to his forehead and, with his eyes closed, imbues the object with a closing farewell to the man that taught him so much.

Hermes' navy eyes fall upon mine, and he gives me a tight-lipped smile. The weight of his pain darkens his gaze. Inserting the lock, he fastens it.

His hands caress mine in the gentlest of touches as he takes the book from me and inserts it into the shelf. Closed and forever standing firm next to Apollo's, the mates have finally reunited.

The sun will soon dip below the horizon, and I'm anxious to feel the darkness of night upon my skin. After three days in the harsh sun of Tartarus, I nearly run out of the library doors and climb the tall steps to the top of the pyramid, using the wind to help me surge up the last few steps.

Reaching the top, I circle the final level, wanting to face the setting sun. As I round the corner, I find Medusa already there, sitting with one leg hanging over the edge, the other tucked close to her chest. I start to apologize for intruding but stop myself, realizing there is so much more I need to apologize for.

Medusa is still in her battle gear, her long locks twisted into a mound at the crown of her head. She stares at the horizon, stoically watching the sunset. The sky is cast in gold and soft pink from the setting sun.

"Are they still alive?" she asks, her jaw tightening as she pauses, asking if her sisters survived all this time apart.

"Yes."

Medusa turns back to the sunset, and I notice the relief in her shoulders. She doesn't tell me to leave, so I sit beside her, dangling my feet over the edge. We sit in silence as the glow of the sun gets smaller and smaller, the sky slowly consumed by deep purple.

"I'm sorry," I say, breaking the silence. This apology is no longer about intruding on Medusa's solitude but about casting her in the role of the villain.

"You have been his victim, just like I was," Medusa cuts me off, excusing my behavior before I can fully apologize. "Just like all of us."

Her words hang in the air as the night envelops us. While I don't deserve her forgiveness, I vow silently to ensure each of us will have a chance to exact our retribution, to make sure Loki pays for every ounce of suffering he has caused.

"He's let go of me since you peeked past his curtain and unmasked the deception." I say nothing and wait for Medusa to continue. "I never realized he always had a tether in my mind, waiting to pull on the strings when he wanted." She looks down at her hands. "But now that it's gone, I feel its absence."

Medusa huffs a sorrow-filled laugh, shaking her head as if in disbelief. "I have so many centuries of lost time. Parts of my past where I can't recall what happened."

She lets go of the lock of hair she was twisting around her finger and looks back to the horizon. "I used to think it was my anger or depression over Athena that I just blocked out large portions of time in my grief." Anger takes over the disbelief. "But now I know Atlas... Loki... had just tucked me away while he acted in my place."

I think about Medusa, sitting in a cave, staring at a stone figure of a mother and daughter. Hermes said she stayed in there for centuries.

"Hermes told me about one story." I keep my voice steady as I test the waters of this conversation. Medusa doesn't cut me off, so I continue. "He said Athena came, and eventually you left the cave."

Medusa picks up the lock of hair again, a sad smile spreading on her face slightly. "Yeah, that's one of the times." She finally looks at me and tells me the story that is returning to her memories, now that Loki dropped the tether he had in her mind.

"I was evacuating mortals from the gladiator pits. Loki was waiting inside the cave and hit the mortal woman and her child, petrifying them. He had hoped to strike me and turn me into the stone figures created from my own power. Then he took over my mind, as he had done before. He made me stare at their stone bodies and made me believe I had murdered them."

Medusa twists the lock of hair between her fingers, adjusting the stone bead and using it to occupy herself as she shares the story. "I knew Hermes kept coming, trying to get me out, but nothing would pull me from the grip of Loki. Until Athena arrived. I still couldn't move. I couldn't run to her and take her in my arms like I wanted to, but I heard her. 'Be better.' She told me."

Medusa snorts a laugh. "That became the thought that echoed in my mind until I could pull myself out of the trance. Of course, when I came to again, I had no idea it was Loki's control that put me there in the first place. But I worked each day to be better, just like Athena wanted me to. Just as she believed I could."

"I should have believed in you too. And I'm sorry I thought you were capable of betraying us."

"Ah, you weren't too far off though." Medusa puts both hands behind her and leans back, turning her green eyes to the darkening sky. "I helped my father betray Hyperion. I didn't realize he would go so far, but he talked of a radical overthrow of the Titans' power, and I wanted to please him so badly. I was foolish to follow him, and I regretted leaving the second I stepped away from my mother."

Medusa is watching the night take over the sky, but her gaze seems to be millions of miles away. "The pain in her eyes made me pause, but it was my stubbornness that pushed me to keep walking away." She shakes her head, pulling out of the memories before she sinks too far into them. "I overheard him, striking a deal with the Harpies and agreeing to slaughter our people." As the sky turns dark, so does her demeanor.

"I killed my father." Medusa whispers. "He was mad in those moments before Tartarus was attacked, but now I wonder if Loki hadn't taken over his mind too."

The thought strikes my gut like a two-ton boulder.

I had no idea she carried this burden on her. Among everything else, the destruction of her bond to Athena, the thought that her home and family had been decimated because of her part in the downfall of Hyperion, and now this. The death of her father by her hand; it's so heavy.

Now, the understanding that Loki had woven a thread of control through her mind and incapacitated her while he massacred across the realm, using her as a disguise and causing destruction in her name.

Hermes' footsteps on the stone of the pyramid echo in the stretching darkness until his tall form comes into view. Just the sight of him alleviates the heaviness in my chest, and his nearness helps me breathe a little easier.

"We need to watch out for each other, now that we know the truth." Medusa and Hermes lock eyes, and a silent exchange passes between the old friends.

Medusa moves first, raising her hand to Hermes, who takes it in their familiar handshake. The one reserved for only them, and it reaffirms their loyalty to each other. As if Hermes is apologizing in his own way, and Medusa is reciprocating.

"Everything changes now." Hermes' deep voice is laced with the promise of retribution he'll bring against Loki. Of what we all will bring to him.

"Damn right." Medusa turns back to the sky where dozens of stars dot the celestial body above us. "That asshole killed my mate." The gravel in her voice and the heavy rise and fall of her chest show her rising anger. "It's time for that motherfucker to pay."

I steel my resolve with them, knowing we are bound by festering wounds that will never heal. Our scars run deeper than anyone can ever understand, and they are all inflicted by the same attacker.

The attacker who will never again have a chance to infect our minds and will soon come to an end by the might of our power. Loki's reign ends with us.

I needed some air. As I stormed out of the Library, my heart ached with the weight of betrayal. How could someone I revered like a father, who guided me through the darkest times, weave such a web of deceit? Every memory with him feels tainted now, every lesson learned under his tutelage has turned into a cruel joke. The trust I placed in him now feels like a knife twisted in my back, leaving a wound that may never heal.

The aftermath of the battle deepens the shadows that swell around Hecate as I passed by her on my way out. She helped tend to the bodies that died on the Sahara sands.

Odysseus.

Penelope.

The battlefield echoes in my mind, the screams, and the clash of steel, a haunting symphony of destruction that soon will be forgotten by the land that soaked up today's bloodshed.

My mother met Hecate at the library's entrance, and they rushed to hug each other, crying. Two sisters, separated by centuries as my mother was hidden away, Hecate living her life believing her sister had died. There is much to catch up on after four hundred years apart, but I needed to find my mate.

Without having to pull on that tether that binds us, I knew exactly where she would be: basking under the night sky. Rhea has been stung by the harsh daylight of Tartarus, and the goddess of darkness needs to absorb the power of the moon and bathe under a shower of stars.

Sitting next to Rhea, the world falls away. Her presence is a balm to the torment of today's truths, my beacon of light in the midst of darkness. The feel of her against me, the simple act of her leaning into my embrace, grounds me in a way nothing else can.

"You're going to be insufferable now that you can turn into a dragon, aren't you?" Medusa asks blandly as we lay on our backs looking at the stars.

"You better believe it," I answer just as plainly.

After talking with Medusa and resolving to bring our fury down upon Loki, I just want to lay in bed and hold Rhea. She releases a deep sigh, and I can feel her exhaustion stretch across our bond. Placing a kiss on the side of her head, I whisper against her soft hair, "Let's go home."

She hums in agreement, and we bid our goodbye to Deuce. With her commune abandoned, she's going to stay at Lucas's territory in Wyoming. Aside from Alexandria, that seems to be where all our allies are going, and we'll need to fortify it against Loki.

Standing, I offer my hand to Rhea, and she takes it. I help her rise and pull her to me. My hand rests at the small of her back as the other threads through the tendrils of her hair.

Her golden eyes trap me, and I know in an instant, I'm completely consumed with her. I would bring realms to total destruction just to have one last feel of her silky hair.

My power swells, enveloping us in blue light as we teleport to Mount Olympus.

The wards and shields that protect our home are strong and remain in place, but I'm not taking any chances. Loki had been here countless times, and there is no limit to the depths of treachery he would employ to get to Rhea.

Pushing the pulses of my light through the home and around the barrier of my shields, the blaze of sapphire starlight turns to a radiant white. I burn away any trace of elemental residue left behind and strengthen the shield that surrounds our home and land. The ground tremors as my power builds, taking the form of a dragon that rises like a plume of smoke.

Circling our property, the Titan power of light fortifies a new shield of protection. Rhea and I watch from the balcony as the beast soars the perimeter, climbing higher with each pass until a large dome is formed.

Reaching the top, the form of the dragon bursts and sparks of light shower upon us. Everything glows in a rich blue sheen, and Rhea holds her palm out, catching the clumps of lumos in her hand like falling snow.

"Show off," she chuckles at me, and I can't help but smirk.

Raising her hand to my mouth, I place a kiss on her palm. "Behave yourself, and I'll bring the dragon out to play with you." I cock an eyebrow as I watch the idea of that prospect wash over her with intrigue.

Taking in a deep breath through her nose, she clears her throat and feigns indifference. I smile at her attempt to remain in control of her expression as she pushes against my chest, taking a step toward me.

Retreating back, my legs hit against a chair. Rhea keeps her pressure against my chest, wanting me to sit, so I do. She places her boot on my knee and fixes her hands on her beautiful hips. "I seem to recall I was promised help in taking off my boots."

Pulling back my grin, I match the serious expression Rhea is forcing on her face. She's hiding her amusement, so I do also. But Rhea is also hiding her anger and grief. The immense guilt she is holding around her like a shroud.

"Anything you command, my goddess."

Starting at her ankle, I run my hand up her calf, pausing when I reach the buckles at the top, still fortified with our shields. I kiss the inside of her knee, still covered by her leather pants, but I hear the hitch in her breath from my affection. "I trust the shields served you well?"

"They did." Her fingers meet mine as I unfasten the clasp and unzip the sides, her tender touch on my hand warming my desire.

Casting the boot to the side, I pat my knee for her other foot. With another prolonged caress of her leg and a kiss on her knee, I remove the second boot.

With her hands on my shoulders, she nudges my legs apart and stands between them. I can't help but stroke her thighs and lean into her, savoring the warmth of her aura as her nails scratch along my head. We hold each other in the silence with nothing around us but the soft breeze.

The thought of losing Rhea, even for those brief seven minutes, was an eternity of torment. Each second stretched into an agonizing void, where the fear of her absence clawed at my sanity. Knowing she fought through Tartarus for three days to return to us fills me with awe at her strength and determination. Now, I just want to hold her until she remembers that she is home and within the shield of my power; she is safe.

As she unfastens the ties of my chest plate, trembles overtake her fingers. Her chest rises and falls heavily as her heart starts to hammer. The veneer she has hardened around herself is cracking, and she is fighting to hold onto it.

I pull her to my lap, and straddling me, her arms cling to my neck as the final thread of her false armor breaks and she frees herself to the emotions flowing within her.

"I was so scared," she whispers as tears take over her eyes.

"You were so strong," I counter and wrap my arms around her. She buries her face in my neck and weeps, finally letting go of the days of torment that she survived. The journey to rescue herself and the pain of Tartarus, left alone to suffer in the aftermath of the Titans' battle, she lets it go.

I hold her and stroke her hair as she clings to me.

Pulling away suddenly, she fumbles with her chest plate, trying to remove it. With a sniffle, her voice cracks as she pleas for my help, "Get it off me." I feel her panic beginning to rise within her as her breathing hitches.

"Hey, shhh." I brush my lips against hers, taking her hands and placing them on each side of my face. "Look at me."

Her brows knit together, and her eyes are wide with fear.

"That's it, focus on me." I speak in a soft tone and hold her with my stare. Feeling along the bindings of the chest plate, I loosen it, and as I do, she breathes easier.

Her thumbs stroke along my jaw as she keeps her hands on each side of my face. Her eyes remain firmly locked on mine, and the panic slowly fades.

"Arms up, goddess." I whisper, and she listens, each breath coming easier.

Pulling the chest plate from her body and sliding my hands under the compression shirt, I free her of the rugged and protective clothing.

She crashes her mouth against mine, and our tongues collide. Her tension immediately gives way to her passion, and I meet her fervor with my own. I run my hands along the bare skin of her back, and she pulls at my own armor.

"Take it off," she breaks our kiss for a chaste command, and I move to her jaw, then her neck as she pants. "Please. I need to feel you."

We work the leather ties, and I'm freed of my armor quickly. Rhea wraps her arms around my neck and pulls at my hair as we devour each other. Chest to chest, her pert nipples brush against me, and my dick strains in my leather pants.

With greedy hunger, I take her breast in my mouth and swirl my tongue around the peak that is begging for my caress. I moan against her soft skin when she grinds her pelvis against me, threading her hands through my hair and throwing her head back in enjoyment.

Using a beam of light from the bathroom, I bend it like a ribbon and turn on the shower. Savoring the salty taste of her, I move to the other breast before I grab her thighs and stand up. Her hold tightens around my neck as her lips instantly find mine again.

As I push her against the wall of our house, I pull back on her hair, nipping and licking her neck. My free hand unbuckles her pants and then my own. When I sense the shower's steam fill the bathroom, I teleport us there, our mouths never parting.

I set her down long enough to remove the rest of our clothes, then I back her into the shower. I kiss her like each embrace is the source of my life because it is. The water runs down her beautiful body, and I slide my hand along her wet skin, cupping her plump ass and moaning at how soft she is.

I take her neck again, licking and sucking the water from

her skin. Rhea tips her head back, letting the rainfall shower head drench her in cleansing, hot water.

Pulling back, I just look at her. The dew drops of water that collect on the end of her long eyelashes frame her rich amber eyes, darkened by her arousal. "You're so beautiful."

Smiling, she makes herself taller, standing on the tips of her toes, and I bend down to meet her. We wrap our arms around each other, letting the water wash away the tension from our bodies.

Palming a dollop of shampoo, Rhea rubs her hands slowly across my chest as I wash her hair for her. With my fingers spread wide, I massage her head as I work the lather into her hair. Closing her eyes, she relaxes into my touch, and with her mouth parted, she exhales a satisfied moan.

My cock hears it and twitches between us, as if reminding her my erection wants her attention. With her eyes still closed, the corner of her mouth tics up in a half smile as she continues to savor my hands as I clean her.

"Mmmm, did you like that sound, Herald of the Gods?" She teases me.

My hands move down her body, my thumbs brushing against her nipples and pulling another breathy gasp. I slide my hand between her legs, slick with soap, and gently rub her arousal.

"I could live off that single moan for a millennia." My lips are so close to hers; I can feel her breathing hitch as I insert two fingers into her. At the same time, my thumb circles her clit.

She widens her mouth, and I taste her next moan on my tongue as I devour her with a kiss. My tongue works her mouth in time with my thumb and fingers working her pussy.

"Gods, I missed you." My lips move against hers as I speak,

unable to pull away from her. Then I push my tongue into her mouth again. Pumping my fingers into her, I hold them there, stroking inside her as the tip of my thumb vibrates against her.

"Oh gods, Hermes." Rhea moves her pelvis in small circles as my hands work her closer to an orgasm. Throwing her head back, the water washes away the shampoo and soap as her moan bounces across the tiled bathroom.

"I think Titan will be sufficient." I work her faster as her needy pussy clenches around my fingers, driving me crazy. "Or commander of Light," I keep teasing.

She looks at me with hooded eyes, her bottom lip, full and parted as she pants with ragged breaths. "How about, 'mine'." She claims me. "All mine."

Possessiveness courses through me, and I pick her up. Hanging on to me with her arms around my neck, I watch her eyes as I slide her down on my cock. She's so close to cumming, the walls of her pussy squeeze and pulse against my dick.

"Mine." I repeat before I give her a bruising kiss. My hands holding her hips as I drive into her with brutal force.

Her orgasm builds and she starts to close her eyes, hiding them from me. With one hand tugging the hair at the base of her neck, I force her gaze back on me. "Keep your eyes on me."

She does. I reward her with rhythmic strokes down our bond that enhances the pulsing waves of pleasure taking her over. Rhea opens her mouth and moans, keeping pace with the cadence of my thrusting.

Her orgasm squeezes me, and I follow after her. Grunting and moaning as I pump my release into her. She watches me as intently as I watch her.

Our hands work each other's bodies as our breathing and the pounding of our hearts move in time together. The fated bonds within us, forever woven together, stretch and slide with seductive movements between us.

Remaining connected, together as destined lovers, we share our breaths, locked in the depths of each other's eyes as I keep myself seated within her.

A shade of mischief slides over the gilded eyes of my greedy little goddess, and she smirks. Clenching me with her thighs, she moves her pelvis.

My dick, still buried inside her, answers as my blood rushes within me, ready to consume her again. I meet her with a thrust as my piercings slide along her.

"Wanna go again?" She nearly purrs, pinching one of my nipples and biting the curve of my neck.

With a growl, I fist her hair and pull her back so I can see her beautiful face. "Always."

Everything around me is on fire. The heat is unbearable, a searing force that seems to reach into my very soul. Never have I felt flames this strong before; they roar and crackle, an untamed beast devouring everything in its path. Panic surges through me, a cold dread in the pit of my stomach, as I realize I am powerless to stop them.

"Rhea, help me!" Callie's voice cuts through the inferno, carried on a gust of hot, turbulent air. It swirls around me, just out of reach, like a cruel taunt. "You have the power to save us."

Her voice echoes, distorted by the heat, like the haunting call of a siren to a lost sailor. "Where are you?" I scream, my voice raw and desperate. The words feel futile against the raging inferno. The fire bites at my skin, its scorching tendrils tearing at my fighting leathers.

"Don't worry, Rhea," Achilles' voice is unnervingly calm, almost soothing, as if the flames were a mere illusion. "I made sure your leathers were resistant against Soul Fire." His words do little to comfort me. The heat intensifies, and through the dancing flames, his face appears, a sinister smile etched across it.

I look down at my arms in horror. My flesh is a grotesque canvas of red and black, blistering and oozing with blood and pus. The pain is excruciating, my skin boiling under the relentless heat. "Where are you, Callie?" I cry out, turning frantically, searching for her beyond the fire's fury. But all I see is an endless burning expanse.

"We are all going to go together, Rhea." Achilles' voice is closer now, a whisper that sends chills down my spine, as if he's right behind me. Spinning in a circle, there is no one.

Somewhere in the distance, Callie screams. It's a sound that pierces through the cacophony of the blaze, filled with terror and agony. I inhale sharply, but the air burns my throat. Another scream, and I realize with horror that it's coming from my own lips.

A deep boom resonates on the horizon. Blue clouds rush toward me, a stark contrast to the fiery inferno. The wall of fog crashes into me, cool mist kissing my scorched skin with a flash of Hermes' blue light. The relief is almost as overwhelming as the fire, and for a moment, I am suspended between two worlds, one of unbearable pain and one of soothing coolness.

I sit up with a gasp, the lingering scent of smoke and burning flesh still vivid in my nostrils. My throat aches as if I've been screaming for hours, and my skin prickles with phantom burns. Clutching at my throat, I frantically inspect my arms. They're whole, unblemished. I'm not on fire.

The room is dark, the only light emanating from the dimming aura of Hermes beside me. His breath is ragged, sweat glistening on his forehead. "Are you okay?" he asks, his cerulean eyes scanning me with concern. At the edges of my vision, I see the pulsing shields of his Light, a comforting yet eerie glow.

"He's near." The words escape my lips, filled with a certainty that chills me to the core. I can feel Loki's presence, a vile, oily sensation that slithers through the night. It's a familiar deception, similar to the night Moros attacked with the Shifters. Loki is here, testing Hermes' shield for weakness, prowling like a predator in the dark.

Our powers surge, Light and Dark intertwining and spreading out in a defensive wave. Hermes is on his feet in an instant, twin swords of Light gleaming in his hands. I sense the exact moment Loki slips away, teleporting back into the shadows where he has lurked for ages.

"He's gone." The adrenaline courses through me, my heart pounding fiercely in my chest.

"He'll be back," Hermes states, his voice steady but laced with determination.

"Then let's be ready," I reply, the lingering fear from my nightmare transforming into a resolve as strong as steel.

10

Hermes

I **'m fucking pissed.** That asshole tried to attack my mate while she slept. Like a coward, he tested the barriers of my shield, trying to worm his way in and steal what he wants when her guard is down. Loki is the epitome of a parasite. I want to wrap him in the chains of my power and syphon the life from his immortal, black heart—if he even still has one beating in that cavern he calls a chest.

Ares was right to call him a monster all those ages ago, and regret surges through me in a suffocating wave of sorrow. Gods, I wish I had known. I think about the last moment my father and I were together with Ares. It was the day of their battle when my father had been poisoned first.

Closing my eyes, I recall every detail of that day as if it just happened. Loki...Atlas...insisted on a hearty breakfast and was overly joyful. I thought he was just trying to boost my dad's spirits before he left to battle their former mate. But no, he was relishing in the torment he was causing, bringing his mates to fight when my father was already dying from the poisonous meal he was served.

I saw my father stagger and stepped in to intervene, but it was too late. Ares and I watched my father take his last breath as Ares's fatal wound consumed his immortality. But now we know Ares was under Loki's total control, forced to kill the man he loved and made to watch the life drain from his eyes. And I'm the one that brought him here.

Guilt for delivering Loki to the Grecian beaches of Gaea nearly chokes me, and I blink away the tears that wells in my eyes. I had been so consumed with saving as many souls as I could, my mind racing with the urgency of our mission. When I saw Medusa standing back on Tartarus, I never paused to think how she could have gotten back there. I should have known something was wrong, but my desperation blinded me.

The realm of Tartarus was quaking so violently, and the mountains were crumbling. It seemed the world was on the verge of being pulled apart as a deep crevasse split the ground. But it wasn't just the realm of eternal sunlight tearing at the seams. It was Loki, shredding the natural order, having just consumed two Titans as his mates tore their bond apart. He had the audacity to take on the form of someone familiar to me, exploiting my trust and memories. And like a fool, I delivered him to the shore of our refuge, believing I was aiding a friend.

I remember that moment with painful clarity. The way Medusa's eyes glinted with eerie satisfaction, the subtle shifts in her demeanor that I ignored in my haste. I can still hear the deceptive sweetness in her voice asking for help. I still feel the chill that ran down my spine too late. My heart aches at the thought of the lives that could have been spared if only I had paused a single second to consider what I was seeing. But there's no changing the past. I pull myself out of the darkness that lurks there, determined to make things right now.

Holding Rhea in my arms and wrapping her tightly in my

power, she was finally able to go back to sleep. She needs rest. Tartarus was grueling, and I fear we'll not have a reprieve until this battle with Loki is over. The sooner we can bring this to an end, the safer everyone will be, but especially the goddess sleeping in my arms.

As Rhea napped, I worked to strengthen the barrier of my power. When she woke, Rhea challenged the shield with the combinations of elements she commands with the strength of the Titans.

Satisfied with the shields, we stand back, looking over our home, and she breathes a sigh of relief. I feel the sense of peace she exudes within our space, and something primitive takes me over. I want to puff my chest out like a caveman and howl into the sky.

My entire purpose narrows in to be her protector, and feeling her emotions through our bond, knowing my shields are keeping her from harm fills me with pride. As I tuck a stray lock of hair behind her ear, she looks at me with an appreciative smile. In this moment of peace, a rare tranquility settles over us, and I allow myself to savor it, however fleeting it might be.

But as we stand there, our thoughts seem to collide and intertwine. The peace is abruptly shattered by a jarring realization that crashes into my mind with the force of a tidal wave.

The Shifters.

"Aw, fuck."

"We need to get Lucas some shields," Rhea and I speak at once. Mine is an exclamation, driven by the sudden urgency that we must leave the safety of our small fortress to help the others. Hers is the voice of reason, steady with determination to assist.

The weight of our oversight hits me hard. How could I

have forgotten about them? All the elemental powers have the ability to cast shields of some kind, with the exception of the Shifters. There is nothing within their powers that deflects the other elements or helps safeguard them from attacks. I should have thought of this vulnerability sooner.

The image of Lucas and his people, defenseless against Loki's mind control, gnaws at my conscience. Their powerlessness could easily turn them into pawns in Loki's cruel game. The thought of them, trapped and forced into servitude as they once were in the Underworld, tears at my frustration.

Rhea's voice pulls me from my brooding. "We need to get going."

Nodding, I push away the lingering guilt and focus on the task at hand. We dress quickly and I send a call to Lucas with my falcons as we prepare. My messengers fly overhead, patrolling the Wyoming skies until we arrive.

"Way to scare the shit out of everyone before the sun can even rise, H," Lucas barks, his deep voice rough from sleep. Wearing only pants, his tanned skin is marred with white scars, and a tattoo covers his shoulder and arm.

"Way to be cliché and get tattoos of animals," I tease, though my heart stings with a sharp pain seeing the immortal ink that decorates his skin. The memory of the last time I was here was with Achilles rushes through me.

I stare at the place on the porch where we sat next to each other, eating lunch. My eyes glaze over a moment as the memories wash over me. I'm pulled out of it when Lucas pats my shoulder with more force than needed.

"You're welcome here anytime, buddy," he says in a lower tone, all teasing gone as if he knows what darkness pulled me away from our jest. The same words he said to Achilles.

"We have some important information to share, and I need to check your packs to make sure they are safe." Rhea wastes no time in letting Lucas know why we're here.

"Do whatever you've got to do." Lucas spreads his arms wide, inviting her to sweep his lands and giving her permission to check the Shifters under his command.

Rhea pushes into the minds of everyone within Lucas's property and communicates with them about the threat. She also ensures no one's mind has been secretly tethered by one of Loki's dark tendrils and places a shield of her own around each of them.

I look at my mate with pride at how effortlessly she is wielding her elements. I hope she is beginning to accept them as part of what makes her amazing. Rhea is disheartened by the violence of the Titans' death but it's clear she is using their essence for the good of others.

I believe it is what the Titans would have wanted and that she is honoring the very reason such magnificent power was created somewhere across the horizon of time.

"I can't believe it," Lucas sits on the steps of his vast home. His legs spread wide as he rests his elbows on his knees. He looks at the ground, slowly shaking his head back and forth in disbelief. "Atlas, this whole time."

"Yeah." I answer blandly as I watch Rhea talk with Kai and Naomi.

Long ago, my mate created Lucas in the belly of this realm. She shared the essence of Fenrir with him so he could save the others and become a general in her army. Loki likely sensed it the second it happened and used Lucas to create his army, trapping them in the Underworld for eons, tormenting them, and breeding them like cattle for slaughter. He enjoyed watching them do his bidding while drugged by Demeter's depraved concoctions and doing it all with the facade of Ares to shield him.

The webs of deception just grow and get more convoluted the more I think about things. We need to get the boundary of Lucas's territory secured and talk about the rest of the immortals dispersed across the realm. Loki will be coming for them all and we need to make sure our army is just as big as his, if not bigger.

Aside from that, the Shifters of the realm are converging here to fall within the protection of their Titan. Their homes and buildings are overrun with cots and mattresses, so families have a place to sleep. They need more homes, and while Lucas has an abundance of land, he lacks teams to construct the buildings fast enough. And I have a feeling we're going to see the number of residents here increase significantly.

After we erect this shield, we'll see what we can do about their facilities today too and I know just the ladies to call.

We've been here several hours as Rhea worked to shield the packs and I made her stop to eat breakfast. Medusa left for Alexandria to get my mother and Hecate. Taking a deep breath, I stand and look at the bright blue sky. "Let's get this show on the road."

For the first time since Rhea returned the essence of the Titan within me, I'm going to call upon the form of the dragon within me. During the reunion in the sky, I had no control over the transformation to the dragon. As the power knit back into my soul, becoming one with me as it had so long ago, it felt as natural as breathing. But I would be lying if I didn't admit I was a little apprehensive to call upon it now.

With Lucas watching, Titan of the Shifters, he would never

let me live it down if my dragon suddenly had stage fright. But I need to get high and project a shield large enough to cover all of his territory. Stepping into the opening and away from the large pack house, I call upon my Light while I open a portal high in the sky. As if the stars from the farthest reaches of the cosmos rush to me, the power surges through me. The wave of Light surrounds me and rushes out of my body.

My physical form turns to starlight, and massive wings unfurl from my back. My legs are replaced with the heavy limbs of a great beast, tipped with razor-sharp talons. The long scaly body writhes with the long tail behind me, providing me balance and power as my wings beat against the wind.

The sapphire-jeweled eyes allow me to see across the realm as everything turns to energy and particles of light. The buildings below, the surrounding forest of trees, everything is made of Light. I can distinguish it with extreme detail, seeing even the fine nails driven into the long wood planks of Lucas's home.

There, shining brightest of them all, is the radiant beam of silver stars that is my mate. Rhea stands, gazing at me in this form. Her hand is shielding her eyes from the sunlight as I fly high overhead, but her smile blazes at me brightly, in awe of the dragon soaring in the sky above her.

Circling the vast property of Lucas's territory takes only a moment. Building the power of Light within my chest, I form it to a central mass of raw energy within me. Threading the strong Lumos into an impenetrable forcefield, it erupts from my body like rain. Falling down to the ground below in a large dome of protection, my element showers the Wyoming territories of the Shifters.

Rhea matches my power with her own. Dark mist and fog

careen out of her, rushing across the ground and coating the space with her dark shield. Our powers collide and roil against each other, fusing into an impassable obstruction against Loki. We continue to push our energy outward, hardening the shield with additional tethers of security.

At the edges of my dragon vision, I see the strong aura of Lucas, pulsing like a beacon in a storm. He stumbles into the clearing, tearing at his shirt, and my senses spike to a heightened level of alertness. The muscles in his neck strain as if he's choking and the Shifters around him look on with confusion.

Within a heartbeat, the raging form of Fenrir breaks out of Lucas's body. The giant wolf, more than fifty feet tall, stands with nothing before him... except my mate. Rage and protectiveness drive me into a downward spin, into a portal that instantly opens up before her.

As Lucas's beast takes in a deep breath, ready to release his roar, the ground tremors with the impact of my arrival. Rhea, frozen in shock with a look of horror on her face, as my massive dragon form shields her from Lucas. The red eyes of his beast look at me as if something has taken him over and Lucas is no longer in control.

With a deep inhale of my own, our bellows of warning to each other rage into the atmosphere of Gaea. The trees shake as birds fly away. The ground quakes and around me, I'm aware that the others have shifted, answering the call of their Titan who is no longer in control.

Fenrir is challenging the cosmic dragon.

Men, and their godsdamned egos. I swear to the goddess, we don't have time for this. The giant wolf, stands on one side, muscles rippling beneath its shaggy auburn coat. His eyes, no longer the friendly hazel stare of Lucas but glowing a fierce amber, are locked onto the dragon with a mixture of challenge and rage.

Saliva drips from its bared fangs, each drop hissing as it hits the ground. Every growl that rumbles from his throat vibrates through the air, a warning of his raw, primal power.

Opposing the wolf of Lucas, Hermes' dragon stands majestic and terrifying, his scales shimmering with iridescent hues of sapphire. Hermes' massive wings are partially unfurled, casting a shadow over the clearing, while his eyes, burning with a deep, otherworldly light, stare unflinchingly at the wolf.

Smoke curls from his nostrils, and the ground beneath his talons is scorched from the heat of his breath. The dragon's tail, long and whip-like, sways menacingly, ready to strike.

Standing between them, I feel the ground tremble beneath their weight and the scorching heat of their breaths on my skin. The tension is palpable, thick enough to cut with a knife. My patience snaps, and with a rush of silver aura, I all but slap the two imposing beasts towering above me.

"Stop this!"

Lucas falls to the ground, his wolf form shifting instantly into a great brown grizzly bear. Returning to his four large paws, the bear is just as massive, towering above the trees that surround us. Hermes' dragon and Lucas' bear are evenly matched in size... and pigheadedness. The sight is surreal, like witnessing the clash of titans in an ancient myth.

"Enough!" My voice echoes through the clearing, but my command does nothing to quell their tempers. The bear reacts to the impact of my Wind and lunges for us. With a spin of his giant body, the dragon's tail whips around and slams into Lucas, sending him crashing into the forest. The trees are leveled in his wake, splinters flying like deadly shrapnel.

As his large form comes to a sliding stop, I catch my breath, the adrenaline still coursing through my veins. Each heartbeat pounds like a war drum in my ears.

Hermes' telepathic voice cuts through the chaos, a mixture of anger and desperation. *What the fuck is your deal, Luke?*

"I—can't..." Lucas's voice is a strained whisper, his bear form slithering into a gigantic anaconda. His struggle is palpable, each word a battle against the primal forces within him.

Oh shit.

Unable to finish his thought, the snake surges forward. I widen my stance and prepare to do... something. My mind races, grasping for a plan. Hermes' Light begins to wrap around me, preparing to teleport us into the sky, but movement from within the forest catches my eye.

Tunneling up from the ground, another snake, equal in size and made of dirt and rock, careens into Lucas. The two snakes become a writhing mass of quick-moving serpentine bodies, hissing, and snapping massive jaws at each other. The ground shakes with their ferocity.

"What the fuck has gotten into you two?" Medusa's voice rings out as she arrives through a dark portal with Daphne and Hecate. Her eyes are sharp, taking in the chaotic scene. Calling upon her Earthen powers, she conjures a snake to entangle Lucas.

"*Can't—control...*" Lucas's voice is a strained growl, his beasts governing him, and he tries desperately to fight them back. His eyes, now dark with turmoil, plead for help.

"The dragon," I exclaim, finally understanding the presence of the dragon was calling out a territorial response from Lucas' animals.

"*Hermes, put your dragon away,*" I tell my mate through our bond as I step out of the shadow of the beast protecting me. Raising my hand, translucent waves of calming aura pulse at Lucas. The red rage in the eyes of his snake widens as my Sensory power over emotion surrounds him. The snake's face appears to strain as Lucas fights to reign in his animals.

Medusa eases up on her earth-cobra as I continue to blast the Titan Shifter with waves of calm, nearly lulling him into a state of sleep. With a brilliant flash of Light, Hermes returns to himself, locking away the cosmic dragon within him.

Lucas stills, the reptilian body slithering back into the form of a man. His breaths come in heavy, ragged gasps as he slowly moves to his hands and knees, covered in mud from fighting Medusa's snake. He puts out a hand of resignation, letting us know he is getting back under control. The earthen snake of dirt and rocks falls apart as Medusa releases her power.

Around us, Shifters are still in a frenzied state, snarling and growling, ready to protect their Titan. Lucas commands them to stand down and return to their human forms. The transition is almost as awe-inspiring as the transformations themselves, a testament to their unwavering loyalty.

"I'm sorry." Lucas huffs; his shredded clothes lay in tatters on the ground. He and his Shifters stand before us naked, taking in the downed trees that are now little more than piles of splinters. "I don't know what happened. I lost total control."

"Well, we need to figure that the fuck out before one of us ends up killing each other." Hermes gruffs, frustration pinching his brows together. He still stands just slightly ahead of me, trying to put something between me and Lucas should he lose control again.

"Hermes," I grasp his shoulder with a calm tone. "It was an accident."

Cappa and Delta rush toward us on four-wheelers, skidding to a stop and surveying the scene of destruction, confusion etched on their faces. Kai and Daphne emerge from the large pack house with robes and coverings for the naked Shifters, some of them speaking low in muttered grumbles when an idea blooms in my mind.

I put this power within Lucas, and I should be able to recognize it. Walking up to him, I extend my hand.

"Rhea," Hermes issues a warning, but I had trusted Lucas long ago to hold this power, and I trust him still.

"It's okay," I call back to my worried mate. "Lucas, do you mind if I check around in there?"

Tying a knot in the belt of a brown robe and still panting from the exertion of a moment ago, he nods in agreement.

Placing my hand on his shoulder, I cast a gentle wave of my aura into him along with a pulse of reassurance. As if the beasts he called upon live within his blood, I can sense them. So many forms of familiar animals reside within his immortal body. Pushing deeper, I sense a darkness within him and feel the beast that lurks in those depths. With a gasp, I pull my hand back and step away from him.

Hermes is by my side in an instant, his proximity pulling a growl from the threatened monster hiding inside Lucas as his eyes begin to darken. I can see the edges begin to rim with deep crimson.

"What is it?" Lucas also takes a step back after shaking his head, his hazel eyes returning to their kaleidoscope of blues, greens, and browns.

"You can shift into a dragon too."

The words hang in the air, and for a moment, there is silence. Then, the reactions come all at once.

Medusa's eyes widen with a mixture of excitement and curiosity. "I vote we see the dragon," she says, leaning against Kai's jeep, raising her hand. "Two dragons would be better than one," she adds, her voice filled with enthusiasm. "We have no idea what Loki has in his arsenal, so whip it out, Luke!"

Kai, however, looks apprehensive. She crosses her arms and frowns. "Is that really a good idea?" she asks, glancing at the others. "I've never seen Lucas not be able to control his animals like that."

Daphne, standing beside Medusa, nods in agreement with Kai. "Kai's right. We need to make sure it's safe first. We can't have a dragon battle on top of a war with Loki."

Cappa and Delta, meanwhile, exchange a look and start discussing amongst themselves, their voices a mix of excitement and apprehension. "That's incredible," Cappa says, shaking his head in disbelief. "Do you think he can breathe fire?"

Delta nods, glancing at Lucas. "Oh, yeah. Or lava maybe? A lava dragon would be badass."

Hermes, his face a mask of concern, steps forward. "It's not safe," he interjects, his voice firm. "We can't risk it right now."

"Hermes, his dragon was threatened by your dragon. How could anyone know Lucas possessed such a beast?" I argue on his behalf, trying to convey the urgency and importance of understanding Lucas' full potential.

"What else are you hiding in there?" Hermes asks, snapping him out of his trance.

"Hm? Oh, uh, I used to go swimming in Loch Ness, but I stopped once cameras got a lot more accessible." Lucas answers so matter-of-factly, a small, hesitant smile playing on his lips.

"You're the Loch Ness monster?" I balk, unbelieving at how casual he makes the confession. Mortals are obsessed with the lore of a prehistoric water giant rumored to live in the ancient lake.

"Can you shift into a T-Rex?" Hermes asks, suddenly excited by the prospect of other animals, his concern momentarily overshadowed by curiosity.

"So, a dinosaur is fine, but a dragon is not?" I tease, pushing him as he pulls me in for a kiss. "Stop being ridiculous."

Cappa and Delta, who have been listening intently, burst into laughter. "A T-Rex? Seriously, Hermes?" Cappa chuckles, shaking his head.

Delta smirks, nudging Cappa. "I'd still place my bet on the dragon being more impressive."

"I can handle this." Lucas finally makes the decision for himself, stopping everyone's arguments on the matter.

Shaking his head in resignation, Hermes walks away,

joining us as everyone else steps back. Cappa and Delta sit in rocking chairs under the covered porch, eating sandwiches and placing a bet on the color and size of their Titan's dragon.

The clearing is huge, and with the trees destroyed in the quick skirmish, there is even more room available. Lucas takes deep breaths before discarding his robe to the side. His naked body still marred with dirt from tussling with Medusa's dirt-cobra. Lucas looks around, ensuring there is no one nearby.

I keep my Sensory waves of calming at the ready and can blast him to sleep should I need to. I give him a knowing confirmation in my glare, and he nods once, nervous to try and pull this beast from the dark recesses within him.

Seeing Lucas shift into his wolf was instantaneous. The mighty beast was called out of him and took over his body within the beat of a heart. I recalled Lupo as he slowly transitioned from the form of an onyx wolf back into a man.

I didn't have my memories about me then, and watching the fur recede within Lupo and the twisting of his bones was gruesome. He did it to terrify me but had to have been painful to slow the transformation down so intentionally. Each of the bones broke and shifted, elongating into the beast they conjured.

As Lucas begins his transition into the dragon, he falls to the ground in agony. His back arches dramatically, the sound of cracking bones echoing across the clearing. He grits his teeth, sweat forming on his brow as his flesh shifts between red scales and tan skin. The sight is both mesmerizing and horrifying.

"Told you he would be red," Cappa murmurs to Delta, who hands over a bill with a smirk.

"I think we should stop this," Hermes says quietly. The

concern on his face is no longer from the unknown of how Lucas's dragon will behave, but sympathy for the pain he is witnessing Lucas endure.

Stepping forward, memories of turning Lucas into an immortal flood my mind, the weight of that decision heavy on my heart. Seeing him in pain now, just as he was then, tears at me. Determined, I encase him in a sphere of healing waters, adding my silver aura to soothe him. Lucas fights against his beast, and together, we coax the dragon out, our efforts melding in a dance of power and will.

Skin is taken over by scales. Arms and legs shift into the paws of the beast, and a pair of red wings sprout from his back. Dispersing the bubble of water, the newly emerged dragon flaps his wings twice, rustling the splintered wood and grass of the clearing as he sets his paws on the ground. With eyes shining like two red rubies, Lucas's dragon looks over the immortals standing before him.

As I look on in awe, the immortals around watch, equally amazed. We have not only one, but two dragons. Something we have never had before in this battle and the thought sends a surge of excitement through me.

Hermes' Titan powers have been guarded on Tartarus and until recently, Lucas has remained a captive of the enemy's army. But they have both been set free now and both are equally motivated to enact their vengeance on the god that has tormented their immortal lives and brought them immeasurable pain for eons.

And I plan to use them and their vengeance to our full advantage.

12 Hermes

Now, Gaea is home to two dragons–sort of. It seems not all of Lucas' animals are as cooperative as others. The transformation to the dragon was hard-fought. It seemed to resist Lucas summoning the beast to the surface.

As a result, I would call this smaller transformation more of a dragonet than a dragon. No larger than a cow, the crimson coloring of his scales and ruby eyes are striking. The impressive wings and powerful tail would be formidable if only he were slightly larger than this. Based on the size of Lucas' wolf, bear, and other animals, I expected a much grander beast to unfurl. From the looks on everyone's faces, so did they.

I smile and throw a sly look at Medusa.

"Don't you dare." She warns me, but I see the grin sliding over her face too. Medusa knows me too well, and I can't resist this opportunity.

"Look at you, special little guy." Stepping out from the cars, I tiptoe toward Lucas. I raise the tenor of my voice and snap my fingers, as if calling a canine. "Who's a good boy?"

If I could describe the facial expressions of an annoyed and bored dragon, it would look just like Lucas does right now.

With half-lidded eyes and his mouth set in a flat line, Lucas flares his nostrils, huffing in irritation.

"Oh, quit." Rhea smacks at me, but I dodge her.

Chuckling, I bend down and pat my knees. "Are you a good boy?" I keep my pitch high as the dragon looks away, and I swear he rolls his eyes.

"I'm going to bite your face off." Lucas speaks to me in my mind, and I throw my head back in amusement.

"With that tiny mouth? No, you're not." Retrieving a stick from the forest floor, I wave it in front of him. "Do you want to fetch the stick?" Tossing it to the side, Lucas follows its path and then looks back at me. His ruby eyes glinting with the movement. "Go get it, boy!" I exclaim once more.

The snickers around us settle as Lucas looks to his packs of Shifters and then back at me.

Taking in a breath of air, Lucas' chest begins to burn like the embers of a fire. His throat glows, and I watch a red blaze with bright yellow flames ascend toward me. He puffs a small ball of fire at me, the size of a volleyball, and it lobs across the clearing, landing halfway between us with a very anti-climactic splat on the forest floor.

"He's a fire-breather." Cappa holds his palm out expectantly to Delta, who turns over another bill.

"You're adorable." I call out as Lucas sits on his hind quarters.

Rhea extinguishes the flames with her elements. Water puts out the fire, and Wind clears the smoke. She looks around to the shredded forest with her hands on her hips. "We need to clean this up." She says more to herself than anyone.

Earth and Life powers work together as she repairs the

charred ground. The dirt and mud churn, consuming the shattered bits of tree that litter the space.

The splintered and busted tree trunks grow, reaching toward the sky once more. Their canopy of leaves unfurls right before our eyes, adding shade back to the clearing.

"Nice." Medusa gives her approval with her arms crossed over her chest as she watches the fast-growing trees.

Lucas shifts back into his human form. The transformation quick as his dragon is all too eager to return to the den of solitude within him.

"Well, that was underwhelming." He says with a huff as he brushes errant bits of grass and dirt from his legs.

"It's not the size of the dragon that counts, right Lucas." I jab him with my elbow, and he pushes back against me, retrieving his discarded robe and heading toward his house.

"It's settled." He calls back, not stopping his path to his home. "I hate you; final decision."

"You're terrible." Rhea pokes my side, but the humor in her eyes gives away her amusement.

"I'm hysterical." I pull her in for a kiss, unable to keep myself from showing her affection for too long a period of time. She reaches up on the tips of her toes and wraps her arms around my neck.

With a smile, she rubs her nose across mine and gives me another kiss. The gesture fills me with a wave of sorrow that constricts my throat.

"Achilles used to do that to Pat and Callie." My tone comes out more somber than I intended as I blink away the moisture threatening my eyes.

"I know." She does it again and this time warmth rushes

through me. A small gesture of their love that we can continue in their memory. "I'm hungry." She declares.

"Well then, let's see if these Shifters can rustle up something to eat." My hand travels down to her ass and I cup her with a squeeze before pulling away. "Gods, you drive me crazy."

The look she gives me drives fire to my core and heats my longing for her. Putting my arm around her shoulder and giving her a kiss on the temple, we head toward Lucas's house. Recalling the amazing lunch Cappa prepared, I nod toward the Shifter.

"Hey Cap!"

He takes notice and nods in return.

"Do you think you could feed the Goddess of the Twelve Realms? She requires sustenance before she saves us all from certain death."

"Stop it." Rhea jabs me again as her cheeks flush.

"Never." My hand trails down again, and she does nothing to stop me as I steal another feel of her gorgeous ass.

Cappa and Delta spring up from their chairs. Adding on to my teasing as they take up positions on each side of the door. "It is our eternal honor." Cappa answers as they both stand to attention and salute.

Opening the door, I gesture for her to walk ahead, smiling at the Shifters.

"If you guys don't stop, I'm leaving, and you can fend for yourselves." She huffs, her pink cheeks flaring to a proper shade of red.

"If you leave, you don't get any delicious lunch." Cappa counters.

Narrowing her eyes, Rhea considers, then resigns. "Fine."

With a chuckle, we follow her inside, the others stomping up the stairs behind us.

Lunch in Lucas' pack house seems cozy but vacant at the same time. While the food is hot and abundant, the conversation is rowdy and the company is welcoming, it's just not the same without my sister and my best friend.

I find myself looking to my right where Achilles would always be, ready to shoulder each other when someone said something funny or to exchange a knowing glance.

A frigid current hangs low to the floor without the sunny demeanor of Callie, making everyone smile and feel light-hearted with her presence.

Then my gaze finds my mother and my heart leaps.

Seeing her here, living and breathing is still a shock, and I'm not sure how long it will take for me to get accustomed to the fact she is alive. Just like I know I'll never get accustomed to Callie and Achilles being gone.

But then I think about Pat.

Losing him was a devastation that rocked us all. I suppose we tried to move past it quickly for Achilles' sake. But I almost don't want this hurt to settle. I never want the pain of their deaths to leave me.

Rhea is sitting in my lap with her arm across my shoulders. She is playing with my hair close to the nap of my neck and laughing at Delta as he recounts stories of their past. He and Cappa seem to be as close as Achilles and me.

Everything that happens around me is bringing me back to the recent loss of some of the most important people in my life. I feel like I'm a blotch of darkness ruining the lightness of the atmosphere, and my chest tightens like the room is closing in on me.

Patting Rhea's hip, I shuffle her off me. *"I'm going to get some fresh air."* I speak into her mind and kiss her quickly.

"You okay?" She occupies my vacant seat, holding me with her honey eyes, filled with concern.

"Yeah, I just need a minute." I know my sad smile does nothing to fool her, but I don't need to hide my grief. Especially not from Rhea.

Keeping my feelings from her almost cost me everything. Before the eclipse, before Ares attacked, I vowed that if her life ended again, so would mine. I was so fixated on the possibility of never seeing her again that I was blinded to other possibilities of how she could make it back.

I had felt the presence of my father within the wards, but Callie picked out the power of Ares as well. Together, the bond of Apollo and Ares wove a shield of protection, just as strong as the love they shared. A love Callie and Achilles were lucky to also have.

And they broke those shields with a power just as strong as Ares' and our father's, allowing my mate to return back to me. A gift I don't feel worthy enough to receive but one I'll cherish and protect for eternity.

But walking out to the front porch of the Shifters' main pack house, the pine-scented breeze of Wyoming swells around me and it feels like Callie should come bounding up the stairs toward me.

The heat of the sun feels like Achilles' warmth, and I look to my right again, only to see an empty expanse of porch that almost darkens with his absence.

Turning to my left, Lucas is leaning with his forearms against the railing. He's tearing splinters off a piece of wood and flicking them into the grass.

"Little too loud in there?" He doesn't look at me as I join him by the railing.

"Something like that."

We sit with the calls of nature around us. The muffled sounds from inside the pack house float out occasionally as someone says something profoundly funny and the occupants laugh.

Taking a deep breath through his nose and clearing his throat, Lucas breaks our stillness. "So, you're a Titan too, huh?"

I snort a laugh. The memory of Theia, laying in her palace within the clouds, dying, spills into my mind just like the golden blood that oozed from her wounds.

I never saw her in any other form than the great cosmic dragon, so I'm not sure if she had another form. I was nothing more than a youngling. An apprentice for barely an age before the Archangels attacked.

My father was away with most of Theia's army, likely a diversion staged by Loki so he could steal another Titan's power. But I was there, invisible within my Mirage and told her I would teleport to my father. I begged her to hold on and that he could save her.

But she knew her fate and didn't want the power of Light to be stolen by the god-killer. She wasn't strong enough to finish passing all her power to me when she detected his invasion.

With the last of her strength, she sent me to my father in an instant. I collided into his arms with the gong of Theia's trumpets blasting their final warning across the realms. I cried so hard and apologized to my father for failing our Titan.

"Oh, son." He tried to comfort me, but I couldn't be

consoled. As soon as he put his hand on my head, he felt it. He knew Theia had transferred her Titanic might into me.

But the god-killer got what he wanted. There was still some of Theia's power remaining in her weakened form and Loki consumed it. I wonder in that last moment, if she knew.

If any of them knew who it truly was that came to consume them: Loki, Apprentice of the Mind, became the killer of Titans.

"What did it feel like?" Lucas' voice snaps me out of the memory and I startle. Shaking my head to clear the darkness, I watch the splinter that Lucas flicks as it arcs across his lawn and falls into the green grass.

A small bead of blue light forms on the tip of my finger and I flick it. The beam of Lumos becomes a streak of starlight as it races into the forest and pings off several trees before we lose sight of it.

"When I turned into a Titan?" I ask and Lucas nods his head. "It was like every light in the twelve realms amped up to a burning blaze and surged into me. I felt bigger, even though I know I didn't grow in size, but still, I felt like a giant."

I think about the memory Lucas shared of my mate turning him into a Titan within the shadows of the Underworld. "What about you?"

"Ah, it was the scariest and most amazing thing that ever happened to me." He flicks another splinter of wood. "But sometimes the world gets too noisy for me." Lucas points to his ears, "Heightened senses and all."

I nod my head in understanding. Even in his human form, he has the instincts and senses of the animals that lurk within him. "I'd like to be able to just turn the volume down sometimes."

"Yeah, I get that." The silence stretches on again as I think of the dragons within us both. "What's up with Tiny?"

Lucas huffs a laugh, flicking another splinter. "I knew there was something else in there, but that beast never wanted to come out." He shakes his head and finally turns to look at me. "To be honest, I've always been a little afraid to see what it was. But now that I know what it is, and how it responded, I'm not sure I can control it."

I look across the vast expanse of Lucas' territory.

Rhea and I just fortified his entire property with a protective shield. "You've got thousands of acres here, surely that's enough room."

"Room for what?"

I stand and adjust the waistband of my jeans, pulling my shirt down. I stretch my neck to one side and then the other. The gloom of my mood lifting as I cock an eyebrow at the Zeta King of Shifters.

"To train your dragon."

"**A**re you fucking crazy?**"** I balk at the Herald of the Realms as his blue wave of Light settles around us. In a blink, his portal swallowed up where we stood on my porch and delivered us to a cliff that looks over the valley of my territories.

The cobalt sky is full of white fluffy clouds that cast shadows over the ground as they roll above us. The wind billows in my hair and I gather it on top of my head with the elastic band that is always around my wrist.

"I don't know if this is such a good idea to shift in such close proximity to each other, H."

"Lucas, are you just going to stand at the edge of a cliff every day, wondering if today will be the day you finally take the leap?" Hermes leans forward, looking over the cliff. His deep blue eyes scan across the grounds as the rings of his iris glow with his aura.

I narrow my gaze at him, feeling the familiar mix of irritation and camaraderie that Hermes always seems to evoke. "You know as well as I do, it's not about the leap. It's about what happens after."

Hermes chuckles, the sound light and almost musical. I

really don't think there is ever much that can ever bother him. "True, true. But sometimes you have to embrace the unknown, trust in your power, and just... fall."

Hermes turns around, facing me. The heels of his boots are just barely hanging off the edge of the cliff as he casts his arms out wide.

My gaze drifts to the edge of the cliff as the shadows of the cloud-filled sky roll across the green grass below. "Some of us don't have that luxury. Some Titans actually have packs of Shifters relying on them."

"And some of us have the fate of the realm weighing on our shoulders." Hermes shuffles his feet, moving closer to the cliff's edge. "If you never fall, you can never rise stronger the next time. So, let's see what you've got."

Then that crazy son-of-a-bitch falls backward with a shit-eating grin on his face.

I stand there, my heart pounding in my chest as I watch Hermes plummet. The air around the cliffs thickens, tension mounting like the pressure before a storm. Then Hermes' form blurs, a shimmer passing through him as if reality itself wavers. I can't tear my eyes away from the transformation that seems to happen in the fraction of time it takes to blink.

He doesn't shift as my pack and I do. Where our bodies break and morph into the animals that live within us, his body elongates, reshaping under the guise of a brilliant glow. The Light brightens to an almost blinding radiance, then coalesces into the vibrant, shimmering blue of starlight. It's unlike anything I've ever seen—magnificent and terrifying all at once.

The transformation is both majestic and eerie. His limbs appear to stretch, morphing into powerful, scaled legs and arms, each movement accompanied by the crackling of static energy. A tail unfurls, sinuous and sleek, trailing sparks that remind me of shooting stars streaking across the night sky.

Then the wings—they're fucking amazing. They unfold like sails catching the wind, immense and otherworldly, glowing with an inner light that pulses with every beat. The sight is so overwhelmingly beautiful it takes my breath away.

As Hermes' head reforms, his jaw extending into a snout, crowned with a row of starlit horns, a low growl escapes me, unbidden. On his great wings, the beast soars down toward the valley. The shadow of his wingspan on the land below nearly reaches each side of the sloping land.

My body reacts on a primal level, instincts awakened by the raw display of power. I feel an urge, a need to match this spectacle, to transform and expand, to feel my own body taken over by such sublime force.

"Let's go, Zeta." The growl of Hermes' voice, taken over by the deep gravel of the dragon, rings in my mind. *"Show me what you're made of."*

I take a deep breath, the air crackling with static as I prepare myself. The energy around me still pulsing from Hermes' explosion of power, and it calls to something wild within me. It's my turn, and the challenge rushes through my veins.

As I edge closer to the cliff, my heart races with a mix of trepidation and excitement. I'm determined to embrace the grandeur of the dragon that lives within me.

My mind has been opened to the possibility of what other creatures of mythology that are real and within my ability to call forward, but first, I need to conquer this dragon.

The cliff looms ahead, a sheer drop into the jade valley

below of green grass and strong pines. With a deep, steadying breath, I leap forward, just as Hermes did, aiming to soar.

But as I fall, the familiar power of the Shifter eludes me. My bones don't break and bend to the shape of the animal I'm summoning. My skin doesn't mutate into the hide of the great beast that I want to shift into.

The ground rushes towards me, a terrifying blur of inevitable impact. My mind scrambles, trying to latch onto something, but panic clouds my thoughts.

In sheer desperation, my instincts kick in.

Suddenly, my body compresses, a sensation like being squeezed through a narrow tunnel. The transformation happens rapidly, my form shrinking and condensing as if the very essence of my being is being distilled into something entirely different. My bones and muscles contract, the once familiar structure of my human body rearranging itself in a blur of motion and instinct.

My skin tingles, the surface texture changing from soft flesh to a hardened, delicate exoskeleton. Wings sprout from my back, unfurling with a delicate whisper, their iridescent membranes catching the light and shimmering like a thousand prisms.

A breath away from colliding with the ground, my vision fractures into a kaleidoscope of images as my eyes morph into multifaceted orbs. I see the world through countless lenses, each capturing a different angle, a different perspective.

The rush of the fall is replaced by the dizzying sensation of flight as I surge upward, my wings beating with a speed and precision that defy human comprehension.

The air around me feels different, each current and eddy a tangible force I can navigate with agility. My body is now light, almost weightless, and I dart through the air with the grace and speed of a creature born to it.

Soaring, not with the mighty wings of a dragon, but with the delicate, iridescent wings of a dragonfly. The relief of not crashing is palpable, but it's quickly overshadowed by a sting of disappointment that the dragon within me has retreated further into its den of solitude.

The sky above me darkens as the cosmic blue dragon banks back toward the cliffs. The head of the large beast looks back, searching for me. I know the instant the heavy gaze of the dragon lands upon me, as if it can see every truth of the darkness within me.

I'm never going to hear the end of this.

I need to regroup, to understand why I can't call upon the dragon form. For now, though, I flutter above the ground, racing toward the top of the cliffs, vulnerable and small, yet alive and determined to try again.

The ground complains as Hermes' giant form impacts the tall cliffs. I brace myself as I flit closer, the buzz of my wings a soft hum compared to the thunderous beating of a dragon's wings I had hoped for.

I land delicately on a nearby leaf, my body light but my ego heavy. The irony of my transformation isn't lost on me, aiming for a dragon, and becoming a dragonfly instead—a cruel little joke of the animals within me.

My body expands and I lay on my back with my arms splayed wide. Looking up at the rolling clouds high above me, I release a sigh of frustration.

Hermes shifts back from the majestic dragon to his human form, the glow of starlight fading around him. As he approaches, a smirk plays on his lips, and I know the teasing is imminent.

"Well," Hermes starts, his voice laced with amusement as he towers over my minute perch, "I must say, your idea of a dragon is a bit–different–than I expected."

I can't help but grimace, even as the corner of my mouth twitches in a reluctant smile. "Yeah, I guess I missed the mark a bit, huh?" I respond, trying to beat him to the punch with my own self-deprecation.

Hermes chuckles, shaking his head. "Just a bit. But look on the bright side, you're probably the fastest dragonfly this side of the mountain. And surely, the most fireproof." The Herald holds his hand out to me. Grasping his wrist, he helps pull me to my feet.

A portal flourishes next to me, delivering my clothing as a pile on the ground. I dress as Hermes stands next to me looking across the valley.

The jest stings, but the lightness in his tone softens the blow. Despite his teasing, I know it's Hermes' way of cushioning the disappointment of my failed attempt. It's a reminder that while the failure is obvious, it's not the end of the world.

"I'll get it next time," I assert, more to convince myself than to inform Hermes. "Just you wait. I'll be a dragon that'll make even your starlight form look dim."

"We're counting on it." Hermes grins, clapping me on the back.

It's not just my Shifters now that need me, but Hermes and Rhea too. The entire realm is being upheaved by a force more powerful than we could have ever imagined.

As Loki has lurked within our crowds and our minds, he's shielded himself away, pretending to be smaller, weaker than most of us. Now that his mask has been ripped off by the goddess, he'll respond like any trapped animal, and I fear we only have only begun to see a glimpse of the chaos he has planned.

Hermes steps closer, placing a reassuring hand on my shoulder. "Keep trying, bud. Remember, it's not the transformation that defines you, but the will to keep fighting for it."

He's right. And if anyone knows the truth in that statement, it's Hermes and Rhea. They have fought this battle and been knocked down a thousand times. And each time, he stands back up, waiting patiently until the day his goddess returns.

And when she does, they march hand in hand back to the front lines of war.

Each failure is a step closer to success, each setback a lesson learned.

I glance at the horizon where the dark clouds gather, knowing that our greatest battle lies ahead. So, I will keep fighting for it, every day until this dragon is as familiar to me as my wolf.

When the day comes that we face Loki, and Hermes' dragon flies over the horizon, I will be flying with him. Our roar will take over the skies, our fire scorching the very ground his army will stand upon.

This time, we will bring the storm to Loki and this time, there will be no escaping us.

"**G**ood evening. Tonight, we face the reality of a new world—a world where the mythic and the modern collide with catastrophic consequences. In the wake of a mass assassination event that claimed the lives of numerous global leaders, we are now confronted with the emergence of beings long thought to be the stuff of legend. Gods and monsters are real, and they walk among us.

Just last month, the ancient city of Venice was lost, not to time, but to a creature of myth—a massive giant squid that dragged the city into the sea in a display of terrifying power. Across the ocean, New York City lies in ruins, a victim not of gods or mythical beasts, but of human conflict, as nations turned their weapons on what was once a bustling metropolis.

The fallout from these events has been devastating. Civil wars and riots have erupted worldwide, as fear and uncertainty drive humanity to the brink. Our societies are unraveling, our cities are battlegrounds, and amidst this chaos, the question on everyone's lips: where do we go from here?

As these immortal beings reveal themselves, some have shown hostility, while others plead for peace, proposing coexistence. But with the world in turmoil, their voices are lost in the cries for vengeance and the clamor of war.

Tonight, we stand at a crossroads. With every city that falls, with every life that is lost, the fabric of our global community frays even further. We find ourselves in desperate need of a savior, or perhaps what we truly need is to save ourselves.

As we continue to report on these unprecedented events, stay with us. Stay safe and stay informed. For now, we look to tomorrow with hope that from the ashes of today, a new understanding may arise between humans and the immortal beings among us. Good night."

I feel the looming darkness of Loki's depravity stitching together and weaving a plan of disaster that will draw me out. It's like thunder that whispers on the horizon. Far away at first until you hear it again and it's closer. Then before you know it, you're taking shelter from the storm.

He'll work to tear this realm apart, knowing I won't be able to stand idly by and let him do it. Then, once I'm no longer within the safety of my power, he'll make his true move and strike me with his hunger to consume me.

The only reason he's delaying is the power we both know he craves is not yet within my grasp. Death: the final feast he's waited for so patiently.

I could let the last of my powers remain in hiding, safely stored away from him, but with it, the final sliver of my immortality would continue to elude me. Perhaps I could live to an old age and avoid being violently torn from my life, but the outcome would be the same. Without it, this vicious cycle will only continue.

Hermes will mourn the loss of his mate again, and I'll watch from the Void for the chance at another lifetime with him. Another mortal shell that I can fill with my hope of finally defeating my hunter.

So, as we gather our plans, the Librarians pull archives of our past battles. We've spent several days at Lucas's pack house, working hard to provide a safe haven for our allies.

Medusa and I used our Earthen powers to ready a massive load of lumber. With Daphne and Hecate overseeing floor plans and directing elementals, a dozen houses are being constructed for Lucas's packs every day.

Lucas has a vast amount of land and has always respected the boundaries of his human neighbors. But in a realm wrought with fear and on the verge of war, we need everything we can get for the immortals that will fight alongside us. A sanctuary that will keep their minds shielded from Loki and safe from the mortal conflicts he's inciting.

We lost so many in the Battle of the Triple Moon Eclipse; that is the name Thoth and the Librarians are giving the fight against Ares. Penelope and Odysseus were leaders of Delphi Commune, its large army of immortals and their leadership was invaluable.

But they were consumed by the Shades of the Labyrinth under the shadow of the eclipse. Their deaths left Delphi at risk, the Elementals and Shifters residing there in peril.

With our shields of protection around the Shifters' region in Wyoming and the ancient Library of Alexandria, we can't afford the expense of energy and risk of exposing ourselves for all the communities of Immortals. It's safer to just move them here.

So, as we finish up the last home of the day and Hermes is teleporting the furniture into the home, it's stocked in an instant and ready for a family. Three families, actually.

There are so many needing homes and with dozens becoming ready each day, people are still sharing.

The immortal community on Gaea has never come together like this since the exodus from Tartarus. Since this war on this realm began, a rift was driven between the factions of immortals, and they have been pitted against each other ever since.

The Shifters were held as captives just like the prisoners of the Labyrinth. But now that they are free, not only of their physical captivity but a mental captivity as well, we are working together to end this.

It gives me hope that the future of this realm will be one of peace and free from war. The immortals will no longer hide themselves and finally share the value they can bring to this realm.

Kai hands out home assignments to the new families. Three families of Shifters stream into a home, thankful for a safe place to stay. The parents carry the dark shade of worry but it's the kids I notice. So carefree and excited, they rush inside, eager to take a look around their new surroundings.

The blemishes of this war have not yet darkened them and if there is anything I can do to make sure that remains the case, then I will do it.

The army Loki implores is varied and vast. Sure, many of them are fighting against their will, but most are not.

He is surrounded by the filth of immortals that would

press their power upon those without. Shifters and Elementals alike that would be happy to see this realm turned over for their tyrannical control.

The dark creatures that seep into the realm from Elysium are starving for Loki to unleash them. When Loki adds his own powers to the mix, the ability to control most of the elements, they create a formidable legion, ready to kill.

Hermes' warmth wraps around me a second before his hands burn a path around my waist. He feels as soothing as being wrapped in your favorite comforter that is fresh out of the dryer.

I relax into him with a heavy sigh of relief. He kisses the side of my head and joins me as I watch the families tucked inside our dome of tranquility.

But outside of this territory, the realm is suffering, and they are going to suffer more if we don't force Loki into action, before he forces us.

"What are you thinking about?" Hermes asks, moving my hair aside and running his lips up the curve of my neck before placing a kiss behind my ear.

"Currently? I'm thinking you should keep doing that." My voice is low, and I bend my neck, letting him keep up his exploration.

"And before?" He smiles against my skin.

"We need an army."

Medusa and Hecate abandon the new homestead and walk toward us. They could not be more of a contrast from each other if they tried. Hecate continues to don the colorful stola of ancient Greece while Medusa embraces her black leathers of modern clothing.

"This one is done." Medusa puts her hands in her back

pockets. Her green eyes moving between Hermes and me. "What's next?"

"An army, apparently." Hermes releases me from his hold but takes my hand in his.

"A Dark army, to be specific." I clarify.

After a moment's hesitation, Hecate seems to know where my thoughts are heading. With a chuckle, she moves the errant strand of grey hair that frames her face and tucks it back with the rest of her raven locks. Patting Medusa on the back of the shoulder, Hecate readies a deep purple swirl of her Dark portal. "You have fun with that, Medusa. I've got a neighborhood to oversee tomorrow on the other side of the territory."

"What the fuck is she talking about?" Medusa throws her hands wide, expressing her confusion.

"Loki has Shades and all manner of darkness under his control." I begin. "He controls the Labyrinth and goddess only knows what lives in there. The prisoners are forced to fight under his control, but the Darkness of Elysium is all too willing to follow his bidding."

"The Morrigan said she sensed the Titan of Elysium among us, just as the Mabon ceremony was starting." Hermes suppresses a yawn as he chimes in.

Medusa's eyes flash with anger as she begins connecting the strings of our separate thought processes. "Was that bastard trying to take the powers from The Morrigan as well?"

"Either that, or just pull her into his control." Hermes rubs his thumb across my hand, but his irritation is mounting as he pieces together Loki's endless deception. "He was cloaked and hiding within the darkness under a tree, but she sensed him. She said she could not call the Dark beings here because they would answer to their Titan, over her."

"But you're a Titaness of Darkness too, Rhea." Medusa points out. "Can't you call them?"

"I don't know. Darkness has many shades. Most would follow Loki over me if given the choice." I respond.

"So, you want to go talk to another army and give them the choice as well?" Understanding wraps around the bond between Hermes and me as he figures out where my thoughts have taken me today.

"Yup."

"What if Loki has gotten to them first?" Hermes asks, his concern valid because it could mean instant death for us.

"We'll just have to risk it." My mate and I share a look of agreement. We'll take the chance. We're too close to restoring my powers and ending this to not try.

"Can someone fill me in on what the fuck you two are talking about?" Medusa's irritation laces her question.

"We need the Vampires to fight with us." I hold her gaze as I reveal my idea. "We're going to make a truce with Vlad the Impaler."

The green flare of my portal fades, and Eris is cowering in her office, as she always does when my hooks are not controlling her mind. A line of drool hangs from her partially open mouth, and her clothes are damp where the slobber has pooled. She rocks rhythmically, humming under her breath, either mumbling some repetitive phrase or singing the same line of a song. She keeps herself company until I have need of her.

"You really are pathetic." I kneel next to her, and while her vacant eyes move to me, I know she is too far gone to process anything around her. "Let's get going, little marionette."

With my mental command, her body answers as if life is breathed back into her. She stands with rigid posture. Her pursed lips look like prunes, and her darkened eyes are filled with the contempt and discord I course through her. With her hands clasped in front of her, Eris waits for my next instructions.

No one would know it from her withered appearance, but Eris is the younger sister of my newly deceased mate. She has never needed a Thaumium collar because I completely took over her mind and broke her so long ago. The detriment to her physical form has been great, prematurely aging her and giving her the appearance of a much older immortal. Eris has long served as one of my several guises, being a figure others could openly detest and keep their prying eyes away from me. Now, I have one more show for her to put on.

"You fucking stink." My mouth turns down at the putrid stench emanating from her. Considering the hour, I allow her a few moments to bathe and put on new clothes. It's only for my benefit so I don't have to smell the stench.

Pulling her hair into a tight bun and securing the last button of her stark white pantsuit, Eris looks the part of my devoted assistant and will serve my needs for the next few days.

"Now, you stay right here, and I'll be back soon for you." Leaving Eris in a much more presentable state, I know she'll remain comatose until I return.

Teleporting to Washington, D.C., I arrive at my first stop. The news station hosting my interview is one of the top national broadcasts. The humans that greet me believe me to be an emissary of the immortals who have recently been unmasked. Today, I will warn them of what is to come and offer them a refuge. When the time is right, I know they'll take it.

Walking through the throngs of workers, satisfaction rushes through me as I soak in their admiration and terror. It's a small feast compared to the banquet of power I'll be consuming soon but enough to stave off my cravings. It's imperative I keep control over myself and my need for consumption. All my sacrifice will be worth it soon.

"This way, Atlas." A young woman chuckles as she gestures ahead of her. "Mr. Atlas? I'm not sure how to address you."

"Atlas is fine." I push up the gold-rimmed glasses I wear for show, so they sit higher on my nose. People subconsciously perceive those with corrective eyewear as trustworthy and intelligent. Immortals are no different.

My smaller stature always made them see me as weaker. Even though I was the youngest apprentice named by a Titan —until Hermes. Standing with my mates, both of them tall and strong, built for war, I was always seen as their *other mate*. Someone the Fates tied them to as a cruel joke. But everyone stopped laughing when they discovered the slain Titan Artemis. As I collected the powers of the Titans, the whispers of the god-killer made me smile. Someone powerful enough to take down a Titan must surely be one to fear. And they were right. I should be feared. Soon, I will be feared and worshiped as I should be.

Donning my friendly smile, I follow the young professional with a stack of yellow file folders in her arm. "And you are?"

"Ashley." She answers with a polite nod.

She ushers me into a room where attendants refresh my hair and pat my face with powder to ensure the studio lights do not cast a shine for the cameras. Escorting me to the newsroom, the bustle in the atmosphere is one of excitement and anticipation. Ashley, the brown-haired woman assigned to attend to my visit today, fidgets with her hair and straightens the folders in her arm for the tenth time. She wants to ask me a question but she's nervous, so I break the ice for her.

"It's okay to ask your question, Ashley." I shove my hands in my pockets as I stand next to her. We wait on the sidelines as the current news segment is underway.

Ashley chuckles, a flush rising on her cheeks. "So, I suppose you are reading my mind then?" Her eyes dart around with suspicion as she runs through a list of topics to hide the thoughts of the affair she is having with her boss. He's married. Three kids. Plus one on the way. Ouch.

Of course, I'm reading the minds of everyone, always. At least those who are unshielded.

"Body language is sometimes easier to read than a mind." I answer with a slight chuckle, and it puts her at ease. "You seemed nervous. I assumed you had a question, as I'm guessing you've not encountered someone...like me." I add the pause for compassionate effect, avoiding drawing attention to my immortality. The fragile minds of mortals crumble so easily. While I love breaking them, I like to savor the experience.

Ashley emits a nervous laugh. "But you are a mind reader?"

"I have the ability, though I feel it's unethical to scan the thoughts of everyone without just cause." I sense her excitement at my confirmation. "Would you like to test me?" I lean to the side, closer so she can hear my whisper. "Something small wouldn't hurt anyone." I wink, and her eyes widen with eagerness to experience a display of immortal power.

She scans the room, landing on the news anchor who straightens a small stack of papers as she reads her lines off the teleprompter.

"What about her, Olivia? What does she think about me?"

"Oh, she hates you." A simple swipe through the mortal woman's mind tells me what she thinks of my host. But I also know what Ashley is hoping to hear, so I entertain her. "She thinks you're having an affair with one of the producers and that your potato salad from last summer's potluck tasted like shit."

"That bitch." Ashley sneers but then straightens up as her lover/producer gives her directions in her earpiece. "They're ready for you, Atlas." Sticking out her hand, she smiles warmly. "It was a pleasure meeting you."

"Likewise." I should tell her she'll be dead soon, so will Olivia and the producer. The global panic would be such a delectable feast, but controlling so many minds at once will be easier with their compliance. And I need to conserve myself for the main course.

Taking my seat and ignoring the rush of final instructions from the technician fitting my microphone to my shirt and hiding the wires behind me, I take a calming breath. The lights of the studio brighten as we receive the cue that our interview has started and is broadcast live to the world of mortals.

"Welcome to tonight's special broadcast." Olivia begins with her practiced tone and poised professionalism shining for the camera. "With us is Atlas, a figure many thought was only a myth but is now known to be very real."

She turns to face me with her false smile. "Atlas, thank you for taking the time to speak with us today. The recent revelations about gods and monsters living among us have shocked the world. What are your thoughts on this?"

"Thank you, Olivia. It's understandable that these recent discoveries are unsettling. However, it's important for everyone to know that not all gods and mythical beings seek to cause harm. Many of us wish to live in harmony with humanity and offer our guidance and protection where we can. In fact, we have been living among you, quite peacefully for a very long time."

She offers a forced laugh and places her hand on her chest as if releasing a pent-up breath. "That's reassuring to hear. Atlas, with all these powers of the mind at your disposal, can you predict the future for us?"

"I'm afraid predicting the future is beyond my capabilities, Olivia. My role has always been one of counsel and support, not foresight. However, I can offer a warning—humanity itself stands at a precipice, facing conflicts that could escalate into a global war. It is a crucial time for all to strive for peace and understanding."

My interviewer changes her expression on a dime, reacting to my answers and putting on a show for the cameras. She wears her masks almost as tightly as I wear my own. "In these challenging times, what advice would you offer to our viewers?"

I pretend to contemplate for a moment, looking off to the side before pushing my glasses up my nose and answering. "Seek to understand each other, find common ground, and build on it. In the event that peace remains elusive, I urge everyone to find a sanctuary, a place of safety where communities can support each other. Remember, amidst the turmoil, strength often lies in unity and resilience."

"Such true words, indeed. Thank you for that insight, Atlas. Thank you for taking the time from your day. I can only assume the schedule of an immortal is a busy one." Insert obnoxiously fake laugh here. "Any final words for our audience tonight?"

"Indeed, Olivia. As we navigate these tumultuous times, remember, we may not control every aspect of our destinies, but we can always influence our paths with courage and hope. Thank you for having me, and to everyone watching, stay safe and stay united. Should your world leaders be unable to find common ground for peace, I warn you to find refuge, and may the Fates be with you."

Crossing the threshold into Transylvania, a shiver travels down my spine—not from cold, but from crossing into a land so steeply rooted in both history and myth it seems as if thousands of years of ghosts fill the space. The land of the Vampires is warded, protected by enchantments that whisper just beneath the audible range, making my ears ring with a silent promise of secrecy and danger. The frigid air bites against our exposed skin as if assaulting us until we abandon our path forward and turn back.

Hermes insisted we wear cloaks and I'm glad he convinced me to. The weight of it hanging on my shoulders is comforting, and I feel like it won't just protect me against the chill, but against the Dark powers that swell around our ankles.

Hermes walks beside me, his usually light-hearted demeanor replaced by a mask of concentration. Even Medusa seems subdued, her writhing braids restless beneath her hood, sensing the ancient power that saturates this place and ready to protect her.

"I don't understand why we can't just teleport to the front door," Medusa says, irritation pushing through her hushed tones. "Do we really have to walk the whole way on foot?"

"We aren't exactly best friends, Deuce," Hermes answers.

"I don't want our arrival to seem like a threat," I add as my eyes roam the foggy sky above. "This meeting is important."

As we walk deeper into the heart of Transylvania, the presence of Darkness becomes palpable, almost a physical touch against my skin. It's not merely the absence of light but a sentient force that seems to breathe along with the landscape. The wards that protect this land are saturated with it, each step forward resonating like a pulse through the soles of my boots.

This Darkness is different—it doesn't merely lurk or threaten; it beckons. It swirls around me, threads of shadow playing at the edges of my vision, whispering in a language felt rather than heard. It recognizes the Titan in me, and the Darkness here doesn't want to overpower or frighten; it seeks a ruler, a focal point for its vast, nebulous energy.

It's as if the very shadows have been waiting for someone like me, someone who could channel and direct its force. A god to worship, not just a commander controlling it.

It's just as I suspected here in the territory of the Vampires, where their wards provide them eternal night, a refuge from the harshness of daylight. It is a haven for the element of obscurity and trapped within these confines, it's deepening into something more. Something that longs for a release. It's an opportunity, a tool that could be pivotal in our war against Loki. But it's also a risk, a dance with a partner whose embrace could be as final as the grave.

"What if we are too late, and Loki has secured the alliance of the Vampires already?" Medusa says what we are all thinking. We could very well be walking into a trap; into the waiting hands of Vlad who will turn us over to Loki or even take my power for himself. But we've got to try.

"There will be no end of this earth that anyone, mortal or otherwise, could hide from Loki."

Looking to the grey sky above me, a thick curtain of white fog blocks out all sunlight from reaching the ground. The grass is brown as if frozen in an eternal state of hibernation, never again longing to burst into green blades and soak in the sun beams that fill a blue sky.

The village seems almost like a phantom emerging from the embrace of the fog. The mist curls lazily around the weathered stones and ancient timbers of the buildings, which stand as silent witnesses to centuries passed. Shadows flit and flicker, playing tricks on the eye, as if the village itself hesitates to fully reveal its secrets.

The air is damp and cold, the kind of pervasive chill that seeps into your bones. The fog muffles the sounds of our arrival, lending an eerie quietude to our footsteps on the cobblestone path.

As we continue, the outlines of the town become clearer, but the fog remains, a constant companion that softens edges and blurs lines, and it seems the village itself might vanish should the fog lift, taken back into the folds of legend from whence it came.

Among the white haze and curling shadows, the Vampires stand like stone columns. I nearly missed them until I saw the slight turn of their heads as we passed by.

Millennia old yet cloaked in the garb of today—they watch us with undisguised curiosity and cold disdain. Leaning from windows or pausing in their nightly routines, their eyes following every step we take, expressions ranging from wary to outright hostile. Here, the modern world seems to have brushed only the edges of the Vampires, leaving the heart of this place as timeless as the stories that haunt it.

As I pass by the lingering figures in the dimly lit streets of the village, my gaze inevitably meets theirs. The eyes of the Vampires are not just watching but assessing, calculating with an eerie precision that sends a chill down my spine. They have peculiar, slitted pupils that I find unnerving—reminiscent of a feline predator lying in wait.

Even in the subdued light, their eyes catch and reflect it as if capturing every stray beam, giving them an otherworldly glow that further alienates them from mortals and Elementals alike.

As I hold their gaze, even briefly, there's a moment where I feel as if they're peering into the very core of me, seeing past the façade of composure I'm struggling to maintain.

The intensity of their stare is unsettling, yet I can't look away. It's as if their eyes, those narrow slits, are not just windows to their souls but doorways to something older, wilder—something untamed and untamable.

A wave of cold runs down me as I realize the ethereal blood within them. "They're made from demons," I whisper to my two companions.

Hermes keeps a steady pace beside me, his gaze darting casually from one face to another, an almost imperceptible tension in the set of his jaw. "Yeah, an unnatural alliance forged between a mortal and a demon long ago. Vlad was the first, the rest he created after."

Medusa's presence, usually so formidable, is muted here; even her serpentine tendrils seem to sense the need for discretion, barely rustling under her hooded cloak.

As we pass a particularly ancient-looking tavern, a whisper reaches my ears, the sneer unmistakable even in hushed tones.

"Elementals," a voice hisses, the word laden with eons of grievances and unspoken accusations.

I turn slightly, addressing Hermes and Medusa without breaking stride. "Seems promising."

"They haven't forgotten the old wars," Hermes keeps his voice low, though I doubt it does anything to keep his words from ringing in their immortal ears. "The times we stood apart when they needed allies."

"The air here is thicker with grudges than mist," Medusa's jade gaze watches one Vampire particularly close. His slitted pupils are blown wide, and the whites of his eyes are bloodshot with prominent red veins. "And that one is dying of thirst."

I lift my chin and steady my pulse, not wanting my nerves and shaking fingers to give away the unsettling dread knotting in my stomach. "Let them stare. Old resentments won't keep the gates closed should Loki come bursting them down. Vladimir should understand the stakes better than anyone that his people will face."

Medusa's voice is a soft murmur, her tone dry. "Let's hope his sense of survival outweighs his memory of the past. Otherwise, this might be a shorter visit than planned."

Hermes nods, a slight smirk playing on his lips. "Especially for you, should his Gargoyles still hold a memory of your past slights against them."

Medusa's stone facade cracks and the corner of her lip twitches with the smallest of smirks. "They liked being partially petrified, and in the end, it worked out to their advantage, so they should probably thank me."

"By the Fates, please tell me you didn't turn his people into stone." I roll my eyes toward the second story of the ancient buildings as the number of Vampires lining the streets and watching our small parade grows.

"Not all of them." Hermes finds no humor in the tension building as we near the castle. His bright blue eyes are a deep navy, and he thrums his fingers against his thighs as we march toward Castle Dracula. "Just Vlad's personal guards."

"Oh, wonderful."

Beyond the village, the ancient castle of Dracula looms ahead, its black turrets piercing the sky like accusing fingers, and I can't shake the feeling of a heavy gaze upon us. It's as if the castle itself watches us, its stone eyes wary of outsiders.

The long parapet leading to the castle gates is a daunting stone path flanked by statues that have watched over countless tales of treachery and alliance. As we approach, the gates— massive, iron-bound, and seemingly impenetrable—stand firm. Yet, there's a stirring in the air, a sense of anticipation, like the castle is holding its breath.

I square my shoulders, feeling the weight of our purpose and send out a tendril of my aura. "Vladimir will see us. He must. Too much depends on this alliance. Whatever the past missteps, we can offer a chance for redemption—not just for us, but for all sides."

I say this, trying to convince myself more than anyone.

We stand as still as time trapped within this protective territory, waiting for Vlad's answer of passage forward. I sense Hermes' growing frustration and take his hand in mine. Lacing our fingers together, we lock eyes and give each other a reassuring squeeze.

"He'll open the gates." Another promising reassurance that I can't guarantee.

My heart jumps as a rusty squeak echoes across the obscurity, bouncing along the white clouds curtaining the land. The gates creak, beginning to open slowly, and we release a collective exhale that makes the fog curl.

As they open wider, we step forward, ready to bridge the gap between centuries of grievances, my faith in Vladimir's wisdom serving as our only escort into the heart of Darkness, into Castle Dracula.

17

Hermes

Stepping into the castle feels like crossing a threshold into a forgotten era.** Torches flicker along the opulent corridors, their weak flames barely piercing the suffocating darkness. Shadows writhe and twist across the walls, making the rich tapestries and ancient armor seem like sinister phantoms watching our every move with hollow eyes.

There's a palpable sense of dread here. The air here is thick and stale, as if untouched by a breath of fresh air for centuries. The oppressive weight of long-festering betrayal lingers in every corner, a tangible force that presses down on us, making each step feel like a journey through a tomb.

Rhea moves ahead with a determined stride, her posture rigid against the oppressive atmosphere of the castle. Medusa scans the shadows, her jaw set, and her forest eyes are cautious with alertness. I keep pace behind my mate, my thoughts racing on a fast extraction should we need it.

We chose not to teleport inside Vlad's territory as a courtesy and a sign of respect to his position. But Rhea's safety will be at the forefront of my attention until we leave here. I'll happily blast all of these Vampires to Elysium where they can rot.

We navigate through a labyrinth of corridors, each turn and archway meticulously crafted, a testament to a time when this castle was not just a stronghold but a statement of power. The deeper we venture, the more palpable the feeling of Darkness becomes, whispering through the cracks of the stone.

The grand hall yawns before us, a cavernous space where the ceiling vanishes into inky shadows. Long tables stretch out like dark sentinels, their surfaces stained with centuries of feasts and the echoes of long-forgotten celebrations. The scene unfolding before us is an open expression of Vampire bloodlust in every form.

The hall, despite its towering arches and ancient relics, is a macabre theater of unrestrained bloodlust. Vampires are entwined in a grotesque dance of sensuality and consumption, their bodies moving with a predatory grace that makes the air hum with dark energy. The sharp, metallic scent of blood mingles with the musk of their desires, creating a heady, intoxicating atmosphere.

Rhea's steps falter slightly, her gaze darting from one group to another, each scene a vivid display of sensuality where the lines between pleasure and sustenance blur.

I think back to Rhea's visit to the Land of the Lotus Eaters; Penelope and Odysseus' nightclub and haven to immortals of all natures. Rhea had never witnessed such open displays of lovemaking, and I recall the warm rush that flooded her face as she watched a Vampire feast on his lover.

Much like that display, a mortal woman is splayed naked upon the table, serving as the feast for several Vampires. Her legs are spread wide, and a woman has her mouth fixed firmly between the mortal's legs. The woman sits on the lap of a man, her hips riding him in circles.

She gives the mortal on the table pleasure while taking her own from the man in the seat. He sucks on her neck, pulling her blood and feasting as she rides him. Her eyes watch Rhea as we walk down the center aisle toward Vladimir, almost asking Rhea if she would like to be their next course.

Rhea's cheeks flush a deeper shade, a mix of embarrassment and a hesitant curiosity that she tries to mask by focusing her attention away from the intimate exchanges.

The mortal woman's moans of pleasure are stifled as her head hangs off the table and is filled with the erection of another Vampire. He thrusts into her mouth, and she hollows her cheeks, sucking him in as he enjoys the sensations of her around him.

With a piercing appendage fixed onto his thumb, he opens a small wound on the mortal woman's wrist and pulls on her blood as she sucks him deeply. Their moans of satisfaction increase as the foursome orgasms together, enjoying their feast of blood and lust.

Raising her head from the mortal woman's legs, the female Vampire wipes blood dripping from the corner of her mouth and sucks it off her finger. She had bitten the woman and gave her oral while consuming her fill. The man she is still sitting on leans forward, licking the mortal woman slowly and igniting a fresh wave of lust from her.

I take a place next to my mate, unaffected by this display. My eyes observing but not lingering as I'm scanning for dangers and marking those who are haunting the shadows of the great hall.

"Remember, Rhea," I murmur, low enough so only we can hear, "for them, these acts are as natural as breathing—perhaps even sacred. It's a blend of their nature and culture, a ritual of survival tinted with pleasure."

The woman Vampire rises from the man's lap and fixes a sheer robe of lace around her. The man stands and inserts himself into the mortal woman as he bites the side of one of her breasts. Her mouth, no longer filled, is being kissed deeply by the man still standing at her head. His free hand kneads her nipple deftly between his fingers as they resume their feast, and their mortal continues her pleasure.

Medusa's stoic expression cracks into a fleeting smirk as her braids sway and twist more animatedly, as if feeding off the chaotic energy. "I always did love a good show," she murmurs, her eyes gleaming with a mischievous glint. "It's not solely indulgence," she adds softly, her voice a calming anchor in the sensory storm. "It's an expression of their immortality, their way of embracing the eternity they're bound to. We must not judge it by mortal standards."

Rhea nods and takes a deep breath, "Their *food*," she emphasizes the word as if not sure how to reference the mortal having her blood let by the Vampires, "is willing? Consenting?"

"Always." Medusa confirms, further putting Rhea at ease. "It is Vladimir's first law."

At the far end, seated upon a throne that seems carved from the very shadows themselves, is Vlad the Impaler, King of Vampires, the first of his kind. His presence is a palpable force, as commanding as the darkest legends suggest. His icy blue eyes gleam with the cold light of uncounted years, each one a silent testament to the blood-soaked history he embodies.

He regards us with a measured gaze, his expression unreadable. The stillness in the air is thick, charged with anticipation as he raises a goblet to his mouth. The ornate base is silver holding a clear glass half-filled with a mixture of wine and blood.

We stop at a respectable distance. Beyond, a few steps lead up to his dais. As Rhea takes in a breath to speak, Vlad cuts her off, ensuring he is the first to address us.

"Are you here to throw me against another wall?" He raises a dark eyebrow at my mate as if in challenge. The dragon within me stirs and Vlad flicks his eyes to me quickly before putting them back on Rhea.

"That depends on you." Her voice is calm and sure, ringing across the hall. "Put your hands on my mate again and we'll see."

Gods, I fucking love her.

Crawling above us, the familiar sound of stone nails grinding on bricks pulls the attention of Medusa and me at the same time. High above us the partially petrified legions of Vlad's personal guards creep along the edges of the great hall and its tall rafters.

In a skirmish long ago, Vlad learned the extent of Medusa's powers as she began solidifying his guards. Before she could finish, Shifters attacked them both and they were forced to turn their fighting on a common enemy.

Turns out, Vlad's guards benefitted from the stone veneer as it protected them against the sharp fangs of the Shifters. Medusa offered to return them to their fleshy state, but his guards wanted to keep the stone coating like armor and better serve their ruler.

Flicking her head at them, Medusa greets her former opponents. "What's up, boys?"

"Gorgon." One responds with resentment in his stare and gravel in his voice.

"We have a common enemy, Vlad." Rhea begins but Vlad cuts her off again. He's really going to piss me off if he doesn't let her speak. Instinctively I take a half step toward the dais.

"I don't care about the war of the gods. It doesn't concern the Vampires, just like our struggles of the past were never a concern for your kind."

"This is about the fate of the entire realm."

"You can leave." Vlad cuts her off again and a rush of irritation flows out of me in torrents. This asshole better watch how he treats my mate. "On second thought, stay. Entertain me with your pleas and bargains. Let's see just how far you're willing to go."

The shadows around Vlad darken, extending their tendrils into an impressive display. While he has not physically moved, the darkness that ebbs around him is intended to be a threat.

A threat I don't appreciate. And based on the tension building within Rhea's power, neither does she.

A cascade of silver starlight erupts from Rhea, illuminating the hall in a blinding, ethereal glow as she takes a step forward. Her hair rises, caught in the unseen currents of her power, shimmering like a river of liquid moonlight against the encroaching darkness. Rhea's anger is palpable across our bond but so is her control.

Without hesitation, Medusa and I move to keep Rhea's path to Vlad clear.

The stone walls come alive under Medusa's powerful stare. Bricks slide and crawl from the wall, trapping the gargoyles like chain restraints.

Turning behind me, I cast a wall of Light so brilliant, the Vampires behind us hiss and shield their eyes. One especially angry woman reaches into the shield, pulling away with a shriek as her hand sizzles. The tips of her fingers, black and burned but already healing.

As Rhea takes her first step toward the Vampire King, she opens the ceiling of the great hall. Ancient timbers and stone blocks float in the air, exposing a bright blue sky. The fog that covered the atmosphere is gone, and sunlight fills the darkened hall for the first time in thousands of years.

Rhea moves quickly and unexpectedly; Vlad only has time to look up before she takes a second step onto his dais.

A strong current swells in the center of the hall, blasting Vlad's agitated vampires into the tunnels and sealing the entrances with long tables.

Turning my wall of Light into a shield, I encase the hall. Swells of shadows dissolve instantly as Vlad's people attempt to portal into the room.

With the hall barricaded by my Light, his gargoyle guards held captive above by Medusa, and Rhea ascending toward him, Vlad is nearly cornered.

"I'll handle this," Rhea says, her voice controlled and steady, calming me through our bond. I keep my position behind her, my eyes never leaving Vlad as I observe her powers with the surrounding light.

Vlad unfurls his large black wings of onyx. Shadows erupt from him, but instead of obeying Vlad, Rhea calls them to her.

With her arms spread wide and her palms up, the darkness flows into her like ink spilled into water. Confusion paints Vlad's face as he processes what is happening to the power that usually obeys him eagerly.

Taking the final step to his dais, Rhea's power explodes, and the richest black fills the hall in a rush. Surging to Vlad, Rhea binds his large wings against him with ribbons of shadow, encasing his body and slamming him into the stone wall behind him. The old stone cracks with the impact of his body.

"Seems like I did come to push you against a wall again." Rhea strides up to Vlad, craning her neck to look up at him. The Vampire King opens his mouth, his face twisted with rage. Before he can speak, she wraps a veil of shadows around his mouth. "I'll speak now, and you'll shut the fuck up."

Rhea uses a Mirage to push the events of recent days into Vlad's mind, flooding him with visions and sounds of the battle and exposing Loki.

Vlad has pissed her off, so while she doesn't hurt him, she's not gentle. "Loki has an army of Darkness, a legion of captive immortals at his disposal, and an entire realm of your food supply that he's willing to kill."

Vlad's pale blue eyes strain as he tries to push out of Rhea's hold, but he's powerless against her. With every shove, my mate wraps him tighter, pushing him harder against the wall.

"We're going to fight him, and we would have a better chance of defeating him if you joined us." Rhea holds Vlad in a fierce gaze, as strong as the darkness binding him.

They hold their stare as Rhea slowly returns Vlad's castle to its original state. Fog rises again, and white obscurity blocks the sun once more. Bricks and timbers reform as the ceiling is stitched together, and the tables of the great hall move back in place, ready for the next feast of the Vampires.

I lower my shield, allowing Vlad's warriors to return to the hall but keep Rhea and the dais covered with my Element. They stream in from every open door and passageway, but Medusa and I stand back-to-back. With her braids unfurled, I draw two swords of Light, and we hold them with a look of warning.

Rhea lifts Vlad higher on the wall, making sure everyone has a good view of the bound King. The Vampires watch as the Goddess of the Twelve Realms attempts to reason with Vlad.

"You have two choices," she begins, folding her arms over her chest and jutting her hip out. "You and your people can join Loki and become mind-prisoners, doing his bidding and watching your Vampires die for his cause."

This sparks a hiss from the observing Vampires.

"Or you can fight with us. Keep your minds free of anyone's control and take your freedom back." Rhea removes the binding around Vlad's mouth so he can speak, but she keeps him bound.

In that moment, I feel her power weave around the massive shield covering Transylvania. Silver starlight intertwines with the existing protective forcefield, fortifying it. Even if Vlad rejects her today, she is still protecting the Vampires from Loki.

"Such a naive little girl." Vlad turns his head and spits on the stone. The venom in his saliva hisses, a thin tendril of smoke rising. "There is always a third choice, and it's the one we will take. Inaction will be our path."

Rhea takes a sharp breath, her brows furrowing in disbelief.

"You would stand by and do nothing as the world burns?" My mate bites back. Her frustration with the Vampire grows, and I pass my encouragement to her through our bond.

"I will take the same road the Elementals took when I was first bound to this realm. When my people begged for help against the suffering forced upon us. We will sit on the shores of Limbo and happily watch you burn with the rest of the realm. Upon your deaths, my contract will be broken, and I can return to Elysium."

The icy stare of the Vampire King is cold enough to burn, but Rhea doesn't back down. Even as Vlad's eyes and veins turn black as he calls upon his deeper Dark power, trying to break out of her hold. "So, leave me and my people here to our peace. We have earned it with our lives."

Rhea shakes her head in disappointment as her power slithers away from Vlad. He stretches his wings, his fists clenched by his side, but he doesn't move. She takes a step back, the sting of Vlad's rejection apparent.

Filling her with my warmth, I come to her side and take her hand. We take the small steps down the dais, and I hold Vlad with eyes as cold as his. "If you change your mind, you know where to find us."

My power swells, and we leave the kingdom of the Vampires without a truce.

"**W**hat a fucking asshole!**"** I slam the closet door with my powers, causing the glass doors leading to the patio to tremble.

"You can't make the Vampires forget millennia of dissent. Vlad is right. We didn't help them back then." Hermes leans against the wall, arms folded, one ankle crossed over the other.

The way his arms rest push his biceps out, and it takes effort not to look down his lean body. His tight slate-gray tee clings to him, highlighting his muscles.

"But I wasn't the cause of any of that."

"No, but we didn't help because we were caught up in our feud with Loki. With the Shifters, actually. We couldn't split our forces."

Hermes is only trying to help, but my anger is too hot to reason. I take off my boots and throw them at the closet door. Hermes' power flares around them, teleporting them to the closet.

Ugh! I don't even get the satisfaction of taking my irritation out on inanimate objects.

The conversation with the Vampires couldn't have gone worse. This is not a time to remain divided over long-standing vendettas. It's exactly what Loki has done to us over the ages, and it's time to put things aside.

I roll my eyes at the situation and think of Callie. My throat tightens when my first instinct is to talk to her, and the realization that I can't hits me like a freight train.

Grabbing my shirt by the hem, I pull it over my head and throw it to the floor, unbuckling my pants next. Hermes' gaze heats me as I unzip my pants.

I'm angry, frustrated, and tired of these petty strifes. I'm tired of being hunted, forgotten, and weakened with each lifetime. I just want a release and I want my mate to give it to me.

Closing the distance between us, I jump into his arms and slam my mouth against his. My tongue battles his as I bite his lip. I thread my fingers through his hair, pulling gently and extracting a growl from him with my urgency.

He crosses the room with me in his arms and climbs onto the bed. His large hand holds the small of my back as I cling to him, legs squeezing his waist and arms around his neck.

With his free hand, he braces himself against the bed, finally dropping me where he wants me on the mattress. I pull at his shirt, and he grabs it behind his neck, pulling it off in one fluid motion.

His mouth burns my skin, his hand squeezing my breast, the fabric of my bra in the way. Hermes removes the clasp in the center of my bra, freeing my breasts.

He licks my nipple, biting gently as I grind my core against him. Hermes returns to my mouth, and our kiss is hungry, desperate to consume each other.

I unfasten his belt and unbuckle his pants. Moving the zipper down, I work my hand into his pants and grab his cock. Squeezing and massaging his erection, his groan of approval rumbles against me, and my nipples harden as a chill cascades down me.

The bars of Hermes' piercings slide along the palm of my hand as he thrusts into my hold. I rub myself against him, desperate to release the mounting pressure within me. "Just fuck me, Hermes. Make me forget."

With a sigh, Hermes stops and pulls my hand away, holding it over my head.

"What are you doing?" I protest as I move my other hand down his chest, but he grabs that one too, holding it above my head as well.

"No, what are you doing?" His breathing is heavy, matching the racing pulse of my heart. His rich velvet eyes dart between mine, and his hesitation pulls my anger out again.

"What do you mean, what am I doing?" I know I'm raising my voice, but my body heats as my mind seethes with today's failure. "I'm trying to have sex with my mate."

"No. you're using me as a distraction." Hermes loosens his hold on me, and my anger mounts. "I don't want to be a distraction, so tell me what's going on?"

I can't explain why I'm so pissed because I'm not sure why.

The truce with the Vampires was important. Reinforcing the shield around the Shifters' territory is critical. Loki is going to cause some form of mayhem any day now, and we're not ready for it. We need a fucking army. I need my best friend, and she's not here. She'll never be here again, and I'm angry about it!

Tears begin to spill over my eyes as I cross my arms in front of my chest. Biting the side of my cheek, I refuse to utter these words. Voicing them may make them more true in my heart.

When Hermes sees my facade begin to break, he shifts us

and pulls me into him. I cover my face with my hands and crumble. Sobs wrack my body as I release the pain of losing Callie, the defeat of Vlad's rejection, and my worry of what will happen if we don't have a force that can hold out against Loki.

But most of all, I feel humiliated and like a failure. Everyone is looking to me for answers I don't have. Power that is out of my grasp and understanding. The people I love are dying because of me, and I can't stop it. I can't stop them from believing they have no other choice but to give over their life.

It's crushing me, and I almost want to let it.

I feel like an avalanche is perched precariously above me, and I'm holding it up for as long as I can, but maybe I'm only postponing the overwhelming defeat that is inevitable.

I weep across our bond, letting Hermes in on the truth I'm refusing to talk about.

"Baby, you have nothing to be embarrassed about." His voice is soft and low. He shifts me in his arms, and somehow I melt even closer into him, hiding away from the crumbling world around us.

"I failed today." I cry out. "I couldn't make an alliance, and we need it." My sobs grow heavier as the weight of my botched negotiation slams into me. "We need them, and people are going to die if we don't have an army big enough to combat Loki."

"Then that is on Vlad, not you, baby." Hermes strokes my hair and holds me firmly against him.

"But I don't want anyone else to die for me." I cry for several minutes, and when it's clear I can't stop, Hermes removes my pants and then his, allowing us to lay together more comfortably. He puts his leg over me, and the weight of his body on mine helps to keep me tethered here.

But it also forces me to stay in the moment and feel the emotions raging through me. Confusion, frustration, and shame collide within me. My mind races with what I could have said differently or if the show of my powers was the wrong move.

I had hoped it would help Vladimir see the strength we could have together and give him hope of our defeat with our aligned forces.

But as Hermes works the tension from my body with his tender embrace and I work through the emotions wracking my nerves, I realize Hermes is right. There would have been nothing we could have said to change Vlad's mind.

He knew the moment we crossed his wards that we were coming to talk to him about an alliance. The Vampire King let us walk through his fog-covered village as his subjects stared us down. He had them put on a spectacle as we walked the great hall but it turns out, we were the spectacle on display. So, Vlad could flaunt the Elementals to his people as we came groveling for his help.

Then he purposefully angered me, interrupting every word I spoke until I lashed out. I gave him a reason to reject us, but he set me up, and I walked right into his trap like a fool.

"I'm such an idiot." I mumble into my hands and release a frustrated sigh.

Hermes shifts my legs apart with his knee and settles over me. With his nose, he nudges my hands away from my face and smiles at me sadly when I finally look at him.

"You're not an idiot." He kisses the tip of my nose, which I know is red from crying. "You're incredibly intelligent." He kisses my cheek. "Powerful." He kisses my other cheek. "You're determined and strong-minded." He kisses my neck. "You're the greatest force of nature that no immortal can contend with." He kisses the other side of my neck and surprises me by biting me. It tickles, sending a rush of goosebumps down that side of my body, and makes me chuckle despite the gloom in my mood.

Hermes stops his teasing, having accomplished his mission of breaking through my wall. Holding himself up on his forearms, he strokes my hair and looks at me with a combined expression of adoration and concern.

"I miss them."

Hermes gives me a tight-lipped smile as grief clouds his eyes. "So do I."

I put my hands on each side of his face and return his gaze with one of my own. After a moment, I wrap my legs around him and pull him into a hug. He envelops me in warmth and surety. "We're going to figure it out, okay, little goddess?"

I nod and wrap my arms around his shoulders, burying my face into him. Featherlight kisses skim my neck as he runs his soft lips over me. His spicy scent cocoons me. Inhaling as much of him as I can, my arousal warms low in my core and floods my body.

With every gentle rub of his hands and peck of his kiss on the tender parts of my neck, I exhale my tension. "I just don't know where we are supposed to go from here." As my breath brushes against his skin, I feel the effect it has on him as his cock hardens between my legs.

When he raises up, his eyes have darkened as our arousal caresses the bond between us. "It's the beginning of the end, right?" He breathes a little heavier as I run my power down our bond, stroking it just as I did his dick moments ago.

My lips part when Hermes brushes his growing length

along my pussy. His eyes move down to my mouth, watching as I react to his movement against me. Only my thin panties and his boxers are between us, and it's torturous. Licking my lips, I pull my bottom lip and drag it between my teeth. "Yes," I nearly moan my answer as I feel my core moisten.

"Maybe to get to the end, we have to go back to the beginning." Hermes whispers against my flesh as he moves down my neck. He hovers over my skin, not touching me, igniting my need to feel him.

Reaching my peaked nipples, he flicks his tongue across them quickly, sending a jolt of anticipation directly to my core.

"Okay," I respond in a breathy moan. "We'll go back to the beginning." I arch my back, needing more of him, but he follows my movement and remains a breath away from me.

He reaches my pussy and runs his nose up the center of my panties, inhaling my scent deeply as if it's the very oxygen he breathes. I sit up on my elbows, shocked but needing to watch him.

I'm so wet and desperate for his caress against my skin that I want to see his tongue lavish me the way I want him to. With a gleam of mischief in his eyes, his tongue skims along my panties so gently, right on my clit.

Gods, it's not enough. When my face flushes from need and frustration, his smirk grows. He wants to tease me and get me wild for him. He wants me to beg for his touch, but we'll see how much he enjoys being teased.

With a swift movement, I catch him off-guard and flip him over. In a second, I'm straddling him and run my center along his erection.

"Move up on the bed." I tell him, licking his lips. He comes after me, wanting a kiss, and I pull away from him. He cocks a crooked grin, knowing I'm going to give him exactly what he's been giving me.

With a hand on my hip, he does as I ask, and when he's reached the pillows, I lash out with my powers. Chains of silver starlight wrap around his wrists, fixing him to the bedposts.

I run my nails down his muscled chest and tight abdomen, rubbing my pussy along his cock. He grinds against me, his mouth popping open as he exhales with the sensations.

Leaning forward and bracing against him, I keep my pelvis hovering just above him. I can feel the phantom touch of his hardness against my core as I move my hips in a circle along him.

"Oh goddess, I want to feel you."

I lick him again along his lips. They are so soft, and while I want to lavish his mouth with my kiss and feel his tongue sweep into my mouth, I want him to beg for me.

Opening my mouth as if I'm going to kiss him, I hold just above him. Our breath mingles, our lips so close to touching.

Holding his stare as long as I can before I avert my gaze to his body, I let my lips run a featherlight caress down his chest. I flick my tongue across his nipple, and he gives me an approving hum.

Running a hot breath down his abdomen, I reach his boxers and slide them off. The length and girth of his cock make my mouth water, and I wonder how many barbells of his piercings I can devour before I'm choking on him, so I ask him.

"You can take every inch of me, little goddess."

I move his legs apart and settle between them, and he watches me with a hungry obsession.

"That beautiful mouth was made just for my cock, and I want to watch how gorgeous you are stuffed full of me."

His words seem to stroke my pussy, and I feel myself get wetter. With the tips of my fingers, I run them tenderly against his thighs, and power courses through me when I see his skin pebble with my touch.

His eyes track my every movement as I lean down. My hair tickles him as it falls in front of me, and I open my mouth as I near his cock.

Releasing a long, warm breath up the length of him, his erection surges toward me, stimulated by the nearness of my mouth and the prospect of my touch.

When I move toward his hip, Hermes relaxes into the bed and exhales. "Baby," his breathy voice, full of want, makes my core pulse.

"Do you want me?" I ask, not looking at him or waiting for an answer. I run my tongue along the dip of his pelvis, and he groans. Reaching his hip, I swirl my tongue and suck on his skin.

I feel the bed dip as he leans his head back, closing his eyes to the feeling of me. "Gods, yes."

I move to his other hip but pause when I reach his dick. It's so close to my mouth, and he lifts his head to watch me. The desire flooding him has turned his eyes deep sapphire, shining in the darkness as he watches me.

"Yes, what?"

"Yes, I want you," he answers breathily, full of need.

"Good boy." I reward him by wrapping my lips around the head of his cock. My tongue swirls around him twice. I taste the salty tease of his cum that leaks from him, and I moan in approval. "Mmm." I remove my mouth with a pop, and he releases a breath with the absence of my mouth on him. "So delicious."

I continue my path over to his other hip and repeat my actions. Running my tongue along the crease of his pelvis, I kiss and suck at his skin, pulling his body tight as he enjoys the attention my mouth gives him. Slowly, I work him until I reach his hip again, wrapping my arms around his legs.

My breasts graze his erection, and I move my nipples along the veins and ridges of his cock.

Finished with his hip, I center my mouth close to his dick again. He hasn't stopped watching me, and it makes me wet knowing how much he desires me.

Emboldened by his hot gaze, I sit up on my knees, my panties soaked, and my pussy throbbing with arousal.

I hook my finger on the fabric and move it aside. His eyes are drawn to my center, and he runs his tongue along his lip. "Let me taste you."

Without answering, I run my finger down the slit of my pussy, wetting it with my juices. Sliding my finger back up to my clit, I rub circles on the bundle of nerves, groaning at the pleasure that rushes through me.

"Oh, my fucking goddess, you are so beautiful playing with your wet pussy."

I close my eyes and let my head fall back. My long hair brushes against Hermes' legs as I swirl my finger around my clit. I moan as warmth rolls through me, hearing my mate exclaim while watching me.

As I think about Hermes' tongue on me, the feeling of his piercings rolling along my walls as he thrusts into me, I build myself to an orgasm. Thrusting my hips as I roll my finger around my clit, I cum.

"Fuck, baby, yes." Hermes pulls against the ribbons binding him to our bed, keeping him from touching me. As the waves of pleasure course through me, each of Hermes words coax the climax to a higher peak. He tells me how beautiful I look, how much he wants me, how he needs to taste me and its only drives my desire higher.

I pant with heavy breaths as my orgasm subsides. Returning my eyes to him, I take three fingers and run them up my soaking pussy.

With my arousal wetting my fingers, I grab his cock and use my juices to wet him as I slide my hand along his length. He groans in appreciation, finally feeling my touch on him, and I love the surge of power that rushes through me at this control.

"What does my mate want? My mouth on your cock?" I ask as my hand slides up his length.

"Yes, my goddess. Put my dick in your mouth and suck me until I cum down your throat."

I lean down and lick the length of him. Starting at his base, I flatten my tongue and move up to the head of his cock, then I stop. "Then beg for it."

Hermes' eyes darken at my command, and his cock jumps, already missing the feel of me. "Please, baby." Hermes squirms again, the muscles in his arms pulling tight.

The sight of his strong body at the mercy of my power, my words igniting his arousal so deeply, makes my pussy tighten.

I move my finger along my slit again, making a show to push my breasts together and deepen my cleavage. "Beg for me, baby." I moan out as I play with myself again.

"Fuck, Rhea. I need you," Hermes pleads. "I need your warm, wet mouth on me. Please, baby, stroke my cock and let me fill your mouth with my dick."

I swear I could cum again if he keeps talking to me like that.

Instead, I lean forward, letting my tits rub along his erection as I let him taste my fingers, wet with the juices from my pussy.

He laps up the taste of me like a starving man, groaning as he sucks my fingers clean.

"Such a good boy," I compliment him, lowering my mouth to his dick. I reward my mate and give him the pleasure he begged for.

"Ah," he groans as I take him in as far as I can. "Yes, fuck me with that beautiful mouth."

I wrap my hand around his base and move up, creating suction with my mouth. Gliding back down, I push him further into my mouth each time until his long dick moves past my gag reflex.

"S-s-shit." He draws the word out as I hollow my cheeks and suck him. Taking him fully, the head of his cock is in my throat as the barbells of his piercing roll along my tongue. I fight against the choking need to remove him and squeeze my eyes shut as they water.

"Yes, my greedy little goddess." This time, it's me that moans as he talks to me while I work his cock. My tongue slides around his dick while I suck him. "You were made to take me, baby."

He grunts as I suck harder, moving my mouth up and down his length, each time fitting him in fully. "Gods, Rhea, you take me so perfectly with those beautiful lips."

His breath gets heavier, and he thrusts gently as I move along him. "You're going to make me cum. Are you ready to swallow me, goddess?"

I hum against him and pick up the tempo. I work him, feeling his muscles tense as he nears release. I squeeze and suck him, pulling his orgasm out with my lips around his hardness.

When he cums, it's not in my mouth but down my throat. The long length of him reaches so far into me, and I work to swallow him down.

Finished, I slowly ease him out of my mouth and lick him, cleaning him off as I look at him through my lashes.

"Such a perfect little goddess," he pants as his chest heaves and relaxes with the waves of his pleasure rushing over him.

I feel it down our bond. It makes my nipples harden again, and I move to straddle him. He pulls against the bindings, leaning forward, keeping his eyes on my mouth. My lips are warm and swollen from sucking him so vigorously.

I lick his lips, still holding back my touch as I rub my hardened nipple against his chest. "Do you want a taste of this perfect little goddess's pussy now?"

I flick my tongue against his bottom lip quickly, and he thrusts his pelvis up, his cock, still hard, rubbing against my swollen clit.

"Yes, goddess." He leans forward again, so close to touching me, but I keep just out of his reach. "Let me lick you until you cum on my tongue." This time, Hermes darts his tongue out and tastes me. At the same time, his powers travel down our bond, feeling exactly like he's flicking his deft tongue on my clit.

Now it's my turn to release a groan of pleasure as Hermes keeps his molten stare on me. "Please, goddess? Please cum on my face and my fingers." He licks me again, sending another sensation down our bond. "Please let me feel that tight pussy around my cock." He licks again with three flicks of his tongue on my lips, and I feel each one along our bond, thrumming on my clit. "I can't breathe without you, my beautiful goddess, so sit on my face and let me worship that pussy the way you deserve."

His words make me wet and fill me with need. Leaning forward, I run my wetness along his shaft and roll my sensitive nipples along his chest. I pull back on his hair, tilting his head back and bringing my face down to his.

We hold each other in a heated stare before I break the intensity and look at his soft lips, no longer able to stop myself from feeling them.

"Such a good boy," I whisper against him as I release the bindings of my power and let the beast I've teased ravish me

To get to the end, we've got to go back to the **beginning.** I can't stop thinking of that phrase. It's like an itch in the back of my brain that I can't scratch. Sitting at the top of the great Library, I watch the rays of the sun dance across the realm. Gold bursts of Lumos shimmer and move across the sky in an unending wave of light.

At night, the gold turns to silver as the light of the moon watches over the realm, giving the mighty sun its rest until tomorrow. The exchange of power reminds me of my parents. My father, Apollo, the Sun God from the realm of Light, and my mother, Daphne, the huntress from the realm of Night. My mother's calm temperament could always cool my father's blistering determination.

While they weren't mates, they were strong companions. A great deal of love and devotion bound them together as my parents, but it's my father's power that I channel, soaking in the warmth of the sun and trying to think with his wisdom about how to help my mate. The path to restoring her powers and immortality has been burdened with danger at every step. But never before have we come so close, and we must keep pressing forward. My staff, the Caduceus, is the final relic that safeguards what may be the most precious of her powers. It's hiding somewhere among the realms, waiting for the day Rhea reunites with it. We cannot stop until we find it.

Looking at my hands, I still feel the imprint of the cool metal of my ancient staff. The beacon of Hel and signet of the Herald, my Caduceus accompanied me as I traveled between the immortal realms. Anywhere I landed, the power inside my staff would light my route, guiding me wherever I needed to go. If only we had it now. I release a frustrated chuckle, running my hands through my hair. How ironic, needing such a tool and wandering along a pathless journey searching for it.

Somewhere in our past, we infused the immortality of my mate into the Caduceus and hid it away. My mother has spent the last four centuries meticulously searching through the archives of the great library, finding no trace of it. We have been searching the Library for hours and I know we're looking in the wrong place.

My instincts tell me the information is long gone. Missing, perhaps stolen, or destroyed. It's likely the reason Rhea hid the library to begin with—to keep Loki from destroying anything else that may help us find the keys needed to unlock her spell.

But a road was traveled with the staff in our hands, and at the end of that road is the salvation we seek. We only need to find the start of the path, and I'm confident we'll find the Caduceus at the trail's end.

Footsteps behind me scrape the stone, and the familiar aura of my mother envelops me. A smile crosses my face, the scent of candlelight and parchment mixed with the scents of the forest heralding her arrival. I turn to see her rounding the corner, offering me a smile that makes her eyes crease at the corners. She takes a seat on the large stone next to me, leaning her head on my shoulder. I take her hand in mine, kissing the back of it and placing it in my lap.

"I don't know that I'll ever get over seeing you again." I watch the sun inch closer to the horizon, the sky exploding in ribbons of pink and orange light.

"It's been a very long time." Her voice is filled with sorrow, each word an apology for her absence. "I'm not sure I'll get over feeling the sunlight on my skin again."

We sit silently for a few moments, both enjoying the final rays of sun before it drops below the horizon.

"How did this even happen?" My mother's last role was as nursemaid to my mate when she reincarnated as Juliet, the daughter of a wealthy Italian merchant. The last memories we had of them both were falling victim to death. For four centuries, the memory of Juliet's death was so profound. She fell on an immortal blade, her power and life siphoned from her.

But that terrible night, only a few weeks ago when the wolves attacked us at Medusa's commune and I hurled my sword across the plain, driving it into Rhea's chest, the truth of her lives cascaded through me. I saw the truth of Juliet's death. She ended her own life with poison, the depiction in Shakespeare's play inspired by our love story was correct.

I've thought about why my memory was tainted, only to be revealed when the first of her power was unleashed. It is now that I suspect Loki altered our past recollections as a way to enact subtle control over our minds so we would repeat the past when the time was right.

He knew my sword held the first of her power and I needed to unlock it. So many of my mate's former deaths ended on the tip of a blade–just not the right one.

"We were on the hunt for the artifacts that hold the power of the goddess, of course." My mother's rich brown eyes stay fixed on the beams of sun as she recalls the final moments before she disappeared from my life for four centuries. "Juliet discovered a long-forgotten parchment from the ancient library. Touching it, memories surged into her, and we came looking for the hidden building. But Loki was there. As well as Demeter."

My mother looks at our laced fingers, rubbing the top of my hand as she continues her account. "As soon as I saw my sister, I knew she had betrayed us. I readied my bow, but Loki struck first." She pauses, laughing through her nose and shaking her head. "His talons in my mind were ripping me apart, diving into my memories to see what I knew. Your mate couldn't stand to see the pain he was inflicting. She didn't know what she was doing; she just wanted to protect me."

My mother smiles at me with eyes aged with patience. "The remnants of the Titans' powers still reside within her. With each lifetime, they thrum, barely alive under the surface, guiding her to find the scattered pieces of herself. She used the full might of those fragments and teleported me to safety. I was forced through the blend of her shields and fell upon the stone steps of the library. Thoth and Seshat brought me inside, and we've watched your lives ever since. I've searched the accounts of the library and gathered everything I could piece together, waiting for the day she would find her hidden castle in the sky and recover us."

I found Juliet moments after that. She was sobbing and frantic, her cheeks wet with tears. She gasped when she saw me.

"I'm so sorry," she said, a small vial dropping from her hand and rolling across the stone floor. She was in a burial vault that belonged to her mortal family. "This is the only way." Her eyes drooped, and her head sagged. The poison worked quickly. "I'll find you. I'll always—"

Those were her last words, and she died.

As I think back to that vault, I take in every detail of her. The candelabras with dozens of ivory candles held golden flames that danced and cast long shadows over the cryptic vault where the dead Capulets lay. It seemed all too happy for the solemn occasion, and I dropped to my knees in disbelief. Her dark hair was splayed across two books, and I see them within my memories as clearly now as I did that day. It is the bottom book that sends a chill racing down my spine as I let the memory absorb into me. Rubbing my hands over my face, I run my fingers through my hair in exasperation.

Fuck.

"Where is Thoth?" I ask my mother as I stand, startling her. Suddenly alarmed by my reaction, her eyes widen and her aura flares, searching for threats.

"Inside the library. What is it?"

"I think this just got a lot worse, if that's even possible." Holding out my hand to her, my mother takes my grip, and together we walk down the tall stones and enter the library.

Rhea and Thoth are looking over a series of tomes that recorded our various departures from the realm to hide her powers from her hunter. Rhea notices me, and with a look, she knows something is going on.

"What is it?" she asks, instantly alarmed.

"When you died as Juliet, you collapsed over two books." I try to urge her with the intensity of my gaze, hoping she will think back to that time and add more pieces to the puzzle.

I watch her eyes as she holds my stare. A million thoughts

race through her mind as if she's flipping through hundreds of lifetimes, recalling the few moments before those deaths and hunting for the right one. Her face lights up with recognition. Her eyebrows shoot into her hairline with understanding before she rubs her brow with her hands.

"Oh, by the Fates, can this possibly get any worse?" Rhea nearly whispers the prayer, and I can feel her understanding pass through our bond.

"Don't say that too loud." Medusa enters the library with Kai, both standing with their hands on their hips. "The Fates may take that as a challenge."

"Loki is in possession of the Book of the Dead." Rhea informs our small assortment of allies. "I didn't realize it at the time, but he also had it in his office at the Atlanta Commune." My mate shakes her head in disbelief as if she should have recognized it. But her mind was still locked tightly in a vice, her memories withheld from her.

I see the recollection as Rhea passes it to me through our bond, and my breath catches, seeing Athena with her.

"Sorry, Atlas, for being tardy. We decided to take the long way and lost track of time." Athena smiled warmly at Rhea as they entered the office of the greatest deceiver we've ever known.

"No harm at all." He answered back, closing the large book, bound in human skin, sewn together and aged like leather. He kept his mask in perfect place, calling no attention to the book filled with spells of darkness and curses of necromancy.

"It was the day he tried to pull my memories of the car crash that killed my mortal family." Rhea speaks to me through our bond. I can feel the guilt washing over her.

"Don't you dare start blaming yourself. It's impossible for you to have known. But at least that is the day you knocked his ass across the room." I chuckle to myself as she rolls her eyes, and I feel her irritation across our connection.

"Yeah, if that was even real. He was probably faking it." Rhea shivers, and the look in her eyes seems like she is a thousand miles away. "Ugh, I feel so gross. I just let him in my mind like that. Goddess knows what he planted in there."

"How would he have gotten such a book?" Kai asks. The lore of Ancient Egypt's famous Book of the Dead is known by all across the realm, even among mortals. The true book has been searched for but never recovered, and now we know why. A god that hunts death has been hiding it, using it.

Thoth turns and speaks to us. His black void eyes seem to be looking over us all at once as he stands stoic like a tree in a great windstorm.

"The Book of the Dead is one of two relics recovered from the fallen realm of the Morrigan." Rhea's eyes snap to mine as we share a single thought: Mor.

"What was the other relic?" I ask quickly.

"Not *what,* but *who.* A being of great power is the other relic."

"The Morrigan." Rhea's thought confirms my suspicion as well. Mor's ability to shift into a being of darkness is like nothing else I've encountered. The auras of three souls that share a single body are unnatural, and if this great book of darkness was the only item retrieved from her realm besides her, I can only assume it had something to do with her creation.

It also makes sense why Loki attacked us as we watched over the Mabon ceremony. He wanted The Morrigan to add her to his collection alongside the book. As my mind races with the prospects of what could have happened if Loki had succeeded that night, a new terror rolls down my spine. "If Loki has the Book of the Dead..."

"The implications are severe. The power contained in that book... it's not just about controlling the dead." Thoth paints a grim picture of the possibilities, each worse than the other. "The dark world of Elysium is like a spider's web that spans the shadowed ether of nothingness between the realms. Occasionally, the monsters within the shadows seep into other worlds."

"The Labyrinth is like a siphon that protects Gaea from the dark creatures that find their way into the realm." Hecate joins us with Cerberus. The fierce Doberman of shadow and burning embers for eyes trots over to my mate.

Turning into a puppy as he walks, Cerberus rubs his head against her calf, his tail wagging so vigorously that his butt wobbles as well. Rhea chuckles and picks the dog up, cradling him in her arms as he nuzzles against her. He is a literal killing machine, a demon that can grow in size until he's large enough to swallow you whole, yet he reverts to an excited puppy at the sight of her. *Unbelievable.*

"The Book of the Dead is more like a codex." Hecate continues as she takes a place by my mother. The sisters look so much alike, standing next to each other, the most discernible feature setting them apart being the strip of white hair that frames Hecate's face. "Instructions of necromancy and dark spells, the ability to create power and store it in amulets. The magic was tested and refined over eons of time. It was the obsession of mortals who inhabited a realm overrun by shadow creatures."

"Amulets just like the ones that unleashed the ten plagues

of Egypt?" Medusa all but shudders recalling the Great Exodus; the battle that took the life of Cleopatra, my mate of that lifetime.

"Precisely. So, there is no telling what ancient knowledge Loki has access to, as the current owner of such a book." Daphne adds to the gloom of this revelation.

"We need to get the book from him." Rhea declares with resolve firing in her gilded eyes.

"Goddess, the restoration of your immortality is our only saving grace." Thoth counters Rhea's idea to rob Loki of this stolen artifact. "You can be assured; Loki will guard the ancient codex with the full might of his stolen power. To challenge him without your immortality restored would be your imminent death."

"So, we focus on finding the Caduceus." I nod at my mate as I speak to everyone gathered within the library. "But if we take Loki down, can we destroy the Book of the Dead?"

"A book of such power cannot be destroyed, only safe-guarded." Seshat stands by her mate with her hands clasped in front of her like intertwined vines running into her dark cloak. "Should you recover the book, Alexandria's vault can hold the codex and keep it from the hands of those like Loki who seek to use it with malintent."

With a deep breath in, Rhea releases her desire to recover the book. Her shoulders drop, and she gives me a nod of reassurance, letting me know she's okay with the decision. "The accounts of where we took the Caduceus are not here, but I know what powers we hid within it." The four relics hold not just Rhea's immortality, but the divided powers of the Titans.

"Fire, Mind, and Death." Rhea's tone is as steady as the

tides that follow the moon. It makes sense these are the last powers to recover.

For ages, we have been misled to believe Ares is our greatest foe, but he's only been a captive of our true enemy. Keeping the power of Fire and Mind from Loki would prevent him and his prisoner from becoming stronger. As for Death, it's the ultimate power Loki has yet to consume. The power he craves most and will stop at nothing to have.

"I have searched these archives day and night for four centuries," my mother begins. "The last mention of the Herald's staff was on the Grecian beaches; the day Tartarus was overrun."

Opening the tome stacked on the table before us, Seshat gestures with her wood-like hand, drawing our attention to the pages. Several pages appear to be blank, like the ink scrawled across them was erased.

"Loki has somehow manipulated some of the written records from Alexandria." Rhea confirms. "Before the library was hidden, anyone was welcome to the knowledge inside."

"The great deceiver visited the library just before The Eclipse of Shadows." Thoth recounts the last visit Loki made to the library before the battle with Nyx. The first death she would suffer at his hand. "It was upon this visit that the great deceiver requested we record his actions under the new name of Atlas. Unbeknownst to the Librarians, he tampered with several volumes of tomes. The instant the Library records an account on them, the ink is destroyed, the information lost. Effectively hiding his actions throughout the realm but also hiding your actions taken to safeguard your powers."

"I am afraid the information is unrecoverable, great

divine." Seshat bows with a solemn nod to my mate. Rhea returns her gesture with a kind and understanding smile.

"We'll just have to look elsewhere. History can't be erased, no matter how hard you try to conceal it." Rhea pats Seshat's hand. "We just need to read between the lines of—" Rhea's words are cut off, and she gasps.

Covering her mouth with her hand, her cheeks turn pink as her emotions run through her. Every eye in the library turns to her with alarm and curiosity. But through our bond, I feel hope rush through her. She's thought of something she believes will be of great help to us, and I watch expectantly for her to share her idea. Whatever it is, we'll pursue it with everything we have.

"Someone else has been recording the events of this realm." Rhea raises her eyebrow as realization washes over me.

"Pan."

"Oh goody," Medusa interjects as I release a huff of irritation. "Looks like we get to visit what's left of the Mortal Counsel."

Rhea sighs, her eyes filled with a mix of hope and wariness. "I hid the great library to keep Loki from accessing it. He needed a solution and found a partner in Pan. Pan has powers over Sonus and Life. He can hear everything that happens in the realm and endlessly transcribe it onto papyrus. Pan has essentially become Loki's replacement for Alexandria's library."

I frown, considering the implications. For ages, we tried to access the archives he guards within the Vatican. Even Aphrodite and her fleet of Sirens have attacked the walled city, trying to access them, without success. There is no telling what he could have locked away in there. "Pan could have the information we need."

Rhea nods, her expression serious. "Yes, but it's risky. His loyalty to Loki makes him a dangerous ally. We need to be prepared for anything."

Medusa crosses her arms, her eyes narrowing. "We'll need a solid plan. Pan is an asshole, and he won't give up his secrets easily."

Rhea meets Medusa's gaze, determination in her eyes. "If Pan holds the key to finding the Caduceus, it's a risk we have to take."

I squeeze Rhea's hand, offering her silent support. "Then we go in ready for anything."

The SUV glides down the crowded street, the hum of its engine a subtle undertone to the chaos outside.** I watch through the tinted windows, my eyes narrowing at the sight of protesters and supporters clashing on the sidewalks. Signs wave, voices shout, and the air buzzes with a mixture of excitement and hostility. Typical mortals, so easily swayed by a charismatic speech or a well-placed whisper. They never change.

Eris sits beside me, her posture rigid, eyes unseeing. My control over her is absolute, her will bent entirely to mine. She has been a potent weapon, masquerading as a goddess of discord, but in reality, she is reduced to a silent, obedient passenger.

I glance at her briefly, a smirk curling my lips. "You have a big day today, Eris. Are you ready for it?" Amusement widens my smirk to a grin when she doesn't answer. Of course, she can't. There is nothing left inside her mind except my net, holding her together.

I lean back, allowing the leather seat to cradle me, and return my gaze to the spectacle outside.

On one side, a throng of radicals wave banners emblazoned with my name, shouting praises, hailing me as a savior, Christ returned. Their fervor is intoxicating, and rightfully placed. I did author the mortals' collective works of religious texts, always portraying myself in the role I'll hold: their redeemer. They look to me as a beacon of change, a leader who will steer this world through its current turmoil. In truth, I will steer them into the turmoil, then I will steer them out of it.

On the other side, a seething mass of opposition, their faces twisted in anger, voices hoarse with rage. They see me as a threat, an embodiment of chaos seeking to unravel the fragile threads of their society, the Antichrist. Their hatred is palpable, almost as delicious as the adoration from my supporters. Both are necessary, both feed into the grand design I have set into motion.

The driver inches forward, navigating the throng with practiced ease. The United Nations building looms ahead, a monument to human diplomacy and the illusion of control. Today, I will stand before them, speak words laced with just enough truth to be believed, and nudge them further down the path I've laid out. They are puppets, all of them, dancing to a tune they cannot hear.

The SUV finally comes to a halt. The driver, an unexceptional man who knows better than to meet my gaze, opens the door. I step out, straightening my suit, the picture of elegance and authority. Cameras flash, reporters shout questions, but I pay them no mind. They are background noise, insignificant in the grand scheme.

Eris follows, her movements mechanical, eyes fixed ahead. The crowd surges, security personnel struggle to maintain order. I walk forward, every step measured, exuding confidence and control. The United Nations awaits, and with it, another opportunity to shape the world to my design.

As I approach the entrance, I can already envision the speech I will give. Words crafted with precision, designed to instill both hope and fear. The humans are predictable, and today, they will take another step toward their destiny. My destiny.

I glance back at Eris, a shadow of a smile playing on my lips. "Come, Eris. The world awaits."

The grand hall of the United Nations is a spectacle in itself, a vast chamber designed to symbolize the ideals of unity and diplomacy. I stand at the podium, the weight of countless eyes upon me. The assembly is filled with representatives from every corner of the globe, their faces a mosaic of skepticism, curiosity, and outright defiance.

I begin my speech, my voice a measured cadence that echoes through the chamber. "Esteemed leaders of the world, today we stand at a crossroads. Our world is beset by conflicts, by strife that tears at the very fabric of our societies. But I come to you with a vision—a vision of peace, a world united under a common banner, where differences are celebrated, not condemned."

I see the shift in the room, subtle yet palpable. Some lean forward, intrigued, while others cross their arms, their expressions hardening. This is the moment I relish, the moment where words can shape destinies just as easily as powers do.

"For too long, we have allowed our divisions to define us. But what if, instead of focusing on what sets us apart, we embraced what brings us together? Imagine a world where borders are mere lines on a map, where resources are shared, and where every individual can thrive regardless of their nationality or creed. This is not a dream; it is within our grasp."

Murmurs ripple through the assembly. I can see the gears turning in their minds, the possibility taking root. But as expected, opposition soon follows.

A delegate from the United States rises, her face stern. "Mr. Atlas, while your words are inspiring, they are also naïve. The world is not so easily swayed by idealistic visions. Our differences run deep, and history has shown that true peace is unattainable."

The hall fills with nods and murmurs of agreement. I allow a moment of silence before responding, my gaze steady. "History is not a chain that binds us, but a lesson from which we must learn. The path to peace is not easy, nor is it quick. But it is possible if we are willing to strive for it."

Next, a representative from China stands, echoing similar sentiments. "Your vision, Mr. Atlas, is admirable, but it fails to account for the complexities of our world. Peace cannot be imposed; it must be earned through mutual respect and understanding."

I nod, acknowledging the truth in their words while steering the conversation back to my narrative. "Indeed, respect and understanding are the cornerstones of this vision. It is not about imposing a single way of life, but about creating a framework where diverse cultures and perspectives can coexist harmoniously."

The debate continues, with voices rising in opposition, each argument a blend of caution and cynicism. It is a dance, this exchange, one I have choreographed with care. And then, the moment I have anticipated arrives.

The Russian delegate stands, a figure of calm amidst the storm. "Russia believes in the potential for a united world. We have seen the destruction wrought by division and are prepared to offer our land as a sanctuary for those who seek peace and unity. Let our actions speak louder than words."

The hall falls silent, stunned by this unexpected support. I allow a smile to touch my lips, the subtle victory savored. Then like the blast wave of an explosion, a cacophony of voices rises, a chaotic blend of surprise, outrage, and confusion.

The representative from the United States, stands abruptly. Her voice cuts through the clamor, silencing the room. "How can we speak of peace when the very fabric of our leadership has been torn apart? President Sims, along with other world leaders, was assassinated in a heinous act that has left our nations reeling. We suspect the hand of immortals in this atrocity. How can we trust, let alone negotiate, with beings whose power makes them seemingly invincible?"

The room falls into a heavy silence, the weight of her accusation settling over the assembly. I can feel the eyes of every delegate on me, their collective fear and suspicion palpable. I let the moment stretch, savoring the intensity, before addressing the room.

"Your fears are understandable," I begin, my voice calm and measured. "The loss of President Sims and other leaders is a tragedy that has shaken the world. But to lay the blame at the feet of all immortals is to succumb to the very division we seek to overcome. Yes, there are those among us with great power, but power does not equate to malice."

A murmur ripples through the assembly, a mix of agreement and dissent. I press on, knowing this is a critical juncture. "The immortals, like mortals, are diverse in their intentions and actions. Some seek only to live in peace, to contribute to a world where their abilities can be a force for good. Condemning an entire group based on the actions of a few is a path to further conflict, not resolution."

The U.S. delegate remains unconvinced. "And what of those who wield their power for destruction? How do we defend ourselves against beings who cannot be killed, who laugh in the face of our laws and our weapons?"

Her words strike a chord, the fear in the room thickening. I raise a hand, a gesture of reassurance. "You speak of beings who cannot be killed, who wield their power without consequence. Allow me to correct this misconception."

At my signal, the grand doors at the back of the hall swing open. A transparent cell is wheeled in, drawing the attention of every delegate. Inside the cell stands Eris, her hands bound by thick metal cuffs, her eyes vacant and unseeing. The sight of her, restrained and contained, sends a ripple of shock through the assembly.

"This," I announce, my voice resonating through the chamber, "is Eris, a goddess who controls the emotions of others. She has sought to rule over mortals, to spread chaos and destruction. But even immortals are not beyond the reach of justice."

The room buzzes with whispers, the delegates exchanging glances filled with both fear and curiosity. I let the anticipation build before continuing. "Today, I offer you proof that immortals can indeed be killed. We abide by your laws, and under those laws, Eris has been sentenced to death for her crimes."

I pause, letting the weight of my words settle. "Would you like to see a display of how an immortal can be brought to justice?"

There is a moment of tense silence before the U.S. delegate nods, her expression a mixture of skepticism and intrigue. "Proceed," she says, her voice carrying the authority of the assembly.

I step forward, placing a hand on the transparent cell. "Eris, you have been found guilty of crimes against humanity. Your punishment is death, to be carried out here, before these witnesses, as a testament to the rule of law."

With a subtle gesture, I activate a mechanism within the cell. Appearances must be maintained and I'm careful not to allow the assembly to see it will be my powers carrying out the execution.

They believe me to be the docile figure I portray, and I need that illusion to continue just a few minutes longer.

The metal cuffs around Eris's wrists and ankles begin to glow, a searing light that intensifies with each passing second. Her body trembles, the energy coursing through her, but she remains silent, her mind still under my control.

The light within the cell grows blinding, a stark contrast to the dimness of the hall. Eris's form begins to dissolve, her essence being torn apart by the energy. The delegates watch in awe and horror, their faces a tapestry of emotions.

Finally, with a brilliant flash, the light subsides. The cell is empty, save for the lingering wisps of energy that dissipate into the air. I lower my hand, the display complete.

"You see," I say, my voice steady and authoritative, "even immortals can be held accountable. This is the future I propose

—a world where power is balanced by responsibility, where justice prevails, and where peace is not just a dream, but a reality we can achieve together."

The assembly breaks out in enthusiastic applause, the sound resonating through the grand hall. I stand tall, my expression calm, though inwardly I relish the moment. With one act, I have solved two obstacles. Eris has been disposed of under the guise of justice. And more importantly, I have gathered all the leaders of the world in one place, their defenses lowered by the promise of peace.

I raise my hand, signaling for calm. The applause gradually subsides, and the room falls silent once more, every eye fixed on me. "Thank you," I continue, my tone now soft, almost intimate. "Thank you for your trust, for your willingness to see beyond fear and doubt. Today marks the beginning of a new era. An era where we can end the wars that have plagued our world, where we can take the first step towards lasting peace."

I let my gaze sweep across the assembly, seeing the flicker of hope in their eyes. "I call upon the nations of the world to meet immediately, to set aside our differences and work together for the common good. Let this be our legacy—an end to conflict and the dawn of unity."

The delegates nod in agreement, their faces reflecting a newfound resolve. The path ahead seems clear to them, a future shaped by the vision I have laid out.

Inside, a dark satisfaction coils within me. Mortals are so easily led, so eager to grasp at the promise of peace that they fail to see the strings guiding their every move.

The doom I am guiding the world towards is inevitable, a grand design they are blissfully unaware of. They believe they are marching towards harmony, but in truth, they are stepping into the abyss I have meticulously crafted.

And so, with each step I take, I savor the silent symphony of destruction that only I can hear.

My lips curve into a sinister smile, the echo of applause still ringing in my ears as the delegates settle. The world is on the brink and I am the conductor of its fate.

Hermes holds my right hand, taking long strides with me down the echoing corridor of the Vatican. Medusa's black boots thud with purpose as she walks to my left. The fast clicks of the immortals' heels work to rush past us, trying to hold us off from entering the inner chamber of the Mortal Council.

We heard Loki's news broadcast just before we teleported to the Vatican. He made sure of it. Flexing his Titan powers of the Mind across the realm, he projected his interview into the atmosphere of Gaea. His answers bombarded us as if warning us that he is coming—not just for me, but for the mortals of the world too.

"I warn you to find refuge, and may the Fates be with you."

Urgency drives me forward now. There is a clock ticking somewhere and I don't know how many hours, minutes, or seconds are left. But when the countdown is over, and Loki strikes, the devastation will surround us all.

I dismantled Circe's shields as soon as we arrived. On the outside, they protect the ancient city from being bombarded by elemental attacks. But once inside, her wards serve to dampen elemental powers and should we need help, I don't want anyone feeling as if they have been locked in a set of Thaumium bindings.

The strength of Circe's wards surprised me; they were much stronger than I had anticipated. The magic of witches is perhaps more formidable than I realized. A note I keep at the front of my mind as we prepare for our encounter, but beyond that, they could be a great asset against Loki.

Circe visited me in the stolen library in Delphi before the eclipse. Her cryptic clue, *"reading between the lines,"* now feels like a puzzle I need to solve. Her visit had a greater agenda, and I'm determined to uncover it.

The lower-powered elemental reaches the large double doors and turns to face us. Splaying her arms wide, she knows she can do nothing to keep us out, but bless her heart, she's going to try.

"You're forbidden from entering unless you have been called upon by the Mortal Council." To her credit, her tone is steady.

"Haven't you heard?" Medusa calls ahead to her. Her voice carries far across the white marble encasing the building. "Archangel Michael has been eaten alive by dark beings, so as I see it, the Mortal Council doesn't exist anymore."

"Damn, Deuce, that's cold." Hermes chuckles.

"Don't act like you are mourning him. He was a cock-sucker and you two despised each other."

Scanning the young woman's aura, I sense the faint element of Water within her. Nowhere near powerful enough to heal, like Athena, but she could still be helpful. I don't sense the power of Loki has tainted her, and I assume Circe's shield is to thank for that.

We reach the doors and I pause. "You're a healer," I declare with a polite smile.

She shifts her eyes back and forth, dropping her arms before she answers. "I mean, not really. But I can pull the moisture from the air and use the dew drops to make images of animals and things."

"How fun." I think of the orphan Shifter children, and an idea blooms in my mind. "Go to the new Commune we have formed in Wyoming and find Kai. Show her your power and tell her I sent you. She'll have a job for you."

"What?" She shakes her head, partially confused, and partially offended. "What makes you think I want to go to Wyoming?"

"Because if you stay here, you're going to die." I tell her flatly. "We're not going to kill you, but a war is coming, and you'll be safe there."

A current of my Winds carefully moves her aside. Wrapping a tendril of my power around the knob of the door, I open it and stride forward. The Wind is a little enthusiastic and billows around me. The long strands of my hair flow around me as I enter the chamber. Medusa whispers to Hermes something about making an entrance, and I think back to the Shifters auction when Bridget arrived. Using the single feather of a crow like a portal, she manifested right before us.

"Entrances are made to be dramatic." She said when Callie remarked about her arrival. So, for good measure, I add a billow of my black mist and it fills the chamber immediately, coating the marble floor in a wispy blanket of my dark power.

Circe sits on the arm of a large marble chair that resembles a stone throne. Her eyes flare with a spark of interest when she sees me. Pan, who sits entwined in his marble chair, roots and vines binding him to the very core of the earth, has a tree-like appearance. Similar to the Librarians of Alexandria, I'm curious if they come from the same species of Immortals.

Pan is a powerful Sensor and Life elemental. He has some ability to morph his body using the power of Life, making vines and thorns grow from him, as well as a never-ending stream of parchment. The creeping branches act like appendages, furiously writing without ceasing.

Circe wears a red stola with an exaggerated slit up the thigh that reveals her hip. With her elbow propped on Pan's shoulder, she lifts one side of her mouth in a crooked grin as she raises an eyebrow. "I wondered how long it would take until you came for a visit. Welcome, goddess." She tilts her head, offering a small semblance of tense hospitality.

"I'm here to *read between the lines*." I tell her, holding her gaze as Hermes takes his place next to me. He crosses his arms over his chest, and I feel the irritation seeping off him.

"Mmm, we'll see if that is true, goddess." Circe answers.

My footsteps echo softly against the ancient stone floor as I near the long marble table where they sit. At the far end, I sense the echoes of disdain and the smug demeanor of Michael. The Archangel was devoured when Flint released the Shadow Lurkers from the Labyrinth. He was also a member of the council that is now made of only Pan and Circe.

Using my powers of Sensory, I try to pick up on their emotions, wanting to get a read of their sentiments toward our visit. Oddly, I feel nothing from Pan. Not a single emotion is exhibited from him. Likely because he is a Sensor himself and is able to shield against me. But Circe's emotions flow off her in torrents, and what I find confuses me.

Hope.

She pretends to be unaffected by our visit, and I realize that couldn't be further from the truth. Circe was counting on us to arrive, and she was nearly suffocating on anticipation. So why play coy now that we are here?

Squaring my shoulders, I address her mate. His black void eyes look nowhere but see everything as he serves as the eternal scribe of the realm.

"Pan," I begin, my voice steady despite the gravity of my request. "I need to know about Hermes' Caduceus. All accounts of it have been erased from the Librarians of Alexandria, and I believe the answers I need are within your records."

Pan regards me with a serene expression. He shifts slightly, the rustling of parchment accompanying his movement. "The past is a vast forest, goddess. Many paths are overgrown, and not all can be traversed again," he replies, his voice like the wind through the trees—there and yet elusive.

Circe's lips curl into a small, knowing smile. "What Pan records, the world knows, but not all knowledge is free to be plucked like fruit from a tree," she says cryptically. Her gaze is sharp, almost challenging.

Frustration flares within me as I struggle to find patience. "What the fuck does that mean? I need specifics, not riddles," I insist. "This is not a game. The very fate of the realm hangs in the balance. What was written here?"

Pan looks pained, his eyes flickering with a hint of something like regret. "Some words are caught in the thorns," he murmurs, almost apologetically.

"What the fuck is going on?" Hermes interjects, his frustration mounting with mine.

In a burst of energy, Pan hits me with a torrent of feelings. Pain, strangulation, confinement all bombard me, and I grasp the tall back of the chair in front of me to keep from toppling over. Then, like a lid snapping closed over a container, it stops.

Pan's chest rises heavily as does mine, and I look to Circe. The ribbons of hope continue to flow from her as if almost begging me to put something together that she can't tell me. Their cryptic responses bounce around in my mind as I look at them both with intense focus.

"Not all knowledge is free to be plucked like fruit from a tree."

Maybe they want to barter a deal and are asking for a payment of some kind. But from the surge of emotions Pan blasted at me, one stands out—*confinement*. Pan himself is very much like a tree, rooted to his throne and with his role as the realm's scribe, he is the knowledge of Gaea. Pan is telling me he is not free.

"You're under a spell." I whisper the words, knowing they are true. When Demeter put me under her curse, the nature of it prevented me from talking about the torture Ares inflicted upon me. I nearly choked to death when Lucas tested me on it. The Shifters of the Underworld were also filled with her toxins, silencing them with her power. "Loki has cursed you under a spell, hasn't he?" My tone rises with eagerness as Hermes and Medusa look at each other.

"All this time?" Medusa asks in disbelief.

Circe can't answer. She only lifts her chin, keeping her mouth closed. The only noise filling the space is the scratch of Pan's thorns across the eternal flow of parchment. Walking around the table, I'm determined to get what I came here for. If they can't physically speak and give me the answers I want, I'll find them within the rolls of parchment.

Circe watches me, keeping her perch next to her mate.

Following the flow of parchment, it's stored in a chamber beyond the room we are in. A forcefield ripe with the power of the Witch behind me is protecting the space and the secret writings within. Looking back to Circe, she returns my gaze as if challenging me to try and break her wards. While I took down the ones around the Vatican city, I have a feeling these wards are going to be much more of a challenge.

With my hand hovering above the shield, I send a pulse of my power into it, testing its strength, and I'm shocked to find I can shatter it with ease. Her shield disintegrates like smoke trapped within a bubble that was ruptured. Stepping into the chamber, Hermes is with me.

Medusa remains with Circe. The serpentine tendrils of her hair alert and almost begging Circe to make a move against us, but the Witch remains at her seat by Pan's side. I turn to the vines that sprawl across the floor, heavy with thorns, they work to roll and store the segments of paper in a vast cavern of knowledge. With a determined grasp, I pull the long stream of parchment towards me, the vines resisting slightly as if reluctant to give up their secrets.

Unrolling the scroll, I scan the ancient script, each line a whisper of the past, each word a piece of the puzzle I need to solve. Scanning the text, I decipher Pan's penmanship as he records our visit today, just as it's occurring. Looking further, he records Lexi as she travels alone, and I look back to Circe. Lexi is her daughter, but I'm not sure if Pan is Lexi's father.

Circe watches me, her eyes gleaming with a mix of admiration and amusement. "Be wary, Rhea. Some shields are in place for a reason. I would hate to see your treasure destroyed before you find what you seek," she warns, her voice low.

Ignoring her, I continue to read. Pan's cursive writing is

difficult to decipher. Each line varies with no consistent pacing or flow. Within this great chamber, there is too much text for us to search through ourselves, and I push my powers through the rolls of parchment. Illuminating the scribe's work with silver starlight, my aura sifts quickly through the endless rolls of paper, hunting for mention of my mate's Caduceus. I find the scroll that recorded Triton's life, and my powers fumble as I detect his name, written with the black ink that weeps from Pan's thorns. My heart races as I read the record of my power moving into him and taking his life.

Closing my eyes, I rush back farther into the chamber, working backward in time and searching the history of the realm. As I pour over the dense script, something strange catches my eye—a pattern emerging amidst the swirl of ancient letters.

At first, it's merely a shadow, an echo of words that seem to hover just beyond my direct line of sight. Focusing too intently makes it vanish like mist under the morning sun.

So, I soften my gaze, letting my eyes relax and drift slightly out of focus, and there it is. Hidden within the seemingly random spaces between words, a secret message materializes: "Please free me."

My breath catches. The words repeat, a silent plea woven into the text with a desperation that is palpable. Each "please free me" is meticulously embedded, only discernible to someone searching beyond the superficial.

Read between the lines.

I glance up at Pan, whose ancient eyes meet mine with a depth of sorrow and weariness now impossible to ignore. His appearance, so intertwined and rooted, had initially seemed a natural extension of his immortal nature—a god forever bonded to the seat of knowledge. But now, understanding dawns—this is not devotion but captivity. The roots and vines, the very chair that seemed his throne, is a prison.

"Pan," I whisper, my voice barely audible. "Why are you bound like this?" The questions hang heavy in the air, charged with the newfound knowledge of his plight.

Pan's eyes flicker with a flash of fear and caution. He glances briefly at Circe, who remains inscrutable, her gaze now fixed on me with an intensity that feels like a challenge. Has Circe bound Pan here, perhaps aligned with Loki and holding her own mate captive for my hunter? But why?

Taking a step back, I ready my powers.

"She's holding Pan here like a prisoner," I tell Hermes and Medusa with my mind. *"When I move, hold her back. I'm going to free him."*

"I've got her." Medusa keeps her sharp gaze focused on Circe. A sinister grin plastered on the Witch's face as she watches me and yet she remains silent.

Pan's silent plea for freedom has reshaped the purpose of my journey here. No longer is it just about finding answers for myself. But this is also a time to liberate this immortal from the eternal life of caged suffering he's been forced to endure.

I step closer to Pan, my eyes locked on his, searching for any sign of opposition. He meets my gaze steadily, an unspoken agreement passing between us. Turning my attention to the vines and roots that bind him, I extend my hands, palms outstretched, feeling the ancient magic pulsate through the air. The energy around us thickens, charged with anticipation and the raw power of elemental forces at my command. Power surges from deep within me, a torrent of force guided by my will to sever his bindings.

The roots and vines begin to shudder, twisting and writhing as if in agony. A low groan emanates from the very walls of the chamber, the sound of old magic being undone. Circe rises swiftly, her expression shifting from seductive calm to sharp concern. "Rhea, think about what you're doing! You do not understand—"

Medusa's long braids bind the Witch as Hermes casts a shield of Light around Pan and me. With a final push of my power, a resounding crack fills the air as the roots snap, the magic that held them dissipating into the ether. Pan gasps, a sound of relief mixed with pain, as he slowly stands, free from his marble prison for the first time in centuries. A rich green blanket of smoke covers the ancient city like a thick blanket of fog. The suffocating grip around the Vatican has been eradicated.

I turn to face Circe, ready to confront her, but the look in her eyes stops me. It is not anger that I see there, but profound fear. "You think I did this to him?"

Confusion twists inside me, and I look back at Pan, who is now slowly regaining his footing, his expression one of deep relief as he regards the Witch beside him.

Before another word can be spoken, a deep boom resonates beyond the Vatican walls. It's a deafening burst of Wind, rupturing like a cannon and soaring toward us. It's powerful and looking to the ceiling high above us, dread runs down my body. I've torn down the wards that protect the city. I left us vulnerable.

Propelling my aura beyond the Vatican building, my shield emerges above us just as the impact of the assaulting Wind slams into my power. I grunt and strain to hold back the force until it dissipates as Hermes responds to the assault. With a flare of his Light, he conjures his sword and holds a shield made of blue starlight in his hand.

"It's Aphrodite." He looks at me sternly, seriousness in his sapphire eyes. "She's come to challenge you for the death of Calypso."

The chamber's atmosphere changes suddenly; a rush of wind swirls around us, stirring ancient dust into the air.** The gritty particles scratch my skin, mingling with the salty tang of Aphrodite's aura. It carries the scent of sea salt mingled with roses, an intoxicating blend heavy with the tension of unspoken grief and palpable anger. The air crackles with an electric charge, raising the hairs on my arms and neck.

"Show yourself, goddess." The Wind carries her message, spitting the last word at me as if it offends her to speak it.

Turning to Hermes, I soften slightly, understanding what I must ask of him. I just returned from a harrowing journey alone through a volatile realm. And now I'm going to ask him to stay behind here, in the archives of Pan's transcriptions, while I leave him to go to another potentially dangerous conflict.

"Hermes, keep searching for the transcription we need." Our eyes lock, and I know I don't need to convey the importance of this task. Everything is lost if we can't recover the Caduceus. "This is between her and me."

"Hey, you've got this. I'm not worried." He places a chaste

kiss on my temple. "Show her who she's messing with." Hermes' whisper wraps around me in reassurance.

The dome high above us tremors, shaking violently before a resounding crack echoes around the chamber. Large fragments of the dome's masonry and glass are picked up by the currents of Aphrodite's power as she strips away the building that was shielding us. Taking a deep breath, I gather my hair at the top of my head and twist it into a bun. Looking at my wrist, I don't have an elastic to secure my long locks.

"Here." Circe interrupts, pulling a long bronze spike that was securing half her hair away from her face. Her raven tendrils fall beyond her shoulders, and she flings the ornament at me. It soars through the space between us like a dart, and I catch it with a ribbon of Wind, placing it gently in my hand. Flicking my eyes to hers, she meets my stare with an amused expression.

"Good luck." She moves to stand by Pan, placing her hand on his chest as he wraps his arm around her for the first time in many ages.

Securing the spire in my hair, I teleport to the plaza outside. The screams of mortals clearing the space are stifled by the rushing Wind carried in by Aphrodite's power. It roars in my ears, a deafening howl that drowns out all other sounds.

As I face her, my heart tightens. Every fiber of my being aches at the sight of her. She looks so much like Callie that it rips my heart open. The resemblance is haunting, a cruel reminder of the friend I lost. How can I confront her without seeing the ghost of Callie in her eyes?

Just survive.

The mantra my chosen sister and I shared across the ages

rings in the back of my mind as I steel myself with a deep exhale.

Aphrodite's long platinum hair is the main feature that pulls her apart from my friend, so recently torn from me. Twisted into locks and secured with wrapped twine, shells and beads adorn her hair. One of her teeth is boxed with a shining gold frame that glints at me with her sneer. Where Callie's eyes were soft and full of love, shining blue like the aqua waters of the Mediterranean, Aphrodite's stare is harsh as stone with eyes the color of hardened amber.

The determination in me solidifies, prepared for the confrontation, as Aphrodite speaks. "You have much to answer for. Calypso was my sister, and you—you let her die," she accuses, her voice like a whip.

My stomach lurches, and my throat burns with tears that I refuse to let fall. Aphrodite has lost much, and while I know her true anger is not directed at me, I can't help but connect myself to two people she has cared about and lost.

Calypso, her sister, and Triton, her former mate.

She doesn't know the truth of why Triton was removed from her side and imprisoned in the Underworld. The love that turned her heart to stone and hardened her against the world.

Triton wanted Hermes and me to make sure she knew the truth of his departure. That he did it to protect her, believing she was in mortal peril. But that means I will have to confess my part in ending his life, even if it was done in mercy and at his request. I would be pouring fuel on this proverbial fire of revenge if I tell Aphrodite the truth of Triton.

So, I just need to resolve this, then we'll cross that other bridge later.

Stepping forward, I meet her gaze, my voice steady but threaded with my own pain. The words are heavy on my tongue, each one laden with the weight of my sorrow.

"I mourn her as deeply as you. She was like a sister to me, too. Her loss is a weight I will carry every single day. But her death was not by my hand, nor was it something I ever desired." The air around us thickens, making it hard to breathe, and I taste the salt of my newly shed tears on my lips.

Aphrodite's eyes blaze with a mix of pain and accusation, hands clenched at her sides as if holding back a storm within. The tension between us vibrates like a taut string, ready to snap. I feel the heat of her anger radiating off her in waves, contrasting sharply with the chill of the wind. The angry gale whips around me, howling with Aphrodite's grief and fury.

Her power wraps around the tall obelisk that stands in the center of the plaza of the Vatican. The long ornament carved from red granite and inscribed with ancient Egypt's hiero-glyphs is hurled at me like a spire. With a wave of my hand, I deflect the heavy stone and send it to one side of the colon-nades that encircle the plaza. The tall pillars acting like bars caging us inside an arena. The eyes of the saints carved into the stone statues above watch our battle like spectators.

"Aphrodite!" I shout over the roar, my voice straining to stay calm, desperate to reach the sister of someone I loved so dearly. "Calypso wouldn't have wanted this! She wouldn't want us to tear each other apart!"

"What the fuck would you know about what she would want?" Aphrodite spits back, her voice a mixture of fury and anguish. "I bet she wanted to live, but she didn't get that, did she? You failed her, just like you're failing everyone now!"

The words slice through me just like I had been cut with Flaying Wind.

Aphrodite's eyes are alight with a tempest's wrath. She controls the Wind as if it were an extension of her own turbulent emotions, hurling fragments of ancient architecture toward me. I dodge a flying column, feeling the rush of air as it passes inches from my face.

Aphrodite is beyond hearing, her sorrow manifesting as violent gusts that tear more stone from the sacred structures around us. I raise my hands, summoning my own power to deflect the assault, creating barriers of force to absorb the impact of the stone and wind. Each block of marble redirected, each shattered column caught in mid-air, is a plea for reason.

Beyond our skirmish, I sense the arrival of Aphrodite's Sirens. Her faithful sailors who have sailed the open waters of Gaea for eons are here to ensure their admiral is victorious. But as I told Hermes, this is between Aphrodite and me.

Ensuring they don't join the fray, I block them out with an impassable funnel of Wind. Building the swirling currents higher, I encase us in the epicenter of a raging vortex of the element I share with Aphrodite.

Just as Calypso used Mirages on the walls of her hurricane to pull me from my toxin-induced rage, I show Aphrodite the gleaming images of her sister. Shining like sunshine within this dull storm of our shared grief, Callie smiles upon us, my memories of her filling the dome around us like the fresco paintings inside the ancient buildings of the Vatican City.

The winds falter, just for a heartbeat and Aphrodite's expression falters with them. Her eyes, wild with the storm's rage, meet mine, and in them, I see the flicker of pain that runs deeper than vengeance.

"I wasn't there to stop her." Her voice breaks through the howling wind, ragged and torn. "But you—you could have saved her."

I fall to my knees, crushed by the heavy weight of grief collapsing my heart. "I would have." I whisper, and the Wind carries my reply to her. "I would have given my life to keep her safe. But tearing the world apart won't bring her back."

Locked in a standoff of our powers, I call upon the Winds only enough to hold Aphrodite within my protective dome. The world outside this sphere of swirling currents goes on as if we are not decimating this revered plaza with our misery.

The air trembles with the power of our confrontation, the square now littered with the remnants of what was once respected and untouched by time. Slowly, the Wind begins to settle, the pieces of stone dropping heavily to the ground as Aphrodite's control wanes.

She drops to her knees, mirroring my pose, unable to stand against the emotions surging within her. Pounding her fist upon the stone, the ground cracks against the force of her blow.

"I'm not your enemy." I say, unafraid as I dissipate the Winds answering to the Siren confronting me. I hold the power of the Wind Titans within me, and should I command it, I could strip her of her elemental powers. Not that I would. But I'm not going to allow her to destroy the city or harm innocent mortals with her rage.

"I'll grieve with you, but I'll not fight you," I say, my voice trembling as I swallow the knot lodged in my throat. Tears stream down my face, but I hold her gaze. "Calypso would want us to come together by her death, not be driven to violence by it. We owe her that much."

Aphrodite looks at me, the storm in her eyes dissipating with her rage. The Winds die down around us, and in the sudden stillness that follows, an eerie chill cascades down my back as if the eyes of a predator are on me. The sensation is so palpable, I scan the plaza but see nothing. I don't drop my guard because something is amiss, I can feel it.

Hermes appears on a blue wave of light. A section of parchment, torn at both ends, in his hands. The strain in my face relaxes and hope resides within me. The question lingering in my expression, the words unable to leave my lips. Hermes offers me a gentle smile and a soft nod of his head.

"You found it." Even speaking through our minds, my voice cracks with a sob. *"You found the record of your staff."*

A tremor vibrates the ground under me, the vibrations traveling up my legs and settling into my bones.

I still, every muscle tensing in anticipation. The gentle quake under my hands feels like a heartbeat, pulsing with a life of its own.

Movement catches the corners of my vision. I focus on the small fragments of broken marble, littering the destroyed plaza around us. The pieces of stone shake, a faint clattering sound that grows increasingly violent as the trembling earth turns to a growling roar high above us. The air is filled with the acrid smell of dust and debris, stinging my nostrils with every breath.

I lock eyes with Aphrodite, both of us on our knees with our hands firmly on the ground. The strain in our eyes, creasing our foreheads with concentration. "This is not me." She breathes heavily as we keep assessing the shift in the atmosphere.

The realm goes silent, like the seconds before an avalanche gives way and races down the mountainside, consuming everything in its path. Surging winds race in from all directions. Screams carried on the currents blast into us, forcing us to cover our ears as we cower closer to the ground.

Pushing against the walls of Wind, I extend my aura outward. Calling upon the elements within my control, I cascade my aura with a brilliant silver flare to the skies above. Dread grips my throat in a vice at what I find.

Standing, I look to the blue sky above. Cold takes me over as my blood rushes to my feet. No longer does the screaming Wind assault my ears because the beat of my heart takes over everything else.

"R–r–r–reah–h–h–h!" The echo of Hermes' voice pulls me from my daze as his grip on my arm turns me to him. His blue eyes are wild with urgency. I stare at his moving lips, not hearing the words he's screaming at me.

It's nuclear holocaust.

Every weapon of mass destruction in possession by every mortal government has been fired. Missiles and bombs of all sizes are screaming through the air, crisscrossing in the skies above us.

"I warn you to find refuge, and may the Fates be with you."

This is what Loki planned. This is what we must take refuge from. New York was only a prelude to his greater plans. A taste of how he intended to destroy the world this time. It would not be a great flood that circled the globe or a volcano that cast the realm into centuries of darkness.

It would be total destruction by the weapons of the mortals.

Hermes grasps both sides of my cheeks, making me focus on him. A rush of his power pours through me and my Winds swirl around me. With it, I take in a deep breath of air, not realizing I had stopped breathing.

My senses rage through me like a flash flood. My heart pounds in my chest, booming through my ears as the sounds of the world assault me again.

"We've got to go!" Hermes screams at me.

"No!" I yell back, grasping his wrists with my hands. "We can't just let them all die."

Hermes fights his instincts only a second before I see him visibly concede. Pressing his lips into a thin line, he releases a breath of air and drops the tension mounting in his shoulders. Pulling me into a bruising kiss, his lips crush mine. "Keep your bond open to me and whatever happens, we stay together."

Nodding my head, I squeeze his hands as if I can physically push my love and worry into him. "Together."

23

Hermes

I **turn into a raging column of blue starlight as my aura races in an instant across the realm.** Within a heartbeat, I survey the world and the terror about to befall the mortal race. This is an attack aimed to end as much life as possible, and Gaea will forever carry the scars of this day.

Rhea responds instinctively. Her first thoughts are to the shields protecting the Shifters' Wyoming territory and the Library of Alexandria. She fortifies the wards against the impending shockwave of bombs racing across the atmosphere of Gaea.

Panic spreads among the people of the realm as they run for shelter, praying to deities that don't exist. The gods among them rush to save them as another god seeks their destruction. Immortals wielding teleportation wands gather trembling mortals, transporting them to any nearby commune.

"Tell the immortals to go to the Shifters' territory or Alexandria," I command, releasing falcons of starlight to spread the message. A quick thought to Lucas is all I can spare as my light swarms the skies. Building my Titan power of Light, I raise my hands and open portals across the realm. Swirling blue vortexes appear in major cities and small islands. In Vatican

City, a portal connects to Alexandria. The desert sun blasts me as my mother rushes through. Medusa guides Pan and Circe to the desert.

"We'll save as many as we can, just hold them open, son," my mother and Medusa shout, directing mortals through the portals. Some flee in fear, but others, driven by desperation, rush towards us and safety. I watch it all through the light encasing the globe. Immortals near the portals help direct people into them. Despite our efforts, some will perish, either by the bombs or the initial waves of heat.

Rhea rises into the atmosphere, held by a vortex of wind as she combats the bombs. She redirects them into space, damaging their components to prevent reentry. Silver portals of starlight make two bombs collide, encasing them in a bubble before they explode. Each blast drains her, sweat forming on her brow, determination etched on her face. As my powers scan the realm, the sheer scale of the attack is overwhelming. Thousands are racing toward the ground.

"We won't be able to stop them all," I warn.

"I know," Rhea grunts, struggling against the man-made weapons. *"But we'll stop as many as we can."*

Loki has planned this carefully. Every button has been pushed; each key turned to ensure the bombs will detonate at once. He counters my portals with his own, luring mortals into his sanctuary in Russia.

He attacks my Light with his Titan power of Darkness, closing my portals and consuming mortals passing through. Rhea senses the assault, dividing herself to fight on two fronts. She detonates bombs and places shields around Loki's portals. I back her up, strengthening my portals and opening more.

We have minutes left, and we're pushing ourselves too far.

"We've got to go, Rhea!" I scream down our bond against the strain of my abilities, stretching my power further and pushing harder.

"Just a few more seconds." She yells back, grunting as she too pushes her powers further.

Reaching within, I call upon all the stars of the universe, my aura surging into brilliant light. I replicate myself into multiple forms, converting each astral projection into a portal and pushing panicked mortals to safety. Rhea is doing the same until I realize she is being selective.

She's not gathering the mortals; she is gathering her army.

Bridget and Lexi are swallowed in silver starlight and dropped to Wyoming. Aphrodite and her fleet of Wind Sirens are plucked from their ships and fall into the soft sand surrounding Alexandria.

Following suit, I search for those we know will fight with us, ensuring the immortals of the realm make it to the safe harbor of our warded territories. Kellan is shifted to his lion form, gravely wounded in South Africa. His sister is defending him against enemies that are surrounding them. Leaving their foes to the bombs, I blast a portal through them, a message to my mother for a healer echoing as I return to my search. The bombs are seconds away from impact, and Rhea is relentless. Exploding them, they detonate against buildings, shattering glass onto the streets below.

"Enough!" I beg her to stop. My power flares, sending a wave of starlight across the realm. The living being it touches is transported to Alexandria or Wyoming, human, immortal and animal alike.

With a final surge, I race to my mate, encasing her in my arms and power. I steal her from the skies and with the next beat of our hearts, we're on the ground in Wyoming as the earth stands still.

We kneel, embracing each other, our bond flaring, our elements combining and pulsing into the ground with each breath. Unyielding, we push our elements into the shield that covers the vast reaches of Lucas' territory. It grows thicker and stronger for one heartbeat, then two when the first explosions light up the horizon.

The ground trembles, and the tension-charged air is filled with a silence that stretches across the world. In an instant, the silence shatters. Explosions bloom across the landscape like deadly flowers. Massive fireballs erupt upwards, belching thick, black smoke into the sky.

It's deafening, a concussive series of blasts that seem to never end, rolling over one another in a relentless tide. Each explosion sends shockwaves through the ground, strong enough to knock the breath from our lungs and rattle our bones. The air heats up alarmingly. Waves of it hit us with great power, carrying the acrid scent of burning metal and scorched earth.

Above, the sky is obscured by a growing canopy of smoke and debris, casting everything into a twilight gloom punctuated by the flashes of further explosions. The world seems to tilt, disorienting, as if reality itself is fracturing under the strain of such widespread devastation.

The first impact against our shield arrives with a terrifying force. The bombs explode just outside our protective dome, and the resulting shockwaves hit like a physical assault. The dome vibrates violently under the impact, the energy rippling like water disturbed by a thrown stone.

I grit my teeth, focusing deeply, channeling my energy to

reinforce the protective shroud. Rhea's grip on my arms tightens as she adds her power to mine. Her Darkness fuses with my Light, strengthening the barrier, interlacing our powers to create a denser, more resilient weave.

The relentless bombardment tests our resolve. Inside the dome, the mortals' fear and panic rise. Their wide, frightened eyes look to us, and in their gaze, I see a silent plea for salvation. As the attacks continue, the protective dome becomes a symphony of light and shadow, each wave of energy dissipated with a flare of light that briefly illuminates the frightened faces around us.

Rhea and I share a glance, a wordless agreement, as we pour every ounce of our divine strength into the dome, willing it to hold, to protect, to persevere. And in her gaze, I remain locked, lost in the golden abyss of her eyes. Resolution hardens my purpose to keep her safe from these blasts as the assault reaches a crescendo.

The very ground beneath us pulses with the waves of our power, splintering out through the veins of the earth. The battle to keep the dome intact is exhausting, a test of endurance and willpower, but Rhea and I hold on to each other. Together, we are a barricade against the apocalypse, defending the last lights of life in a world consumed by darkness.

As the cacophony outside finally begins to ebb, the tremors subside, and the roar of destruction dwindles into an eerie silence. We relax our embrace, breaths heavy with relief and exhaustion. We linger for a moment, arm in arm, gathering our strength, reassuring ourselves through the simple contact that we are indeed alive and safe. Not only us, but those we managed to save.

Surveying the aftermath, we see the shocked faces of

immortals and mortals alike, a myriad of emotions. Children clutch their parents, strangers share quiet nods of thanks, and amidst them all, there's a palpable sense of uncertainty. Nodding, we look around, the reality of our situation setting in. Surviving was one thing; what we should do next will be another.

There are injuries to tend to, and healers immediately disperse through the throngs of survivors. I find Lucas as he trots through the crowd. Pausing when he sees me, relief is evident on his face as he nods once, then resumes giving orders to his packs. This makeshift commune of the Shifters was already a strain to house the daily arrivals of immortals being rescued. And we just delivered thousands here in a matter of minutes. The enormity of what lies ahead of us is unfathomable.

Looking to my mate, a slow trickle of blood seeps out of Rhea's nose, and she wipes it away. She's exhausted and falls into me, holding back a sob as we embrace. Weariness seeps off her as she trembles in my arms. I cup her face in both my hands, splaying my fingers through her hair and savoring the soft feeling of her against my hands.

"You pushed yourself too far, little goddess." I barely get the words out of my mouth before I place a kiss on her lips. "Are you okay?"

She nods, resting her head against my chest. Slowly, chatter from the crowd rises as mortals brave their new future, but I remain encased in the presence of my goddess. Breathing in the gentle scent of sweet berries that always lingers on her skin, I absorb the nearness of her and use it to recharge myself. I feel her doing the same, and slowly the tremor in her hands begins to ebb away.

"We had to save as many as we could." Tears streak down her face as the adrenaline of our final moments washes away. Wrapping her arms around my waist, she hugs me tighter. "I couldn't just leave them out there to die."

I rock back and forth, rubbing my hands up her back in a soothing motion. Both of us staying in this nest of protection before we face the magnitude of destruction we will find outside this shield. Closing my eyes, afraid of what I may find, I send a soft wave of my aura across the realm.

The atmosphere is a haunting shade of burnt orange as fire and smoke rise into the sky in an endless parade.

I sense small pockets of life that reached safety and survived the explosions. But as my power approaches Alexandria, I hold my breath. We pushed just as many survivors into Alexandria as we did Wyoming. Even considering we could have lost them all, as well as the great library we just recovered, is a fate I don't want to entertain.

As my light rushes across the horizon, Alexandria emerges through the smoke, calling back to me. Our forcefield withstood the bombardment, and everyone inside is safe. Dropping my head back and closing my eyes, I release a large breath.

"The other dome is safe too, baby." I look down to my goddess as she lifts her gaze to mine.

"I know, the Vampires too" she breathes. "Thank the goddess."

"No. Thanks to you." I offer her a sad smile as I stroke her cheek.

"And you." She returns my smile with one of sorrow as well. Her expression lightens only a fraction as she raises her eyebrows. "What did the parchment say?"

Her curiosity about the recovered scroll from Pan's archives gives her a momentary distraction, but the news she will find will be no less dreary than the desolated lands of Gaea.

Pulling the crumpled parchment from my back pocket, I work to flatten it for her. In my earlier haste, I shoved it away, carelessly wrinkling it. Handing it to her now, Lucas finally makes his way to us from the mass of mortals. We clasp hands, and he pulls me into a quick embrace.

"I'm glad you're both safe." He says quietly, placing a hand on Rhea's shoulder. "You okay?"

She nods but otherwise doesn't answer as her golden eyes rake over the parchment, reading the last written account of my Caduceus before it disappeared from history.

Looking up, her mouth gapes open and the color drains from her face.

"What the fuck is it now?" Lucas exclaims, curious to know what is going on and tilting his head to read the parchment clutched in Rhea's hands.

"I found the location of the Caduceus and where we need to recover the last of Rhea's powers," I say solemnly.

There is no way to dance around where this path will take us. I take a deep breath, knowing my next words will cement this fate for us.

"It's in the Labyrinth."

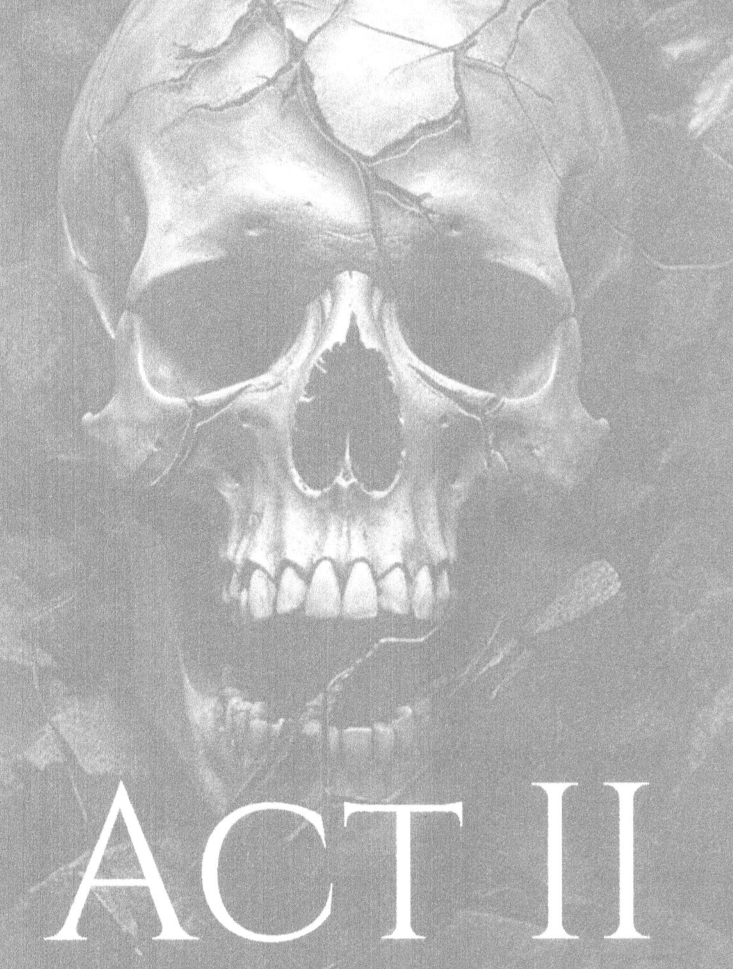

ACT II

THE LABYRINTH

E mpty. Utterly and truly empty. My mind, my emotions, my ability to comprehend what just happened and what I'm looking at have retreated so far within me, I'm just empty.

Others who are empty, just like I am, stand with me, shoulder-to-shoulder at the edge of the forcefield. Silence is our only companion as we look out at the once lush forest, now just a flat expanse of charred land.

Thick clouds of smog and soot diffuse the sunlight, casting an eerie burning glow across the atmosphere. The devastation of Gaea stretches forever until our eyes can't track it anymore beyond the horizon.

My powers roam the world. Small wisps of silver starlight and rolling black mist make a somber parade through the air. Empathic Echoes show me the moments of detonation. The bright flashes of light that disintegrated everything in the immediate vicinity. Towns, neighborhoods, animals, people, just gone in an instant.

Death, there is so much death.

Hermes and Lucas are somewhere behind me, directing people into organized groups for those that need medical attention or support. Those who can help. Others find places to sit and rest, waiting for someone to tell them what to do.

The sound of children chuckling to my right acts like a tether, turning my head away from the destruction. A brother and sister poke at the forcefield, giggling as the iridescent waves of my power undulate at their touch. Nearly the same size, they can't be more than four or five, perhaps twins or otherwise close in age.

A woman behind them, I presume her to be their mother, stares at nothing, her eyes unseeing. With one arm crossed over her chest, she holds the other over her mouth.

Closing the small distance between us, I approach her carefully, slowly extending my hand to touch her shoulder. "Excuse me?"

She startles at my touch, snapping out the heavy thoughts weighing her down. "Oh!" The woman exclaims, looking at me and then quickly to the children who are now pushing against my wards, making them wobble like a bowl of Jell-O. "I'm so sorry. Children, stop that."

"No, they're quite alright to have their fun." I reassure her. This barrier just survived the blast of hundreds of nuclear explosions. I'm sure it can withstand these kids. "Are you okay? Is there something I can do to help you?"

Shaking her head, she dismisses my offer. "We're fine, thank you. I just–" The woman pauses, tears filling her eyes as she looks back at the barrier and what lays beyond it. "I can't believe this."

A tear falls, and she quickly wipes it away. Her eyes moving to the children for a moment, then back at me. "Do you think– anyone could have survived out there?" The end of her question is almost choked off by her emotions.

Straining and trying to keep her composure, she swallows hard, holding back the turmoil inside her.

"Is there someone you are looking for? Perhaps I can help look them." I know there can be no promises. The majority of the world's population has been incinerated in a flash. The likelihood of finding people will be a rarity. But there were thousands pushed into our protective wards. I send a prayer to the stars for a miracle that they perhaps got separated.

"My husband." She smiles, but the tears that surface betray the brave face she is trying to put on for her children. "He was right next to me, and then we were just–here."

I hold out my hand, and she grasps it firmly. "I understand. My name is Rhea."

"I'm Avery."

"Avery, I have abilities."

"I was watching. It's... hard to find the words." She looks up as if searching the sky for answers. "Remarkable comes to mind. Terrifying."

"A lot has happened in a very short amount of time, but trust me, many of us are here to help and pose no threat."

"But others are not." It's a statement, not a question.

I nod. "Correct, others are not."

Avery reflects on my words a moment, her hand still clutching mine.

"If you would allow me, I would like to see your husband, in your mind." I say the words slowly, letting her absorb them. "It's painless and will help me know who I'm looking for."

Her control is slipping as she creases her forehead, but taking a few deep breaths, she steadies herself again. "We were just going to the mall for new shoes." Avery scoffs, shaking her head, still unable to process everything. "And now–" Several tears fall.

The conversation is colliding with her mind that is struggling to absorb the enormity of the past few minutes. She may be going into shock, and I need to help keep her grounded. Conjuring a cool breeze, it wraps around us. "Hey," I squeeze her hand and it pulls her back from the darkness of her thoughts. "Just take a deep breath." I inflate my lungs, and Avery follows. Blowing out a shaky breath, she nods her head, as if telling me she is calming.

"I can't tell you everything will be fine, but I'd like to help you if I can." Holding gaze with patience, Avery thinks for a moment. Her brown eyes study mine before she agrees.

My sweep into her mind is effortless. Being a mortal, she has no innate abilities to shield herself as most elementals do, and in an instant, I know everything about their lives. I discard the details, looking only for her husband and his name. The residue of his faint mortal aura lingers ever so dimly on the family before me, and I use it to search for him. Holding my breath and starting from the protective dome we are taking refuge in; I don't find him.

Releasing the huff of air, I push my powers out, searching across the realm and hoping for a miracle. Anxiety builds, and I bite my lip to alleviate the tension. When my aura reaches Alexandria, the impossible happens.

He's there.

Gasping, I feel my cheeks flare as my disbelief surges.

Within the wards surrounding Alexandria, he stands, his hand on the thick shield, and his face downcast as if in prayer.

"What?" Avery says, clutching onto me with both hands. "Dear god, please." She begs.

"I found him." I smile. "He's okay and alive."

She all but falls to the ground, and I brace her in my arms, helping ease her down as she sobs. Her children turn from the shield, worried looks of concern on their sweet faces as they see her weep. "What's wrong, Mommy?"

She can't even answer for her cries of relief.

Hermes comes to see if I need his help, and Lucas is following behind with a basket of snacks and bottles of water.

"You kids hungry?" Lucas turns their attention to the promise of food and smile as their faces light up.

"Everything okay?" Hermes says quietly as Lucas kneels down, presenting the goodies for the kids to make their selections.

"I found her husband at Alexandria; we should bring him here for her." As I speak, a realization hits me. "So many of them will be searching for survivors, and most will find no one."

Hermes rubs his hand up my back in comfort as we look across the thousands that made it inside our protection. "We should organize searches. Use the elementals that can read auras and have them look."

I give him a small smile and a nod. Thankful for his compassion toward these mortals, caught in the crossfire of our ages-old battle. This has an oddly familiar taste. An event we have repeated several times throughout the history of this realm. It was not me who flooded the earth all those ages ago, unable to control my powers and drowning the realm. It was Loki.

As the waters rushed in, elementals surged to the forefront of the shores. Water and Wind Sirens worked to hold back the waters. Earth elementals conjured boats, and we raised the mountains bringing as many mortals as we could to safety. But like today, so many died. I felt as helpless then as I do now.

Pushing the crushing memories aside, I tell Avery to wait here. The kids' eyes widen as they watch Hermes' power wrap around us, opening his portal that will deliver us to Alexandria. Before we disappear from their sight, a ball of sapphire blue light forms above their heads, exploding in a gentle burst. Miniature sparkling stars turn into dozens of blue butterflies that flitter around their faces.

Their giggles fade away as Wyoming turns to Alexandria in a flash.

Things are no different here.

A sea of mortals takes up seats around the great library and the sandy surroundings. Thoth and his Librarians are standing guard at the entrance to the many stares and gaping looks of the humans that have never before seen creatures such as them.

Dark shadows bound toward me from three directions. Cerberus has split himself into the forms of three dogs, but as he nears, they merge together. Kneeling down to greet him, he puts his snout in my waiting hand, sniffing hurriedly before walking a circle around me.

Once he's satisfied I'm okay, his nub of a tail wags excitedly as I pet him. Rubbing his head against me, he's glad I'm here, and the shadow pup brings a happy smile to my face.

Hecate and Daphne stand together dozens of feet away from us. Taking notice of our arrival at the same time, the sisters smile, their bodies relax in relief. We begin making our way to each other, hugging tightly when we meet.

"You both were so amazing." Daphne lets go of Hermes to hug me. "I'm so proud of you." She whispers, giving me another squeeze before letting go. The sentiment warms my heart, and tears want to rise within my eyes, but I blink them away.

"How did you guys do here?" Hermes asks, moving his gaze to the mass of people as he scans them, taking mental inventory of any needs.

"Everyone is fine, son." Daphne joins Hermes, looking over the survivors. "Thanks to you two, thousands are alive. It's difficult to see the blessing in that among so much loss. But hold on to that and remember it when you need it."

Hermes puts his arm around his mother's shoulders and hugs her as they survey the people a second longer.

When we arrived, I found the location of Avery's husband. Flora and Zephyr were close by, so speaking into their minds, I asked that they walk him here to us. It will give us a few minutes to speak with Daphne and Hecate about the parchment we found.

Hermes is always in tune with my feelings and seems to always know what I'm thinking. Taking the folded parchment from his back pocket, he hands it to Hecate. "I think you'll find this interesting."

She pushes her long dark hair behind her ear as she looks over the ancient account of events. Pan detailed our arrival to the doorway of the Labyrinth. It was not the first incarnation of my life as Nyx but my second, Eve.

Together with Hermes, we walked into the darkness. His faithful staff in one hand and the other held on to mine. There is no further account as the massive wards surrounding the Labyrinth prevent Pan from hearing or seeing inside.

Sometime later, Hermes and I exited the Labyrinth, and the scepter was gone.

Sitting beneath the surface of Gaea, the inverted pyramid

not only houses immortals too dangerous to live among the humans, but it also plays host to a pantheon of dark creatures that seep through the cracks of Elysium.

The Labyrinth is like a realm of its own, and its inhabitants are constantly starving. Somewhere within their haven of shadows, the final piece of my immortality awaits me.

Hecate finishes and hands the parchment to her sister. "Well, I suppose you'll need a path through the Labyrinth, then."

"Hi Jacob," I extend my hand to the mortal man who looks between us nervously. "I'm Rhea."

He wipes his hand down his pant leg before shaking it. "Nice to meet you." He keeps looking down at Cerberus, then quickly diverting his eyes away.

"Your wife and children are safe in another refuge, much like this one." I cast my hand in an arc, and his gaze follows my path, looking upward at the great dome that covers the large area of Alexandria. "We'll take you there in just a moment, if that is okay with you?"

"Yeah, sure. Uh–" He pauses, uncertainty at what to say pausing his words as his nervousness brings a flush to his cheeks. "Thank you so much, you know... for everything."

With a smile and a nod, I greet Flora. Her fated mate, Zephyr, walks alongside, their hands clasped, fingers woven together.

Hermes and Hecate are speaking of the Labyrinth and hearing the name of the immortal prison, Flora pales.

Falsely accused of disabling the Atlanta Commune's protective shield, Flora was cast into the dark cavern of the Labyrinth until Hecate snuck in and retrieved her.

Like all things as of late, we know now it was Loki, pulling the strings of different puppets, playing everyone against each other and moving us around like chess pieces so we would look everywhere but at him.

The short time within that dark prison had sucked so much of Flora's essence out of her, she was barely recognizable. Some immortals have been imprisoned within the tomb of darkness for eons, and I can't imagine what they would look like after all this time.

Thaumium collars withhold their elemental powers from them, but they are immortals. They can only be killed by elemental powers, so they rot, forever starving, never sleeping and never able to die. In a constant state of vigilance, they hide from the dark monsters that live inside their prison.

"We should talk more once the mortals are settled." Hecate gestures to the great library. "Within are the structural plans of the Labyrinth's interior. I can show you the pathway in, but I cannot help beyond that. What you seek could be hidden anywhere. You'll have to find your own way once inside."

Hermes nods in agreement, folding up the parchment and returning it to his pocket.

Beyond him, a disturbance within the crowd of humans takes my attention.

They part like the Red Sea as Pan walks among them, Circe at his side. Similar to the Librarians, Pan looks like a living tree that's shed its leaves. His height makes him head and shoulders above the mass of humans.

Lexi emerges opposite them and rushes to her mother's arms. Circe embraces her daughter as Pan puts his long arms around them both. Lexi spots me as I watch the family reunite.

With a stoic expression, void of any emotion, it would seem as if she still holds a grudge against me. Until I see the almost imperceptible nod of acknowledgment before she turns her head up toward Pan with an affectionate smile.

Despite our past turmoil, I'm happy to see the reunion and know a family is able to take refuge in each other's presence.

Returning my focus back to the small group around us, Flora and Zephyr asked to come with us back to the Shifters haven in Wyoming. So, with Hermes holding my hand and our new human companion standing nervously with us, the bright flash of blue starlight delivers us back to Wyoming.

A wave of emotions washes over me, watching Jacob rush to his family. The kids squeal, excited to see their dad again, oblivious to the gravity of recent events. They bounce, hugging his leg. Avery and Jacob hold each other tightly, knowing they came so very close to losing each other forever.

"It's nice to see a happy moment blooming among all this sadness," Flora says softly, a gentle smile on her lips as we watch the family reunite. "I only hope we get to see the world blooming again soon. I already miss all the green."

"I don't think the realm can recover from the poisons of the mortal bombs so easily, Flo," Zephyr interjects. "But if I could blow the clouds of smoke away for you..."

Flora leans her head against her partner, her smile growing with the sentiment. "I know you would."

Zephyr nods toward a group of mortals waiting for someone to help them find missing loved ones. "We're going to go see if we can help."

As the couple leaves me, I watch them walking away, noticing a small pinecone in Flora's hand. She turns it over in her palm, and a small black seed drops from it, landing somewhere in the grass. I recall a fact about forest fires and pinecones: during a fire, they close up, protecting the seeds within. After the blaze, they open, reseeding the forest so it can start anew.

I kneel at the edge of the wards, placing my hand on the ground. Closing my eyes, I push my powers into the earth, sensing seeds and roots waiting for sunlight. Without help, it will take years for the skies to clear and wake the seeds from their slumber.

The air outside the dome tastes like metal on my tongue with all the toxins in the atmosphere. My mouth turns down at the corners at the pungency. Keeping my hand on the ground, I look to the darkened sky above and form a swirling vortex within the clouds. The churning winds work to clear a small patch in the dark clouds, and a beam of sunlight breaks through. Hope swells around me as the emotions of onlookers pour out of them, and a plan comes to mind.

"Zephyr, let's gather the Wind and Water Sirens over here," I call to them in my mind, catching the attention of my mate who joins me in curiosity. "Oh, good idea. I'll need the Light and Life Bearers as well."

"Give me a few minutes, little goddess, and I'll bring you the realm." Hermes places a kiss on my temple and vanishes to Alexandria. Within minutes, the edge of the large dome is lined with immortals of all the elements.

An immortal is responsible for this destruction, but we're not going to let this realm struggle for ages to recover. We will use our powers to help clear the atmosphere and jumpstart the realm's recovery.

Looking down the line on both sides, I feel their powers calling the essence of the Titans that reside within me. Light and Life, Wind and Water churn as immortals wielding those elements wait for my command. Medusa joins us, bringing with her Earth elementals and an added sense of resolve. With a nod, she turns her focus to the world beyond, ready like the others.

The elements are braided together within me like silken ribbons, and I call upon each of them individually. Speaking with my mind, I ask the immortals to join me as we summon the powers of the realm.

Raising my hands to the ashen sky, I close my eyes, focusing on the winds. The Sirens, creatures of the air, join me, their power connecting with mine, strengthened by the Titan within me. A gentle breeze picks up, growing steadily stronger with each passing moment. A haunting melody rides on the stagnant breeze, like the lingering cries of mortals as they lost their lives only moments ago. The thick clouds of smoke and debris disperse, torn apart by the relentless winds we've summoned.

The toxic clouds churn and roil under the assault of the wind, gradually being driven back, dispersing into nothingness. Through the thinning gray, shafts of gilded sunlight begin to pierce the gloom, spreading across the devastated landscape.

The warmth of the sun on our skin is an encouraging touch amid the wreckage. Around us, mortals and elementals alike raise their faces to the sky as if we haven't felt the heat of the sun in ages. Looking to my mate, Hermes meets my stare, his eyes steadying me and giving me faith that we can set this right.

"Ready?" I ask with a smile, already knowing the answer.

With our hands clasped together, our Titan powers of Light swell, and the elementals around us follow suit. A collective energy builds to a tangible warmth that tingles in our fingertips. The air shimmers as if heated by an invisible fire. The light intensifies to beams of energy that shoot upwards and spread out across the sky. The Light Bearers' merges with us, creating a radiant network of rays that crisscross above.

This light is not just illumination—it is purification. The toxic particles disintegrate, evaporated by the intensity of the sun's brilliance. It's a spectacular sight, the beams acting like cleaners scouring the sky, leaving behind nothing but purity in their wake.

We continue, our focus unyielding, as the energy demands more from us than ever before. Hermes' hand firmly holds mine, his grip strengthening me, reinforcing our shared resolve. Together, we amplify the power of the Light Bearers, pushing their element further, ensuring no corner of the sky remains untouched.

As minutes pass, the air not only clears but begins to sparkle with a newfound freshness, the toxic threat neutralized by our combined efforts. Slowly, we lower our arms, the network of light gradually fading, but its work complete.

As the winds have cleared the smoke and light has purified the air, healing waters rain upon the world, washing away the final residues of destruction. As the Water Bearers heed my call, it's as if the world is collectively crying, mourning the tragic loss of life. The mighty rivers and raging oceans swell and rock at our beckoning. Rain cascades from the sky and drenches the land, giving drink to the thirsty roots and seeds nestled within the soil.

Throughout the realm, small pockets of survivors, human and animal alike, emerge from their hiding and raise their faces to the rain. Washing away the grime and healing their injuries.

The Earth Mages and Life Bearers need no calling,

knowing it's time to renew the world of what was lost. The ground tremors, and briefly, the mortals fear another round of bombs are coming for them. Using my Sensor powers of emotions, I fill them with calming serenity, assuring them of their safety.

The rubble of collapsed cities and debris of shattered homes litters the realm. The Earth Mages command elements within the wreckage and churn the earth to break down and consume the destruction. With a nod from Flora, the Life elementals join me.

Murmurs of fear are taken over by gasps of amazement as spears of grass grow in an instant. Spreading out like a green wave, the grass overtakes the brown dirt. Sprigs of trees rise up, growing in height and expanding to replenish the abundant forest that stood here just this morning.

Laughter and cries of joy echo within the dome as the Life and Earth elementals around me keep their focus. Feeling the renewal sweep the realm, we weave the fibers of our abilities together, pushing them across every landscape. Hermes wraps his arms around me, and his awe and pride bring warmth to me as he watches the tall trees grow to their full height.

Only when we know we have renewed the earth as much as we can do I ask one final favor of my mate. Fusing our powers again, we expand the bubble of our protection. Increasing our enclosure to allow more space for the larger number of residents.

By keeping them here, we risk the chance they will grow restless, demanding release to rebuild civilization. But knowing Loki has destroyed the world before, raising the waters so high, he drowned the realm, we must keep a constant vigil against the chaos he might still unleash.

But just as the sun shines with hope through the gray clouds of despair, I feel a sense of peace and readiness now that we know the final location of my powers. Soon, we will bring the fight to Loki, and no longer will he be able to hide behind his charades and masks. No longer will the immortals and the humans of the realm suffer or live in fear of extinction because of his craving for power, because a craving of my own has emerged.

A yearning that has grown with each recovered memory and recalled lifetime. A longing to take back my life. And with it, I hope I'll be able to bring peace to this realm.

"**M**an, I'm so fucking glad I'm not you.**"** Lucas pats me once on the back as he sits down with a plate of food and a sigh of relief. Rumors about our quest to the Labyrinth are spreading with a mixture of responses from the immortals. Some look at us as if our death is certain while others are intrigued.

"You couldn't handle being me." I scoff back, adding a few extra beef skewers for Rhea.

"Oh, what, like it's hard flitting around with your flashlights and your little winged sandals?" Lucas chuckles, jabbing at the mortal's representation of my mythological lore. "How did that come about anyhow: sandals with wings?"

The question is not what makes me pause, but the memory it evokes. Like so many things, Achilles is at the center of it. From the second we became friends; we were rarely apart from each other.

Lucas notices my hesitation and takes a breath to interject. "Look man, I'm sorry—"

"No, it's okay." I wave him off and tell him the story. "Achilles was just a sore loser." I chuckle, recalling that one race when he stepped down on a rock, hurting his heel and tumbling for yards. I won and he always claimed we should have raced again. "Achilles never could live down losing that race, so he would always draw graffiti on the stone walls of the towns, like I had wings on my feet. He said that was the only way I could have beaten him, somehow cheating."

I can hear his voice taunting me, knowing exactly what he would say if he were here; but he's not. The thought that he'll never be by my side again tightens around my throat, and I drop my head, blinking away the pain. "It was just harmless fun, but it stuck."

"It's funny how twisted stories get over time." Silence falls between us as we begin eating.

Shelter and food are the priorities of the immediate need; then, the Labyrinth.

We've been working nonstop for hours to help the mortals prepare for their first night in the dome, but we need to make a plan to enter the immortal prison. The urgency to ensure Rhea is fully immortal is burning within me. Not just so we can defeat Loki before his plans worsen, but to ensure we never have to be separated again.

Elementals of all kinds are coming together to craft shelter and prepare food. Amazement seems to overtake the humans at every turn as they watch the Life Bearers grow fields of plentiful crops in minutes. Or accelerate the growth of fish until the lake on Lucas's property is nearly over-flowing.

Keeping our lives hidden among the mortals was always imperative. They can reproduce; we can't. All it would take is mortals gaining possession of immortal metals, and they could eradicate us all from this realm.

But now I'm hoping for a new life where mortals and

immortals can thrive together. Peace is required first, and that means Loki must be defeated.

Rhea joins us, sitting on my knee and snagging a skewer. Sliding the grilled beef off the stick, her eyes close, and she breathes a sigh of exhaustion, finally sitting down for the first time in hours. Cerberus has been staying close to her since we checked on Alexandria after the bombardment. The shadow pup curls up at our feet, closing his ember eyes and falling asleep quickly.

Between Wyoming and Alexandria, I have kept a large portal open continuously, allowing the mortals and immortals alike to move between the two strongholds as they wish.

It's working for now to keep the mortals calm, but we'll likely need to branch out beyond these two domes and create more. Lucas took center stage, speaking with groups of mortals openly about the threat we are facing and the need to remain protected within these wards.

We'll see how long the mortals' willingness to comply lasts.

Walking out of the portal from the sands of Africa to the lush green forest of Wyoming, Medusa wipes her brow with her hand, sitting with us and drinking her water heavily.

My mother and Hecate are already sitting with Flora and Zephyr, eating and talking of plans to keep a food supply replenished for the needs of the mortals.

The echoing caw of a bird catches Rhea's attention, and she turns, looking behind us. Beyond the dome, Kai has taken to her shifted form, scouring outside the wards for survivors and wildlife.

Rhea opens a silver portal of starlight, and Kai flies through it, arriving back inside our haven. The mortals watch her shift back to a human form, mothers covering the eyes of children from Kai's naked body. Those of us sitting around the table chuckle in amusement. It will take the mortals some time to get used to walking among gods and legends.

Bridget welcomes herself to the table with a more tentative Circe, who hesitates before finally deciding to sit as well. Pan has been occupying himself inside the library with Thoth, and Circe's daughter Lexi has been keeping to herself.

Betta and Cappa make room for Kai, who is now dressed. Joining us, the Shifters dig into the assortment of beef and fish, taking hearty servings of roasted vegetables as Fire Mages monitor grilling pits, churning out more food.

The conversation is on one thing: finding the Caduceus.

There will be no celestial event to mark the occasion like Mabon or the Triple Moon Eclipse. I have a feeling that the keys to the doorway this time will be brute force and unwavering determination. The Labyrinth will have no leniency for anything else.

"Everyone knows our next step is the Labyrinth." I begin, now that our assembly of allies is gathered. Those who are not here scorch my mind like their absence is branded inside me.

Callie and Achilles. Odysseus and Penelope. Athena. My father.

So many others gone over the ages that I have to push the thoughts of their loss to the back of my mind. "We should talk about what you guys will do to help the mortals and defenses while we're gone."

"They can talk about what they will be doing for the mortals and defenses," Medusa begins, pulling a piece of fish from Hecate's plate and taking a bite. "I don't need to talk about that, because I'll be coming with you."

"Deuce..." I begin to argue.

"I'm not asking. I'm telling you. I'm going with you both to the Labyrinth."

"I'll go as well," Kai adds herself to the party.

"Yeah, we're in too." Cappa elbows Delta, who was not listening, too busy eating.

"Sure." He answers, cheeks stuffed full of grilled food. "Where are we going?"

"To your deaths," Hecate deadpans, making Delta stop his chewing, swallowing hard. "The Labyrinth is not a vacation spot that welcomes tourist groups. The more of you that offer to enter the doors of the eternal prison, the more will never walk out."

Silence falls over the group as the architect of the inverted pyramid offers her warning. In the distance, Pan and Thoth arrive. The crowd of mortals parting for them easily, watching the two tree-like beings stride casually to us.

"No one should sign up to go inside," Rhea breaks the quiet, her voice small, and I know her worry is growing over the prospect of what we'll find once we're inside. "Hermes and I went in last time and came out just fine. We can do it again."

"The last time, Loki did not know you entered the immortal prison," my mother offers her counsel. "This time, he will know, and rest assured, he'll have prepared for you."

"Loki wants me to find the staff. He wants Death more than anything else." Rhea's voice rises in volume, her earlier anxieties swallowed down by the surety of her thoughts. "He's just as starved as the dark beings inside the prison, and he's waited long enough for his meal. I don't think we'll face any greater problems once inside than what should be expected."

"I agree." As I rub Rhea's back. "If anything, it's everyone above the surface that we need to worry about. He's shown there are no limits in this game he's playing."

As we talk of creating two more protective domes and keeping them open with portals, a coalition forms of volunteers that want to join us in the Labyrinth. I'm not going to turn away others that can also help keep Rhea safe once we're inside. But the thought of those we may lose is a heavy risk, among all the loss we've already faced.

Loki must be stopped, and enough of us need to be alive at the end of this to make sure that happens.

Medusa and Kai have decided to arm wrestle to see which of them will be coming with us. They are both strong fighters, and leaving the surface without those capable of defending the mortals is a poor plan.

So, the winner is coming with us, and the loser is staying here.

The pair of immortals are locked in a battle of wills. Both of them too stubborn to give up and concede that perhaps they are equally strong. But I know my friend. There is no way Medusa will ever let herself come in second place.

A buzz floats around the crowd of mortals as some look on. Perhaps guessing which woman will take the victory. Sweat beads on their heads, but slowly, Kai's arm begins to move toward the table.

Just as I suspected, Medusa will dig just a little deeper, making sure she comes out victorious. Inch by inch, the Gorgon overtakes the Shifter until the back of Kai's hand hits the table.

"Best two out of three?" Kai interjects playfully as the buzzing crowd grows more restless, stealing our attention.

People are walking quickly to one side of the warded dome, pointing at something, and straining to see.

"Something is riling up the natives," Lucas stands, putting his hands on his hips. His keen senses taking in everything going on. "Something is outside the dome." He warns.

Rhea and I send a rush of our powers beyond the barrier we have created, investigating to see what is going on.

Rolling shadows, so thick they look like smoke, churn and dance close to the ground. The small group of our immortal friends pushes their way through the crowd, made easier when Cerberus divides himself into several large Dobermans, fanning out and barking at the humans.

We reach the dome and watch the shadows collect. Gathering in a swirl like a churning eddy of darkness, the form of a man takes shape. Great leathery wings protrude first from the obscurity.

"Oh great, the bloodsuckers are here." Medusa jests, amusement teasing in her tone.

"Don't call them that." My mother scolds, pulling a chuckle from Medusa.

Rhea keeps her eyes forward, her arms folded over her chest, and one eyebrow raised in defiance. Jutting out her hip, she stands with most of her weight on one leg as the manifestation of the Vampire King takes shape.

When I first petitioned Vladimir in the plaza of Venice, he blended in with modern society, wearing a sleek tailored suit, his icy blue eyes shining against his tan skin and long chestnut hair.

But he appears to be going for dramatics today, sporting a regal black suit and leather gloves befitting older times. The

Victorian tailcoat jacket is double-breasted, buttoned, and hangs down mid-thigh.

His black vest showcases black satin detailing while the tufts of his black lace shirt spill out of the vest's top. Complete with top hat, Vlad looks like he's stepped right out of ancient Transylvania.

With one ankle crossed over the other, he leans against a black walking cane with a small silver raven's skull fixed at the top.

His wings are the most impressive statement, and he's making every effort to stretch them out to their full span. The mortals can't look away, both transfixed and terrified by the Vampire before them. That is part of their allure.

The visceral reaction the Vampires provoke helps excite the blood of the meal they will soon consume, richening the flavor and drawing out more nutrients critical to their existence. It's often why sex and bloodletting are common companions for Vampires and their familiars.

Rhea holds Vlad's unimpressed gaze, standing in the lush green landscape of Wyoming as if it's the most boring thing he's done in centuries. Just as Medusa won her showdown with Kai, Rhea is just as determined to win this showdown with Vlad and get the truce she wants with the Vampires.

"I apologize." The King of the Vampires dips his head to my mate, tipping his hat, then waits for her response.

A smile creeps across her beautiful face as she slowly releases her stoic demeanor. Pride from her earlier attempt that seemed a failure at first, now coming to light, causes her to push back her shoulders and jut her chin ever so slightly before she answers him.

"I accept."

As the velvet night blankets the sky, my sense of accomplishment swells, filling me until I'm nearly bouncing. Just this morning, the world came to a standstill as Loki unleashed his own version of death across the realm.

But working with the elementals to clear the destruction, helping the mortals and securing the alliance with the Vampires, hope is blooming within me, just as fast as the quick-growing plants, at my fingertips.

Lost in thought, I didn't hear Hermes enter the greenhouse but the constant tether binding us together thrums, making me smile. His warmth cocoons me just before his arms do and I lean back into him. "You were amazing today." He whispers, nuzzling against my neck and taking in my scent.

We sway back and forth as I rub the fine petals of the white lilies that just bloomed. "Is it bad that I feel...happy?" The hesitation in my question makes me visibly cringe as I scrunch my shoulders and furrow my brow.

"Of course not. You're allowed to feel happiness, baby." Hermes moves my hair aside, revealing my pale skin that looks almost pearlescent in the moonlight. The faint touch of his lips, barely skimming my neck, sends a wave of gooseflesh down my back.

"But today was probably the most terrible day this realm has ever seen." Tears prick at the edges of my vision. "I shouldn't have anything to smile about today."

"Yes, you do." Hermes turns me, bringing me around to face him and bracketing me in with his strong arms. His triceps flex and he thrums his fingers on the wooden workbench behind me.

I'm hypnotized by his forearms and the way the muscles move under his veins. Running my hands slowly up the length of his arms, I move my eyes back to his. With a tick of his eyebrow and a crooked smirk, I know he's caught me ogling him and he loves it. *Cocky bastard.*

"You reunited a family today; that alone is worthy of a small grin, at least." He's teasing, and it brings out a shy smile. Standing, he pulls me to him, wrapping his arms around my waist as I continue rubbing my hands along his biceps.

"I just feel bad. So many terrible things have happened; I feel like I should be in a constant state of sadness." Biting my lip, a habit I do when I'm anxious, pulls his eyes down to my mouth. A jolt rushes through me knowing such a simple gesture can drive him crazy with longing for me.

His thumb and forefinger find my chin and his head dips down to meet me. Taking my lip between his teeth, he tugs it free. Releasing me, I'm rewarded with a quiet growl, his chest grumbling under my hands. "That's my lip to bite, little goddess."

Picking me up, Hermes sets me on the bench. His large hands splay across my legs, massaging my tired limbs.

"It's okay to go through sad events and not feel upset the

whole time." He tucks an errant lock of hair behind my ear, letting my long hair run through his fingers. "You know, each time you died, the world turned dark for me. But every now and then, there would be a small sparkle that brought the smallest bit of illumination back."

His eyes are a rich navy hue surrounded by night and there is a symphony of crickets, playing a melody for us in this otherwise quiet greenhouse. "I held on to those small moments with everything I had, and do you know why?"

I shake my head, no. "Why?"

"Because I knew you would want me to be happy. I knew you would want me to live." His answer brings a sad smile to my face. "And among everything happening, life goes on. Those small moments will sparkle around us, and it's okay to enjoy them." He puts his hands on each side of my face and I cover his hands with mine. "Callie would want you to keep enjoying them."

With the mention of her name, my chest bursts open and tears flood me. Hermes holds me, stroking my hair and rubbing my back. "I miss her so much." I choke out.

"Me too, baby. Me too."

"Is it always going to hurt this bad?"

His chest rises, then he releases a sigh, as if my words weigh him down, but along our bond, I sense that he feels the same way I do. "I think so, but maybe we just get used to it."

Pulling away, he rests his forehead against mine. For a moment, we let the heaviness hang in the air, and oddly enough, the quiet comfort he's giving me helps settle my sorrow.

A moment passes, and he rubs the tip of his nose against mine and the gesture warms me.

Leaving the greenhouse, I feel no less guilty about my earlier sentiments of joy, and milling over the remorse has brought a shadow over me. Maybe eventually I can free myself to enjoy the life that takes place around me, but I feel like there is such a long path ahead before I can be released from this prison of guilt.

Late into the night, the work to help settle the mortals continues. Massive efforts to erect large buildings for shelter take place within both domes. Life Bearers work in a constant stream of elemental power to grow forests for lumber. Earth elementals shape and move the wood, standing up structures in minutes.

But there are thousands that need homes and bathrooms and as I walk to the home Hermes and I will be staying in, my guilt only worsens. Though it is a small house, several families could stay in here together, yet it's reserved for Hermes and me.

Lucas wouldn't hear my complaints. "You two saved the world, so you get your own place."

Tired and unable to think clearly from exhaustion, Hermes finally convinced me to go home and lay down. Staying with the others, he wanted to help finish up the last two buildings so all the mortals have a place inside to rest for the night.

The small log home has two bedrooms that share a bathroom and an open living space with a small kitchen. The giant bed in the main bedroom is so tall I nearly have to jump into it. But it's so soft, and the quilted comforter is warm.

Showering and dressing in a satin chemise with thin straps and lace trim, the split that rises up my leg showcases my curves.

One of Lucas' Shifters brought me a small trove of books earlier this evening from their collection. Those with a love of reading seem to be able to find each other anywhere. Picking up a reverse harem, I read about a goddess who reincarnates, just like me. Each time, her four mates reincarnate too, and they work to find each other.

The story is all too familiar, but as the main character is being enjoyed by several of her partners at once, I think back to the mortal woman, spread across the table with Vampires feasting on her from every angle.

It was exciting to watch and makes me think of Hermes filling my mouth with his cock while he eats my pussy, his fingers stroking my insides and consuming me everywhere. Just before I reach the part of the book where all four mates take the main character in their oversized bed, the door to our bedroom opens, startling me.

My face heats, and I shut the book quickly. Hermes pauses, as I attempt to hide what I was just doing. Hermes has already shown me that he loves recreating the spicy scenes in my books, but I reacted on instinct.

"My, my, my little goddess." In a flash of cerulean starlight, Hermes uses his speed to quickly shower, reappearing before me a second later wrapped in a towel, his dark hair dripping wet. "What were you up to?"

"Nothing," My answer is breathless and does nothing to convince him. I watch with fascination as a drop of water falls from his hair to his firm pec. Slowly rolling down his skin, I resist the urge to run my tongue along the path of the water droplet.

I follow it until it disappears into the towel circling his narrow waist. Only then do I raise my eyes to meet his glare. Heavy with desire, he looks at me as if I'm his prey and he's starving to consume me.

I put the book onto the side table next to the bed, and he watches my movements as intently as I watched the water drop. His mouth quirks up when he sees the title.

"*The Goddess Fourtold*. Hmmm, interesting way to spell foretold, don't you think." He keeps the towel around him and walks to the corner of the bed. Sitting up on my knees, he gets a full look at my silky nightdress and his eyes hood with his arousal.

"It is." I agree, my husky voice giving away my own desire. Biting my lip, I crawl to him. His hands reach for me on instinct, and as our bodies meld together, we're a perfect fit.

One hand squeezes my ass, the other squeezes my thigh as he presses into me. His erection is ready to satisfy me in any manner I could possibly desire and with my heart pounding, I gather the courage to let him in on my thoughts.

"She has four mates." My voice is low as I trail a finger down the path of the water droplet. Reaching between the folds of the towel, I grip his long hard length and feel the barbells of his piercing rub along my palm as I stroke him.

"Mmmmm," He closes his eyes, enjoying my touch on his body. "Does that make you curious, little goddess?"

My cheeks heat as I flush at his question. My earlier bravery wavering. When I only reply with a nod of my head, Hermes opens his eyes. Taking my chin tenderly, he holds my gaze close to his.

"Tell me your fantasy, and I'll make it come true," he murmurs, his lips grazing mine but not kissing. "Do you want more hands caressing your body?"

As he speaks, his aura gleams and splits away from him, forming another Hermes, also in a towel. This translucent blue projection comes to my side, his hands sliding up my ribs to cup my breast and rub across my nipple.

"Oh," is all I can say while Hermes keeps a tender grip on my chin, locking my gaze on him.

I think back to the Underworld, weak and trapped after battling Ariyana. A projection of Hermes reached me then, sharing his power in the most intimate of ways to restore me.

"Do you want more tongues worshipping your perfect body?" Another projection splits away. This one kneels behind me on the bed, his hard cock pressing against my ass. Warm hands move my hair aside as the projection licks and sucks my neck, sending chills down my body.

I want to lean my head, but Hermes holds me still. His free hand slides from my ass to my pussy, toying with the lace band of my panties before reaching inside. His expert touch circles my clit, making me drop my mouth open, a rush of pleasure tightening a knot in my stomach.

"Do you want more cocks filling your holes?" he asks, then kisses me.

His tongue sweeps into my mouth, possessing me as his finger maintains a steady rhythm, massaging my clit with the gentlest vibration.

"Yes," I answer breathlessly when he pulls away.

"Tell me," Hermes demands. "Let me hear your filthy mouth say the words." The vibrations on his fingertip increase, and so does the climax building in my belly. "Open your eyes and tell me how you want to be fucked, you greedy little goddess."

Mouth parted, I open my eyes against the caresses igniting my body, nearly rendering me speechless. "I..." The sensations overwhelm me. Several hands stroke my body and my pussy. Two mouths suck my nipples at once.

"Tell me," Hermes' quiet demand is like silk across my lips.

"I want what she had." I share the image of the mortal woman on the table at Transylvania. Her head hanging back, a vampire's cock down her throat, another lavishing her breasts while her pussy was being devoured as if she were the vampires' last meal.

Hermes' work on my clit builds my orgasm, and I tighten my grip on his shoulders. My pelvis moves in small thrusts as I release a moan of pleasure. But he's not going to let me off the hook so easily. With a grin, he lessens the intensity of his vibrating finger and slows the circles around my clit. The orgasm ebbs away before it can crest.

"Be a good girl and tell me," Hermes whispers, pecking at my mouth. Sliding two fingers into my wet pussy, he adds, "Tell me, and we'll make you cum so hard you'll see all the stars of this universe right here in this room."

"Oh, my gods, Hermes," I pant as his two fingers fill me, words pouring from my mouth. "I want you to fuck my mouth until I choke." He vibrates his thumb against my clit as he pumps his fingers into me. "I want your cock to fill me while your mouth sucks on my pussy."

Gods, I'm so close.

My hips move with Hermes' hand, my muscles tightening as my climax builds again. Hermes claims me with a kiss, and I whimper, pulling at his hair as he owns my mouth with his tongue.

Again, he eases away, teasing me with the promise of release, then pulling it away tenderly. He slows his movements and slides his fingers from me. Pulling his lips from mine, he groans in approval, rubbing my clit with his soaking fingers. "You're so wet for us, little goddess."

Hermes pats the corner of the bed. "Lay down and put your head right here." He takes off the towel, and the two astral projections follow suit. His sculpted body is on full display, his long dick standing tall and ready. Looking between them, my fingers tingle, wanting to touch their astral forms.

"Can I?" My question is shy, and Hermes watches me closely, nodding and tracking my hands as I touch them. Running my hands down the lengths of their cocks, I cup their balls, giving them a gentle squeeze. The projections feel solid, just like touching him. Hermes dips his head back, moaning.

Wrapping my fingers around their shafts, I stroke them, my movements a mirror image on the two forms, making Hermes' breath quicken. The sensations from the projections travel to Hermes through our bond, as if I'm stroking him.

"Lay down, baby, so I can stuff this cock in your mouth."

Having Hermes move deeper and deeper into my mouth while the astral projections worked my body was the most intense orgasm I ever had. Each inch he moved into me, he let me acclimate before going deeper. With my head hanging back, my throat opened, welcoming his impressive size. The astral projection licked and sucked my clit as Hermes fucked my mouth. The other projection pinched and bit at my nipples. When I came, so did Hermes. My legs twitched with the intensity of the pleasure coursing through me, his aura holding my knees open.

"On your knees." Hermes' demand makes me shiver with anticipation. One projection fades away as I get on all fours. The bed dips as Hermes positions himself behind me. He runs the head of his cock along the slit of my pussy, rubbing the evidence of my orgasm on his tip and teasing my still-throbbing clit with the promise of more pleasure.

With a single thrust, he's inside me. My back arches as I release a satisfied groan. Pulling me up with his hand on my throat, he turns my face, giving him access to my mouth. I reach behind me, holding onto his neck and lightly pulling the short hair at the nape of his neck. "Do you want more, little goddess?"

I follow the path of Hermes' eyes to the astral projection standing just on the other side of the bed. Tall and strong, a perfect replica of my mate is ready to join in my pleasure if I want it. And gods, I do.

The projection fades and appears below me, laying on his back between my legs. "Widen your knees, baby," Hermes whispers, nipping at my earlobe. I follow his directions, widening my knees and bringing my needy pussy to the mouth of the projection below me. Hermes thrusts into me and rubs my nipple as the projection sucks my clit. My back bows dramatically as Hermes pulls back on my hair, making his cock rub against my walls perfectly.

The pair work in tandem, edging me closer and closer to another climax, then pulling me back. Finally, my second orgasm careens through me like a freight train. One hand holds Hermes' neck behind me, the other fists the projection's hair below me as I ride them through the waves of pleasure. Hermes' grip on my hips tightens as he growls with the intensity of his release, our bond thrumming with combined satisfaction. The pulsing prolongs as I keep thrusting against them.

Finally, when the crest of my enjoyment subsides, my vision turns static, showing me all the stars of the universe, just as Hermes promised.

Sunlight shining through the crack in the curtains **draws me from sleep.** Stretching, the smell of bacon beckons me to the kitchen of our small cabin. Rhea's side of the bed is empty and cold, and I place my hand on her pillow in the divot where she laid her head.

The late hours of last night play through my mind, pulling a grin to my face. Gods, she is so beautiful wrapped around me, giving over her pleasure to me.

Last night, she wanted to be filled in every way possible by me, and I gave her everything she desired. Splitting my aura and casting my Mirages, I pleasured every inch of her body again and again until her legs were too shaky to stand, and I carried her to bed.

Our last round of the night was her favorite. I sat across the room watching her while she sat on the lap of my projection. Sliding down onto the cock waiting for her, Rhea's face blushed when I groaned from across the room.

Moving her hips in slow circles, she kept her heated eyes on me every second. Fisting my dick and stroking myself as I watched her, she opened her legs and held them wide so I could see her glistening pussy take my cock. My second projection feasted on her, and my mouth salivates just thinking about how delicious she is.

I felt every slow stroke and tasted each caress of her sweet skin.

When I came, she wanted to devour me. Striding across the room, bringing myself to a climax at the sight of her, those full pink lips opened for me, and she took every drop.

Her own pleasure cresting at the same time, I could barely stand it as she sucked and moaned against my dick. When her orgasm subsided, she looked at me with contentment and satisfaction in her weary gaze.

Scooping her up in my arms, I took her to bed, laying her down gently and holding her until she fell into a deep sleep. Keeping my treasure in my arms, she stayed there all night.

Brushing my teeth and putting on some linen pants, I join her in the kitchen.

Steam rises from the stove as she stirs a pan of scrambled eggs. Her hair is twisted in a sloppy bun, and the globes of her ass peek from the hem of her satin gown as she reaches for a plate.

Coming up behind her, I palm one of her cheeks with a squeeze as I nuzzle into her neck. Reaching above her, I get the plate for her. "I was going to make you breakfast, beautiful."

With a giggle that warms my heart, she leans into my kiss, momentarily distracted from her task. Turning around, she wraps her arms around my neck with a smile that lights up the morning, her eyes sparkling with joy. "You looked so peaceful; I didn't want to wake you."

Taking the spatula from her hand, I give her a long kiss before releasing her. "I'll finish up. You sit." I hand her a half-drunk cup of coffee from the counter, and she sits at the table, propping her feet up and taking a sip.

I would give anything to make sure she could always feel this way: content and happy, knowing how much she is loved. But a shadow clouds the warmth of the moment as the truth tries to push its way to the forefront of my mind. The reality of our present is that she is anxious and in mourning, feeling responsible for things she can't control. And hunted; always hunted.

That fact is a constant itch that can't be scratched, forever hanging over every thought.

She is masking the tension growing inside her, but I feel it, slowly squeezing our bond, and I wish I could take all this away from her. But the only way to end it all is to reunite her with the last of her powers.

And the only path to do that appears to be traversing through the dark twists and turns of the Labyrinth. The most perilous domain created, designed to entrap and confuse its occupants as they try to survive in a constant state of danger.

Dividing the eggs between two plates, I butter her toast and sprinkle a mixture of cinnamon and sugar on it. Cutting it just the way she likes it, right down the middle, I set it in front of her and smile when she wiggles in her seat, excited to dig in.

Finished preparing my own plate, I sit with her, and we enjoy a lazy breakfast. By the time we're finished, her feet are in my lap. I massage her while she tells me every detail of her book, complaining about the ending and waving her hands excitedly as she explains all the things she would have done differently.

"I'm sorry, I'm sure this is boring you."

With a stupid smile on my face, I pull her into my lap. She

straddles me, and our arms find their way around each other. "I can't wait for an eternity of mornings just like this with you."

Standing in the large atrium of the great library, the assembly before us is one I've never seen here on Gaea. Immortals from every race are huddled around a large stone table with the blueprints of the Labyrinth laid out.

Vlad returned with an entourage of his gargoyle guards and high members of his court. Lucas is next to me with a wide stance, his arms crossed over his chest, with his Beta on his right, and Cappa and Delta on his left. Kellan and Zara stand behind him.

Medusa leans against a wall, her legs stretched out with one ankle crossed over the other. Picking her nails, she acts like she doesn't have a care in the world, but her braids tell another story. Several writhe like snakes, observing the gathering of immortals. Another long tendril curls around her pinky finger, then uncurls, repeating the motion as if soothing her.

Pan and Circe are quiet in the corner with Bridget.

Most surprising of all is Aphrodite and several captains of her crew. My mother has never given Aphrodite any leniency for her treatment of Calypso.

Their mother abandoned Aphrodite at birth, leaving her to be raised by the spirits of the Wind. But Calypso was dropped off at our father's doorstep as a youngling. Aphrodite was always resentful of Calypso for having time with their mother that she didn't get. But in the end, they were both abandoned by her. A fact Callie tried to convince Aphrodite of many times.

The standoff at the library's doorway between my mother and Aphrodite was brief when my mother offered her sorrow first. "I'm sorry for your loss."

Nodding in acceptance, Aphrodite did the same. "And I yours."

Rolling up the blueprints, Hecate joins her sister, standing with Thoth and Seshat. "And so, you know everything that you may face once inside, but I have to warn you, nothing can truly prepare you." She runs her dark eyes over each person's face.

"No one is expected to join us," I begin. My mate looks at me with pleading eyes, guilt already choking her at the thought of others joining us. The prospect that they may never leave the Labyrinth is very real. "But you know the path Rhea and I will go down, and you join of your own will."

"Before anyone gets excited to jump to their deaths," Rhea interjects. She doesn't want anyone in danger, but as long as Loki lives, no one is safe. "The surface needs strong warriors to defend against Loki, should he attack during our absence. It may be better for you all to remain here and protect each other and the mortals."

"We have as much to lose in a fight against Loki as we do risking your death." Medusa looks plainly at Rhea, firm resolve in her tone. Pushing off the wall, Medusa squares her shoulders to Rhea and crosses her right arm over her chest, placing her fist over her heart. "I give my powers and strength to shield the goddess, and should I fall, may the Void claim my soul...for my heart already resides there."

A tear rolls down Medusa's cheek as she recites a vow spoken by so many warriors during the Titans' battle. The last part Medusa added on. Half her heart died when her fated bond to Athena was severed. The other half died the day Athena did.

Pan is next to stand, stepping away from Circe, who doesn't appear to agree with his decision. Following Medusa, he recites the vow. Cappa smacks Delta's chest, bringing his attention back to the conversation, and the pair of Shifters join in the guard, along with Kellan, who receives a firm nod from his sister.

Aphrodite steps forward, her captains behind her, as she looks directly at Rhea. "My sister would have walked by your side, and so will I." Crossing her arm with her fist over her heart, she bows her head, then steps back.

The Vampire King clears his throat before interjecting. "Well, I'm not dumb enough to join you in death and leave my Vampires without protection, but I am bound by the contract that holds me here and am forbidden from entering the Labyrinth." Vlad deadpans, looking at no one as he pulls a piece of nothing off his all-black ensemble. "But you can have my guards. They will defend you with their lives."

Rhea trembles more with each person that offers their life to her.

Taking her hand in mine, she squeezes tightly as I pass my reassurance to her through our bond. *"They have as much to lose as we do, baby."* I try to calm her, but I know she just needs a moment to process the willingness of those around her who want to help. *"We don't have to do this alone."*

Forcing back her tears, she finally looks at me and nods, though the trepidation hangs heavy on her heart, and I can understand why. Looking across this group of warriors, we know some will see their vow to completion.

Once they walk inside the Labyrinth, they may never again walk in the realms of the living.

The spinning portal of my starlight shines like a silver eddy of turbulent waters. On the other end is the cliffside cave entrance that will take us beneath the surface of Gaea. My mate is by my side, a granite pillar of surety and strength. Behind us stands an odd assortment of immortals who have been at civil war with each other for eons—a war carefully orchestrated by a god of deceit and mischief.

It is that strife that now brings these enemies together as allies, ready to lay down their lives in search of my power. The final piece needed to face the Titans' hunter and bring this ages-long torment to an end.

Hecate and Daphne stand at the entrance of my portal, each passing final sentiments and reminders of our path through the Labyrinth. Cerberus lays at Hecate's feet, his head resting on his crossed paws. Occasionally, he whimpers as if sad we're leaving.

As Hecate embraces me in a final hug, Cerberus sits up and paws at her crimson stola that flows in the gentle current of the day. Looking down at him with soft eyes of affection, she smiles as if a silent message has passed between them.

Hecate nods at the dog formed of shadow and smoke, and

he wags his tail with excitement. He spins in circles and rubs his head against her.

Laughing, she scratches behind his ears. "Cerberus demands he join your party." She looks with longing affection at her faithful companion. "He knows the path well and can serve as a helpful guide."

Kneeling down, he rubs his head against her, and she speaks to him in a quiet tone. "Stay with the goddess and help her find her way if she becomes lost." With a kiss on his head, she stands. Backing away from the portal, she joins her sister, and they clasp arms. A tear flows down Daphne's cheek as she looks between Hermes and me.

Hermes and Lucas exchange a very manly handshake and one-armed hug. "Work on that dragon while I'm gone," Hermes says quietly as he adjusts the strap of his scabbard, his faithful sword secured at his back. Instinctively, my hand moves to the hilt of my daggers, securing them in my thigh holsters.

"I will. You guys make it back in one piece so I can challenge you," Lucas smiles faintly, but worry keeps his face grim. He looks at me, his expression softening before he steps back with the friends that we're leaving behind.

Taking a deep breath, I face my entourage of shields. "Ready?"

Looking between their stoic faces, each of them nod. Taking Hermes' hand, he gives me three squeezes, bringing fond warmth to my heart. It's become our coded message, used when I sent three taps down our bond when we were separated between the realms of the Crimson Eclipse.

"I love you." His sapphire eyes are rimmed with concern. I know it's not for the journey we are about to take, but the prospect of death that could await me inside. "As long as we stay together, we'll be fine."

Nodding, I take the first step forward and halt as I receive a call from the Wind.

"Wait!" It's Zephyr. Jogging to us wearing the same tactical gear as us. "Wait." They call out as they near. "I'm coming too."

"Zephyr, you don't have to do this," I begin, but they hold up their hand. "Flo and I talked about it. I'm coming too."

Flora stands to the side, as gentle as the petals of a rose, eyes red from crying. But she nods. Covering her mouth, she waves goodbye to her mate as Zephyr joins us, standing with Aphrodite and the captains of her fleet of Sirens.

"All right, let's go."

Walking through my portal, the pine-scented Wyoming air is replaced with the salty brine of the Mediterranean. I close my eyes, feeling its freshness on my skin. But the quick reprieve is soon overtaken by darkness when I walk into the entrance of the cliffside cave.

The air thickens as we approach the threshold, a shimmering barrier that separates the known from the depths of the hidden world beneath us. My heart pounds with a mixture of dread and determination. I reach out, my fingers brushing against the barrier. It ripples under my touch like disturbed water. A deep breath, a shared glance with Hermes, and I step through.

Instantly, a strange vertigo seizes me. The world flips startlingly, my stomach lurches, and quickly, down becomes up. We are walking on the underside of the world, our steps cautious on this new, inverted plane. The sensation is disorienting, the world around us a mirror image of normalcy.

The Labyrinth hangs ominously from what should be the ground, a pyramid of daunting size and palpable darkness. Its stone surfaces drink in the surrounding darkness, making it seem less a structure and more a void cut directly from the night sky itself.

The crunch of frost-laden ash beneath our feet punctuates our progress towards the gaping entrance of the Labyrinth. I can hear the distant clanking of chains and the eerie howls of creatures that call this dark prison home—sounds that send a chill down my spine.

As we near the entrance, the air grows colder, the darkness deepens, and the foreboding presence of the pyramid looms larger. This prison is a fortress of forgotten horrors, a place that tests both the strength of one's mind and the resilience of the soul.

With Hermes by my side, our fingers intertwined, we step into the yawning darkness of the Labyrinth's mouth.

Each breath turns to mist in the chilling air as we begin our journey. Behind us, the entrance vanishes, swallowed by the blackness, leaving us with only one direction to move— forward, into the heart of this ancient, dark prison where my destiny, bound to the Caduceus, awaits. Our journey into the abyss has just begun, and every step takes us deeper into the unknown.

As we advance into the vestibule of the Labyrinth, the air grows thick with the musk of ancient stone and dormant malice. The walls, ceilings, and floors are made from sleek black stone that seems to absorb any light that dares to touch its surface, leaving only darkness in its wake. The silence is oppressive, hanging heavy around us like a suffocating cloak.

Ahead, a towering structure of stairs emerges from the

shadows, leading up to a solitary throne that dominates the space. It's an imposing sight, the throne sitting regally atop its grand staircase, crafted from the same black stone, imbued with a cold authority that chills me deeper than the air around us.

As we pass, I keep my eyes fixed on the throne, feeling a wave of ominous energy emanating from it. My power of Sensory, a curse in moments such as this, allows me to perceive the layers of discarded emotion that escape the normal senses.

Now, it draws me to the essence of death that clings to the chair like a second skin. This was no mere seat of authority; it was a perch for a tyrant, a would-be king of prisoners who ruled through fear and pain.

Hermes notices my hesitation and places a reassuring hand on my shoulder, his touch grounding. "What do you feel?" he asks quietly, his voice barely a whisper in the chilling silence of the vestibule.

"Death," I reply, my voice steady despite the dread that tightens its grip on my heart. "The throne... it's soaked in the essence of Archangel Michael. The Shadow Lurkers ripped him apart."

Hermes looks to the chair, his eyes darkening with the weight of what my powers allow me to see. "Let's keep going. The Lurkers are still here, and they will not hesitate to tear us apart too."

Nodding, I draw a deep breath, steeling myself against the creeping fear as Cerberus nudges his head into the palm of my hand for a scratch. He takes the next several strides keeping his body next to my leg before trotting ahead a few paces.

We came prepared for danger, but the reality of the threats

lurking in the shadows presses in from all sides, making the air feel even colder, the darkness deeper.

Narrowing my eyes at a dark corner, the obscurity plays tricks as I think I see movement. Still, when my eyes are on it, it's when I look away that I sense the beings hiding in the constant night that cloaks the inside of this formidable realm.

"Keep your wits about you and stay close. Don't let your guard down, not even for a moment."

As we step beyond the throne, the air shifts slightly, heralding the presence of others within the vastness of this dark corridor. The shadows part to reveal two figures, each a surreal amalgamation of nature and something ethereal. Their heads, resembling the hollowed-out skulls of deer, sit atop bodies that look as if carved from ancient trees, rough and gnarled. Dark cloaks drape over their forms, stirring gently with the air we disturb as we move.

The group halts, a collective breath held as we assess these new entities. Pan steps forward slightly, his voice a whisper yet carrying clearly in the hushed silence.

"These are the Leshy Clerics, the record keepers of the Labyrinth," he explains, his gaze steady on the towering figures. "They are guardians of knowledge and lore here. As long as we do not harm the Labyrinth itself, they will not hinder our passage."

Reassured yet still cautious, I step forward, leading the group past the Clerics with a respectful distance. Their eyes, deep within the shadows of their skull-like faces, follow us, an unnerving sensation that makes the hairs on the back of my neck stand up. Yet there is a calm about them, a stillness that speaks of millennia—if not longer—of watchful silence.

As we pass, I pause and turn to address them. "Can you

show me the entrance to the inner prison?" I say, my voice clear and composed. The Clerics remain silent, their gaze unsettling. After a moment that stretches like eternity, one of them slowly turns its head, pointing with a gnarled finger towards a set of formidable double doors at the corridor's end.

I nod, murmuring a thanks that feels swallowed by the darkness surrounding us. Our group resumes walking, the heavy sound of our steps a stark contrast to the eerie quietude maintained by the Clerics. Cerberus, already sitting in front of the doors, a steady guide, just as Hecate promised.

As we stand before the heavy doors, the inscription etched deeply into the ancient wood sends a chill down my spine.

"Abandon every hope, all ye who enter here."

The words, dark and foreboding, echo in my mind—a grim echo from Dante's vision of hell in the Inferno.

An old collection of cantos, written long ago from the point of view of Dante, who traveled through the nine levels of Hell. Nine: just like the levels of the Labyrinth.

I wonder if somehow the mortal passed through these levels, escorted by some charitable entity inside. If the Inferno he depicted will be a representation of what awaits us.

I take a moment to steady my breath, feeling the weight of the warnings Hecate told us.

Turning to face Hermes and our band of resolute warriors, I see the concern mirrored in their eyes. They too understand the gravity of the inscription, a portent of the trials we are about to face.

"This is no ordinary prison," Hermes speaks with a low tenor, the strain in his voice a reflection of the anticipation of the treacherous journey before us. "The Labyrinth has likely been twisted further by Loki's influence."

Our group nods, Medusa's gaze hardening with resolve. "We'll face whatever comes," she assures, though I catch the brief flicker of doubt that clouds her eyes—a reflection of the unease we all feel.

"Remember what Hecate warned: What we see, what we hear, even what we feel inside may be manipulations meant to lead us astray or drive us to despair."

The warriors shift, the stone gargoyles gripping their weapons tighter, a silent acknowledgment of the danger. I can see the resolve setting in, the readiness to confront the illusions and mind games that surely await us within.

"Trust in each other," I urge them. "Not everything you see or hear is real. Doubt what is doubtful, and cling to what you know."

With a final, collective deep breath, we cross the threshold, the air growing colder as the darkness seems to swell around us. The door closes with a resonant thud behind us, sealing us inside the Labyrinth.

As the doors clang shut, a dirt path unfolds, winding into a foggy woodland.** The trees loom large, their branches like the outstretched fingers of giants, clutching at the mist that shrouds their forms. This forest feels alive and otherworldly, each tree breathing ancient secrets.

We step onto the path, the soft crunch of earth underfoot replacing the echo of our footsteps on stone. The fog thickens, weaving between the trees, obscuring our vision and dampening sounds. Silence hangs heavy around us, pressing in with a tangible presence.

I glance at Rhea, the Titan powers within her alive and swirling in constant motion. She's searching for the call of her powers secured within my staff. With a shake of her head her expression is resolute yet tinged disappointment. She had hoped to detect the essence of her powers and use it as a guide through the maze of this prison.

But hiding her immortality within the darkness, one has to suspect it wouldn't exactly be a blaring trumpet, signaling her so obviously. Wherever my caduceus is hiding, we'll be certain to find it.

As I carefully project my own aura, the dark fog swells

around me, blocking out everything and swallowing the illumination of my light. Rhea takes my hand, her fear of alerting the dark beings of the prison evident in her tight grip on me.

"I'm okay," I reassure her, and she releases a shaky breath.

Hecate has warned our abilities will be of no use as we walk down our path. Different levels of torment will dampen the use of certain elements, further depressing the prisoners. But it's not just our powers that will suffer here; we must also take great caution to keep our presence unknown. Everything here is starving, not just the living beings. And we are walking in with a powerful group of healthy immortals—a bountiful feast for the Labyrinth should the darkness here discover us.

We proceed, our group tightly clustered as the path narrows, the underbrush grazing against our legs, leaving traces of dew. The air is cool, moist, filled with the earthy scent of damp foliage and something unsettlingly metallic.

The path twists and turns, leading into an endless enigma. Visibility dwindles, and I strain to see any sign of the way ahead. Our surroundings blur into shades of gray and black under the mist.

Whispers of unease begin to stir among our group. The unexpected environment, so unlike the anticipated labyrinthine corridors, sets everyone on edge.

Walking in the front with Rhea, I carefully watch the ground where we step. The path seems to disappear under a particularly dense bank of mist. I halt, holding up a hand to signal the others to stop as well. "This doesn't seem right," I murmur, squinting into the fog, trying to make sense of the terrain that now offers no clear direction.

Sweeping my hand low to the ground, I try to clear a patch of earth, hoping we've only stepped a foot or two off the path.

With each swipe of my arm, the fog that rolls back into place seems heavier and denser.

Rhea steps forward, her eyes narrowing as she surveys our surroundings. "The fog," she says thoughtfully, "it's weird—thick, disorienting. It feels...alive."

Her words resonate with a cold trickle of realization. Of course, the fog. It's not merely a companion to this dark forest but a manifestation, possibly a guardian of this place to ensure we can't reach the depths of the prison; our first challenge.

"Let's stay close," I suggest, my voice low, as I reach for Rhea's hand, ensuring we maintain physical contact. The others draw nearer, their faces etched with concentration and the unspoken agreement that unity is our best defense in this obscured world.

As we trudge deeper, the ground becomes obscured by thickening fog and foliage. Natural markers look eerily similar, and soon, it's clear—we are lost. Our group's weak unity begins to unravel.

Tensions flare as Medusa, her eyes flashing with frustration, turns her sharp tongue on the gargoyle guards. "This is your fault! Always too slow, too heavy!" she accuses, her voice harsh.

The gargoyles, their expressions rigid and unreadable, protest in their gravelly voices, blaming Medusa. She is the reason for their partial stone facades, a curse cast upon them by her anger.

Nearby, Aphrodite is embroiled in a heated debate with Cappa and Delta, the Shifters. Arguing over direction and using the skies above to navigate our way out.

"What sky? We should have turned back ages ago!" Cappa snaps, his features shifting subtly with his agitation. Delta nods in agreement, his eyes darting around as if expecting the woods to reveal a path. Aphrodite, lost in her temper, argues for pressing forward, her voice rising, a clear note ringing against the quietude of the forest.

The noise grows until Pan clamps his bark-covered hands over his ears. His elemental power of Sensory overloaded with the arguments ricocheting off the forest. "Enough!" he booms, his deep voice resonating with the power of an ancient deity. "Quiet! I need silence to listen—to hear the path we've lost!"

Just as I'm about to intervene, Rhea tugs at my arm, pulling my attention to the ground. "Look, Hermes," she whispers, pointing to a set of deep impressions in the soft dirt mound that rises just above the foggy covering. I kneel beside her, examining the tracks more closely, running my finger around the edge of the impressions. A cold realization washes over me as I recognize the distinct shape and size of the prints.

"These are the tracks of a minotaur," I murmur, my voice lost among the bickering group behind me. "I've seen these before, battled such a beast during the Titan wars in the realm of Darkness." I pause, the memory of that ferocious encounter sending a shiver down my spine. "It's a huge and relentless beast. Once it catches your scent, it never stops hunting you. It will pursue its prey tirelessly, consuming them alive."

Rhea's eyes widen as she watches me, the haze of my expression alarming her. "Can you tell which direction it's headed?"

"I can't even tell which direction we're headed, baby. But we need to get out of these woods, now."

The disorientation deepens, and it feels as though the fog is not just around us but within us, clouding our thoughts and weighing us down. Our steps become sluggish; our arguments pointless as we circle back to the same patches of eerie, mist-covered ground.

"Fuck," Delta stumbles, catching himself on a nearby tree. Hissing, the Shifter pulls his hand away from the tree, his blood dripping to the ground below. Where it touches the ground, worms flood the area, like a spring bubbling up out of the dirt. Consuming the blood, they bury themselves in the black dirt, hidden again, waiting for their next meal to drop to the forest floor.

Rhea stops abruptly, her brow furrowed in concentration. "Of course. It's the fog," she murmurs, almost to herself, "it's more than just mist. It's a shroud for the mind." She looks at me, her eyes clear despite the haze. "Keeping us here until we fall to the ground, for sleep or exhaustion, then the Labyrinth can consume us."

Everything here is starving.

Without waiting for a response, she raises her arms, her posture commanding and determined. There is no current within this forest, so she generates the wind from herself. A gust begins to stir, at first gentle, then swiftly gaining momentum. The air around us swirls, whipping the fog into nothingness. Branches sway and leaves flutter wildly in the tumult she creates, the very atmosphere bending to her will.

As the fog dissipates, so too does the confusion it carried. A wave of calm emanates from my mate, flowing outward like a soothing balm. It washes over us all, easing the tension, silencing the bickering, and smoothing the creases of frustration and fear from our brows.

Everyone pauses, taking deep breaths and looking around as if seeing for the first time. With a clear forest, and darkness above, the path we searched for is found directly under us, as if we had never strayed from it.

"Let's move on," Rhea says, her eyes flicking to the forest

floor, scanning the retreating trail of minotaur impressions left in the soft ground. "Hecate said our first goal should be to pass the judgment of Minos."

Judge of the prisoners, Minos is eternally bound to the interior chambers of the Labyrinth. He measures the immortals' crimes and weighs their souls, casting them into the level of the prison that befits their crimes.

While we are not prisoners, Hecate has warned to keep a keen eye for Minos, regardless. He passes judgment indiscriminately and will cast his ruling on all he finds. But passing by him, the path deeper into the Labyrinth will be found.

We regroup, following Rhea as she steps confidently onto the now-visible trail. The path is narrow and winding but unmistakably marked, leading deeper into the woods. As we walk, the trees seem less daunting, the shadows less menacing. Our progress is swift, our steps sure, as we leave behind the place where the fog had nearly undone us.

As we leave the deceptive calm of the woods behind us, the terrain shifts, and the landscape becomes increasingly barren and grim. It seems as if it's twilight, like there is a sun somewhere beyond the haze of fog. The darkening sky burns orange as it sets for the day.

Walking for hours, the ground beneath our feet hardens, and the sparse vegetation gives way to cracked earth and the distant silhouette of crumbling structures.

One of which looks like the ruins of an old castle. Seven bridges, most crumbled and impassable, lead to seven large doorways. With a grumble of thunder, large blocks fall from one of the bridges, making no sound as they crash to the ground below.

In the remoteness, an ominous structure emerges: a set of

gates, towering and formidable, though clearly damaged. They hang partially askew, their iron bars bent and twisted as if subjected to great force. These gates, crooked and unwelcoming, mark the true entrance to the labyrinthine immortal prison —a threshold to deeper dangers.

As we approach, a figure catches my eye. A solitary immortal, gaunt and with a haunted look in her eyes, stands briefly at the gates. A metal collar encircles her neck, its dull sheen a testament to the length of her captivity here.

Wounds on her neck and stomach, gruesome and raw, are a clear sign of her suffering. The magic of her collar, designed to suppress her powers and inflict endless torment, ensures her wounds remain fresh, never healing—a perpetual punishment.

Passing a silent signal to Rhea through our bond, she also finds the figure. A gasp leaves her mouth at the terrible state of the immortal.

The immortal notices our approach and, with a look of desperation mixed with fear, quickly slips through the gates, disappearing from view into the shadows of the prison.

"Wait," Rhea mutters, stepping toward the spot where she disappeared, but it's too late—she's gone, her presence swallowed by the Labyrinth's dark embrace.

"How cruel." She whispers with an unbelieving shake of her head, the anguished state of the prisoner sinking into Rhea's compassionate heart.

"You heard what Hecate said, this place... it's designed not just to confine, but to torment. The enchantments here are potent and cruel."

Rhea nods, her expression grim. "I know. I just didn't expect them to look so gaunt."

With resolve, we pass through the askew gates, the metal

groaning. The atmosphere shifts as we enter the prison, the air cooler and heavier, charged with a subtle malevolence.

Cerberus whimpers, looking to the darkness that would be a sky. His burning ember eyes seem to hold a palpable sense of dread. The faint churning of water takes over his cry and in the near distance, a wide river awaits us.

Thirst comes to me as soon as I set my eyes on it, but I know not to drink the waters. Hecate was clear to avoid ingesting even a drop at any cost.

"There are five rivers that flow through the Labyrinth but do not be deceived by them. While driving you to thirst, they will do nothing to quench your needs. The riverbeds are not filled with water but Lethe, a powerful potion of forgetfulness. Drink, even a drop, and all your memories will be lost."

Standing at the top of a ridge, the line of our gathering looks over the flowing river. Several of them licking their lips, feeling the pull of the water as I am.

"I wonder if this is what Loki uses after my deaths." Rhea wonders out loud, addressing no one in particular. "He has the Titan power of Water. He can easily cast a small drizzle across the realm and poof—no more memories." *Damn.*

We look at the river with new eyes.

This very well could be the poison that sweeps the realm and steals the memories from our minds. As the realm returns to a state of waiting, all its inhabitants forget the savior we are waiting for. We forget the monster that lurks within the harbor of our friendship.

We forget.

I rub my thumb over the top of Rhea's hand, and she gives me a tight-lipped smile full of sorrow.

Cerberus whimpers again, pawing at Rhea's pants as if

asking to move on. He turns his head and looks above us. Beyond the river, his gaze is watching the distance. The shadows that form his body undulate faster.

The dog of darkness and shadow is trying to warn us to keep moving. His eyes, an eternal burning fire, remain on the dark sky above as if looking for something. Perhaps something we should avoid.

The ground below us trembles as a growl rises into the atmosphere. Quickly, the tremble erupts into a massive earthquake, and the ground below us rocks and bucks.

The growl becomes a collective cacophony of screaming and wailing as confusion takes over. Standing at the edge of the ridge, Cerberus barks, but the sounds of torment filling the skies drown him out.

"Oh my gods." Rhea's eyes are filled with terror as the blackened sky lights up with bright fingers of lightning. The multitude of flashes filling the sky bring light to the darkness that has cloaked us since we arrived.

Within roiling clouds and between endless flashes of light, hundreds of bodies soar through the air as if thrown a great distance by a giant being.

Like starved ghouls, the prisoners of the Labyrinth have been caught in some kind of force that is expelling them toward us. Arms flailing, metal collars clanking, they are helpless to control their path.

Cerberus barks, and it echoes around us, pulling our eyes from the horror occurring in the skies. The shadow pup takes off running toward the banks of the river Lethe, which is now churning rapidly with the anger of the Labyrinth.

His deep calls slice through the chaos, urging us towards

the small cluster of rowboats bobbing precariously at the water's edge.

"We need to get out of here!" I call out as I jump down from the ridge. Taking Rhea's waist, I help her down, and we run.

Panting and with hearts pounding, we race to the shoreline, dodging debris and shifting earth from the quake as the bodies of immortal prisoners fall around us.

On the opposite bank, the ground is still and free of the prisoners dropping from the sky. While I can see no discernible path from here, it's clear this bank is not the place where we need to linger and find our way.

Some bodies are coated in rich red blood; others are smoking as if they had been set on fire and their course through the air has extinguished the flames. Exclaiming with a scream, Rhea quickly moves to the side, barely missing being hit with a falling body.

"This is really fucked up!" Medusa yells when a blood-coated body slams into the ground next to her with a heavy thud.

Pan, with his long legs, reaches the boats first. He works quickly, untying them and righting the ones that have capsized. The urgency of the moment is palpable, the ground beneath us a constant reminder that time is a luxury we do not have.

I help Rhea into the first boat. The river's edge is slippery, the sand and mud loosened by the quake. I grip her hand tightly to steady her as she climbs in. Cerberus jumps in after her, his large form taking up the front of the boat, his barks now more determined, as if he can sense our desperation. His muzzle pointed toward the opposing shore reaffirms my thoughts on it as our destination.

Medusa and Zephyr scramble aboard, their faces set with grim determination. Pan gives the boat a strong shove, and we grab the oars, paddling with all our might as the wide river fights back, its waters swirling and white-capped waves crashing against us.

The other boats are in chaos as our group rushes into them. One of the gargoyles slips on the mud, tumbling into the frothy waves. The Lethe's waters close over him, and when he resurfaces, there's a blankness in his eyes, a haunting void where once there was recognition. He stands, motionless, as the waters lap at his feet, his memories slipping away with each wave.

His brother calls out, reaching for him, but it's too late. The waters of forgetfulness have claimed him, and he stands lost and uncomprehending on the shaking shore.

"We have to leave him!" Pan shouts from another boat, his voice heavy with regret. The final boat pushes off, its occupants casting sorrowful glances back at the stranded gargoyle.

From our boat, halfway across the river, Rhea's voice breaks with emotion. "We have to go back for him!" she cries, tears streaming down her face as she watches the tragic scene unfold. But the river is merciless, and our boat is already being carried away by the strong currents. We keep rowing forward despite her pleas.

From a distant bend in the river upstream, a new terror arises—a massive wave, spawned by the relentless quake, races along the riverbed. It towers over the shore, a wall of water fifty feet tall, poised to wash away everything in its path.

"No!" Rhea gasps, her voice drowned out by the roar of the approaching wave.

This tsunami seems to only crash upon the shore we just

abandoned. As we row harder, pushing stronger against the current that battles us, the shore of our salvation grows near.

We have to make it across before the forgetting waters overtake us and we emerge on the bank, a mindless sentinel like the gargoyle we just lost.

Pushing the oars against the strong current with everything we have, we make it to the opposing shore. Cerberus jumps from the boat to the shore, taking the loose rope in his mouth and pulling the boat from the waters.

The other two boats arrive with merely a second to spare. Leaping from the boats, we rush up the shore, ensuring errant tendrils of this deadly river can't reach out and ensnare us.

Turning behind us, to the beach we just left the imprisoned immortals crawl to the poisonous river, thirsting to lap the waters with greedy fervor. They want to forget. Or perhaps they have given up fighting against the beckoning call of the river.

The wave crashes into the shore with devastating force, obliterating everything in its wake. The sounds of the water's rage fill my ears as I strain to see through the spray and foam. When the view clears, the shoreline is unrecognizable, reshaped by the wave. The pitiful prisoners hurled onto the beach and the abandoned gargoyle are nowhere to be seen.

The aftershock of the wave is still vibrating through my body. I barely have time to mourn the loss behind us before our next challenge introduces itself. My gaze is drawn inexorably to a dark, swirling storm that rises with a ferocity and chills my blood. A hurricane more massive in size than any I've seen before. The sky churns with dark, ominous clouds streaked with fiery tendrils. Within the funnel, an orange glow dances across the scorched earth as it heads toward us.

The funnel is impossibly wide, its edges lost to my sight, and within its furious heart, dark forms are caught in its relentless churn. As we watch, horrified, bodies are flung from the top of the vortex, soaring through the air like macabre debris. The starved, tortured forms of immortal prisoners are tossed helplessly in the storm's grip, their fates left to the whims of this unnatural hurricane.

My heart pounds, a mix of fear and anger coursing through me as I grip my oar tighter. Cerberus whines, his body tense as he too watches the approaching disaster.

"Hermes!" I shout, needing to hear his voice, needing his strength as the storm readies to bear down on us. He looks over, his face set in a grim line, his eyes mirroring the storm in their dark intensity.

"We can't outrun it," his reply is barely audible over the storm's roar, his words snatched away by the wind before they could fully reach me. "We need to find shelter!"

I scan the banks of the river, desperate for any sign of refuge, but there is nothing—only the bare, scorched earth left by the previous wave. The realization sinks in with a dreadful finality; there is no escaping this monstrosity.

Turning to the rest of our group, I see the resolve in their eyes, a fierce determination not to cower before this new threat. "We need a shield!" I call out, my voice as commanding as I can make it amidst my own fear.

Hermes grabs the rope of one of the boats, wrapping it twice around his forearms and tugs it further up shore, away from the waters. "Medusa, drive the boat half into the ground and turn the mud to rock."

Her powers respond in a second and a chasm opens in front of her. Manipulating the wood, the boat moves with her command. Its end sinks into the mud before it swirls, hardening around the boat and making it an anchor.

Kellan and Pan retrieve the other two boats, lining them up, creating a sort of wall we can use for a stronghold against the beast raging toward us.

"Hold on to anything you can!" I scream over the wind as we crowd behind the scanty refuge. Hermes drives his sword into the ground and holds it firmly. His other arm is wrapped around me, his body acting as a second shield.

The heat is unbearable, searing my skin and making the air around us shimmer, while the wind lashes at us with brutal force, threatening to suck us into its funnel. I use my powers to conjure a shield of protective wind around our fortress, an attempt to deflect some of the flames and debris. It's a meager defense compared to this monstrous tempest, but it's all I can muster in the face of such overwhelming power.

Aphrodite, Zephyr, and the Sirens join me. A wall of currents helps to dispel the flames and heat from us.

The storm engulfs us then, a maelstrom of fire and wind. Immortal bodies fly past us, their expressions frozen in terror, reaching toward us for help. We cling to each other, to the boats, to anything to keep from being thrown into the chaos outside.

Through the blinding heat and the roar of the storm, I keep my focus on the faces of my companions, until I hear a familiar voice, one that stills my heart and stops my breath.

"Calypso!" Achilles calls out. His voice fading as if he is trapped in the vortex, a slave to its endless churn. "I'm sorry."

"Hermes." I gasp, my eyes wide and scanning the grey clouds streaked with smoke and flame. This can't be.

They're dead.

My breaths are ragged and my heart rages in my chest. Hermes is frozen, his eyes locked on the funnel with me.

"Callie!" The next voice that swirls in on the rushing winds makes me cover my mouth with my hand, a gasp of my shock lost in the rage of the storm. Patroclus. "Callie, you're hurting me!"

"Oh, gods, Hermes." I cry.

"This can't be real." He shakes his head, disbelief widening his gaze as he searches the clouds. "There." He points and I see the gleam of gold armor, the crimson of a flowing cloak and the face of our friend twisted in pain. The grit of sand and raging winds eat away the flesh from Achilles' face. The funnel streaks with his blood until his skin reforms, only to be ripped away again.

"We have to get them out!" I try to move from behind our wall of boats, but Hermes pulls me back.

"Rhea, no."

Pushing against him, I stop when I see a second set of gold armor, the sandy brown curls of a man I've not set eyes on in ages. "I can't take it anymore, Callie." Patroclus cries as the storm carries him around the vortex. "Just kill me, please."

But where is she?

Too afraid of what I may see, I creep inch by inch, looking beyond the boats, searching for the center of the hurricane. Every nightmare I could have ever dreamed comes true when I see her. And all the breath in my lungs leaves me.

Suspended high into the air in the center of the spinning churn is my best friend, my chosen sister, the Temptress of the Four Winds. Tears of blood streak her face and with her arms cast wide, she releases an eternal scream. Her anguish is to suffer an eternity, a servant to the Wind that once obeyed her, listening to her mates beg for her mercy as they suffer in agony within her currents.

I can't take this anymore.

I can't stand here while they suffer like this.

They sacrificed themselves for us, for me. They were supposed to rest in the sanctuary of the Void, together. Not this. Never this.

Tears fall freely down my face, quickly flung into the rage of the wind.

Ducking under Hermes' arm, I rush out and the second I do, I realize my mistake.

"Stop!" Medusa calls out but it's Zephyr's fast grip on my

arm that pulls me harshly back. But they expose themselves to the storm, to the truth of judgment waiting in the eye of the hurricane.

It's not Calypso but a giant. With skin the color of onyx and eyes crimson red, his sharp fangs protrude from his mouth like those of a sabertooth tiger. His body dissolves from the torso of a man to the body of a snake. Nine tails lash about, capturing the prisoners sucked into the vortex and ejecting them out.

It's Minos, here to cast judgment.

The long tail of the beast whips out, wrapping around Zephyr's body four times.

Plucked from our hoard of warriors, the fading scream of Zephyr is the only thing that remains of the Siren, vanished in an instant, consumed into the vortex with the other souls trapped in its swirling mass.

The stillness following the storm is unsettling.

Sitting on the beach with sand and dirt stuck to my sweaty face, my eyes are locked on the water in an unfocused stare.

The storm conjured our most guilt-filled memories and turned them into vivid, torturous illusions. For a moment that felt like an eternity, I was caught in the throes of a nightmare so real, so palpable, that it left me gasping for breath and clawing for escape.

Hermes shared the same vision I did, both of us seeing the three people we are heavily mourning, our friends...family that laid down their lives for us.

Medusa saw Athena, burning and begging for her help to put out the flames. She tried to rush to the waters of the Lethe, but Kellan fought her back and held her down.

Zephyr was our only victim to the storm. And it's my fault.

The image of their determined, brave face, as they pulled me back to safety, haunts me as I stare at the ground. *How can I face Flora when I caused her mate's death?*

As we sit in the eerie calm, the beach around us betrays no sign of the cataclysm we just endured. Back is the eternal darkness that fills the sky, clear of constant lightning and rolling clouds. The waves gently lap at the shore with a soothing rhythm, as if to wash away the traces of our ordeal.

Looking to my left, Delta sits with a glazed stare, just as I have been.

"Are you okay?" I ask, my voice cracking as if I've not spoken a word in weeks. Delta turns his hand over, inspecting a gash on his palm that is inflamed and red, white around the torn edges of his skin, but he doesn't answer my question. "That looks bad."

"Nah, it's nothing."

"I can heal it. It's no problem, really."

Thinking on my offer, Delta turns his hand to me. Placing my hand under his, I pull on the threads of my Titan power of Water but there is nothing. Searching within me for the rejuvenating element of Life, I don't feel it answer me either. Confused, I furrow my brow and try again.

My power, usually flowing freely like an erupting geyser, feels like nothing more than a broken and dripping faucet. But a whisper of my element seeps out of me, passing to the Shifter. The cut doesn't heal but it turns from red to pink. Some of the white appears to be puss under the skin and remains.

Disappointment in myself makes me pull away, "Sorry, I'm not sure why it won't heal."

"Hey, don't worry about it. It's probably this place." He's likely right but I'll try again in a moment. Perhaps I can heal the wound bit by bit as we move on.

Cerberus, ever our steadfast guide, stands and shakes as if the remnants of the storm cling to his shadows. He looks at us with eyes that hold a depth of understanding beyond any human or immortal. With a soft whine, he nudges me, urging me to rise, to leave this place of false peace and continue our journey.

I know we need to move forward, not just toward our goal, but away from the memories that now claw at our minds. Now I understand why the tormented souls would scrape their way to the waters, lapping them up, ready to forget the eternal torment they endure.

Hermes stands next to me, holding his hand to help me stand. "It's time to go."

With heavy hearts, we gather ourselves. Each of us is battered, not just physically but emotionally, the echoes of our darkest fears still whispering in our ears.

We follow Cerberus. His pace is steady as we trek along the sandy beach. The path ahead, uncertain.

Cerberus leads us around the wide bend of the river. Each rippling wave is like a plea to our starving ears, begging us to come to the shore for a drink. Looking back at our crew of warriors, they are beaten down, and we've only just entered this maze of torment and shadow.

Medusa is the first to pass me, her green eyes a deep emerald. "This river is a piece of shit."

I huff a quiet laugh, patting her shoulder as she continues on. "We'll be past it soon."

The three Shifters walk together, talking quietly about the bombardment and the exodus into the protective domes. The Sirens walk with their captain, speaking quietly of the river. Pan and our remaining gargoyle walk in silence at the rear.

A heaviness follows them, as if the two members of our party already claimed by the Labyrinth are still with us.

Even with the passing time, the sky remains a burning orange haze of sunset. I wonder if the entirety of the Labyrinth will give us this faint light, but I know it's too wishful. The Titan of Light within me senses the rich darkness ahead.

Not just the absence of light, but the oppressive dark beings moving in shadows, constantly hungry and hunting.

Taking in the terrain we have passed, I look ahead. We're approaching a large bog that stretches as far as the eye can see. I release a tense breath. At least we'll be able to see any threats well ahead of time.

Catching up to my mate, I feel the weight of her guilt, as palpable as the heavy air around us.

"Hey," I start, nudging her gently with my elbow, trying to break her trance. She looks up, her eyes glistening with unshed tears, a deep sadness etched across her face.

"I should have been more careful," she murmurs, her voice barely above a whisper. "Zephyr saved me, and I couldn't save them. This is my fault, Hermes."

I shake my head, reaching out to take her hand, squeezing it reassuringly. "You can't think like that. We're in this together, remember? What happened to Zephyr—they made their choice, a brave one, to protect you. We know we're going to lose more friends on this journey; perhaps all of them. It's harsh and brutal, but blaming yourself won't bring them back and it won't get you to the end of this path."

She bites her lip, looking away, her shoulders tense. "But I'm the reason we're here to begin with. If it weren't for me, none of this would have happened. How do I live with that?"

I stop, pulling her gently to a halt, and turn to face her. "Look at me, Rhea," I urge, waiting until her eyes meet mine. "You live with it by carrying on, by fighting to make sure that every sacrifice wasn't in vain. We're not just trying to defeat Loki but to make sure the suffering and losses we've endured lead to a better future. We owe that to Zephyr. To Callie, Pat, and Achilles. Athena deserves that. Teddy deserves that."

Her gaze holds mine, searching, seeking solace or perhaps forgiveness. "How do you do it?" she asks. "How do you keep going when it feels like every step forward costs another piece of your soul?"

I give her hand another squeeze, offering her a small smile. "I look at you. I remember why we started this journey and who I'm doing it for." My words pull the tears from her eyes, and I wrap her in my arms. "You're my strength, little goddess, just as I hope to be yours. We're in this together, through every trial and every battle. But we're not alone. We have a whole team, a family, helping us."

She nods slowly, the corners of her mouth twitching upwards in a semblance of a smile. "A family," she repeats softly, drawing strength from its implication.

"Yeah, a pretty dysfunctional one, but it's ours," I tease gently, hoping to lighten her mood. It works, a brief laugh escaping her, breaking through the grief if only for a moment. "Let's catch up with the others. There's a long path ahead, and I need you by my side, strong and ready to kick some ass."

She snickers, resting her head against my chest and rubbing her hands down my stomach. Looking at me, a dim light has returned to her golden eyes. Cupping her face, I rub my lips against hers before kissing her. So soft and sweet, she kisses me back and squeezes me tighter, her arms circling my waist.

I rub my nose against hers and turn us toward the group that has walked on ahead. "Come on."

We trudge silently, lagging behind the group. The river-bank has evolved into a dark bog, our boots sinking slightly with each step into the soft, murky terrain. The landscape stretches out endlessly before us, a sprawling expanse of damp earth and dark water clinging to every step.

Ahead, the line halts as everyone looks down into the marsh. One of Aphrodite's generals, a formidable captain of her fleet named Callista, points into the dark waters at her feet. Curiosity piqued despite the heavy atmosphere, Rhea and I quicken our pace to see what has caught her attention.

As we reach her side, Callista steps aside, making room for us on the tufts of vegetation serving as our walk-way. I lean over to peer into the murky depths and catch my breath. "Fuck." Staring back at us is not merely a reflection, but a face—an immortal prisoner trapped beneath the surface, eyes wide with a haunting and vacant stare.

The group murmurs in shock, peering into the water around us. It becomes chillingly apparent that this is not just a bog—it's like a prison within a prison. Countless faces gaze up at us, a sea of immortals submerged and living within the dark waters, each face a story of despair and eternal captivity.

Rhea's hand finds mine, gripping it tightly. Her voice is barely a whisper, "No one touch the water."

"It's like a living tomb," Medusa replies, her voice steady despite the unease of what surrounds us.

One of the submerged faces moves, bubbles escaping his lips as he tries to speak. The muffled sounds are barely discernible, but the message is clear enough—help.

Around us, more immortals stir beneath the surface, bubbles from their silent pleas rising gently at first, then quickly as if the bog is boiling.

Callista kneels beside the water, reaching out tentatively to touch the surface. Before she makes contact with the water, Cerberus snaps at her with a bark and a growl, and she quickly retracts her hand.

"I said don't touch the water unless you want to join them." Rhea punctuates the last word just as a soggy pair of hands shoot out of the water, grabbing Rhea's ankles and pulling her into the bog.

Panic surges through me as I see her disappear, her scream ending abruptly.

"Stay back!" I shout to the others, removing my sheathed sword as I position myself at the water's edge. My heart pounds furiously, my fear for Rhea overwhelming.

Without a second thought, I dive into the dark water, Cerberus barking frantically before following me in.

The water is shockingly cold, its murky depths clouding my vision. Calling upon the power of Light, relief floods me as my aura shines in the dark water, allowing me to see ahead.

As my eyes adjust, I search for her, following the stream of bubbles rising below me. I kick furiously until I finally see her. Eyes wide in fear, her mouth pressed tight as she holds her breath, arms stretched up reaching for me.

Skeletal hands on her ankles and legs pull her deeper as she tries to kick against them. The immortal prisoners with chains fashioned around their necks are dragging her down much faster than I can swim to meet her. Their faces are gaunt, their eyes hollow with despair.

Further and further down we swim. Cerberus pushing alongside me as we rush to save her. The hands of the immortals grip me, each one trying to pull me away from my objective. Reaching the end of the mass of bodies, she is pulled into a dark abyss, her body jerking with spasms.

She'll run out of air soon.

Pushing past the immortals trapped within this hellscape, my light begins to reach her, illuminating the cause of her spasms. It's not air she is losing, but the very essence of her life.

Black ribbons of shadow weave through the water like

sinister eels. Each one striking her and siphoning some of her life force with each pass. Around me, more obscure ribbons of shadow slither, feasting off the immortal prisoners condemned to reside at the bottom of this hoard of people.

They try to push their way to the surface, sacrificing the prisoner above them in hopes to save themselves. They have brought Rhea here as an offering. Likely hoping their deposit of a fresh life source can save them a momentary reprieve from this torture.

Kicking harder, I call upon my powers and conjure a whip of blue starlight. Slashing around me, I clear the stagnant mass of prisoners, kicking my way down to my mate.

Cerberus is swimming ahead of me. The immortals fight against me as I try to reach her. Clearing the hoard, Cerberus is so close to reaching her but a band of shadow wraps around him, pulling him down.

Made of darkness himself, Cerberus splits his body. The tendril pulls and one of Cerberus' forms is dragged down, disappearing into a great abyss beneath us.

Again, Cerberus is captured by shadow and again, he makes another version of himself. This time, both are wrapped in shadow, and he makes another version of himself, and another.

As Rhea spasms with each attack, she continues to endure, Cerberus tries to reach her, splitting himself and giving the darkness another body to feed upon.

Slashing my whip and blasting my aura in a pulse, I stun the bodies around me and clear a pathway to my mate.

Kicking and adding the power of my aura, I swim faster, reaching her within a few seconds. My arm wraps around her waist as she clings to me. Her touch is faint and weak, pulling fear and anger into a tight knot within my chest.

The dark ribbons slice me, and the pain is excruciating. Burning like someone has cut me with a red-hot blade, the sting lingers.

As another ribbon of obscurity comes for me, Cerberus is there, intercepting it. With each attack, the demon dog splits himself, keeping the darkness from attacking us, giving me a chance to swim away.

Cerberus doesn't speak. At least not in a way I have ever sensed, but I feel the pressing urgency to get out of the water. *Save her.* It's clear in my mind, ringing like a bell.

Slashing my whip, keeping the beings away from us, I don't question it. I don't look at the savior below me, splitting himself into dozens of shadowed canines. I just kick with everything I have. Praying to Fates that Cerberus will escape the darkness, I fight to get my goddess to the surface.

Pushing my aura into each movement, I shoot upward. Breaking through the water's surface, we both gasp loudly as the hands of our comrades reach for us. Coughing and sputtering, Rhea tries to help, but she's weak. I push as they pull her.

Once she is out, I pull myself out of the dark water, helping her turn over to cough out any of the water still choking her.

I pull her in my arms and surge my power down our bond to her. Rejuvenating the energy the darkness was consuming from her. Shivering, she settles into me, warming under my power. My eyes never leave the dark ring of water where I first jumped in, waiting for Cerberus to emerge.

Several minutes pass, and nothing.

The bog has calmed. The prisoners within have returned to their catatonic state, floating beneath the surface.

Medusa looks around, and I notice what she does. "It's getting darker." Her eyes rake over the sky, seeing the orange haze is deepening. A violet purple is reaching up from the horizon, pushing its way through the orange. "We should get off this bog before it turns too dark to see anything."

Medusa looks at me, tension rimming her eyes. *"Cerberus is gone?"* She asks in my mind, keeping her question from the rest of the group, but they are all suspecting it. Callista is staring at the water without blinking, still kneeling close to the water's edge.

Nodding my confirmation, Medusa looks to Pan. "Can you hear anything? A possible direction we should go?"

"No, all is quiet. Unnaturally so." Pan answers. "But perhaps that creature is offering a service to us?" At once, our heads snap in the direction Pan is looking.

The same ghoulish woman I saw earlier at the gates is back. Crouched behind a tuft of soggy bush, the skeleton-like figure picks small morsels off the vegetation. She was a woman once but is now starved eternally within this prison.

Her dark eyes shift nervously between us before she turns and flees. The darkness swallowing her again, just as it did before.

"Or perhaps not." Medusa huffs a frustrated sigh. "Let's keep heading in the direction Cerberus was going. We'll figure the next steps out once we're off this bog."

The group moves without question.

Rhea is shaken, trembling, and while my energy has recharged her, she needs a moment before she will be ready to walk again. Picking her up, she wraps her arms around my neck, and I hold her close to me.

"I've got you, baby. Just rest." I kiss the side of her head as she nods. A sob escapes her, but otherwise, she remains as quiet as the settled bog.

Hermes carries me until we reach the end of the **bog.** I've never been happier to see an outcropping of trees and solid ground. The only thing running through my mind is the path Hecate gave us before we left. I keep repeating it, trying to remember all the things she told us to avoid.

Our next two legs of the journey are the Lake of Sorrow and the capital city, Dis. The lake feeds the rivers that run through the Labyrinth, filling them with the poison of forgetfulness. The capital city marks the center of our journey, but it is also where the dark beings that reside in the Labyrinth live.

This place is not just a home for immortal prisoners and a siphon that captures the darkness of Elysium, preventing it from seeping into Gaea. It's also a place for banished beings. Those that lived here before or arrived with the refugees. Regardless, it's home to a pantheon of monsters that dwell within the city and torment the prisoners.

Once we pass the city walls, avoiding it and not drawing the attention of its residents, we should find a hidden path that will allow us to bypass the city unseen.

Aphrodite sits next to me, handing Hermes and me a square that looks like an oversized saltine cracker.

"What is this?" I ask, smelling it. It just smells like flour.

"Hardtack," she answers, taking a bite. "Ship's biscuits. They last for ages, and we pack them full of nutrients." Aphrodite takes another bite. "Dry as shit but you won't be hungry."

Nodding, I turn it over in my hand. I should be starving, but after the bog, I just feel like nothing.

"Eat something for me, little goddess." Hermes' voice wraps around my mind and warms our bond. Sitting next to me, he leans against one of the trees, resting his forearms on his knees.

I bump into him affectionately with my shoulder and then nibble on the corner of the biscuit. It's dry, as Aphrodite said, but it tastes good, like ambrosia-infused honey.

"She feels terrible." Aphrodite nods her head toward her captain, Callista. "She said it felt like something was pulling her to touch the water."

I don't know what to say, so I just nod.

If I were being polite, I would say, "It's okay," but it's not.

Cerberus wasn't just our guide; he was my friend. I loved him, and now he's gone. The third member of our party that won't make it out of the darkness of this twisted maze.

Resting against this tree, we sit around it like the spokes of a wagon wheel. Medusa is lying down, her head propped against the trunk, her chin tucked to her chest. With her feet crossed and her hands folded together at her stomach, I think she's already sleeping.

Cappa and Delta took several biscuits from Callista and are talking quietly about the wound on Delta's hand. I need to check on him again and see if it's getting any worse.

Kellan is making small talk with the gargoyle, and I've learned his name is Alaric. His brother, lost on the shore of the

Lethe, was named Marius. "You were not angry to be turned to stone?" Kellan asks, speaking in low tones about Medusa partially petrifying some of Vlad's warriors a long time ago.

"Don't listen to his griping." Medusa pipes up from her side of the tree. I guess she's not asleep. "I offered to turn them back, but they like it." She finishes without moving a muscle.

Alaric nods, a sly smile pulling up the corner of his mouth. "We do." He whispers.

"I heard that," Medusa says.

Pan and the rest of Aphrodite's generals are spread around our small refuge of trees, scanning the dark horizon for signs of trouble as we rest.

Hours Later

"Rhea," Hermes whispers, shaking my shoulder gently. I don't know how long I've been asleep, but my limbs are stiff, and my muscles are sore. "Pan hears something." In an instant, I'm alert. Warmth floods me as I hope it's Cerberus coming to find us.

"It's relatively far off, from what I can tell," Pan stands tall, half the height of the tree giving us shelter, "but heading in our direction."

Testing my powers, my black mist curls around my feet. The darkness within stretches out, greeting me. Relieved to have access to my powers again, I send a gentle wave of obscurity out in all directions. Faint and slow, I don't want to alert anything that may be lingering in the shadows.

In front of us is the lake, our next objective. Behind us is the bog and beyond that, the Lethe River. Nearing the edge of the bog, I find a large creature.

Standing on two hoofed feet, its body is nearly human but mostly beast. Its large head, like that of a bull, carries two great horns. Just as tall as Pan, the creature's fur is black, and so are its eyes. It bends down, standing on all fours and sniffs quickly across the bog, focusing on one spot specifically.

Dread coats me with a frigid thought as I recall the impressions of a beast in the fogged forest. "Hermes, I think it's the Minotaur," I whisper as I project the image I'm sensing from my powers.

"Fuck. Yeah, that's it." Hermes stands and offers me his hand. "And it's tracking us."

Perfect.

"Maybe we'll lose it on the lake," Aphrodite adds, fashioning her pouch back to her belt and securing it to her thigh.

Walking with quiet steps and purpose, we head to the lake. Reaching its shore, the Lake of Sorrow lives up to its name.

The water is unnaturally still, mirroring the gray skies above with a metallic sheen, unbroken by the breeze that whispers through my hair. It's as though the lake is holding its breath, waiting for us, which only adds to the heavy atmosphere of anticipation.

Four small boats sit along the shore. They're a bit worn, with sails that have seen better days, but they're our only means to cross. We split up into the boats, everyone settling in with silent apprehension. Aphrodite takes charge, and her Sirens follow, their adept hands working the tattered sails to catch the intermittent gusts of wind.

Silence envelops us as we push off from the bank. The only sounds are the gentle splash of water against the boat and the occasional creak of the timeworn wood beneath us. The lake's eerie calm casts a spell of unease over us all, and I find myself constantly scanning the reflective surface for any hint of what might lurk below.

Sitting next to Hermes, he rubs my thigh, a silent exchange of strength as he too scans the horizon. I scoot closer to him, clutching his arm, grateful for his presence and for the unspoken understanding between us that no matter what lies ahead, we face it together.

The sails billow with a stronger breeze, and our boat picks up speed. Aphrodite skillfully navigates, her gaze locked on the destination ahead. The other boats keep pace, forming a small convoy gliding across the vast, still body of poisonous water.

The isolation of the lake deepens as we progress. It stretches out, seemingly endless, the distant shores appearing to withdraw further into the mist as we sail on. I watch the water intently, half-expecting the tranquility to break at any moment, revealing a hidden danger.

Every sound, every movement becomes a subject for heightened alertness in the encompassing quiet. The capital city of Dis will be waiting for us on the opposing shore, but right now, it seems like we are in the middle of an aquatic desert, no sign of a shoreline in any direction.

"We're about halfway." I startle at the quiet sound of Aphrodite's voice, breaking the stillness. In that instant, the winds die, leaving our sails limp and our boats motionless. Dread blankets us as we collectively pause, holding our breath along with the wind.

Hermes is the first to notice the change in the water's texture. "Something's coming," he murmurs, his eyes narrowing as he searches the darkness around us.

I follow his gaze and see it—a disturbance in the distance, a wave slowly forming, gaining height as it approaches. The water's surface, previously a mirror, now betrays the presence of something formidable lurking below.

Rising from the lake's depths, a great creature rages toward us with immense speed. The water breaks as the beast presents itself. The enormity of what is coming for us is unfathomable.

With six heads and a dozen long tentacles, the mighty Scylla rises out of the water. Two long tentacles surge downward, crashing into the surface of the lake as the Scylla wakes up the sleeping lake.

A collective gasp rises from our group, but it's Aphrodite who reacts most profoundly. Her face goes pale, her body rigid with shock. "Triton..." she whispers, the name of her former mate carrying a weight of horror and disbelief.

The powerful Water Siren had the power to conjure a Water Giant that could pass as a twin of the beast emerging before us. But where his monster was created from water, this one is real. With deep crimson hide covering its body, and each of the six heads full of long razor-sharp teeth, we have little chance of slaying a monster so large within these rotting boats.

Dread of what is to come silences us all for a beat before the wind starts again with a gentle tug, blowing in the opposing direction, it threatens to pull us toward the monster.

"Everyone in the boat with Rhea," Aphrodite commands, turning to her Sirens captaining the other boats. "Remain with your vessels." Her two commanders nod once, their hands remaining on the masts of their boats, ready for their captain's next command.

Aphrodite holds out her palm, and a small vortex of white

wind whips around her hand. Her Sirens do the same as if testing they can use their element here.

Callista is commanding our boat, and it rocks as our new passengers hurry into it.

"It can't hold us all." I argue, panic beginning to rise with the prospect of the poisoned water taking our memories should we sink.

"You only need to get to shore," Aphrodite replies, not looking at me or the others, her sharp gaze steady on the horizon.

The wind is sucking us backward, pulling us in the direction we just came. No longer still, the waters churn, angered by the disturbance of the Scylla as waves begin rising around us.

Aphrodite looks back to Callista, "Don't come back." Callista nods in agreement and orients herself to the shoreline of our destination.

Wind whips around us, as if the Sirens are powering their element.

Between us and the raging Scylla, the waves grow as the ribbons of wind agitate the surface. Large waves build, beginning to spin as an eddy forms.

Callista calls upon her power, a force of wind driving into our sail, and slowly, it begins to pull us away. Each manned by a Siren of the Wind, the other three boats turn to face the monster.

"We can't leave them," Medusa calls out over the rising storm.

"Then jump into the water and join them." Callista answers, keeping her focus on putting distance between us and the impending collision of the Scylla and Aphrodite.

Resignation makes me drop my shoulders, knowing we're

about to lose three more members of our party. But this time, it is someone connected to Calypso, and while Aphrodite and I did not know each other well, sorrow hits me hard in my chest. I look back at the Siren, and for a second, I see the face of my friend in Aphrodite's firm resolve.

The whirlpool in front of them becomes stronger. Drinking the waters of the lake as it forms, churning violently, the large mouth of Aphrodite's monster grows, preparing to challenge the Scylla.

Behind us, a monstrous roar splits the air. The Scylla rears from the depths, its many heads poised to strike. But the Charybdis waits—a swirling sentinel that guards our retreat. With a thunderous clash, the two leviathans meet. Water and fury collide as the Scylla attempts to breach the whirlpool's defenses, only to be met with the relentless, grinding force of the Charybdis.

Aphrodite stands firm, directing the battle between the monsters with a conductor's flair. The air around her crackles with power, her silhouette stark against the chaos of her making.

Her Sirens, faithful at her side, issue their own attacks. Flaying wind streaks across the metallic night. Like blades, they sever the heads of the Scylla, leaving the long serpentine necks flailing.

New heads begin forming before the dispatched ones crash into the whirlpool below.

"We need to put more distance between us, or the wave will overtake us too." Callista's voice is calm but edged with urgency. Looking beyond the monstrous battle, far off in the distance, a wave is forming.

Called by the Sirens as they occupy the Scylla with Charybdis, the gnashing teeth of the carnivorous whirlpool are a distraction keeping the Scylla in the lake's center. The oncoming wave is intended to swallow the Scylla down into the darkness of the lake.

With a tear rolling down my cheek, I add my own power to the sail, propelling us to the shoreline. I want to turn back and help them fight, but I know my goal lies elsewhere in this prison of torment.

I watch every second, never letting my eyes leave the Sirens who are giving their lives for us, for our mission.

The Charybdis is huge and can now churn on its own. Aphrodite abandons it, focusing the might of her power to attack the massive beast. The wave grows, pulled larger and larger by the Winds they are directing.

Building to its peak, the wave crests. Its shadow dwarfs the massive Scylla, pulling the beast's attention. At the same time, Aphrodite surges her whirlpool forward to devour the six-headed monster.

The razor teeth of the churning eddy shred the Scylla, pushed into the center of the vortex by the tsunami. And with it, Aphrodite, and her Sirens. The decimating roar drowns out my gasp as I watch them die.

As soon as the waters pull them under, the storm stops as if nothing was ever there. The Lake of Sorrow stills to eerie perfection. The only disturbance is our single boat slicing through the calm water, heading for the shoreline of Dis.

s we set foot on the opposite shore, the capital city of Dis looms on the horizon.** Its towering structures of blackened volcanic rock rise menacingly against the cloudy sky, casting long shadows that stretch to the cliff's edge. The grand and grotesque architecture, adorned with spires and statues, depicts dark creatures—each figure a tribute to torment and despair.

As we approach, the air grows colder, a chill that seeps into our bones, not from the temperature but from the malevolence exuded by the city. Rhea's eyes scan the imposing cliffside, searching for the path that will lead us up to the city pulsating with dark energy.

"We need to be careful here," she whispers to the group, her voice barely audible. "And avoid drawing attention at all costs."

This is perhaps the most dangerous portion of our journey through the Labyrinth so far. A multitude of dark hosts reside beyond the black gates of the city walls. Awakening one of them to our presence would awaken the entirety of the Labyrinth itself. Swarms of starving monsters and legions of obscure Shades would descend upon us, consuming every morsel of our life forces until we were nothing more than shriveled husks.

The cliffs loom high, their rugged faces daunting. Alaric leads our climb—sure-footed and steady. We follow closely, hands brushing against the cool, rough stone for support. The climb is strenuous, pushing our endurance, but the need to avoid the dark denizens of Dis drives us on.

At the top of the cliffs, breathless and muscles aching, Alaric peeks over the edge, taking inventory of what awaits us. "I'll scout ahead," Alaric volunteers. "Better to know what we're facing than to walk in blind."

"I'll go with you," Kellan whispers. The pair of immortals quietly search the clifftop for hidden dangers. Holding our positions, we catch our breath, waiting for their signal to continue.

Rhea is weighted down with the heaviness of guilt. I see it in the shadows beneath her eyes and in the frown that turns down the corners of her mouth. Her remorse grows stronger with each member of our party lost. Sending three pulses down the tether of our bond, it pulls her gaze to me, and she gives me a soft smile, full of sorrow.

"I'm okay," she whispers, but we both know she's not. "She just—" The words get stuck in her throat, but I sense the sentiment that is choking her.

"She reminded me of Callie too." I take my mate's hand and raise it to my lips, offering her a small kiss of reassurance.

She nods, dropping her gaze to her lap, then back at me. "Yeah." Her smile is still forced but slightly less sad.

"It's clear." Alaric creeps over the top of the cliffside, and Rhea turns to follow him.

The city of Dis unfolds before us, a sprawling fortress that commands the landscape with a somber and imposing presence. Its high, thick walls, built from dark stone that absorb light rather than reflect it, encircle the city entirely, standing as an unyielding barrier between the horrors within and the horrors outside.

The iron gates loom ahead, intricate yet formidable, crafted to intimidate as much as to fortify. Beyond them, the city's silhouette against the overcast sky is stark—towers and spires rise like jagged teeth, casting long, oppressive shadows that stretch towards us as if reaching out from a nightmare.

The city sits perched atop the cliffs, overlooking the Lake of Sorrow below—a fitting guardian for such a desolate expanse. The water's surface, a mirror of despair, reflects the city's grim visage back upon itself.

As we move cautiously along the outer wall, I feel the weight of the city's stare. "It's like this city has eyes," Medusa says as her gaze pierces the shadows.

It is as though the very stones are watching us, whispering secrets of the damned in hushed tones that the wind carries away before we can grasp them. Every so often, a cold breeze cuts through the stale air, carrying with it the faintest sounds of chains dragging and mournful wails from within the walls.

"Hermes, Delta, and I can shift. It may make it easier for us to locate the hidden path," Cappa offers, with agreements from his friend.

"Let's hold on. We don't want to draw anything out of the city."

The atmosphere here is thick with a sense of foreboding. Dis is not merely a city; it is a bastion of the underworld, a place where light comes to die. The air is chillier, the shadows deeper, and every so often, a gap in the stone offers a glimpse into the city—the streets are narrow and winding, designed not just for defense but to confuse and disorient. Here, the architecture itself is a trap, a labyrinth within the Labyrinth.

I can't shake the feeling of being watched, of being judged by the city itself. It feels alive, pulsating with a dark heartbeat that resonates against the stone of the cliffs on which it stands. The city embodies despair and torment, a hellish realm where only the darkest creatures could thrive.

As we continue our passage, I keep my hand on the hilt of my sword, not out of expectation of a fight—the path to the gates is as quiet as the dead—but out of an instinctive need for reassurance.

Rhea moves silently beside me, her eyes scanning the horizon and the depths of the city. I can tell she too feels the oppressive nature of this place, her hand fixed on the dagger sheathed in her thigh holster, should she need to use it.

As we reach the imposing iron gates of the city, their formidable structure bars our way. Despite their apparent age, they stand resilient, a testament to the city's intent to keep intruders out—or perhaps to keep its secrets within. I test the gate, but it's locked, the mechanism cold and unyielding under my fingers.

"We need to find another way," I murmur to Rhea, scanning the walls for any sign of weakness or hidden entry. The secret path we seek is just beyond these gates, according to the verbal map we were given, but with every moment we linger, the risk grows.

As we discuss our options, a slight movement catches my eye. From the shadows of the city, figures begin to emerge, one by one. They are the immortal prisoners of Dis, their forms so emaciated, so ravaged by their confinement, that they slip through the narrow spaces between the iron bars with an eerie ease.

The sight of them is chilling. Their bodies are thin, almost skeletal, their eyes hollow with long suffering. They move silently, but with a purpose, forming a growing crowd around us. Their faces are etched with the pain of endless torment, as they look at us soundlessly.

Rhea steps around me but remains close. Holding her hand out with gentle reassurance, the slight tremble in her fingertips is the only sign of her shaky nerves.

"We mean you no harm," she speaks softly to the gathering figures, her voice imbued with compassion. "We're trying to get to the secret path."

The prisoners stop, their hollow gazes fixed on us. A palpable tension hangs in the air, thick and heavy. It's unclear if they understand her, or if they're even capable of communication after enduring the horrors of their imprisonment.

As the mass of prisoners grows, their murmurs become a low, haunting chorus, filling the air with a palpable tension. They press closer, their forms ghostly as they reach through the bars, their touches desperate but harmless. Despite their wretched condition, their presence is increasingly unsettling, not for the threat they pose but for the attention they might attract from the darker forces within the city.

Rhea's anxiety escalates with each passing moment, her eyes darting nervously toward the looming structures of the city, silhouetted against the dark sky. "We need to move now," she hisses under her breath, her voice tinged with fear. "If we wake the city..."

Before she can finish, a loud clang echoes from somewhere behind the walls, followed by a deep growl, making us freeze. I unsheathe my sword, preparing for the darkness of the city to notice our arrival. The blade's blue glow begins to shine, but I dampen it, muting the power of the runes to ensure it doesn't draw the darkness.

The sight of the blade, however, seems to agitate the prisoners further, their murmurs rising in pitch.

Pan extracts his vines, exposing the long-poisoned thorns that tip them. "We need to clear a path," he declares, raising a vine, ready to strike the chained immortals.

"No!" Rhea steps between him and the prisoners, her arms spread wide, her expression one of adamant refusal. "They are not our enemies. They're victims, just like we will be if we don't keep calm. We'll find another way," Rhea continues, her gaze locked on Pan, imploring him to see reason.

I lower my sword, nodding slowly. "Rhea's right. We're not here to fight those who can't even defend themselves."

An ominous thunder booms, rolling continuously above us, a deep and relentless sound that sends a chill down my spine. It's not the normal thunder one might associate with storms; this is something darker, heavier—a foreboding omen that something malevolent is stirring in the distance.

"Can we find another way now?" Callista wraps her arms around herself as if suddenly chilled.

The constant booming grows louder, reverberating through the air and the ground beneath our feet. Rhea and I exchange worried glances. "Something's coming," she murmurs, her eyes scanning the horizon where dark clouds gather with unnatural speed over the Lake of Sorrow.

The air is charged, thick with tension and fear. The immortal prisoners respond to the noise instantly, accustomed to impending danger. With panicked eyes, they scatter, scrambling into shadows and crevices, leaving us exposed.

"Shield her," I call over my shoulder, drawing my sword. Medusa takes my side, Alaric on the other. Pan and Kellan flank Rhea. Cappa and Delta stand behind her with Callista between them.

Every member of our dwindling party is ready to defend the goddess of the realms, their elements buzzing within them, charged by her presence.

As the thunder grows, my blade is cold and heavy in my hand, ready to be ignited with the power of starlight and tear down whatever approaches.

Bracing ourselves for the imminent clash, a streak of white rushes over the lake, disturbing the stillness as the speed of the creature approaching causes the water to shoot up like a jetstream.

Landing with a boom directly in front of me, the dark soil billows up in a cloud as I swing my sword in an arc.

Before the dust settles, the clang of a dark sword meeting mine pings around us. I push against my opponent, holding them locked in a stance of challenge.

A large pair of wings, once white and gleaming, now grey and dull, unfurl. Eyes, once blue, now reflect silver, the whites now black, stare at me with haunting malice.

With a grunt, I push his sword down with my own before standing up straight and taking a few steps back. With the cloud of dirt dissipated, the Archangel sheaths his sword. No longer a weapon of Light, now a servant of Darkness.

"Didn't expect to see you here, Michael."

"Yeah, well, you can thank her son for that." Archangel

Michael gestures with a jut of his chin to a dark set of rocks beyond the gates. "Fucking asshat."

Within the shadows, the emaciated woman we have spotted twice is crouched and shifts uneasily as Michael pulls our attention to her. She hisses at him before retreating more into the darkness.

"Calm the fuck down, or I'll lock you in Cocytus for a millennia." Michael tucks his wings in close to his body. Turning his head, he spits. The rocks sizzle and smoke where his saliva lands, turning black until it burns away.

"Wait, that is Flint's mother?" Rhea asks, her eyes peering into the shadows to take the woman in.

"You died." I sheath my sword as it's obvious Michael, while still an asshole, is not here to pose a threat.

"No shit, numb nuts." Michael pushes his audacious cape away, revealing a large ring fashioned to his belt. Full of keys of various sizes and shapes, Michael removes the ring from his belt and sifts through the keys. The noise is so loud, I look to the dark city behind us as if ready to see it awaken because of the noise.

"Do you have to let the whole city know we're here?" Rhea whispers through clenched teeth.

"They don't give a shit." Finding the key he was looking for, Michael walks to the gate. "I'm still the warden here; they're used to me." Michael pretends like he has just noticed Pan for the first time, but we all know that is just an act. "Oh, look at you. Finally stretching your legs and getting some sun?" He chuckles to himself.

Michael held a spot on the pseudo–Mortal Council for ages while Pan was forced by Loki to sit for an eternity, scribing the events of the realm. Michael was happy to be

Loki's lackey while Pan was cursed, his mind under Loki's control.

"Are you going to turn us over to the city?" I ask, my hand ready to draw my sword if needed. "Because I would love it if you died a second time."

"Mm, bet you would." Michael unlocks the gate and pushes it open. "But you don't get that privilege, sweetheart."

"Just as much a cunt in death as you were in life," Medusa chides the fallen angel.

"Probably worse, to be honest." He puts the keyring back on his belt and strides back to the cliff's edge. "I heard the ring of that godsforsaken sword of yours. I thought I would come to piss you off." He flashes a wide smile, standing with his hands on his hips.

"Gee, thanks, honey." I roll my eyes. He's such a fucking asshole. I'm only pissed Flint is the one that took him out with the Shadow Lurkers. I would have loved seeing him fall on my blade.

"Why would you help us?" Pan's tone is low, but he's keeping his patience, even with Michael's persistence at being as irritating as possible.

Michael looks around as if thinking before he answers. "Death makes a lot of things—clearer." He unfurls his wings, readying to take flight. "Like the fact that puny asshole tricked us all. He crept into my mind, and I had no idea."

"Are you going to pretend like Loki controlled you?" Some of the hold Pan is keeping on his patience begins to slip, his voice rising slightly. "We both know you enjoyed the depravity all on your own."

"We are not going to do this now," Rhea whispers, her eyes darting toward the dark city.

Michael walks up to Pan slowly. His hands are on his hips and a cocky grin is plastered on his face. Sniffing, he looks Pan up and down. "Your mate enjoyed my depravity," his smile widens seeing the fury Pan is trying to fight back, "So. Many. Times." Michael whispers, punching each word into the air.

"That's enough," Medusa interjects, putting her hand on Michael's chest, walking him back and positioning herself between him and Pan.

He holds Medusa's stare a second too long for my liking, and I unsheathe my sword. Michael visibly shudders, as if the exposed sword is clawing at his nerves.

"I'm done here, anyway." Michael backs away, looking at each of us as he gets closer to the cliff's edge. "She'll show you to the path." He nods once again at the hidden prisoner that keeps to the shadows. "Oh, and the Minotaur is tracking you, so—have fun with that."

Michael salutes us with two fingers, then pushes off the ground, shooting into the air at great speed, turning to a white streak as he soars back across the lake.

Armed with a new guide, our band of immortals sets out along the hidden path. Medusa and Kellan lead the way, followed by Alaric and Pan. Rhea and I are in the center, with Cappa and Delta behind us and Callista at the end.

We've managed to reach the midpoint in our journey, and our group has dwindled by half.

The realization is not lost on me that Rhea and I may very well reach the end of the Labyrinth alone. Taking another look at our comrades, I try not to think about which one of them will be next to die.

A s we follow the woman down the hidden path, her skeletal frame sways with each step, every movement a struggle. I can't stop looking at the torn slash across her throat, visible just above the thick collar that suppresses her powers. The jagged opening at her sagging belly pulls at my curiosity as Archangel Michael's words echo in my head—this woman is Flint's mother.

The thought gnaws at me, the connection between Flint and the frail creature leading us, and her imprisonment.

I find myself drawn to her, compelled to understand her story. "Can you tell me what happened to you?" I ask gently, my voice soft. "How did you come to be here?"

Hermes, walking closely beside me, places a hand on my shoulder, his touch cautionary. "Rhea, she may not be able to answer you," he murmurs.

"I just want to know how she got here. What if she shouldn't be here?"

The woman stops suddenly, turns, and grabs my wrist. Her grip is unexpectedly strong, despite the fragility of her form. Our eyes meet, and there's a depth in her gaze, a piercing sorrow that feels as if it's reaching into my very soul. She doesn't have the same distant haze as the other prisoners we've encountered.

In an instant, her memories flood into me—an overwhelming deluge of images and emotions. I see her life before the Labyrinth, filled with laughter and light, the stark contrast to her current torment painted vividly in her recollections. Her days as a warrior, her capture, and the cruelty forced upon her that ended in her imprisonment unfold in rapid succession.

As the rush of her past subsides, I'm left gasping, the weight of her despair pressing down on me. I collapse to my knees, my hands hitting the ground.

"Rhea!" Hermes is by my side in an instant, blocking me from her, thinking she hurt me. Our companions stop, alert that our new guide may be a betrayal.

Tears stream down my face as she watches me, her eyes filled with pain and a hint of gratitude for my willingness to understand her plight.

"Hera." I choke out her name. Medusa gasps, covering her mouth.

"Oh, my gods," she whispers, kneeling down and looking at the ghoulish face that is the result of so many eons in this torment.

She was so beautiful before. Long red hair flowed down to the small of her back, and she often wore long dresses as green as a new meadow in spring. Hera is a Shifter and an incredibly powerful one.

Like so many of the Shifters, she was captive in the depths of Ares' Underworld.

Loki's Underworld.

He sensed her power and wanted to breed her with Ares,

hoping the child would have multiple powers of Shifting and Fire. He took over their minds; he forced them.

Gods, the thought of it all chokes me with sorrow and anger. I cough, trying to hold back the sobs that want to break through.

Loki ensured they knew everything that was happening to them. He forced Ares upon her again and again until she was impregnated, then her captivity began.

First, locked in a chamber with the imprisoned Triton as her neighbor, she carried her baby all that time, living in darkness. As soon as her labor started, Loki slashed her womb open and ripped her child from her body. Loki was angered by the soft power of Fire that Flint possessed, not at all powered to such intensity as Ares and Hera.

So, he punished her.

With her wound still open, he delivered her here. Slashing open her throat before she was bound in her collar.

And each day, she has survived in this desolation, survived Michael and the abuse he inflicted upon her, survived the dark creatures that hunt the prisoners eternally.

And she's never drunk from the river of forgetting. She remembers it all.

She *wanted* to remember it all.

I saw the moment Flint was told who she is. She knew him the second she saw him standing there with a book under his arm. For the first time in so many millennia, joy surged through her.

Hope bloomed within her that he would help her, and the sinking despair when he kicked her away. That was the closest she had ever come to diving into the Lethe and letting the waters wash away every terrible memory.

But then she saw Michael had been killed; she sensed the shift in the atmosphere here and thought to hang on a little longer. That perhaps an end would come soon to her torture.

As I calm myself from the horrors of her life, I put my hand over hers. She just stares at it for a moment before looking back at me. "I promise, I'll get you out of here." Fresh tears roll down my cheeks as I hold her gaze, hoping she realizes the sincerity of my promise.

Hera shuffles ahead of us, continuing to lead us down the secret path. I follow, the weight of her life's story heavy on my heart. Her memories are now part of my consciousness, and I never want to let them go.

She has held on to her past with such ferocity, despite the unending darkness of her life. Just as Hermes said he finds strength in me, I find strength in her. Each step down this path renews my resolve and sparks my anger.

At the end of our trail through the Labyrinth, the rest of my powers are hidden. Once I restore them, once I defeat my hunter, I'll tear down this prison, stone by stone.

But just as I'm piecing together thoughts of how we might dismantle the dark powers at play here, our path leads us into a sudden clearing.

Hera stops abruptly, her body tensing as she scans the expanse before us. The clearing, wide and ominously quiet, feels like a trap laid open under the shadowed canopy of the Labyrinth. I instinctively draw closer to Hermes and rest my hands on my blades, sensing the same wary tension in his posture.

The rest of the group, too, becomes visibly alert, their hands moving to weapons and their eyes narrowing as they survey the surroundings. This opening, while seemingly just a part of the landscape, strikes us all as strategically significant—a perfect place for an ambush.

"Something's not right," Hermes whispers, his voice low and cautious. He glances at me, his expression mirroring my own concern as he reaches for his sword.

My gaze remains locked on our guide. She stands still, her skeletal frame almost ghostly against the muted light filtering through the trees. After a moment that stretches taut with tension, she takes a tentative step forward, then another, her movements slow and measured as if testing the safety of the ground.

"Stay sharp," I murmur to the group, my voice barely a whisper. Every sense is heightened, every shadow scrutinized, as we prepare to cross the clearing.

"Yeah, no shit." Medusa agrees, her tone laced with sarcasm despite the gloom of the moment.

The trees around us seem too still, as if holding their breath, and the silence is too complete. Every step feels laden with risk, and I find myself constantly looking over my shoulder, expecting an attack at any moment.

Halfway across the clearing, our guide suddenly stops again, this time more abruptly. She turns towards us, her eyes wide with an urgent warning.

From the sky, something drops quickly, thudding against the ground as the sound of wings flapping retreats into the darkness.

It takes my mind a moment to understand what my eyes are seeing.

The bloodied body of Callista lies in the center of the clearing, skinned and twitching. Her eyes are still open but unblinking.

My mate curses under his breath as I remain speechless. Medusa growls as our Shifter companions encircle us, watching the clearing for danger.

She was just at the end of our group. I swear every time I looked back, everyone was there. My mind empties as I try to recall the last several minutes, and every thought sails away from me before I can grasp it.

A dark mass emerges from the ground beneath her body. Like a giant slug, it leaves behind a trail of slime along her chest and arm, then across her face as it slithers into her mouth. Her throat expands with the force of the thing crawling into her.

She convulses as if choking.

"She's still alive." I whisper as my feet move on instinct toward her. But the moment I do, Callista's body begins to wither as if she is being sucked dry. Her limbs stiffen, pulled into her body as she dehydrates right before our eyes.

Fully shriveled and dead, her eyes turn black as they weep tar. Her stomach is distended, and there is movement as the slug that crawled into her is still there.

It breaks through her thin, dried flesh and glides onto the dark grass of the clearing. We back away as if it's going to hunt another meal, but satisfied, it burrows into the ground.

Only a second later, from the dark trees that line the edge of the clearing, three figures descend rapidly, their forms cutting through the air with terrifying grace. Their eyes burn with an infernal light, and their sneers are filled with malice as they encircle us, their gaze fixed on one person. Medusa. "Enjoy our present?"

"What's going on, ladies?" Medusa says casually, as if we didn't just witness a member of our party die an agonizing death only seconds ago. One of the three winged beings snarls her response.

"Furies," Hermes whispers to me as he adjusts the grip of the sword in his hand.

Their wings, vast and leathery, beat the air, stirring up a wind that whirls around us, carrying the scent of decay and sulfur. The claws at the ends of their fingers gleam ominously, ready to exact punishment.

Like the Harpies of Tartarus, these bird-like women are a cross between a humanoid form that blends seamlessly into animal. Also, like the Harpies, they look ready to kill.

"Mighty brave of you to venture here, Gorgon," one of the Furies says, her voice a growl.

I take a half step forward, hoping to broker an understanding. "We seek passage, not conflict—"

The blazing eyes of the Furies snap to me as they all screech loudly, cutting me off abruptly.

"THEN YOU SHOULD NOT HAVE BROUGHT HER HERE!" the Fury screams. The winged beasts turn their eyes back on Medusa, and she meets their glare. The tendrils of her braids snake down her back. "The Gorgon knows the debt we are owed."

"Awww," Medusa clicks her tongue, urging the Furies' anger to rise. "Still a sore loser? Come on, girls, we can move past this, can't we?" As she holds her arms out, the echo of flapping wings nears the clearing as more Furies arrive, landing in the trees around us. "I guess not."

"Deuce," Hermes starts, but Medusa half turns her head to him.

"Go."

"No," I answer for my mate, refusing to leave someone else behind.

Medusa turns to me, resolve set in her hard features but her gaze softens slightly. "Athena always believed in you."

"Medusa, stop this," I choke out as my throat tightens.

"And so do I."

"Enough stalling, Gorgon. Face the Furies," the main Fury barks out, and the others gathering around us begin screeching and flapping their wings in agreement.

Medusa looks to Hermes and nods. "Our paths no longer go the same direction, old friend, and you made me a promise."

Hermes doesn't say anything in response but sheaths his sword. They clasp forearms and hold each other's eyes. This feels like a very final farewell, and I can't just walk away from her like this.

"We need to stay together," I demand, but they pay me no attention.

"Get her to the end, brother," Medusa says to Hermes.

"No matter the cost," he responds.

"No matter the cost." Medusa nods her head.

Stepping away from us, the braids tied behind her head, keeping half her long hair out of her face, relax. Her powers flare, and her long locks rise and sway. The three Furies that encircled us form a line, and she walks toward them.

"Let's make it a good one, girls!" Medusa heckles the Furies, raising her voice so it bounces off the trees. "Not dull like our last fight, okay? That one got you banished here."

The Furies growl and screech in reply, making Medusa smirk.

"Hermes, we can't..." I start after her, but Hermes grabs

my arm, holding me back. His grip is gentle, which contrasts with the emotions raging in his eyes.

"We have to see this through, and we can't risk losing you." His blue eyes bounce back and forth between mine. He holds both of my arms at my side, pushing the seriousness of the situation to me through our bond.

Everyone here took an oath and promised to give their lives for our mission. But I can't stand back, running away while Medusa kills herself.

"I'm not leaving her," I snap back at him.

"I know, so, I'm sorry for this." He bends down and picks me up, throwing me over his shoulder and walking away. Our band of warriors follows Hermes without a question or so much as a look back at Medusa as she prepares to sacrifice herself for us.

"Hermes!" I push against him, trying to free myself from his hold. "I will never forgive you for this."

"And I will live with that." He keeps his fast pace, our weakened guide unable to keep up as she wobbles across the clearing with us. "I can't live without you again though, so I'll work every day to show you how sorry I am. I'll beg for your forgiveness for eternity, but we're leaving this clearing."

Amid my screaming and pounding on Hermes' back, my thrashing, hoping to dislodge myself from his iron hold on me, the ground in the clearing quakes before breaking apart.

Medusa's braids rattle their warning to the Furies approaching, but the winged creatures encircle her. The crumbled ground around her rises, taking the shape of two people.

At first, I thought them to be earthen replicas of herself, but upon closer inspection, I see two faces I recognize. Her sisters, Stheno and Euryale. She has fashioned the earthen forms after her sisters, bringing them out to battle with her.

Medusa takes a fighting stance as the three Furies ready their attack. The two earthen casts take a stance with her, and at once, the three beings strike out, igniting the battle with the Furies.

"Hermes, go back for her!" I begin to cry now as Hermes reaches the other side of the clearing and keeps going.

The last image I see of Medusa before she disappears from my view is her unleashing her own fury, fighting side-by-side with the images of her sisters she left behind on Tartarus.

"**B**aby, look at me," I plead with my mate as we take rest on a grouping of large boulders. We kept our pace out of the clearing and down the path until Hera led us into a narrow pass, steep rock walls rising up above us.

The distant echo of falling rocks travels down the narrow pass as we rest. Cappa inspects Delta's hand again. The scrape he received in the foggy forest is worsening.

It's a vibrant red, and the edges have turned from white to black. The veins in his hand and forearm are darkening as if a poison is seeping up his skin.

"I'll be alright once we get out of here," Delta reassures Cappa, tearing a piece of his shirt and using it to wrap his hand.

Rhea refuses to look at me. Her breathing is still heavy, her eyes distant and shadowed with the weight of what just transpired. I know her heart is torn, left behind with Medusa, who stayed to face the Furies and buy us this precious escape.

I cup her cheek, my touch begging her to acknowledge me, our bond thrumming with our combined sorrow. Rhea finally looks at me, her eyes brimming with unshed tears, the pain evident in her gaze.

"Rhea," I begin, my voice soft, trying to bridge the chasm of her thoughts. "Medusa is a warrior, one of the fiercest I've ever known."

Rhea shakes her head, looking away to hide the tears that rise up in her eyes. "I know that, Hermes, but knowing doesn't make it easier to accept. How many more will we lose before this is over?" Her voice cracks with the strain of unvoiced sobs.

I rub her thighs, massaging her sore muscles until she looks back at me again. The guilt over the immortals that walked into the Labyrinth with us that we are leaving behind breaks her spirit more each time.

"I don't know, baby." I admit, my own voice heavy with the same dread. "We may lose everyone. But I do know that Medusa believes in you, in us. She believes in what we're fighting for. Finding the Caduceus, ending this torment—it's everything. It's worth every sacrifice."

I keep caressing her legs, patiently waiting for her to reason with the war happening in her mind. Slowly moving from her calf to her thighs again, rubbing and massaging as I go. She puts her hand on mine, and it feels like my heart starts beating again.

Gripping me tightly with both hands, her emotions begin breaking down the barriers she is trying to construct. Raising her hands to my lips, I kiss them both tenderly as she breaks out into sobs.

I pick her up and set her in my lap. My arms encase her firmly as she melts into me. "I'm sorry, Rhea." I kiss the top of her head. My own grief meets the torment of her pain through our bond, and we rest in our shared suffering a moment.

Leaving Medusa was hard. My instincts wanted to stand with my friend and fight, just like we've done a thousand times over the ages. But the need to protect Rhea, to protect our goal, was greater.

We all understand that, and it is why Medusa made me promise I would leave her behind if it meant the difference between a fight, or getting Rhea to safety.

Everyone asked me to make the same oath. If it came down to a fight, they are ready to remain behind. But nothing makes this any easier.

"It's just so heavy."

"I know, baby." Stroking her hair and rubbing her back, she releases a shuttered breath before looking at me. I push her long golden-brown hair away from her face and hold this space for her in silent patience.

Finally, she relents, and I see the moment she decides to let the weight of her guilt settle. She relaxes the tension in her forehead and brings her hand to my face. Closing my eyes, I lean into her, touching my forehead to hers. She leans forward, rubbing her nose against mine, and it fills me with warmth.

Another rock falls from the top of the cavern surrounding us, this time closer. The small hairs on my neck stand on end as I feel a heaviness above us.

I scan the top of the passage and glimpse the split-second movement of something retreating back away from the top of the cavern. Rhea feels the tension in my body as chills cascade down my spine.

"What is it?"

"Something is up there." The timber of my voice drops as I try to quiet myself, and our remaining group looks up with me. In silent agreement, we stand and leave.

Our guide, already anticipating our departure, is waiting at the mouth of another crevasse. This one is much more confined than the passage we have been walking down in a single line. Reluctantly, we enter, the path ahead so narrowed in places that we're forced to crawl.

The journey through this rocky channel is tense and claustrophobic. The walls press close, rough against our skin, and every few feet, the passage seems to constrict even further, challenging our resolve and our ability to continue. I lead the way, with my sword in hand, unable to keep it sheathed on my back. Rhea is close behind, each of us focused on navigating this natural labyrinth.

Just as we start to adapt to the rhythm of squeezing through tight spaces, I hear a commotion from behind. Pausing, I call back, "What's happening? Is everyone alright?"

There's a moment of strained shuffling and muffled grunts before Alaric's voice, usually calm and steady, echoes with a note of frustration and discomfort. "I'm stuck," he announces, his tone edged with annoyance and a hint of concern. "Can't move forward or back."

I shuffle around to head back toward him, the narrow confines of the passage making it a slow and awkward process. The others make way as best they can in the cramped space. When I finally reach Alaric, I see him wedged tightly between the rocky walls. His broad, muscular gargoyle frame, usually an asset in battle, is now a liability in the tight confines of this passage.

"Let me see," I say, assessing the situation. The rocks around him are unyielding, and his movements have only caused him to become more firmly lodged.

"It's my wing... it's caught!" Alaric gasps between strained breaths. "It twisted when I moved!"

I brace my shoulder against the rock behind me, then push

against him with all my might. He grimaces but doesn't move an inch.

Alaric tries to adjust himself, and when he thinks he has it, nods at me, "Okay, again."

As I brace, ready to push him again, the silence of the moment is shattered by a sudden, heavy snort from behind us. It's a deep, resonant sound that reverberates through the narrow passageway, chilling us all to the core.

Alaric freezes, his eyes wide in panic.

Don't. Move.

I mouth the words to him, and he remains breathlessly still. His body is so close to the color and texture of the rocky formation we're crawling through, I pray to the Fates whatever is lurking behind us will miss him and move along.

Another breathy snort of the animal sounds but this time further away.

The silence that follows is almost as terrifying as the noise had been. We wait, each second stretching out interminably, until we're reasonably sure the creature has moved on. Only then do we dare to stir again, our breaths coming out in quiet, shaky exhales.

As we prepare to attempt another rescue for Alaric, the tension is palpable. I position myself to push against the rock once more. Rhea is turning around, trying to maneuver back to me as well. "Maybe I can help."

Her Earth powers may be useful to help dislodge him, but I try again.

A horrifying scream erupts from Alaric. A gut-wrenching sound, filled with agony and fear, echoing sharply through the cramped space of the tunnel.

Before anyone can react, a massive force yanks Alaric from

the passage. The movement is so sudden, so violent, that for a moment, all we can do is stare in stunned silence at the space he once occupied.

We're momentarily frozen, shock anchoring us in place, as Alaric's body lands with a heavy, sickening thud at the passage entrance.

The massive head and horns of the Minotaur surge into the tunnel entrance, his guttural roar piercing the tense silence, reverberating through the cavern walls.

Pan covers his ears, screaming against the pain of the noise.

The Minotaur, its massive head and glaring eyes filled with bloodlust, pushes toward us. Instinctively, I kick out, my strike landing on the beast's snout as we scramble backward, deeper into the tight confines of the cavern. "Move back!"

As it struggles to advance, its roars of frustration echo around us, a sound as terrifying as the threat of its presence. The large horns and wide shoulders of the beast prevent it from reaching us, and I narrowly avoid its clawed hand as it swipes out erratically.

Our group ascends deeper into the narrow passage, and several feet later, an interior chamber widens, allowing us some space to stand and catch our breath.

Checking for additional openings, there is only one exit, and it's just as narrow as the confining tunnel we just left.

Rhea, visibly shaken, darts her eyes around our refuge to ensure the Minotaur hasn't found a way to breach the passage. "It can't follow us here, right?" She looks to our guide for reassurance, and when Hera sits, leaning against the stone wall and closing her eyes, we take that as a sign of her agreement.

"You okay?" I check on my mate, rubbing her arms as she calms her breathing.

"Yes, are you?" She checks over my body for signs of the Minotaur's talons.

"I'm good." I answer, taking her in my arms and releasing a large breath of relief. "Let's rest for a bit while we know it's safe in here." Looking to the small huddle of skin and bones on the far side of the cavern, Hera has fallen asleep. Knowing how long she has survived here, I trust we can relax for a little while in relative peace.

If such a thing can even exist in a place like the Labyrinth.

Resting against the wall, Rhea scoots in close to me. I radiate warmth through our bond, and she releases a sigh of relief. Slowly, she relaxes in my arms, and within a few minutes, she's sleeping.

Pan's massive form in this small cavern is almost comical, but at least here, he has the space to stand fully. He takes a few moments to stretch his long tree-like limbs over his head before sitting near one opening. Kellen takes up a spot opposite him, both immortals keeping their keen senses alert as they work to rest.

Cappa fell asleep as quickly as Hera did, and Delta sits next to his friend. Cappa uses his shoulder for a pillow, and while we settle, he unwraps his injured hand.

Pan notices the Shifter's hand has nearly turned completely black, the wound is pus-filled and bright green. With both Sonus and Life elemental powers, Pan offers his assistance.

Delta winces but keeps quiet as Pan secretes a salve from one of his vines, letting it drip onto the wound. Several deep green leaves grow on Pan's forearm, and he plucks them. Crushing them between his fingers to release the oils, he places the leaves on the wound and wraps Delta's hand with fibrous fungi that acts like gauze.

Offering his thanks, Delta inspects the new dressing on his hand and his eyes flick to me quickly before he looks away.

That injury is getting worse and worse by the moment, and I wonder if Delta is thinking the same thing I am. The Labyrinth may have claimed him as its first victim; it's just taking a little longer for the immortal prison to collect his death.

You should always trust that feeling you get when you sense you're being watched. When the heavy weight of someone else's observation is bearing down upon you and raises the hair on your arm in warning. Never ignore that gravitational pull to look around because it's likely to save your life.

Or scare the shit out of you.

That sense crept upon me as I slept until finally the need to open my eyes was too much to ignore. I just didn't expect a large pair of nearly all-black eyes to be staring me right in the face.

Jumping back with a start, I woke up the entire cavern and set them on alert. "By the gods, Hera. You scared me."

Hermes' arms tightened around me as he jolted awake. Pan shot out defensive vines, ready to use them like whips. Kellan shifted his hand into the paw of a lion, and Cappa was ready to pounce like a stealthy predator. They all relaxed when I waved my hands dismissively. "Sorry, she just startled me."

The gaunt face of our starved guide filled my vision, then backed away near the other opening, waiting.

"I think it's time to get going, then?" I said, my tone

turning up at the end in question. Hera nodded. Aside from the memory exchange, it's the only real communication she's given me this entire time.

I recalled Hecate telling us about the collars of the prisoners. They hold whatever memories the prisoner has. It enables the Leshy Clerics to keep records, but the dark beings use it for amusement, brutalizing the prisoners and then watching it replay like a movie.

This is a place of cruelty. I wonder if this is what Hecate intended when she created it or if the Labyrinth has become a being of its own, twisting its purpose from confinement to torment.

The weight of the losses we've sustained pressed heavily on my shoulders as we exited the relative safety of the cavern. The air felt different here—heavier, charged with an ominous energy that sent shivers down my spine.

That haunting sense of observation returned, and it felt like a dozen pairs of eyes were watching our every step. The terrain shifted dramatically, the stark, rocky landscape giving way to a dense, unkempt forest that seemed almost to deepen the darkness that surrounded it.

Our guide, a frail shadow of her former self, motioned us forward with a sense of urgency that left no room for hesitation. Yet, stepping into the forest felt like entering another world—a place where the trees loomed like specters and the darkness played tricks on your eyes, making you see movements and shapes that weren't really there.

Hermes gave my hand a reassuring squeeze, sensing my trepidation. "Don't let go of my hand," he murmured, sensing the same unease that was warping my mind with confusion.

Pan, Kellan, Cappa, and Delta followed closely behind,

their expressions grim. They felt it too—the oppressive metallic tinge in the air that warned there was a manipulation of the mind here.

As we pushed deeper into the forest, the sense of disorientation grew. The trees seemed to bend and whisper secrets, their branches shifting subtly in a non-existent breeze. Every crack of a twig underfoot sounded like a warning, every rustle of leaves a threat.

"Keep close," I instructed the group, my voice low but firm. "Don't let the forest separate us."

Kellan, always silently observing, kept his eyes darting from shadow to shadow, searching for any sign of danger. Cappa and Delta used their heightened senses, occasionally pausing to sniff the air or listen to the subtle sounds of the forest.

"Wait." Cappa's tone was low, a clear warning he had detected something.

At the same time, Pan turned his head sharply to the left, squinting his eyes as if trying to see through the forest. "I can hear them. There are a lot. It's–" His voice trailed off as he listened again, focusing his powerful sense of Sonus. "It's like a stampede."

Hera climbed on top of a large boulder that came halfway up my waist. She crouched but then stood up, getting a better vantage point and looking in the same direction as Pan.

It was then that we heard the unmistakable sound of hooves beating against the soft forest floor. Projecting my dark mist outward, I let my power crawl through the forest, helping me sense what lurked.

Hermes kept a keen eye on Hera, watching her for reactions. She was relaxed, her body is not tense but just waiting expectantly.

My dark wave detected the on-comers, and intrigue struck me at what I found. "Centaurs," I warned the group, then looked to Hera. "Are they allies?"

I think she nodded in agreement as she kept waiting on her boulder. The first Centaur came into view, jumping over a fallen tree and navigating the uneven terrain of the forest with ease.

The lower half of his equine body had black hair that gave way to equally black skin. Long onyx hair hung down past his shoulders with a matching beard. There were no whites to his eyes. They seemed to be only black with an even darker black outer ring.

His powerful legs moved with expert ease, and he balanced with his muscular torso and arms. A wooden bow was strapped to his back, and a brown leather quiver was fixed around him with several arrows protruding from the top.

Behind him, the next Centaur was a female with hair like white snow leading up to a white torso. With matching long white hair on her head, she carried her bow in both hands, an arrow at the ready.

Hera leaned forward, sniffing the air. The Centaurs caught sight of her, changing their direction and heading toward us.

Some of the Centaurs were dappled with several colors of brown, black, and white. One was completely brown, and another was black with white patches of hair. All had similar coloring on their torsos and even carried the same patches of various colors along the rest of their bodies.

As the thunderous sound of hooves neared, a flurry of emotions gripped me—fear, curiosity, and a fleeting hope that perhaps we had found allies in this foreboding place. The Centaurs encircled us as the leader approached Hera.

"I am Nessus, leader of this tribe," he introduced himself, his gaze sweeping over us with a mixture of curiosity and calm. "You are far from the usual paths. What brings you to venture into the Pathless Wood and the Labyrinth itself if you are not prisoners?"

I stepped forward, feeling Hermes' supportive presence beside me. "I'm Rhea." Introducing myself first, I gave the names of everyone. Each nodded as I acknowledged them, and Nessus returned the gesture. His gaze lingered on Hermes as if he recognized him.

"Tartarus." Hermes spoke to the lead Centaur, giving him a reminder of where they may have met. They all stomped their hooves at the mention of the realm of the Earth Titan.

"Yes, I remember you," Nessus said thoughtfully. "My father led our tribe during the escape."

Hermes nodded as if that explained something, and an uneasy silence halted our encounter. My heart rate settled with Nessus' strong but non-threatening demeanor. Seeing how Hermes had some interaction in the ancient past with this tribe, I let them know the reason for our journey.

"We're looking for an artifact that may have been hidden in the Labyrinth long ago. Do you know where something like that may be?"

Nessus nodded thoughtfully, his expression contemplative. "The Labyrinth is old, its secrets many and its guardians fierce." Nessus looked to Hera as he continued. "The imprisoned are told salvation lies in the Labyrinth's center. They strive eternally to reach it."

"What is at the center of the Labyrinth?" I questioned him further, hope blooming in me that it could be Hermes' scepter.

"I cannot say. It is impossible to reach, but we did attempt it once." He looked around to his tribe and they stirred. Some murmured to each other as if recalling their journey there. "The tribe is strong, but the forcefield surrounding the center point of the prison is much stronger. If something were hidden here, that is where I would look."

"Can you take us there?" Hermes asked.

"I cannot risk losing any more of my kinsmen. I regret I have to send you off alone." Nessus seemed genuinely apologetic, sparking my curiosity about how they got here if they were able to flee from Tartarus.

"How did you come to live in the Labyrinth, if I may ask?"

Nessus lifted his chin with pride before answering. "Banished, you mean. We refused to bargain with the Titan-killer."

My cheeks heated as they mentioned the Titan wars, but I wasn't sure if they believed the lie that Chaos was hunting his fellow Titans or if they knew the truth. "Loki?"

"An abominable creature of darkness." Some of the Centaurs sneered, and the tribe agitated at the mention of his name.

"Is this all that is left of your tribe?" I looked to them. There couldn't be more than fifteen Centaurs. While there were several females among them, there were no younglings.

Nessus nodded, and my heart dropped for them. Our own group was dwindling by the moment here, and it was nearly an unbearable grief. I could understand his unwillingness to put his kinsmen in danger.

"If you could help us with the best path to the center, we would be grateful."

Nessus bowed to me, as if thankful I wasn't pressing the request for their escort further. "Hera will lead you from the Pathless Wood to a shortcut through the Burning Desert."

"Oh, that sounds wonderful," Cappa murmured to Delta, who snorted an unamused laugh.

Nessus looked to Hera. "Take them to the pit of the Geryon," he instructed her, then turned his attention back to us. "If you can pay the toll for passage, the Geryon will carry you over the Netherpeak Mountains. It is far too treacherous and enormous to attempt to cross them on your own."

"Thank you."

"And do your best not to disturb the darkness that lives in the Malebolge," he added. Hecate had warned us of this too, advising we should avoid passing it at all costs. "It is incredibly dangerous, but the fastest path to the Labythin's center is to scale each pit. Any other route will take you ages to navigate through."

"We understand." Hermes offered his hand to Nessus, and they grasped forearms. The gesture was a common greeting or farewell among allies. "We appreciate the help."

Nessus nodded to the Centaurs on each side of him, and they removed their bows and quivers, handing them to Kellan and Pan.

Nessus turned back to his tribe, and they disappeared as silently as they had appeared, blending back into the woods with graceful agility.

Left alone to continue our journey, our small group gathered around Hera. Despite her own burdens and the chains of her past that she carried, her determination seemed unwavering. She led us deeper into the Pathless Wood, where the trees grew denser, the shadows longer, and the silence more profound.

As we walked, the atmosphere thickened, a palpable tension settling over us. I found myself constantly looking over my shoulder, half-expecting to see a Minotaur or another Fury lurking in the shadows. But there was only the forest, endless and watching.

Amidst the stillness of the Pathless Wood, the occasional cry of a distant bird or the snap of a twig echoed unnaturally loud, each sound magnified by the oppressive silence. Every rustle in the underbrush seemed to herald an unseen threat, heightening our senses as we pressed onward.

As we followed Hera, my senses remained heightened, on edge, as if anticipating an unseen threat lurking just beyond the next tree. Hermes walked closely beside me, his voice low and steady, trying to offer comfort. "I'm sure we'll be clear of the forest soon," he murmured, his hand gently holding mine. But his words, meant to calm, seemed to dissolve into the thick air around us, unable to quell the rising tide of panic within me.

When another twig snapped, this time accompanied by the gentle sounds of a babbling creek, my heart leaped into my throat. The rest of the group finally halted, their previous nonchalance fading into alertness as they too heard the unmistakable sound of footsteps.

It was different this time—hasty, deliberate, as if something or someone was moving swiftly but retreating away from us.

"We need to check this out," Pan whispered, gesturing for us to follow. Kellan nodded, both of them quietly stringing their newly acquired bows, arrows at the ready.

We moved with cautious steps toward the source of the sounds, navigating through the dense undergrowth and around a tall crop of dried and twisted bushes that obscured our view. As we peered around them, the sight that greeted us was unexpected. We shared a collective gasp.

"**Z**ephyr?" I ask cautiously, my voice a whisper. Relief washes over me at finding them alive, but suspicion lingers. The Labyrinth is a place of tricks and lies, and I can't shake the feeling that this might be one of its illusions. The Pathless Wood reeks of deceit.

Hera, our silent guide, notices my hesitation. With a slow, deliberate movement that belies her frail form, she hobbles over to Zephyr and sits beside them. This act is her way of telling us it's safe—or at least, she believes it to be.

Despite her reassurance, my instincts scream caution, and we emerge slowly. Zephyr kneels by the brook, paying no mind to Hera's arrival. The water sloshes as Zephyr raises a hand to their mouth, ready to drink.

"Zephyr, no!" Abandoning my caution, I rush to their side. Pushing their hand down, I can only hope they haven't ingested any water yet.

When they look back at me with rich chocolate eyes, my heart plummets. There is no reaction to our arrival. Zephyr's eyes are glassy and vacant. Their once expressive face is now eerily blank, their gaze distant, as if looking right through us. A chill runs down my spine. The waters of forgetting that flow through the darkest corners of the Labyrinth have already claimed them.

"Zephyr?" I call out softly, hoping for any sign of recognition, any flicker in their eyes. But there's nothing. Their stare remains fixed, unfocused, and utterly devoid of warmth.

Hermes steps forward, his face etched with concern. He places a hand gently on Zephyr's shoulder. "Can you hear us, Zephyr?"

Zephyr doesn't respond, doesn't even blink. They stand motionless, their body present but their mind lost.

My thoughts go to Flora and the moment we reunite with those waiting outside the Labyrinth. I was preparing to tell her how her mate sacrificed themselves to save me, how they died. But Zephyr survived the hurricane, likely thrust out of it like the immortal prisoners, only to end up here, alone. The waters of the Labyrinth must have called to them, and for some reason, they couldn't resist.

These rivers urge us to quench our thirst, but even a single drop wipes our minds completely. Drinking more can drive you to insanity. *How much did you drink, Zephyr?*

"We can't leave them here." I address our group, keeping my gaze on Zephyr. Still no acknowledgment of our presence. "We're taking them out of here."

"Are you kidding? We only add more risk to our lives bringing them." Kellan interjects, igniting my anger. "Is there even a way to reverse the effects?"

Pan shakes his head slowly. "Not that I know of."

Hermes turns to Kellan, a challenge in his glare. "It wasn't a question. It was a statement." Pride swells in me when Hermes supports me, then moves to action. Kellan doesn't argue again but takes several paces back, rolling his eyes.

"I need some thin but strong vines," Hermes directs Pan.

The tall immortal, more plant than anything, points his finger. A thin brown vine emerges from his fingertip, extracting until Hermes is satisfied with the length.

Holding the vine in Zephyr's line of sight, Hermes tries to warn them, but I don't think it makes a difference. Aside from the rise and fall of their chest, Zephyr only blinks and swallows.

Hermes wraps the vine around our comatose friend and ties it. Using it like a lead, he begins walking, careful not to pull too abruptly. When the slack vine is pulled taut, Zephyr's legs move on their own. When Hermes stops, Zephyr stops.

"See, it'll be fine." Hermes turns to the rest of the group. "Someone should turn back and take Zephyr out of here."

Kneeling beside Hera, I place a gentle hand on her shoulder. "I can't thank you enough for your help, and I promise, I'm going to free you from here." Hera blinks but shows no other change. "Can you escort them to the beginning? Help them with the safest route back?"

Hera takes two wobbly steps to Zephyr and takes the vines from Hermes.

Looking expectantly at our group, I wait for a volunteer.

Cappa looks to his injured friend. Delta's wound seeps black discharge through the gauze Pan wrapped around him. "You should go. Get someone to look at that." I hold back a wince, thinking of the pain Delta must be in with the festering wound that none of us can seem to heal.

"No, I'm better off helping them get to the end." Delta looks at his feet and swallows hard. Lifting his shirt, I gasp at the network of black veins webbing across his torso. "I figure when it gets to my heart, I'm done." He gives his friend a sad chuckle, devoid of humor. "Seeing how I don't have much time left, I'll get them as far as I can, then I'll go out in a blaze of glory."

Cappa holds back tears, seeing his friend's condition and understanding Delta is likely right. "You always have to try to one-up me, don't you?" The friends share a somber glimmer of amusement, likely an old joke.

"Well, we both know Luke gave you Cappa because he felt sorry for you." Cappa can't hold back his tears and lets them fall. They embrace, and Delta whispers his goodbye.

Moving to stand with us, Delta waits for his friend to leave. Taking the vines from Hera, Cappa follows her, retreating the way we came. He looks back every few steps, trying to keep his friend in sight until they vanish into the shadows.

Hermes pats Delta's shoulder, giving him a reassuring squeeze. "Let's get going." He looks at Pan and Kellan before holding his hand out to me.

Taking Hermes' hand, I send a wave of my power outward, closing my eyes and letting my dark mist find a way out. Feeling a lightness in the distance, I begin walking, leading what remains of our group deeper into the dark forest.

Using my powers to stay on track, I pause occasionally, sensing the way out has shifted even though we walk in the same direction. As we go deeper, I detect other beings among the trees and work to avoid them. It's slow going, and occasionally I call the group to duck behind fallen trees to hide.

But as we watch the darkness ahead with anticipation, nothing crosses our path. Sending out my dark wave, what I had just sensed is no longer there. The third time this happens, Pan audibly sighs in irritation.

"Something bothering you?" I ask as I stand. The others join me, and we resume our journey.

"Are you sure you know where you're going?" His dark eyes dart from branch to branch, searching for hidden dangers.

"Is that a real question?" My tone rises with my offense at the implication. The Labyrinth has been working against us the entire journey, and these woods are no different. The path moves, vanishes, and reappears elsewhere as if the ground and trees constantly shift.

"It feels like we're walking in circles and we're not getting very far with you being paranoid every few minutes."

"You're welcome to take your own path out if you feel that would be best." I offer him an alternative. "This forest is alive and is a maze that is constantly moving, so sorry this is not the walk in the park you were hoping for."

Pan holds my gaze but ultimately knows there is nothing more to be done. Following my powers is our best bet to make it out in one piece.

"We're heading to the Geryon's pit through the Burning Desert, so I guess we'll see you there!" I add a fake chipper tone and keep walking.

Hermes walks by my side, saying nothing but with a slight smirk on his face. After a few moments, I glance at him and see his grin widen.

"Something funny?" I jab his side, smirking.

He puts his arm around me and turns my head, stealing a kiss as we walk. *"You're sexy when you're pissed off."*

I let out a small chuckle. It's brief, but it cuts through the tension, lightening the load, if only for a moment. Hermes' ability to lift my spirits even in dire circumstances is something I deeply cherish.

I smack his chest playfully. *"Well, he's being an asshole. It's not like this is easy. I mean, it's called the Pathless Wood for a reason, for goddess' sake."*

"You're doing great, baby."

Distracted by my irritation and talking with Hermes, I don't sense the change in energy around us until it coats us in a cold sense of dread. I nearly stumble into what I initially think is another twisted tree. But the shape is too symmetrical, too deliberate. I stop abruptly, and as my eyes adjust, the chilling truth becomes apparent. What stands before us is not a tree, but a person: a Shade.

The realization sends a shiver down my spine. Shades are tragic figures; once humans, they were killed by creatures of darkness. Their souls, unable to find peace, are bound to the dark energies that destroyed them. They are eternally restless, doomed to wander in search of solace that will forever elude them.

Understanding the potential danger, I motion silently to the group, and we quickly find cover behind a nearby large tree. We watch the Shade from our hiding spot. It keeps its back to us, moving almost aimlessly, its form flickering like a shadow against the forest backdrop. The sadness of its existence is palpable, even from a distance.

Hermes leans closer to whisper in my ear but loud enough for the others to hear. "It's new," he murmurs, a mix of relief and concern. "See how it moves? Lost, confused... it doesn't have the resentment that older Shades show. It hasn't turned bitter yet."

The Shade's aimless wandering underscores his point. It pauses frequently, turning in slow, disoriented circles, as if trying to recognize something in its surroundings or itself.

Older Shades develop a drive fueled by their deepening despair and anger towards the living.

Pan nods in agreement, his earlier frustration forgotten in the face of this new threat. "How do we get past it?" he asks quietly.

"The only way you get rid of darkness." A small orb of blue starlight forms in Hermes' hand. "Light."

The Shade turns, revealing familiar features twisted into a spectral form. Hermes and I take a sharp breath in shock. I feel the color drain from my cheeks as chills rush down my body. We know this Shade.

"Odysseus..." Hermes murmurs, his voice breaking with sorrow. His hands, poised to cast the orb of light, now tremble slightly.

My heart aches at the cruel twist of fate that turned a fierce warrior and leader into a wandering shadow. Odysseus and Penelope died recently in the Battle of the Triple Moon Eclipse, and knowing he's condemned to this shadow existence deepens the tragedy.

"Do you think Penelope is here too?" My eyes widen at the thought. Hermes' face darkens with sorrow at the prospect they are both here.

"I don't know."

Composing himself, Hermes casts the faint orb of light just to the side of Odysseus. The Shade, still confused, reacts on instinct to the element that is its opposite. Walking onward, the Shade that used to be our friend disappears to wander forever in the shadows of the Pathless Wood.

We find Penelope, a Shade like Odysseus. Rhea cries as she watches them pass each other. They stop and seem to look at each other. Both reach out their hands as if yearning for the other. Their touch is just a breath away before they drop their hands to their sides and continue on their opposing paths.

"That's exactly how I found them." Rhea has been walking with her head down for the last ten minutes. She sniffs softly, wiping a fresh tear from her cheek. "When I used the Echoes to see the battle. To see when Cal–"

Her voice breaks, and she pauses to compose herself.

"To see when Callie and Achilles destroyed the wards." She avoids saying when they died. "That's how I found their bodies. Right next to each other, looking at the other, hands outstretched but..."

Rhea looks at the ground again, then shakes her head. "In that final moment, they just wanted to hold each other, and they couldn't." She looks back as if they will be behind us. "Now, they'll be like that forever."

Wrapping her arms around herself, a fresh wave of sobs breaks out. I stop walking and hold her, shushing her as I stroke her hair. "I don't know if a Shade can be helped." Putting my hands on each side of her face, I tilt her head up until she looks at me. "But we'll do everything we can to try."

She nods, and I hold her a moment longer. When she squeezes me just a bit more, I do as well. I'd keep her in my arms forever, never letting her go if it were possible.

We find more Shades in various states, and Rhea makes sure we avoid them perfectly. She has a visceral reaction when we happen upon a flock of Harpies gathered around an immortal prisoner. Ripping the prisoner's flesh and feasting on its innards, the Harpies consume the prisoner like vultures feasting on a rotting carcass.

Several hours pass before we finally emerge from the dense shadows of the Pathless Wood. The stark contrast of the Burning Desert stretches before us. The air shimmers with heat, and the ground beneath our feet shifts from rich earth to scorching sand. The sky burns, giving the appearance of a sun.

Sweat forms on our brows in an instant, and the heat increases the second we clear the tree line. We pause at the desert's edge.

"Well, at least we found our way through the woods." Rhea shields her eyes with her hand as she looks across the Burning Desert.

Patches of fire roar without ceasing, spewing black smoke into a column that rises above us. It is a windless flat expanse with a river running through it.

The sound of the boiling water is a low, menacing rumble as bubbles rise up, popping on the surface. Angry plumes of sulfuric steam roll constantly off the surface of the boiling river. The immediate need to rush to the riverbank for sustenance tells us it is poison. The thick, viscous water is so saturated with the toxin, it is like syrup.

Rhea looks at the river as if deciding if it would be worth it to jump in and bathe. She licks her lips and wipes her mouth on the sleeve of her tactical shirt.

I feel her hunger and thirst through our bond. While I also want rest and sustenance, it is not the same weariness that falls over me as an immortal.

Rhea is still part mortal and needs nourishment to survive. What she has restored of her powers and immortality will help, but that fragility remains, adding another sense of urgency to conquer the Labyrinth.

"Can you find the pit of the Geryon?" I ask and watch Rhea concentrate on what she reads from her powers. Opening her eyes when she finds it, she points toward a distant rise in the terrain where the heat distorts the air into wavy lines of obscurity.

As we trek across the desert, the oppressive heat tests our endurance. Kellan and Pan, although visibly affected by the heat, maintain a steady pace. Rhea mumbles something about *"more fucking sand,"* her recent voyage to Tartarus still a fresh memory.

Delta struggles most of all. The injury to his hand and the toxins spreading within him cause a strain that he is trying hard to hide. "What is a Geryon, anyway?"

"I have only heard of them," Pan answers. "Though I have never seen one, I know they are a great winged beast. They are said to be quite hideous."

"Oh, this place just gets better and better," Kellan mutters as he wipes his brow.

The sight of the emaciated prisoners wandering aimlessly

across the Burning Desert adds a haunting layer to the already stark landscape. Their power-suppressing collars gleam dully under the harsh heat. They shuffle past, their eyes vacant, lost to whatever torments the Labyrinth has inflicted upon them.

I maintain a watchful eye as several immortal prisoners near. My hand rests lightly on the handle of my sheathed sword. The air around us thickens with a growing sense of uncertainty if these prisoners have ill intentions.

Delta, Kellan, Pan, and I surround Rhea, ready to protect her should something happen. She keeps her hand on the hilt of her dagger, also ready but restraining herself from pulling her weapon.

The sorrow-filled stare of the prisoners does nothing but fill us with despair for them, and it seems they look upon us with the same pity. As if we share an understanding that the Labyrinth makes victims of all those who pass through its door.

Kellan, adjusting his bow, looks at a passing prisoner. "Let's hope this is the worst we encounter." Though we all know the greatest terrors the Labyrinth holds are yet to come.

"I wouldn't say that too loud if I were you." Delta's tone is sarcastic, but seriousness undercuts his comment. "The Labyrinth may hear you and take that as a challenge."

Behind us, a prisoner, his body worn thin by the endless walking, collapses onto the charred sand with a dull thud. The impact sends a small cloud of dust swirling into the dry air.

The group halts, instinctively turning back as a debate sparks from Kellan of all people. "Should we help?" his voice tinged with concern, yet cautious perhaps due to the interaction regarding Zephyr.

Pan looks conflicted but wary. "It could be dangerous," he

counters, eyeing the surrounding desert as if expecting the landscape itself to turn against us. "We don't know if—"

Before he can finish, the air changes. It crackles with energy, an electric tension that raises the hairs on the back of my neck. My eyes widen as a powerful bolt of lightning strikes down from the clear sky, hitting the fallen prisoner directly. The sight is shocking, almost unreal, as the desert around us is devoid of clouds.

The first bolt is followed by another, then another—each strike a continuous, unyielding assault on the prisoner's body. The sand around him turns to glass, heated to extreme temperatures by the electrical onslaught.

"We need to move!" I shout, grabbing Rhea by the arm and pulling her back as the group instinctively retreats. "It's not safe!"

As we put distance between ourselves and the scene, the electrical strikes continue, a relentless display of power that seems too targeted, too controlled to be natural. "What is this?" Rhea breathes out, her face a mask of horror at the spectacle.

"It's like a punishment," I speculate, watching, unable to look away. "Maybe the Labyrinth itself is enforcing some kind of rule of their sentencing."

The strikes eventually cease, leaving behind a silence that feels as heavy as the desert air. The sand where the prisoner had fallen is nothing more than a glistening patch of glass. The air above it shimmers with residual heat. A wind rises, whipping around and adding a momentary reprieve from the constant burn of the terrain. The surrounding sand covers the spot where the prisoner collapses. The evidence of what has just occurred is erased.

We walk on in silence, shaken from the encounter.

When another prisoner collapses just as the previous one had, and the same gruesome punishment is imposed—a storm of lightning strikes reducing the unfortunate soul to nothing—it cements a chilling pattern in my mind.

Rhea's voice cuts through the heavy silence, her tone filled with sorrow as she voices my very thought. "Do you think... they have to keep walking forever? Is that the punishment here?" Her question hangs between us, disturbing yet making a terrible kind of sense.

The idea that these prisoners are bound by such a relentless, unforgiving imprisonment—walk or be obliterated—casts a shadow over our group, deepening the grim understanding of our surroundings.

I see the weariness of the persistent heat bearing down upon the others. I feel the suppressing scorch weighing down each step we take. The desire to just take rest, even if for a moment, is all too great. I can't imagine an eternity of this, never able to have a moment of respite.

"No matter what, we have to keep going." My voice is steady, but inside, my heart races with the same fears that I see reflected in the eyes of my companions. If we stop walking, will we meet the same fate? "Can you tell how far away the pit is now?"

A momentary pause, and then Rhea answers. "We're not that far away now. Maybe another hour?" Scrunching her forehead, she wipes her mouth with her sleeve. "I'm not sure how much time has passed, actually, but we're close."

With the knowledge that the pit of the Geryon is near, a tangible shift in the atmosphere among us takes hold. The weariness that has draped over our shoulders like a heavy cloak lightens somewhat, replaced by a renewed stamina.

Rhea's estimation that we are merely an hour away from our destination injects a fresh surge of energy into our strides, despite the oppressive heat of the Burning Desert and the haunting memories of the punished prisoners. Even Delta has a renewed pace, the prospect of being done with this desert giving us hope.

As we near an outcrop of jagged rocks that rise ominously from the sands, we take caution. The Labyrinth has taught us that nothing is as benign as it appears, and we approach the pit with wariness.

Peering around the massive boulders, we discover a deep, dark crevasse cutting through the ground like a wound. Its depths are shrouded in shadows, but there is a sense of endlessness to this hole in the Labyrinth.

On a narrow ridge within the crevasse, the massive form of the Geryon rests. The creature is more formidable in appearance than its name suggests—multi-headed, each head bearing massive fangs that pierce the darkness. Its body is a tangle of wings and a long tail, like the body of a snake giving way to that of a bat. But it is the faces on the heads where I think the hideousness comes from. Aside from the fangs, the faces on each of the three heads look human, even capped with dark wavy hair.

"Is it asleep?" Pan whispers, squinting to make out the details in the dim light.

"It looks like it," Kellan replies, an arrow at the ready in his bow. "But we should assume it could wake at any moment. It could attack seeing us this close to its nest."

We pull back, taking cover behind the outcrop to discuss what kind of payment the Geryon would accept.

"Maybe it wants a prisoner, you know, to eat." Delta's

suggestion that it might require the sacrifice of a prisoner causes a visceral reaction within me. I can't stomach the idea, and neither can Rhea, who quickly dismisses it.

"We won't be sacrificing anyone," she declares with conviction.

Pan, looking frustrated, counters. "Rhea, your compassion is commendable, but it might put us all at risk. We need to consider all options if we're to get past this creature and secure what we came for."

Before I can weigh in and support Rhea's stance, the atmosphere shifts ominously as a blast of warm air hits us. The abrupt silence is cut by the scraping of talon on stone. We turn toward the pit, knowing what we will find, causing us all to move slowly.

The winged beast has awakened and is slowly creeping its several heads out of the pit. Rhea stumbles, taking a cautious step back, and I move slowly in front of her.

The Geryon is far more imposing up close than it had been far below, sleeping on its ridge. Its large claws grip the edge of the rocks, anchoring its massive body as several heads rise from the darkness, each one more menacing than the last. The creature's yellow eyes, glowing with a predatory light, fixate on us as it continues to rise over the pit's edge.

The tension mounts as the Geryon heaves its immense body out of the pit. Its snake-like torso and massive arms, tipped with razor-sharp claws, scrape against the sand, sending a shiver of dread through us all. The air becomes as still as death, none of us daring to move.

Kellan shifts to nock an arrow, and the Geryon's three heads snap to him. Rhea's hand shoots out, gripping his arm with a quiet intensity. "No," she whispers sharply, her eyes locked on the Geryon. Kellan slowly lowers his bow, understanding the precariousness of our situation.

The Geryon continues its slow, deliberate advance across our group. Each of its heads, horrific in their own right with slithering tongues and deep-set, calculating eyes, moves independently. They lean in close, sniffing each of us with a curiosity that feels almost exploratory. The moment is surreal, each breath I take laden with fear and awe.

When one of the Geryon's heads hovers near me, it pauses at my abdomen, sniffing more intently. A low, guttural noise vibrates from its throat, drawing the attention of the other heads. Soon, all of them are focused on me, their collective gaze unsettling and intense.

The creature steps back slightly, its many eyes still fixed on me, as if it expects something. I feel the weight of its stare, like a physical pressure. "Okay, so I'm the poor bastard getting stuck with paying the toll, it seems."

"Do you think you are supposed to fight it?" Pan suggests in a low tone, speaking slowly.

"Gods, I hope not."

Putting my hands on the leather strap of my scabbard, the heads of the Geryon lower and issue a defensive growl. Raising my hands in resignation, I move slowly again, feeling for the items I am carrying that it could possibly want.

When my hand touches the silver metal of my belt buckle, the Geryon's heads rise attentively. "My belt?" Watching with caution, I begin to remove my belt with slow precision. Once I remove the strap from my pants and hold it up, the center head of the Geryon leans in.

Its split tongue slithers out of its fanged mouth, then wraps around the offering. Pulling my belt into its mouth, it lifts its head, chewing several times, then swallowing my belt.

"Is this for real?" Rhea says in disbelief.

The Geryon shakes its body, stretching the large bat-like wings. Leaning a shoulder to the ground, it waits for us to climb up.

"Okay, well–" I am just as stunned as Rhea, not sure what to say or do next. "Looks like our Uber is ready."

"Shut up." Rhea gives me a smack to the arm, then heads toward the beast's shoulder. Holding on to the ridges along its back, she climbs on, sitting close to its neck.

I settle in behind her and lean close, speaking into her ear. "Is your seatbelt buckled?" I kiss her neck quickly, then move out of range of an oncoming slap. Instead, she pinches my thigh.

"Behave yourself while we ride a giant monster through a prison of torment." She hides her amusement behind the air of frustration she projects, and it only makes me smile more.

Nessus has warned that the next step of our path to the Labyrinth's center will be the most dangerous yet. My moment of teasing is quickly suffocated by the overwhelming anticipation of what we are going to face in the Malebolge.

Wrapping my arm around my goddess, I send three pulses down the tether of our souls. When she feels it, she leans back into me, her hand covering mine.

"I love you too."

With one mighty flap of its large wings, the Geryon lifts off the sands of the Burning Desert, diving into it's dark and cavernous pit as we descend deeper into the Labyrinth.

The descent into the abyss is nothing short of terrifying. The Geryon dives with a speed that pulls the air from our lungs, causing our eyes to water and our grips to tighten in fear of being thrown into the void. The wind howls around us, a mournful sound that echoes the darkness rushing past. Each of us holds on with a mix of determination and fear, each second of our plunge threatening to eject us.

Hermes' arms on each side of me hold on to the bony ridges of the Geryon's tough hide. My thighs squeeze hard, fighting to remain in place.

Unfurling its great wings, the Geryon's flight path shifts dramatically from a near-vertical plummet to a gentle and even flight. The air rushes out of my lungs, and the change in force pushes my torso down to the Geryon's back.

Sitting up, we all reposition ourselves, each of us looking to the others to make sure we didn't lose anyone. One of the Geryon's large heads turns, the long serpentine neck turning back to us as well, as if the beast is making sure its passengers are still aboard.

The rushing wind is now a gentle breeze as we emerge from the depths of the crevasse, meeting an awe-inspiring sight.

Before us stretches an incredibly large mountain range, its peaks vast and numerous, each one rising sharply against the smoky sky.

Dwarfing any of the great mountains of Gaea, black snow occasionally rolls off a peak, stirred by the violent, rushing winds.

The arrangement of these mountains forms a natural labyrinth, a maze of stone and shadow that spreads across the horizon. The sight is both beautiful and daunting, and I consider the warning from Nessus.

Attempting to cross this mountain range would have likely cost us additional lives and an incredible amount of time. Leaning forward, I rub and pat the hard hide of our transportation. The head on the far right turns back slightly, and I think it passes me an appreciative glare—it's difficult to tell with the beast's harsh features.

The cold wind is like knives stinging my skin, but even still, I am thankful for the time to rest. Hermes rubs his warm hands along my thighs and arms before wrapping me in his embrace. He passes warmth to me through our bond, and I reach behind me, cupping his cheek and giving him a quick peck. "Thank you for taking care of me."

Hermes smiles softly, brushing strands of hair from my face. "Always, little goddess," he whispers, his voice gentle against the cold. "Until the stars fade into the abyss."

The winged beast navigates through the maze of towering peaks with expert ease. Within an hour, the horizon beyond shifts from dull and smoky gray to a dramatic canvas of orange and red hues, an ominous yet mesmerizing skyline that marks our destination.

"The heart of the Labyrinth," I murmur to myself. My

voice carries a hint of dread that resonates across our small group. The closer we get, the more palpable our collective anxiety becomes at what awaits us in the Malebolge.

The Geryon's flight over the mountainous terrain has saved us days of perilous trekking, yet it has also hurried our arrival at what we know to be the most perilous part of our journey.

Delta, clenching and unclenching his injured hand, looks toward the fiery horizon. "It's like flying into a forge."

He's not wrong. It's like this mountain range is nestled inside a large volcano, and we're nearing the sea of magma that lives within it.

Hecate doubted we would have hidden the staff within the Malebolge and then debated herself thinking it could be the best hiding place. Home of the worst beasts and monsters of the Labyrinth, it's the ring of the prison the darkest of creatures avoid.

The ten pits of the Malebolge form concentric circles around the Labyrinth's topmost level. From Nessus' advice, climbing over the tall walls that separate each pit is the fastest route and, with any luck, the safest.

The Geryon changes course, flying to one side of a tall mountain. The burning Malebolge glows on the other side of the ridge. Flapping its large wings and straightening its body to land on one of the sheer mountainsides, we hang on again to avoid slipping off its back and plummeting into the darkness below.

The beast's strong arms and long talons scrape the rocky mountain, and it shuffles along the near-vertical face, clinging to it like a bat, its long tail curled below us. I realize it's creeping toward a large cave opening. Not big enough for the Geryon to land in, so we're going to have to climb off the beast's back.

The Geryon pauses at the opening, the path to the cave precarious as I dig my fingers into the ridges of its back. My boots search for a foothold as I work my way closer to the mountain. Using the dip where the Geryon's wing meets his back, I launch myself off, landing with a roll within the cave's mouth.

Hermes follows my path, landing more gracefully than I did in a crouch.

"Show off," I mutter to him. He gives me a wink, and his crooked grin reveals the dimple in his cheek as he offers me his hand to help me stand.

We move out of the way as Pan follows us into the cave. Delta is next, the climb made difficult by his rotting hand. As he grimaces and climbs, he loses his footing, slipping down with a yelp.

Kellan reaches out, grabbing the collar of Delta's tactical vest and helping hoist him back up as Delta works to find his footing again. My breath holds in my lungs, and my heart stops beating as I watch them strain to hang onto the monster's back. Finally, the immortals reach the top of the Geryon and exit its back together. My shoulders drop as I release my strained breath.

Feeling its payload has been deposited, the Geryon scratches its way along the mountainside, turning its large body toward the ground before taking off into another dive. Opening its wings, the wind catches, and the Geryon soars upward, flying away over the vast mountain range.

Inspecting our landing pad, a pungent odor, warm and putrid, assaults our senses and burns our eyes from deep within the cave. The same reddish-orange glow that burned in the sky is emitted from an opening further into this cave.

A wave of repulsion hits me—the air is foul, tainted with a stench that speaks of decay and forgotten ages. I take the short break as a moment to acclimate to the smell as bile threatens to rise from my throat.

Kellan ventures in to find the opening while Pan takes a moment to tend to Delta's hand. There is not much more that can be done, but Pan tries to help by applying a numbing salve and something for the pain.

"The opening is just around this bend," Kellan announces as he returns, taking a moment to adjust his bow and secure his quiver of arrows.

A pervasive hum fills the atmosphere around us and seems almost alive, vibrating through the very ground beneath our feet, unyielding and constant. It feels like the heart of the Labyrinth is alive, beating within the giant cavern of the immortal prison.

We advance cautiously into the cave, the oppressive darkness gradually succumbing to the dim light from the entrance. As we navigate the uneven ground, our footsteps echo eerily back at us, adding to the tension as we keep watch for the monsters that live within the Labyrinth's center.

The break in the cave's interior is like a burning ember as smoke wafts into the cave. As I look through the doorway to our next journey, the sight before me sends a menacing shiver down my spine.

The Malebolge is a vast and terrifying expanse that stretches out in a series of pits, each more menacing than the last, leading to the center of the Labyrinth. The design is meticulous, an engineered nightmare crafted to torment and contain.

"Remind me to tell Hecate I hate her for designing this."

Hermes leans over, speaking low as he surveys our next series of obstacles. I snort a laugh, but there is no humor in this.

My eyes rake over each pit, taking in anything visible from our spot high on the ridge. Smoke and steam rise from different pits, and we feel an occasional tremor under our feet, like small earthquakes.

"Rhea, look." Hermes points to the farthest pit. Beyond it is a large expanse of open space. Roaming within are three giants. The largest of them, a cyclops.

"Oh, my gods," I breathe out, amazed by their hulking size. The cyclops steals my intrigue most of all for the many arms he has. I count five arms on each side of his torso and can't imagine what it would be like to move around with so many appendages.

Dread takes me over as I think of how we are to get past them, but I don't have time to dwell on it too long before a high-pitched ringing in my ears overpowers the hum. My eye travels upward, just above the heads of the three giants to a platform at the farthest rock wall.

The arched opening, a deeper darkness than the rest of the interior mountain, thrums at me, and I choke a sob. Grasping Hermes' forearm, I raise my hand to my mouth in disbelief while tears brim in my eyes.

"I feel it." Hope floods me amidst the daunting view, and for the first time since we entered this twisted and tormenting prison, I feel that familiar tug—a pull that resonates deep within my soul. It's my missing powers, calling to me. A beacon from the very heart of this malevolent maze.

I can't help but laugh as I cry, turning to my mate. Hermes is smiling, tears brimming in his rich blue eyes. He pulls me into him, his strong arms holding me in a tight embrace as he nuzzles into my neck.

Around us, the others join in our chorus of joy.

"Amazing." Pan mutters to himself, a smile breaching his stoic face for the first time since I've met him. Kellan smiles widely, clapping Delta on the back.

"We're so close, baby." Hermes whispers before he pulls away and cups my cheek with his large hand. "Are you ready?"

I can only nod my head, and he pulls me in, kissing my forehead and giving me another hug.

Pulled out of the reverie, Kellan turns serious as he places his fist over his heart. "No matter the cost." Delta follows and repeats the mantra, then Pan, as our last trio of protectors renew their vow to follow us into the darkness of the Labyrinth.

Hermes takes my chin between his thumb and forefinger. His sapphire gaze searches me, the promise of his steadfast protection evident in his resolve. "No matter the cost."

The weight of the words from his mouth is too much to bear. He's conveying so much more than those four simple words mean. He's telling me, if he dies, that I have to keep going. I can't stop until I'm reunited with my powers.

The thought of losing him to this horror is too much. Thinking of his body rotting here within this tormenting darkness makes my chest pull tight, my heart skipping several beats. Panic tries to wrap its skeletal claws around my throat as the edges of my vision darken.

Blinking quickly, I take several steadying breaths, chasing away the panic wanting to consume me. "When I fight Loki, you'll be by my side. And I'll accept no argument about it." I try to force as much bravado and command into my voice, but it cracks anyway, buckling under the flood of emotions at the thought of losing my mate.

"Anything you want, little goddess." He smirks, but his tone is heavy, knowing he may be making a promise he can't keep. With a final kiss, he rubs the tip of his nose against mine and takes my hand. "The power of Death awaits you. Let's go get it."

We descend from the cave with careful precision. Every movement is calculated to avoid detection, every breath stifled, as we try to move silently through the shadows. The Malebolge sprawls before us, and my eyes rake over the ringed pits as I catalog the dangers awaiting us.

As we reach the ground, our pace quickens to a swift, crouched run, darting along the shadows that cling to the walls. The wails and moans of the tormented souls trapped within the pits claw at my conscience. It's a sound that pierces through the heart, resonating with a pain knowing we can do nothing to help end their torment right now.

We approach the fifty-foot-tall wall of the first pit, the obstacle formidable but not impossible. I pause, pressing my back against the cool, rough earth, scanning the area for any signs of immediate danger. The constant wailing of the prisoners continues to echo around us, a haunting companion to our grim task.

"These prisoners," I murmur under my breath to Rhea, who is crouched beside me, her eyes scanning the horizon for any movement. "They don't deserve this. No one does."

Rhea nods silently, her expression hard with the same

resolve that tightens my chest. "We'll make this right," she whispers back, "We'll come back and make this right."

And we will.

We have a responsibility to the souls suffering within this demented maze. After Rhea has been made whole and Loki pays for the injustice he has spread across the realms, we will return here. We'll dismantle every brick and bring light to every shadow until there is nothing left of the Labyrinth.

I push those thoughts to the back of my mind and lock them up, focusing on the task at hand. Shifting my gaze upward, I assess the wall's structure, looking for handholds and footholds that will aid in our climb.

"Let's move," I signal to Kellan and Pan, who are positioned a few feet away, Delta on the other side of us. Together, we begin our ascent, our movements synchronized and silent, our expressions focused on overcoming the first of many barriers before us.

Reaching the top of the wall, it's thick, wide enough for our party to walk side-by-side if we wished. Crawling on my belly, careful to keep low, I make my way across the wall and peek over, inspecting the first pit we need to cross.

It's like an untamed garden of dead brush and thin dried vines. Shades crowd the space below with vacant, cloudy expressions. Some wander in benign circles. Others are caught up in tangles of foliage, swaying back and forth as the vines wrapped around them keep them in place.

While there appears to be no immediate danger within this first pit, we know that is the great lie of this hellscape. We must be ready for anything and never forget—everything here is starving.

"Shades," I whisper, letting the others know what awaits us.

Slowly, I swing my legs over the wall, carefully trying not to disturb the foliage. Helping Rhea over, we begin the slow climb down as the others follow us.

The thin vines have tiny thorns that act like Velcro, sticking to our clothes and stabbing our hands. Reaching into the foliage, we're able to find our holds to climb down with relative ease.

We keep to the same path, forming a line as we descend deeper into the pit.

Pausing before I reach the bottom, I cast a faint glowing orb, barely emitting any light. It serves its purpose, just as it did in the Pathless Wood, gently coaxing the Shades away from us so we have a crossing point.

Safely on the ground, I help Rhea down and we look down each side of the pit. Our eyes take in every detail and movement, our senses all on high alert. The walls around us are fifty feet tall, and the pit is just as wide. Only the Fates know what traps could be waiting for us.

With my hand on the base of Rhea's back, I urge her forward. "Go." In another crouched run, she hurries across the pit, and I don't blink until she reaches the other side.

The Shades are still subdued and take no notice, so I cross the pit along with Delta. "Let's climb," I urge my little goddess, and she starts working her way up.

"I wish you were more like Achilles." Rhea's voice is like a ribbon, caught on the currents of the wind and stops me instantly.

"What did you just say?" I ask, my voice tinged with a mixture of confusion and offense.

Rhea turns, her brow furrowed as she clings to the wall. "I didn't say anything." She whispers loudly back. "And keep your voice down." She turns back, focusing on her finger-holds, then looking down for her foot placement before hoisting herself up.

With a shake of my head, I release the offending words to the shadows of the Malebolge and start my climb. Delta is by my side, struggling with his damaged hand but trying not to let it slow us down. Sweat gathers at his hairline, and his complexion seems more pallid than usual.

Pan and Kellan dart across the pit as easily as the rest of us. Pausing midway up the wall, I glance back at the Shades. They have filled in the pit again as if we were never there to disturb them.

A slow rolling fog creeps along the floor of the pit that I hadn't noticed before. It swirls as the Shades shuffle along and makes me think of the fog that confused us when we first entered the Labyrinth. "Hey, was that fog there before?" I whisper to Rhea.

"Maybe if you were paying attention, you would have seen it."

What the fuck?

I climb the next few paces quickly, catching up to her. "What is your deal?"

"What do you mean? I'm just trying to climb up." She's breathless with the physical exertion of our task. "Can you wait until we're at the top?"

I nod my head, trying to brush off the irritation in her earlier reply. This is incredibly stressful, and maybe she's just focusing.

My thoughts slow my pace, and looking around, I see the

others are nearing the top of the wall. Rhea is the first to swing her legs over. Delta is next in joining her at the top, so I stretch a little further with each step, meeting them in a few paces.

As soon as I breach the wall, I see Delta with his hand on her cheek. Rhea is looking at him with a smile on her face. He pulls his hand away quickly as Rhea blinks away her smile. My blood heats with anger as I set myself at the top of the tall wall of the second pit.

"This next pit is only prisoners, so I'm going to head on down." Delta whispers and then throws his legs over, starting the track down.

"Did he just touch you?"

"Who? Delta?" Rhea looks at me with confusion. "Why would he touch me?"

"If you mention my mate one more time, I'll rip your tongue from your mouth." Pan is seething as he talks with clenched teeth at Kellan. His finger pokes Kellan's chest to emphasize the last few words.

"I don't give a shit about your fucking mate, but touch me again and I'll burn you like dried shrubs." Kellan sneers back at Pan.

What is happening?

My mind is rattled at how the tone of our small band can turn against each other so quickly. We've had a few disagreements, but everyone understands the greater mission and its importance.

"You two knock it off." My whisper carries along the top of the wall, but they hold their glare on each other a second longer. Kellan is the one to break away first, throwing his legs over and beginning the climb down.

Releasing a frustrated sigh, I look back to my mate. "What

is their problem all of a sudden?" Rhea looks as confused as I am.

"I don't know. Just stay close to me, okay?" She nods, and I reach out, my hand gently holding her neck as I rest my forehead against hers.

"We're going to be okay." Rhea reassures me, and it washes away the aggravation.

Nearing the bottom of the second pit, my stomach heaves at the stench. Brown sludge like raw sewage is knee-deep on some of the prisoners within the pit. Several of them notice us but give no alarm of our intrusion.

Looking to my side, I take a breath, ready to tell Rhea I'll carry her across the sludge, but she's not here. Delta is already carrying her as he wades across the pit. Her arms are around his neck, and she throws her head back laughing at something he said like they are at a fucking party or something.

My stomach flips as shock and anger compete within me. I swear to the gods, Delta won't make it to the next wall touching my mate again.

Moving my foot and handhold too quickly, I slide down the wall as it becomes increasingly slicker. Securing my hold, I look back to the pit again quickly, ready to call out to Rhea. But a cold wave of surprise freezes me.

Rhea is still by my side, climbing down the wall with me, and Delta has just reached the bottom and stands there alone.

I'm losing my fucking mind.

"I really don't want to get in that sludge." Rhea grimaces. Looking at me, she drops her expression as concern washes over her. "What's wrong?" She asks, her question oozing with worry.

My heart is pounding in my chest, and I catch my breath

from the rush of adrenaline. "Nothing." I shake my head, clearing the image from my mind. "I thought I saw something, but it was nothing."

"Okay." She accepts my explanation, but the worry doesn't leave her face. "You're sure you're okay?"

"Yeah, I'm good." My heart is settling, and I'm able to relax some of the tension in my expression. Rhea's worry softens, and she resumes her climb down.

"Okay, let's go get in the shit pit." She scoffs.

"I'll carry you across." Before she can answer me, Delta whistles quietly, getting our attention. We freeze where we are on the wall, unsure if there is an oncoming threat.

"The ledge." He whispers up at us, pointing along the perimeter of the pit. He shuffles sideways, keeping his body against the wall. Following the path of the ledge, it wraps around the pit to the other side.

"Oh, thank the goddess." Rhea breathes a sigh of relief that she will be spared from having to get into the watery sewage below.

When we reach the bottom, I'm relieved to see Kellan is in front of Rhea, and Pan is behind me. Hopefully, with some separation, these two can calm down.

"I heard your little mate likes to get all her holes fucked." Pan's voice in my ear makes me spin around in a blink. Grabbing the edges of his bark armor, I pull him to me. My jaw is clenched to keep from head butting him, which is what I really want to do.

"I don't care what Kellan said to piss you off, but you keep *my* mate out of your mind and her name out of your mouth." I push him back as I release him, keeping my heated gaze on him.

He says nothing but just returns my glare.

A flurry of whispers sound behind me, and I turn back around toward Rhea.

She has not moved across the ledge yet. Her eyes are ignited with shock at what just happened. She grabs my elbow, pulling me closer.

"What the fuck is going on with you guys?" She's whispering very loudly, and several prisoners stop their trudging through the muck to watch us.

"Shhh. Keep quiet." I try to calm her, my eyes darting from the prisoners back to her.

With her hand still holding me, her face turns from shock to curiosity as she moves her hand down my arm. "What is this?" She squeezes my arm, moving her grip down until she is holding my wrist.

Moving back the sleeve of my tactical shirt, a small thorn is embedded in my skin. Probably stuck into me from the first pit. She clicks her tongue against the roof of her mouth as she pulls the barb from my skin.

The second it's out, it feels like clouds lift from my mind. The whispers of a thousand voices silence in an instant, and I release a deep breath, like I've been holding it since the first wall.

"Better now?" She rubs her thumb across the spot where the thorn was and smiles at me sweetly.

"Yeah," Fuck. In an instant I realize how ridiculous I was not realizing I was hallucinating. Toxins from the thorn seeping into my blood and fucking with me. "I'm sorry."

"I need you, okay?" Her expression turns serious. "This place is going to try to destroy us, so we need to stay sharp and call out anything that seems odd, no matter how far-fetched it appears."

"You're right. It just seemed so real." I shake my head in disbelief at what I heard and saw. I should have known it was an illusion. An attempt of the carnivorous prison to prepare us to be its next meal.

"This is real." She puts her hand on my chest, and our bond warms, flooding me with calming reassurance. "It's just you and me." She nods, reaffirming her sentiments with a kiss.

"You and me." I repeat.

Rhea keeps hold of my hand as she starts her path along the ledge, balancing carefully to keep from tipping into the sludge.

Ahead of her, she gets Kellan's attention, telling him to check himself for thorns, and I do the same to Pan.

Kellan pats himself, then shakes his head. "I'm clear."

"I'm fine." Pan seethes, most certainly not fine.

Across the Malebolge, a beast roars loudly. It echoes across the pits, and we pause. Rhea's face turns pink, then red as we listen for the roar to stop. "Was that the Minotaur?"

"I don't know." My eyes scan the top of the pit. "I don't think it could track us over the mountains, but if it did, it would take days to get here and we'll be long gone."

My mate doesn't look any less worried. "Unless there are other paths."

It's a possibility. This Labyrinth is endless and expansive. There is no telling the secrets it holds. "Let's just keep moving." I give her a reassuring smile, hoping the concentration on traversing the pits will be enough to distract her from the dangers that may be hunting us.

The next pit we pass with relative ease, given it was thick quicksand.

The prisoners were just standing, stuck at various stages of sinking. Some were only sunk to their ankles and were still walking, staying in constant motion to avoid sinking further. The prisoners who were waist-deep just stood still as if accepting the sand was going to slowly consume them.

Rhea held on to my back as I walked into the sand. Holding my sword in front of me like a staff, I used it to pull us through. "Oh, my gods, Hermes." Rhea exclaims, her voice tinged with fear. "Look."

Directly next to us, no more than a foot away, is a prisoner. All that can be seen is the top of their forehead, the rest of them swallowed within the sand.

"Don't look, baby."

She sniffs and blows out a strong breath like she's trying to keep herself from crying. "Okay." Her voice strains as she tilts her head up, looking to the rocky ceiling high above us.

Pan used his powers of Life to make his tree-like legs long and walked across with Delta on his back. The Shifter struggles more with each pit, his condition worsening. Kellan used his bow in the same manner I did my sword and crossed with us.

Working our way up the wall to the fourth pit, Rhea is tiring. Her climb is slower, and her arms shake as she nears the top. I help push her up as she heaves herself over.

Her chest rises and falls rapidly with her quick breathing as she lays down. Joining her, I rub her tired arms and reassure her. "You're doing so good, baby."

The others join us, and Pan gives me a pointed look. "Delta needs a break for a few minutes."

Nodding in agreement, I keep working on massaging Rhea's muscles as she catches her breath. "Five minutes."

I wish I had some water and food for her. The ship's biscuits we had from the Sirens wore off long ago, and I know Rhea needs nourishment.

As Rhea and Delta catch their breath, I look over the fourth pit with Kellan. It's deceptively empty, and neither of us trust it. We share a look edged with doubt as a single prisoner emerges from around the bend of the large pit.

Like the others, it's bound with a collar, and its emaciated form shows the toll of its imprisonment. It walks slowly through the empty pit until a Shade erupts up from a hole in the ground.

The weakened prisoner doesn't stand a chance against the Shade. With a powerful grip, the dark being takes the head of the prisoner and twists it backwards. Ripping the arms off the body and tossing them to the ground, the Shade pushes the tormented prisoner to the ground and begins its feast.

Tearing into the inmate's chest with claws and sharp teeth, the Shade reaches into the cavity, pulling out the immortal's organs and eating them with ravenous hunger.

The prisoner is alive until the Shade rips its heart out, saving that for last.

"I'm going to be sick." Rhea holds onto my arm tight as we watch the death of the prisoner.

A dark sludge seeps out of the dead prisoner's wounds, like black tar, and is absorbed fully into the ground. The dirt begins to churn as a sinkhole forms where the body lays, swallowing the immortal.

Within the empty pit, there are likely dozens, if not hundreds, of Shades hiding within the dirt, waiting for the living to cross above them. Unlike the calm Shades of the first pit, or those in the Pathless Wood, these Shades are much older. Their contempt for the living has turned to rage, and they are ruthless in their need to destroy.

Another prisoner walks around the bend, this time

hugging close to the wall. We only set eyes on it for a few seconds before a Shade busts out from the wall, pulling the immortal inside as the dirt covers them as if there was no disturbance at all.

"Well that's perfect," Delta scoffs, watching the scene. "So, how the fuck are we supposed to get across this one?"

W e study the pit, watching a few more prisoners walk through. Some are brutally torn apart and consumed. Others make it through okay, but there is no pattern to where the Shades are located within the ground. There is no warning they are about to spring from their hiding spots; nothing we can use to our advantage.

Sitting on the wall, Pan and Kellan have been bickering for ten minutes, arguing and insulting each other as they fight over ideas on crossing. Pan has tried to put his ear to the wall and listen, hoping to hear the Shades, but they are soundless. Hermes is near the point of losing his temper and saying fuck it all so he and I can just go on without them.

Delta is next to me, and it looks like he's barely hanging on to life.

The black toxin darkening his veins and rotting his hand has spread up his neck and is encroaching upon his face, seeping into his eyes. He's pale and sweating. There is a constant tremor in his fingertips.

I don't know how many more walls he can scale, but he refuses to slow down. He doesn't ask us for help and hasn't complained once.

"Don't look at me like that," he says without turning to me. "My blaze of glory is just up ahead. I can feel it." Delta puts on a brave smile and turns to me. His expression is pleading, asking me to stop feeling sorry for him.

I recall the first time I saw Delta, outside my room in the Underworld. He stood dutifully next to Cappa. They were by my side nearly the entire time, volunteering to keep me safe while Lucas plotted an escape for the Shifters.

If their plan had been discovered, they could have been killed, terribly tortured, or even cast here, damned to eternal suffering. And yet, they remained, just as Delta is remaining steadfast by my side now.

The sacrifices the immortals of this realm are willing to make fill me with so many emotions, but right now, it's pride in being able to fight this battle next to someone so brave.

"Thank you for guarding me in the Underworld."

Delta gives me a sad smile and huffs a laugh. "I said it was my honor and I meant it. No matter what happens, taking you as far as I can, it is my honor." Delta directs his attention back to the pits.

I stare at my fingers as I pick at the dirt under my nails. Releasing a heavy sigh, I fist the wall beneath me, constructed of dirt and mud. Each one is tall and wide but nothing more than packed earth. Rubbing my hand across it, an idea forms.

"I bet I can feel where they are." Only Hermes and Delta hear me, so they both turn their heads to me. "Just have to be gentle so we don't wake up the entire Labyrinth." I tease, but it's laced with seriousness.

Countless dark monsters would swarm us, and we would be overtaken by their relentless hunger. None of us would survive, and starting this cycle of reincarnation over again, I shudder at the thought of Hermes dying, unable to wait for my return to fight this battle again in another lifetime.

Would I even return if there were nothing left for me to fight for?

Closing my eyes, I swallow the bile that rises with the dark thoughts seeping into my mind and focus on the essence of the Earth Titan that flows within me.

Testing the pulse of my power, I send a faint ribbon of my aura inside the wall, and just as I thought, I can feel the Shades lurking within. Well, more like I can feel the dirt and earth wrapped around them. It's like they are dormant, laying in hibernation until a prisoner steps above them and they spring to action.

By some gift of the Fates, there is a section of the wall and the pit that are free of Shades. It's not wide, only about fifteen feet across, but it should work.

"If we climb down here," I point to the section of wall we're sitting on that is clear of Shades, "we should be able to make it across and back up."

"One at a time?" Hermes asks, and I nod.

"I'll test it out first." Delta offers. We all know it's because he's close to death already, but of course, no one says anything.

Following the path, Delta makes it across. I monitor the Shades hiding inside their little dirt coffins, and none of them are disturbed.

"You're next, little goddess." There is a tension surrounding Hermes' eyes, and I know he doesn't like the idea of us being separated. Neither do I.

Before I can argue that we can probably walk across together, Hermes already knows my thoughts. "I'll be right behind you, baby." He whispers, kissing the side of my head.

"Okay." With a deep breath, I make the careful trip across the pit, and with shaking arms, I begin to climb the next wall. Hermes follows, careful to remain on the same path, and he quickly joins me.

Kellan and Pan still sit at the top of the opposing wall, seething at each other. While I can't hear what they are bickering about, it's clear their argument is growing more heated by the second.

Hermes has reached the top with Delta and me as we watch the approaching implosion on the other side of the pit. Pan and Kellan's whispers grow louder, and soon I can hear the occasional word float across the pit and reach us.

"Quiet!" I whisper, but I know it doesn't reach them. "They're arguing about who will go next, like two children." I grit my teeth in frustration.

"Gods dammit." Hermes' glare turns to anger as the pair keep up their feud. "I told Kellan to go first and for Pan to go last. Why the fuck are they arguing about it?"

Pan shoves Kellan back and starts his climb down. My racing heart is already galloping fast in my chest without this added pressure. Dropping to the ground, I feel inside the earth, concentrating on the Shades and making sure they have not moved and are still dormant.

After Pan makes several paces, Kellan decides he's tired of waiting and starts to climb down as well. "No. Tell them one at a time." The strain in my voice is tight with the mounting stress.

Hermes tries to get their attention, but it's like they can't hear us.

Kellan is climbing down quickly, but the cleared path is not wide enough for both of them to walk next to each other.

"Kellan, just wait." I try to call down to him, keeping my voice low. Over the constant groan of the Labyrinth and the ongoing wailing of sorrow from the prisoners, a noise that sounds like a cow grunting makes me look over the other pits.

Slow creeping fog climbs over the walls of the first two pits. Aside from the rising smoke of the burning pits we have yet to cross, there is nothing else up here moving but us.

The next pit is full of bubbling tar, and at the very center of the ring, a long bridge stretches across the remaining pits. We have been staying close to the edge of the rings, near the mountain wall, as Nessus advised.

The Centaur didn't mention a bridge, and it could be a risk if we try to cross it. We would be exposed on all sides, and anything in the Malebolge could spot us.

I think the best course is for us to keep to our path, scaling the tall walls and traversing the dangers within the pits.

Counting the rings we have passed and those we have remaining, I realize I'm on the fifth wall and we're halfway through the Malebolge. Exhaustion is going to be my enemy alongside the monsters hunting us. Steeling my mind, I remind myself of the prize that waits for me in the Labyrinth's center.

As I look beyond the giants to the opening above them, the high-pitch ring of my power rises, as if answering my thoughts. I'm nearly there, so close to my powers, and these assholes are putting us in danger with this ridiculous argument they won't drop.

"Don't fucking touch me." Kellan pushes Pan and stomps angrily across the pit, starting his climb up. Somehow, the Shades in the ground remain still, and we wait on the last two members of our party to join us on top of this wall. Anger is radiating off Hermes as he fights against his aura to remain dull and muted, ensuring his light doesn't draw unwanted attention.

As soon as Pan clears the ledge, Hermes grabs him by his bark armor. Driving Pan to the ground, Hermes draws his sword. By the time Pan's back hits the ground, the point of Hermes' sword is at his throat.

"If you do anything else that puts her life in jeopardy, you'll die on this sword before you can blink again." Pushing the sword slightly to emphasize the threat, Pan flinches. "Do you understand?"

Delta pushes Kellan back with his good hand on Kellan's chest. "What the fuck is your problem, man?"

"Why don't you ask him!" Kellan punches the air with his finger, pointing at Pan. His eyes, seething with anger, blow wide as shock takes over his expression. Looking quickly, Delta and I turn behind us. Aside from Hermes, who is still threatening Pan, there is nothing out of place. "Get behind me." Kellan says, his gaze fixed ahead.

"There is nothing there." I counter as Delta steps away from Kellan.

Pan's tone changes as quickly as Kellan's expression. They shift from anger to fear, instant. "Get your mate to safety." Pan says quietly as he slowly stands, his dark eyes locked on Kellan. Two long spikes of birch wood grow out of the top of his wrists.

In a second, Kellan has removed the bow from his back and is nocking an arrow.

"What are you doing?" I grit through my teeth at Kellan. "Hermes." I whisper back toward my mate.

"Rhea step aside." Fear coats our bond as Hermes worries Pan and Kellan are going to fight each other up here, with me in harm's way or worse, calling the attention of the Malebolge to our position.

I take a few steps closer to the next pit but keep some distance from the wall's edge. Delta takes slow and deliberate steps to Kellan, staying out of the pathway of the arrow.

"Hey, let's just put this down and keep going." He pleads with Kellan.

"There is no need for this." Hermes tries to reason with Pan.

"Monster," Kellan whispers, as time slows down.

I watch Kellan's fingers as they release the string of the bow. The tail of the arrow wobbles in one direction and then the other as it begins its path.

My head turns, and I begin to open my mouth to warn Hermes.

Pan thrusts his arm in an arc, reaching around Hermes as if pitching a ball. The spike protruding from the top of his wrist becomes a projectile, tethered to a vine like a grappling hook.

Hermes' name forms on my lips as Delta reaches for my arm. Kellan is in a dive, both arms outstretched, and he's headed straight for me.

My Darkness shoots out like a whip for my mate. Hermes has turned around, a tether of Light stretching out for me as everything rushes together.

Kellan's arrow drives through Pan's head. Pan's projectile strikes Kellan's chest. The momentum of his dive carries him toward me as his arms go slack. Delta tries to pull me out of the way, but Kellan's lifeless body slams into me, tipping me over the edge of the wall.

Hermes' whip of Light wraps around my wrist, and my whip of Darkness wraps around his. Kellan's body follows me over the edge, and we begin to plummet to the boiling tar below.

Holding onto the whips of our power, the lines pull tight as Hermes wraps them around his body, keeping me from hitting the tar. With both arms raised overhead, my hands firmly holding the tether of our auras, I hit the side of the wall. The air is forced from my lungs as I hit it again.

Delta reaches for Kellan's body, trying to keep him from falling into the tar so we won't draw attention. He grimaces with the strain of catching the dead Shifter with one hand and growls through clenched teeth as he adds his wounded hand.

"He's slipping." Delta warns as Hermes pulls the whips, one hand over the other, and I rise back up toward the top of the wall. Turning myself, I look up. The crest of the wall is within arm's length.

Extending my hand as Hermes reaches over, we lock wrists. With a single tug, I'm in his arms as he moves us away from the edge.

Delta loses his hold on Kellan's body, and it falls. Still tethered to Pan's vine, the momentum pulls the dead immortal over the ledge, and they fall to the bubbling pitch below.

A column of fire shoots up, and Delta rolls away from the edge of the wall to avoid being kissed by the flames. The entire pit emits clouds of white smoke that span the width of the Malebolge. Dozens, perhaps hundreds of beings screech and billow. The secret of our presence here has been revealed.

Demons within the pit of tar have spotted us, and with long hooks in their hands, they traverse the pit toward us. Driving their curved hooks into the pit's wall, they swing forward. Coasting through the air, they ready their hook and impale it again, repeating this as they race through the pit, avoiding the deadly tar below.

"We're running for it." Hermes sheaths his sword and helps me up. With my hand in his, we run. Delta is behind us, and we pump our arms, racing toward the bridge that crosses the remaining pits.

A demon climbs out of the tar pit, meeting us at the top of the wall. My hand is on my dagger, and it's speeding through the air before the demon can take a step toward us. The enchanted blade made of immortal metals strikes the beast in the heart, killing it instantly.

My dark tether wraps around the handle as I pull my weapon back to me, sheathing it in my holsters without losing pace.

Hermes takes the next demon with three daggers of Light that strike the demon in the head, chest, and abdomen. It falls back into the pit they are coming from, and fire erupts as the tar consumes their bodies.

We're nearly to the bridge when a boom echoes across the vast expanse. It sounds like a battering ram is beating upon the rocky mountain wall above us. Striking again, then again, the rock high above cracks as small pieces of rock rain down on the pits below.

It's on the opposite side of the Malebolge from our position and near the first pit. Another booming strike further breaks the hard rock, and a final impact reveals the large head and horns of the Minotaur.

It roars into the Malebolge, and the sound shakes the very walls around us, making the ground under our feet tremble as large boulders break away from the high ceiling and race to the ground.

As if gravity draws the Minotaur to us, his red eyes find us immediately, and the beast roars again. Our hunter is still in pursuit, and there is only one direction we can go.

Reaching the bridge, we turn sharply, crossing over the pit of boiling and smoking tar as we race to the Labyrinth's center. Coughing and trying not to breathe in the noxious fumes, they burn my eyes as we race through them.

A choking cough erupts from me as a large chunk of the mountain crashes down next to me. My hand flies out of Hermes' hold, and I dive out of the way of the crushing rock. Two hands grasp firmly under my arms as Hermes helps me up, and we take off again.

Behind us, the Minotaur beats its mighty fists and horned head against the rock, opening the wall further and pushing its massive body through. With one hand still gripping the rock, the Minotaur hangs before dropping down to the top of the first pit's wall.

Landing on his two hoofed legs, his focus zeroes in on us before he drops to the pit below, and we lose sight of him.

A demon climbs upon the bridge on each side of us. Delta punches one in the face and pushes its chest with all his strength. Hermes grabs for his sword. Two strikes, faster than the eye can see, he slices the demon's body, severing its legs and splaying its torso open. Both demons fall at the same time, and we keep running.

My head spins in a dizzying swirl from the fumes of the tar, but we've reached the next pit as we race on.

Clinking metal chains sound next to me, and I turn my head just in time to see a massive lead block racing through the air. My breath catches in my throat, and time seems to slow as the deadly weight hurtles closer, promising to crush everything in its path—me.

Ducking into a flip, the lead block narrowly soars past me. Standing, I barely miss a stride as I push back into a run. Hermes' sword screams against the chain, easily severing it. Grabbing it, he spins twice and hurls the block back at the demon that threw it.

Striking the demon in the head, the heavy block is driven into the dirt floor of the pit below, completely burying the head of the now-dead demon. Behind us, we hear the snarls and grunts of the Minotaur.

Braving a glance, I catch it dropping down the wall into the third pit as several demons climb onto the bridge, racing after us.

"Don't look back," Hermes yells over the screeches and growls of the dark beings around us. "Just run, Rhea. Run and don't stop."

Tucking my chin, I push harder as I reach the next pit ahead of Hermes and Delta. Something like a whip wraps around my ankle and yanks hard, pulling my feet from under me. My head bangs against the bridge before I'm dragged over the edge. My vision flashes to black as I fall fifty feet into the pit below.

A collection of vines softens my fall, but the landing is far from gentle. The thick, sinewy vines wrap around me, their thorns scratching along my arms and back, leaving stinging trails of pain behind. Each thorn is like a needle, pricking through my skin, and I grit my teeth against the sensation. The vine around my foot tightens like a noose, and another vine snakes up, capturing one of my wrists in its vice-like grip.

Taking my dagger in hand, I slash at the vines with desperate fury. Each cut requires effort, the thick, fibrous vines resisting the blade. The severed pieces fall away, oozing an acidic sap that burns and sizzles upon contact with my skin. The air fills with the acrid smell of the vine's juices, mingling with the metallic scent of my own blood. My heart races as I fight against the tightening grip of the carnivorous plant, each breath a struggle.

Finally free, I pull myself from the predatory shrub and look to the bridge above. I can't see Hermes or Delta, but I hear their fight raging on the bridge.

Growling demons and the clang of Hermes' sword echo above me. Rushing to the wall of this pit, I quickly find a finger-hold and, kicking my boot into the wall, I push up.

A sudden, excruciating pain crushes my ankle, and I scream as a searing burn shoots up my leg. The agony is immediate and overwhelming, like my bones are being ground to dust. Instinctively, I kick out, my boot connecting with something solid before I have time to see what has attacked me.

Turning, fear races through me as I see a large six-legged lizard, its eyes glowing with a voracious gleam. The creature's black reptilian skin glistens in the dim light, its red stripes pulsing with an eerie glow. Its mouth opens to reveal rows of razor-sharp teeth, each one glinting like a dagger, and it emits an odd, guttural growl that vibrates through the air. The sound is a low, menacing rumble, sending chills down my spine as the lizard lunges at me again.

Dropping back to the floor of the pit, I conjure a flaming sword of fire and drive it into the lizard's head. A sharp whistle shoots by me as another carnivorous vine lashes out like a whip. As I surge my arm up in an arc, I morph my flaming sword to a dagger of fire.

Slicing through the vine, I fling the burning blade into the center of the plant. It screeches and cries as it bursts into flames, the vines whipping erratically like a living, breathing creature.

A figure drops down in front of me, and I jump back with a scream, thinking it may be a demon. A new dagger of flames is in my hand and ready to strike in an instant.

"It's me." Hermes says, with breathless urgency. "There's a way up over here."

Oh, thank the gods.

On the other side of the bridge, there seems to be a makeshift ladder formed of woven and dried vines. "There." Hermes points as we run to it, and when I put my boot on the first step, the growl of another lizard sounds.

As I reach for the dagger in my right holster, Hermes takes the dagger from my left holster. My blades cut through the air, hitting our target in the center of the lizard's head.

Hermes takes a few quick strides and bends down, retrieving my weapons. "What the fuck is that thing?"

"Where is your swo—" My question is silenced as a green streak slashes across Hermes.

As if the world stops, his face relaxes, and my heart pauses its beats in my chest. Everything around me blurs into nothingness, the sounds of battle fading into a distant hum. My daggers drop from his hands, clattering against the dirt ground with a hollow echo. Time seems to stretch, each second an eternity, as I watch with growing horror. His head begins to tip off his body, the motion agonizingly slow, as if the very fabric of reality is being torn apart.

I stop breathing. My lungs burn, screaming for air, but I can't move. For the longest moment, I watch my mate fall to the ground, his lifeless eyes still locked on mine, as I remain frozen on the pit's ladder. My fingers grip the rungs so tightly that my knuckles turn white, yet I can't tear my gaze away from the sight before me.

It seems surreal, a twisted nightmare I can't wake from, to witness the head of my mate fall away. His eyes, those beautiful cerulean eyes that once sparkled with life and love, are now vacant, staring into nothingness. Inch by agonizing inch, Hermes' body crumples, as if in slow motion, and I am powerless to stop it.

All the sounds around me muffle, as if I'm submerged underwater. The clash of swords, the snarls of demons, all fade into a distant, distorted murmur. The only thing I can hear is the rhythmic beat of my heart, pounding painfully in my chest.

Bum bum. Bum bum.

Each beat a cruel reminder that I am still alive while he is not.

My body shakes with a tremor that grows each second, and I let go of the ladder. I can't remember my last breath, and my body holds, almost wanting me to run out of air. My fists clench as I drop to my knees. My lungs burn, begging me to breathe.

Opening my mouth, I take in a long, ragged breath of air,

the cold searing my throat. I release it with a scream, a raw, primal sound that tears through my very soul. It rattles my head, reverberating through the empty pit, a cry of pure, unfiltered anguish. My entire body trembles, every muscle tense, as I scream and scream, until there is nothing remaining inside me.

My hands hit the dirt, fingers clawing at the ground as I lower my forehead to the cold, unyielding dirt. I am hollow, emptied of everything but pain. Silent sobs wrack my body, my lungs burning. Each breath is a battle, each exhale a surrender to the overwhelming grief that engulfs me.

In a wide circle around me, my fire erupts and races through the pit. Growing the flames higher and breathing my sorrow into them, they burn hotter. The ground beneath me rumbles, shaking with the anguish that is streaming out of me.

I gasp. In and out, I pull ragged and choked breaths of air into my body, then cough and cry them out, crawling to be by my mate's side.

Hand. Knee. Hand. Knee. Until I reach him.

Maybe this isn't real. Maybe it's another demented trick of this horrible place, and when I reach out, there will be nothing there because I'm hallucinating.

Pausing, I extend a shaking hand to him. My heart fractures when I touch the hand that's lying flat on the ground. *Goddess, please no.* He's still warm.

"We were so close." I can't even speak the words out loud as my throat closes. We were so close.

After all these lifetimes of torment, so much suffering, he's always been there. Forever waiting for my return. Forever, my guiding star. Not wanting to take my touch away from his, I keep my hand on him as I lay down. My body parallel with his and I just look at him.

My mind empty of thoughts, and I reach up, carefully moving a lock of his dark hair that's fallen in front of his eyes.

The noise around me is nothing more than muffled murmurs against the static crackling in my ears. My heart, still the only noise filling the space between us.

Bum bum. Bum bum. Bum bum.

I look at each rivet in his blue eyes. The aqua and silver that breaks up the deep blue, that was a raging ocean is nothing more than still waters now. I want to memorize them. I don't want to forget a single speck of detail.

My body is numb, and I don't even want to feel anything ever again, knowing I'll never feel his touch again.

"How did you do this a thousand times?" I ask my dead mate, wishing I could hear the deep timber of his voice answer me, but knowing he never again will.

The pain burns through me like Soul Fire, and I wish it would just burn me into oblivion and let me go with him.

Over and over again, he endured this. Watching me die, saying goodbye. How can someone survive this pain, so many times? I turn my head toward the ground and weep.

Three more times my heart somehow finds the will to beat against my chest. With each pound, the muffled bark of a dog pierces my ear as if far away.

Bum bum. Bum bum. Bum bum.

One, two, three.

I count the heartbeats to keep my mind tethered here to this moment, so I don't float away from it. I know I should get up. I know there is a horde of darkness waking up all around this prison of desolation, but I can't leave him.

Bum bum. Bum bum. Bum bum.

One, two, three.

I run my fingers through his hair, trying not to think about how long it will take his soft raven locks to turn brittle. How long it will take for the Labyrinth to turn him to ash. Closing my eyes, I try to push that thought out of my mind.

Two sharp barks from a dog, this time closer, intrude on my awareness. The animal seems to be nearing, or maybe I am slipping back into the present.

My still heart begins to race.

Bum bum. Bum bum. Bum bum.

One, two, three.

Like a second heart is pounding in my chest, another three knocks beat in an alternate rhythm to the muscled organ in my chest. My cheeks heat, and I raise up, propping myself up on my hand.

All around me, the pit is on fire, burning white-hot flames as plumes of angry black smoke rise high above me.

Pushing my palm to my chest, I wait.

"This is real."

The words I spoke to Hermes echo in my mind as I feel three more taps against me. A loud bark is right behind me, and I turn around with my hand still over my heart as the cutest little demon puppy bounds toward me, running straight through the flames and jumping into my arms.

"Cerberus!" Tears stream down my face as I hold the dog of darkness and shadow tightly. "I thought you died." I choke out, squeezing my eyes shut, suddenly scared to open them again and see my dead mate behind me.

The sight of his body and decapitated head is burned into my memory forever. What if I turn around to find him rotting away already?

Wriggling in my arms, Cerberus licks at my face, his puppy

tail wagging out of control. Two more dogs emerge from the flames. The larger Doberman versions of the demon dog walk to me, both of them sniffing me as if making sure I'm okay.

One whimpers, his snout nudging my side as it suddenly burns like fire is coursing into me. With a wince, I turn, lifting my shirt. A large thorn of the carnivorous vines is protruding from me.

Pulling it out and throwing it to the ground, it's as if all the noise and excruciating fumes of the Malebolge come rushing into me at once.

Three more taps on my chest steal my breath as I realize it's not my heart.

It's my mating bond.

My head shoots around as I look back at Hermes' body. Gasping, my body floods with shock. Relief and nausea rage through me as I see Delta lying there. His head severed from him, brown eyes open, filled with the black poison that was consuming him and staring into the veil that separates the realms.

I scoot away, choking and sputtering as puppy Cerberus grows to his regular size. The three dogs surround me, watching as I work to compose myself.

"He's still alive." My ragged voice is somehow able to speak. My words are just as much a question as they are a reassurance for my broken soul.

Turning on all fours, I clutch my stomach and take in deep breaths as the wave of sickness subsides. Squeezing my eyes tight, I send three pulses down our bond, and elation floods me when I feel Hermes there.

Relief, joy, and worry rush back at me when Hermes feels me finally answer him.

"Where are you?" I nearly scream in my mind, but it feels like I hit a wall. He's blocked me off. Because he doesn't want me to come to him, or perhaps my agony was too painful, distracting him.

The pockets of blazing fire and plumes of black smoke cover the pit in shadow, and I can't see through the haze anymore.

"Take me to him." I cough.

Cerberus is a beast from the realm that leaks into this abysmal prison. He comes from the same darkness, and it's likely how he survived the bog when I thought him destroyed. Somehow, he found us here and made his way into this pit to help me. I send a prayer to the Fates that he can Shadow Walk in this portion of the Labyrinth and deliver me to Hermes.

Warmth rushes through me when the three dogs surround me, one of them nuzzling by my side, the other two poised to attack. As if the darkness around us deepens, dunking us in a tank of cold water, the shadows swell, and in an instant, I'm no longer in the smoking pit of fire.

My heart beats a thousand pulses at once as I set eyes on the most beautiful sight of my mate.

Sword in one hand, Hermes holds the long horn of the Minotaur with the other. In a single, powerful thrust, his sword, blazing with bright blue light, slices through the neck of the beast that hunted us through this maze of torment.

Hermes kicks the body of the monster and it falls away, slipping over the edge of a tall wall and tumbling into the pit below. He tosses the severed head along with it and flings the blood from his blade as he takes long and determined strides to me.

Her agony was pulling me apart. Ripping my mind in two with her terror. The Minotaur reached the bridge when Rhea was pulled over and I would rip this realm apart before I let a beast like that reach her.

Sending Delta to help, I realized the Minotaur had been hunting him all along, not us. The wound from the forest left a scent trail the Minotaur followed. It stalked us across the bog, beyond the city of Dis, and through the burning desert until it found us here.

Its red eyes locked on him as he chased after Rhea, but Delta was nearing death and couldn't defeat the Minotaur. After consuming him, the beast would target us next, and Rhea would still be in danger.

Then something happened and she nearly drown me in her pain and sorrow. Collapsing under the intensity of her torment, I raised my sword, blocking a swipe of the Minotaur's razor-sharp claws.

Cerberus came bounding down the bridge, entering the Malebolge from the opening made by the beast attacking me. Snarling and sinking his fangs into the Minotaur hoofed leg,

Cerberus distracted the beast for a second, enabling me to get up.

"Go find her!" I called out to the dog as I prepared to dodge another attack from the Minotaur. I kept spending pulses down our bond as I battled the beast on the bridge until she came back to me.

Reaching Rhea, she nearly collapses into my arms, her legs unable to support her as she clutches me and sobs.

"I thought you died," Rhea chokes out. "I saw it." Her words break with cries. "I–"

"Shhh." I squeeze her tight, rushing my powers to her through our bond, calming her aura with my essence. Taking her face in my hands, I kiss her gently. "I know, I know, but I'm here. Look at me. I'm right here."

She opens her golden eyes, red from crying, and wraps her arms around my neck.

"I'm okay. Baby, I promise," I say, pulling her arms off me but keeping a firm hold to steady her. I bend down so our gazes are level and cup her face to keep her looking at me. "When we get out of here, I swear to the gods I will hold you for a decade without letting go, but..." The Labyrinth rumbles again, awakened by Rhea's torment. Dark beings squawk and bellow, racing to the Malebolge from every corner of the prison. "...we have to go. We have to go right now."

She nods, her legs still trembling but working to regain control. I take her hand, tugging her back down the bridge toward salvation.

I rub Cerberus' head, disbelief rolling through me again that he survived the bog and found us. "Good dog."

We take off running, the demon dog matching our pace,

splitting into three and flanking us on both sides as one leads in the center.

A horde of sword-wielding demons rushes out of the last two pits just as the far entrance to the Malebolge explodes behind us. Like insects emerging from a nest, a swarm of dark creatures pours into the mountain's interior.

Rhea shoots a jetstream of fire through the demons ahead, blasting them off the bridge. The pits where they came from blaze bright orange as she fuels her fire, burning them all and clearing our path.

Without regard, I blast a super-heated wave of Absolute Light behind me. The Malebolge lights up as my power radiates, blasting away the creatures starving to consume us.

But more are coming.

Beyond this hallowed mountain, an endless supply of monsters will keep coming with unending hunger and blind rage. We have to reach the center and fend off the darkness as Rhea restores her powers.

Three more obstacles block our path, and they are huge.

"Any ideas on getting past the giants?" We are halfway down the long bridge that spans the pits. Between us and the Labyrinth's center are the giants. The most fearsome is the largest, with ten massive arms.

"I'm working on it," she huffs as we run down the bridge.

I feel her aura rush forward to the curious giants at the end of our path. The Titan powers of Earth race ahead, shimmering with mirages of Tartarus. The giants visibly excite at the images she shows them, bringing them happiness. I see thick collars and heavy chains around their necks and realize they are prisoners too.

"Yes!" Rhea exclaims with elation, smiling as her plan

works. "I thought they might be related to the cyclopes on Tartarus, and they are. They've been prisoners all this time. They'll help us."

We are almost there. So fucking close.

One of the giants leans down with his large hand cupped and waiting at the end of the bridge. We don't slow down. We run and jump into his large, waiting palm.

Our chests heave as we ride in the giant's hand to the center's entrance, high above.

Carefully, the giant lifts us up high above his head. His hand pauses with steady patience as we climb off and onto the waiting platform. The three giants turn their backs to us, the one with many arms in the center, the other two on each side.

When a fresh surge of dark monsters and legions of malevolent Shades race through the large opening, the giants release a billowing roar, readying themselves to fight back.

"They'll give us as much time as they can," Rhea says quickly.

Taking my hand, we enter the inner chamber of the immortal prison.

The power surge bears down upon us as soon as we cross the threshold. Pushing against it, it feels like a literal forcefield beating against us, keeping us from the center. Beyond the strong shielded wards is a turbulent vortex, winds spinning so fast in a tight funnel it seems like a constant swirl of white clouds.

We have to get in there.

Rhea and I strain to lift our hands to the forcefield. Electric energy zaps into us as we push against it. Dark and Light powers burn together, weakening the spot where our elements collide. Beyond the raging wind inside, the interior begins to shine as if anticipating our arrival.

Our efforts create a break in the forcefield. With our arms around each other, we jump with Cerberus by our side. The currents immediately suck us toward the vortex of Flaying Wind.

Rhea surrounds us in a Shield of Current as we pass through the funnel, reaching the center of the prison.

The interior is much more massive than I had thought. Tall platforms stack, creating a step pyramid. At the topmost platform, a pulsing swell of silver starlight dims, then fades away.

Rhea and I look at each other at the same time. Our expressions mirror hope and elation. But Rhea is tired, weary from the exhaustive journey. I see it in her eyes.

At the prospect of finally being made whole again after all these ages of torment, she takes a deep breath, steeling herself to make it this final distance.

"Let's do this." She nods at me, holding out her hand. She tries to conjure a portal, but the wards around us intensify, tampering her powers and preventing the portal from forming.

I try using my Light, but just like hers, my element doesn't work.

Looking to our shadow pup, I raise my eyebrows in question. "What about you?"

Cerberus pauses, perhaps trying to open a portal, then sits on his hind legs with a whimper.

"Okay, climbing it is."

The steps are too tall for Rhea, so I lift her by the waist. She grabs the ledge, and I push from below, helping her pull herself up and swing her leg over the edge. I jump and follow, hoisting myself onto the platform.

We run for several steps, then take the next platform the same way.

The ground beneath us trembles, and we have to balance to remain upright. All around us, dark beams blast against the shield that surrounds the center chamber.

"We have company." I look around, seeing the dark creatures of Elysium working to destroy the veil protecting us. "Let's keep going."

I lift Rhea again, noticing this next platform is not as tall as the previous ones. Hopefully, they'll shorten as we go, quickening our pace. Cerberus jumps along with us, able to scale each level on his own.

Behind us, some of the darkness destroys a small opening in the barrier. It sounds like lightning ripping open the atmosphere.

Cerberus stops his ascent up the step pyramid, locking his burning eyes on the breach. With a growl, the canine of darkness and shadow grows in size before his form splits, making two dogs.

"Go!" I yell to Rhea over the churning tempest surrounding us.

Cerberus divides himself more, sending massive dogs around the pyramid and to the steps below where Shades are entering through the funnel.

Cerberus attacks them as we climb, taking out most but several slip by him.

Pushing Rhea up over the next platform, then myself, two Shades rush us from the other side of the pyramid. Rhea, with her daggers, and I, with my sword, destroy them quickly and set back to our climb.

The shield around us flickers and ripples as the darkness

keeps assaulting it. Soon, it will be dismantled, and we'll be surrounded by the beasts of the Labyrinth.

"It's not going to hold much longer," Rhea yells over the chaos unfolding in the chamber's interior.

The steps are getting shorter as we climb, and Rhea can pull herself up the next one. More Shades and several large lizards with many arms sneak past Cerberus as he combats the monsters entering through the opening.

She needs more time.

I reach within the Titan power thrumming inside me and find the cosmic dragon. The wards and design of the Labyrinth have been suppressing our powers, and as I attempt to pull the dragon from my aura, the Labyrinth pushes back.

More Shades invade our temporary refuge, their numbers growing by the second. Cerberus can no longer hold them back.

Rhea jumps and lifts herself up the next step, but she is slowing down. Her arms shake as she struggles. She looks back, seeing me two levels down. The thought of her being so close and losing it all when her powers are almost within reach rips through me.

"Keep going!" I call out, turning back to the oncoming creatures.

My power surges inside me like a star on the verge of explosion. Pulsing inside me, it feels like the mighty wings of the dragon are beating against the Labyrinth's wards as my core heats. The need to protect her, to ensure she reaches the top, builds until it feels like my skin will burst open.

Everything around me brightens as my aura burns so brightly it turns white. Building and collecting the anger and determination within me, I feel the dragon wanting to rupture out of me, but it can't break the surface.

Pushing more, I scream against the power building within me. I hear Rhea call my name, but it is drowned out by the power of a thousand stars rushing into me. Brighter and brighter, it builds until it feels like my skin is ripping open.

The essence of the Titan detonates, and blue starlight pulses in all directions, blasting against the funnel of wind and the thick barrier protecting the inner chamber. A brilliant flash of light takes over my vision as I feel the dragon wrap around me.

The restrictive wards dissolve as starlight pulses out of me. As my form is taken over by the cosmic dragon, Rhea watches, mesmerized by the transformation.

"Climb." The rough growl that accompanies my voice in this form makes Rhea shiver, snapping her out of the spectacle.

This chamber restricts my wings. The first flaps rake against the sides of the rocky interior, and I know I can't fly in here.

A dozen Minotaur break past the giants and rush into the Labyrinth's center.

The burning star at the heart of my dragon heats, climbing up the column of my throat and racing out of my large jaws. Burning the Minotaur first, I carefully work myself around to the other sides of the step-pyramid, the dark creatures burning to ash under the intense blaze of dragon fire.

As I destroy the Shades and monsters coming after us, Rhea climbs. With each platform she reaches, my determination strengthens, and my resolve cements itself within me.

It ends with us, with Rhea and me. No matter the cost.

I keep my infernal blaze on the opening of the chamber,

destroying the darkness and allowing Cerberus to begin climbing the pyramid again. Pouring the aura of the Titan out of me like a geyser, I form a new shield, weaving everything I have into its fibers to ensure nothing will make it beyond to harm my mate or keep her from her quest.

The shield builds and blocks the Labyrinth's residents, but I keep going as Rhea climbs. She is nearly there, and as I watch her lift herself to the final platform, her face bright with hope drops as her disappointment and confusion squeeze my heart. Her happiness dissolves, and despair floods our bond as she turns in circles at the topmost platform.

"What is it?"

"There's nothing here." She calls out, her voice cracking as she fights back tears.

Within a single stride, I climb to the top platform. As quickly as the dragon formed, I pull him back within myself and join my mate. My confusion mirrors hers.

"I don't understand." She sniffs as tears begin to fall. "It should be here. I felt it."

A resounding boom shakes the platform, and Rhea reaches for me. The interior chamber is being bombarded and cracking all around us. The monsters that live here, unwilling to abandon their obsession with our destruction, are now working to dismantle the Labyrinth's interior.

"Just concentrate." I hold her shoulders, helping to keep her steady through the continued assault. "Let's think, baby."

Rhea closes her eyes as the chamber's interior gives way. Raising my palms toward the top of my newly formed shield, my Light rages out of me in a beam of power, reinforcing the shield as the mountain collapses around us.

The interior is exposed now, open to the Malebolge below.

The masses of dark monsters racing toward us send chills down my body. *There are so many.*

"The records said we had the staff when we entered the Labyrinth, and we didn't have it when we left." Rhea continues to search around the top platform, hoping to find a pocket of power or something that will give her a sign of where we hid it. "So, what did we do between entering and leaving?"

Her voice trails off, and I feel the moment she realizes something.

Beyond the vast mountain range, a massive cloud of Darkness, so deep it seems like a massive void, is heading toward us. With that thought... a void... my head snaps to Rhea.

She breaks into a laugh that turns to tears, nodding at me in agreement.

Son of a bitch.

I join her in the center, running my hands through her hair and tucking a stray lock behind her ear.

"The one place he could never go." She wraps her arms around me, and I pull her against my body. "The one place that only you and I can reach."

I shake my head at the simplicity of it. "Pan couldn't sense what happened once we entered the Labyrinth, so he wouldn't have been able to record it. Loki would never know where we took it."

She smiles at me as a tear rolls from the corner of her eye. "We only used the Labyrinth to hide where we really went."

The giants bellow, under attack by hordes of creatures. With our hands outstretched, we blast our powers at once, sending waves of Dark and Light across the Malebolge to help the giants.

The platform illuminates with the essence of Rhea's silver

starlight, surrounding us in a swell of her magic. Her long honey hair blows as the power spins around us, then fades away.

That is it. We made sure the portal would only work with both our powers. The smile that lights up Rhea's face surges through my body, and I swear the beat of my heart is tethered to it.

Cerberus sits patiently, watching us work out the final piece of our puzzle with his tongue hanging out of his mouth. Rhea kneels down to him, hugging him and giving a few scratches between his pointed ears. "Go back through the prison, find anyone we left behind that is still alive. We'll meet you on the surface soon." Cerberus turns, jumping down the steps of the pyramid and bounding through my shield.

She stands back up and takes both my hands in hers. My mouth is drawn to hers. Her tongue sweeps across my lips as the wind of the oncoming darkness rises around us. Pulling back and looking into her eyes, I see the power of her aura build within her as I call upon mine.

Silver and blue starlight swirl together, surrounding us as our portal forms.

A portal to the realm of souls. The realm of my goddess: the Void.

"Are you ready to go home?" I ask, and she smiles.

"You're my home." She rubs her nose against mine. I wrap my arms around her waist with a possessiveness that will never fade. Our powers flare as the portal opens, swallowing us just as the dark wave envelops the platform.

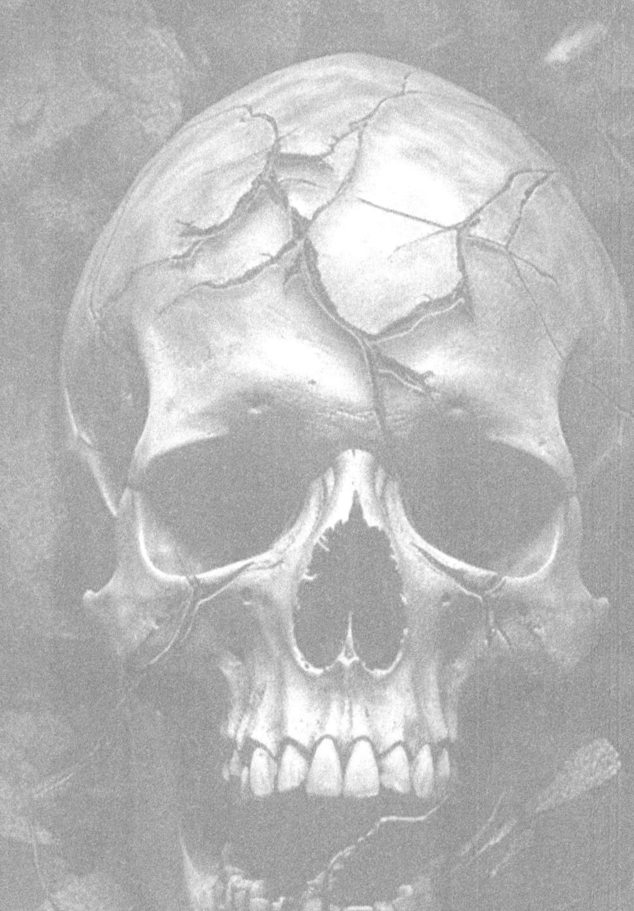

ACT III

PART 1: THE VOID

"**H**ello-o-o-o." My voice carries on, bouncing away from me in an endless echo. A timid breeze swirls around me like an investigation, making me shiver. Goosebumps spread across my shoulders, and I stretch my neck to both sides to alleviate the discomfort.

Black nothingness surrounds us, deeper than the richest obscurity and darker than a thousand nights. It's calming, somehow. A sense of peace and serenity fills me instantly, as if the weight of the twelve realms has been lifted from my shoulders.

"Nice place you've got here," Hermes teases, squeezing my hand.

"Oh, stop it." I give him a playful smack on the arm, which I can't see even though we're standing so close our bodies are touching.

Pulling him with me, I take a few disorienting steps forward. My heart races, and my eyes search for something, anything to focus on. With each step, our boots slosh in a thin layer of water, and I remember being here just a few weeks ago. Though I could argue that was lifetimes before.

I was scared and only had a faint whisper of my cardinal

powers at my control. I hadn't realized then that I had taken myself here by accident, or that I had even teleported to begin with.

After reliving the fatal car accident with Athena and Atlas... Loki as he dug around my mind, the lights within his portlet had gone out. In the next instant, I was just—somewhere else, standing in a void with no clue what to do.

I feel the essence of the same fear and uncertainty that gripped me the first time I found myself here. But so many things have changed since that version of me set foot in this infinite darkness. Now, as I reflect on my journey, I hardly recognize the woman I once was—a woman with a secret power she barely understood and was desperate to learn about. How could I have ever known that last-minute choice to attend a book signing would be the catalyst for everything that followed?

Nothing felt different about that mundane morning when I woke up and dressed. Making my way to Once Upon A Spine, it was just another day, like any other. It truly was my birthday because the second I stepped into that bookstore, I stepped into a new life. And when I sat down next to the most handsome man I had ever seen, there would never be any turning back.

"Would you care to shine a little *light* on where we should go?" Hermes' shoulder knocks into mine playfully, and I roll my eyes, chuckling at the way he emphasizes the word "light."

"Are you making corny elemental magic jokes now?" I tease him back, but his effort to calm my anxiety makes me smile more.

"Maybe." He tugs on my hand, pulling me a little closer

and nuzzling into my hair, taking a deep breath. "But you laughed, so it was worth it. But seriously, I can't see shit."

"Well then, watch this."

Holding out my palm, an orange and yellow ball of fire lights up our faces, and I pull the warmth within me, chasing away the bite of the gentle breeze.

Taking a deep breath and blowing like I'm extinguishing a candle, the embers erupt and fill the sky above us. Hanging in the darkness like a galaxy of stars, their reflection in the dark water below magnifies the wonder of this place.

I watch Hermes as he gazes above us, held in awe. "Beautiful," he whispers.

All around us, as far as we can see, there is just a vast expanse of empty space. The steps I take disturb the shallow dark water that reaches on forever.

I'm dying for something to drink, my throat parched and my body weary. Exhausted from resisting the unending urge to drink the Lethe—the poisoned waters of forgetting—I now find myself surrounded by an endless expanse of water. The irony is bitter, as the liquid that tempts me might hold its own dangers. Who knows if it's safe to consume, or if it too is tainted by the same malevolent properties?

Calling upon my elements, I cast each one into the sky above. Each element adds another color to the prism of stars burning above us. An ethereal kaleidoscope, more beautiful than anything I've ever beheld.

"Are those souls?" Hermes asks without looking away from the brilliant night sky.

"I don't know." We could look at this landscape for hours, never tiring of its allure, but we came here for something. And it's time to find it.

Taking a deep breath, I push my billowing black mist out in all directions. The dark cloud of my power rolls across the water, and I wait to feel the Caduceus answer my call.

The pull of my powers from Tartarus was so intense it took my breath away at times. I expected to feel that same tug when we arrived at the Labyrinth, but I didn't until we reached the center. A small part of me is tense with worry that I can't feel the Caduceus here either, and I send a prayer to the Fates for mercy.

Holding my fingers, anxiously squeezing them together, I wait. Looking across the spread before us, I turn. My eyes search every direction, begging to feel something.

The lights above us shine upon the water, and I watch as gentle ripples move across the surface of the shallow water toward us, mirroring the growing anticipation in my chest. Watching intently, I hold my breath, the weight of the moment pressing down on me. As I bite my lip and squint, a sliver of hope flares within me.

Am I imagining it, or is the horizon truly getting lighter? Slowly, a glow builds in intensity, as if heralding the approach of something significant. This light, piercing the darkness, brings with it a sense of recognition.

Three distinct colors of light. Three.

Gasping, I clutch Hermes' forearm, hoping he can see it too. Watching motionless, tears gather in his eyes, and I know he sees what I do.

The light crests the horizon, exploding like the most beautiful sunrise I've ever beheld, and I drop to my knees.

Frosted green and bronze orbs are escorting the most brilliantly burning ball of yellow sunlight, racing toward us like comets. Barely skimming the dark waters, they streak, a glowing tail of light trailing behind them.

"Callie." I choke out her name as the light collides with me. The presence of Achilles and Patroclus with her, three mates finally together as they are always meant to be.

Warmth, so tender, envelopes me, and I swear I can feel her arms wrap around me. Bursts of images shoot through my mind. Hundreds of our moments together flash behind my eyes as I sob, and I know it's her.

It takes me a moment before I can open my eyes and realize it's Hermes I'm hugging. The light of their auras swirling around us as their memories rush into us both.

"Can you see it too?" I ask, cupping his jaw with my hand while tears run freely down both our faces. Grasping my wrist, he turns his head, placing a kiss on my palm and nodding.

"It's really them." His voice cracks, overflowing with emotion.

The orbs squeeze around us, and it feels like they are pushing us up, wanting us to stand.

Guilt and the sudden need to explain my return from Tartarus nearly crush my windpipe. "I didn't want this—" I choke out, but the words fall flat as I cover my face with my hands. "I'm just so sorry."

Hermes wraps his arms around me, holding me while I cry, and the souls of our departed friends fill the space around us. I wish I could see her...really see her and feel her hug me, even if it's only once.

The images change. Small snips of different moments play in my mind as I hear different phrases. It's like someone spliced together dozens of short movie snippets and strung them together.

I feel like Callie is trying to tell me something, but it's not making sense. Finally, the messages sink in. While she can't speak, it's as if I suddenly understand her meaning and the intention behind the images they're showing us.

It's okay.

It was supposed to happen this way.

The messages are supposed to be reassuring, but they crush me more. My thoughts race through the dozen scenarios of how we could have done things differently. Anything that would have changed the course of their lives so we could stay together.

"I miss you." My cries pour out of me again, my shoulders bouncing with sobs. "I miss you so much."

We miss you too.

"It was Loki—Atlas." I blurt out, wanting them to know the truth of everything. "He tricked us all."

We know.

Hermes and I hold each other as we cry, sitting in shallow black water under an endless sky of stars. The comfort of our friends' souls surrounds us as the light of their auras blankets us. We can feel them, and if I close my eyes, it's almost like they are actually here.

Patroclus' laugh echoes around me while Hermes and Achilles jest over who is the stronger immortal. Whoops ring out as Callie and I cheer the boys on while they prove themselves in a race.

Such a simple moment I would give anything to have again.

I'm not sure how long Hermes holds me like this, but finally, I sit up. The souls of our friends float next to us like little hovering balls of light. "Are you okay?"

Hermes gives me a sad smile and a nod. "I will be."

I wish we could stay here forever in the tranquility of this place with the presence of our friends, our family. Where no one is searching to destroy me for the selfish greed of power, but I know we can't.

There are too many souls back on Gaea that would remain in anguish under the control of Loki, and we have to stop that. We can't allow any more deaths in the name of this war that we didn't start.

"We came for the Caduceus." My voice echoes away from us, and I wonder if I even need to talk at all or if Callie, Pat, and Achilles just know our thoughts.

The stream of images pieced together in my mind relay a response: *Not ready.*

The words ricochet around my mind, filling me with confusion and a growing sense of unease.

"I don't understand," I whisper. "What is not ready?"

You.

The simple answer strikes a chord deep within me, stirring a myriad of emotions. Through all of this, could there be something else we've missed? Another riddle to solve, another quest to embark on? The frustration of yet another hurdle pulls at my heart.

"What else could I possibly do? How much more suffering does this curse demand before I can break it?"

There is no answer, just an image. And it doesn't change.

I see a picture clearly in my mind, just like the day Callie and I were sitting in the library at Delphi. I was just about to remember my first Triple Moon Eclipse and the night Hermes and I protected our bond.

Callie and I were sifting through an endless amount of tomes and scrolls, looking for answers. The stained-glass window of Death loomed over me with its gold inscription that I say out loud now: "Memento Mori."

"Remember, you must die."

I've already died a thousand deaths. There is no way this gluttonous curse demands another. In every life, I have suffered. In every death, I have been scared. Afraid to leave those I came to love. Terrified of somehow never being able to return, to never again have the chance at life. I've been scared of death—

"I'm scared."

My own voice rings in my mind. It's my memory this time. I was with Hecate. I had just figured out that I was Death, that I held the power of the Titans within me.

"I'm scared." I said to her.

"I don't believe you are an instrument of death, Rhea."

"How can you say that? I am Death."

"Death is a misunderstood element of the cycle of life."

The image of Chaos from the depiction of the window is stuck in my mind. Searching the image like it holds the answers, his enormous form, swirling darkness, filled with all the stars of the galaxy, was so beautiful.

Stars surround him, just like the ones that come alive here when I cast my powers into the sky.

It's so beautiful, and yet I'm—I'm scared.

I'm scared of Death.

Warmth fills me, and the image finally fades as I think I understand now. I'm scared of this power. Afraid of what horrors I may have the potential to unleash with it. And I can't accept it into me, as part of myself, because I fear it.

"How do I become ready, then?"

Let go.

"I don't know how," I whisper, but it's more like a plea. How do I learn to accept something so terrifying?

The three orbs of light spin around us again in a gentle vortex.

Callie encircles me as Pat and Achilles swirl around Hermes. They are pushing us together, and when their memories rush into us, we both know why. Despite the rawness of my pain, the frustration building within me, and the weariness of the battles we've faced, the images our friends show us make me smile.

Hermes' navy eyes hold me in comfort and reassurance as he takes my hand. "Dance with me, little goddess." Kissing my knuckles, he holds my waist as I place my hand on his shoulder.

He sways, and we move our feet in a circle. His smile grows when I roll my eyes, reluctantly moving with him. "This is silly."

"Ba-bum-bum, ba-bum-bum," he makes a tempo for us to follow, and I laugh, burying my head in his chest to hide my embarrassment. "Come on, just let go."

"Yeah, sure." I shrug my shoulders as my sarcastic reply keeps a wide smile on my mate's face. "It's just that easy."

"It can be."

"Ugh!" I dip my head back in exasperation.

Hermes laughs and spins me around twice before taking my waist again to resume his steps. "Relax and just enjoy the moment with me, baby." He leans down for a kiss, which I would never deny. I think his soft lips could solve any problem I could ever have. "Just be in the moment."

The gleam of mischief shines in his eyes as he cocks a smile and lifts an eyebrow. He picks up the pace as he moves us around the darkness. We spin and sway, he dips me back and makes me twirl until I'm dizzy.

"These moments are all we bring with us when we die, Rhea. Not victories or treasures. Just moments." He slows our stride as he tucks my hair behind my ear. "Do you know one of my favorites?"

"Tell me." I shake my head.

"That morning I found you in the bookstore." He smiles, recalling it, and shows me the memory. I'm on the phone, looking at books. "The way your aura shined around you, lighting up your hair and reflecting in your eyes. I'd never seen anything so beautiful." His smile drops as he takes a lock of my hair and lets it run between his fingers. "And you laughed. I knew I wanted to be the one to make you laugh like that, forever. I'll never forget that moment."

He twirls me once, breaking the tension, but it tightens again when he holds me securely against him and takes me in so deeply with his beautiful blue eyes.

"Memento Mori is just a reminder to enjoy the moments while you're living in them so you can hold them close to you when death comes."

I release a heavy breath, and with it, some of the tension in my shoulders relaxes. "Okay, let's live in this moment."

Hermes smiles, but a tremble under our feet makes us look to the dark water surrounding us. Ripples race across the surface and grow stronger as the vibrations intensify. The horizon is lighting up like sunrise is coming.

A surge of souls, every color of the prism, bursts above the plain, racing toward us. My mouth drops in awe as I stare with wide eyes. There must be thousands, streaming toward us like a wave of light rushing toward a dark shoreline.

Hermes and I look at each other, and a smile breaks out over our faces, the same idea running across our bond. Turning around, we clasp hands and run. The wave catches us, and orbs of light streak past us. Overtaken by them, the lights skim the surface of the water, and after a moment, we're no longer running through the dark water but on top of the rushing lights.

I lose my balance, and Hermes catches me. We let the lights carry us, and it's like we're surfing on top of a massive wave as it travels across the ocean. He pulls me to him, taking my hand and wrapping an arm around my waist. "Now, dance with me."

My hair whips around us as the current of the souls carries us across the Void. It's like ice skating, and my cheeks hurt from the smile that seems to be a permanent fixture on my face. We spin and twirl, and the wave rises and falls like it's passing over low rolling hills.

We slide across the top of the orbs faster, and on one of the hills, Hermes holds my waist, lifting me in the air as we spin. My stomach drops, and I yelp. "Don't let me fall."

"I would never let you fall without being there to catch you."

Behind him, the wave is rising, and I bite my lip to hold back my grin. "Prove it." And I take off running for the rising wave.

Pumping my arms and pushing my legs, I race him up the hill that keeps climbing higher and higher. Reaching the top, I slide down a steep incline, and Hermes is right behind me.

Like a surfer riding a wave, I hold my arms out to balance

and slide faster. I'm nearing the end of the surge of lights, and I can see how high we are. Nearly high enough to reach the stars that burn in the eternally dark sky above us.

The end of the wave is a ramp, and I shoot into the air. Like a diver, I point my feet and spread my arms. Closing my eyes, I let the wind caress my face as I rise into an arc across the darkness.

Behind closed eyes, the glow of Hermes' brilliant blue light gets brighter by the second. I open my eyes just in time to see the massive body of his dragon shoot beneath me, timing it perfectly so I drop onto his back.

Ribbons of light cross over my legs to hold me down, and I grab the thick ridges of his armor-like hide. "Hold on tight, little goddess."

The rumble that travels down our bond with his gruff voice shoots through me, making me shiver. "I like your dragon voice." The tenor of my voice is a little breathier than I intended.

"I know."

With a powerful flap of his wings, we shoot upward. My hair flies back as he climbs higher, taking us straight up before leveling out. I think he's going to fly straight and coast on the currents. But he doesn't.

His large head points down, and his long neck curves with it. Like cresting the top of a tall rollercoaster, I prepare for the drop and raise my hands over my head.

Hermes can feel what I'm doing, and the grumble of his laugh vibrates through me as we plunge straight down.

My stomach lurches into my throat, and I whoop into the infinite Void. He tucks his wings close to his body, and we streak toward the ground. My hands fly to the ridges of his back to hold on when he puts us in a corkscrew spin.

I'm laughing. My eyes are watering from the whipping wind. Through the blur of our spin, I see the ground rapidly approaching as we plummet. With only feet remaining until we crash, Hermes opens his mighty wings, and we level out in an instant.

Coasting just above the dark water, we soar, and I don't think I've had such a peaceful moment in ages.

With my arms wide, I let my head fall back. Closing my eyes, I enjoy the serenity of being with my mate in a place where I'm finally safe. Around us, I sense the arrival of the sea of souls.

Like a kaleidoscope of color has ruptured, the orbs of light travel with us, soaring just as fast as my dragon and riding just beneath his large body. It's so beautiful, and I lose myself in the wonder of the lights. The souls begin to pass in front of us, and within seconds, we're surrounded by an ocean of light.

In the front of everything, I find Callie, Pat, and Achilles.

I don't know how I recognize them among all these burning orbs, but I do.

Hermes pumps his wings a few times, and I can feel he's going to change directions again, so I'm ready this time.

The wind curling off his wingtips gets under one of the balls of light, throwing it off course. The rich honey-colored ball of light bounces along the top of his wing, and I reach over, catching it.

"I've got you."

Just then, Hermes flies up again, but instead of climbing higher, we keep going backward. Strapped along his back with his power holding me in place, I'm hanging upside down as he flies us in a big loop. Gaining speed again as he levels out, I keep hold of the soul in my arms until we meet up with the others again.

Turning behind me, I carefully let the soul go, making sure it joins the others. "There you go. I won't let anything happen to you."

My smile fades as the image of Chaos slams into my mind again. It's so abrupt, I nearly freeze, unblinking as I see something I missed before.

In my mind, I see the depiction. The outstretched hand of Chaos with silver lightning is what stuck out when I first observed the depiction, like he was reaching for me, trying to claim me. But it's what is in the other hand that I didn't pay attention to before.

Close to his large body, held delicately within his giant palm, are orbs shining brightly with a glow of every color.

I remember Hecate's words, that Death was just a misunderstood element in the cycle of life, and I get it. I finally get it. A dam of emotions rushes through me as I finally understand the power of Death.

Chaos was no killer. He wasn't the harbinger of death; he was a protector of souls, like a shepherd, keeping his flock safe.

Hermes feels the rush of my excitement through our bond. Like a light being sucked into a black hole, the cosmic dragon is gone. I'm in Hermes' arms, and he's opened a portal, delivering us to the ground. We only need to take a few strides to keep our balance.

"I figured it out!" I begin excitedly, but Hermes stares behind me with wide eyes.

"I can tell."

Spinning around, I gasp. My hands fly to cover my mouth as my mind tries to make sense of what I'm seeing.

It's like a veil has lifted, and we can finally see the Void as it's truly meant to be seen. But it's the face I'm looking at that I can't turn away from.

Callie smiles at me tenderly and opens her arms. I rush forward and crash into her. I feel her arms wrap around me, filling me with warmth as she hugs me back. Completely translucent and shining like yellow sunlight, I know she is still nothing more than an astral projection. A soul taking a solid form, but I have her. I still have her.

I don't know if souls cry, but I do for the both of us. I cry more when I hear her voice.

"It's okay." She squeezes me tighter, and I never want to let her go. "Hey, it's okay."

Next to me, the rich voice of Patroclus calls out to Hermes, "Come here, brother." And the friends, separated for so long, finally reunite. Patroclus' aura, the most beautiful shade of frosted green, looks just like he did. And so does Achilles.

Laughing through tears, hugging, and patting each other's backs, they embrace. "Gods, I've missed you," Hermes tells Pat before he looks at Achilles. The wound of this loss still fresh. "You just had to go show off, didn't you?" Hermes kids with Achilles, but his voice struggles to carry the tone of humor above his sorrow.

"Like you can talk," Achilles answers, doing a much better job of maintaining the intended sarcasm. "A fucking dragon? You'll never shut up now."

We all break into laughter, and Callie pulls away from me, cupping my face. The boys launch into an animated discussion as Hermes tells them what it's like flying and about the transformation. It's like we never missed a moment apart from each other.

"No way, you can breathe fire?" Pat exclaims. "That's badass."

But I just stare into the kind face of my chosen sister as grief steals my voice.

"I know you're down there, beating yourself up about us," Callie scolds me, her tone full of warmth. "Don't. It was our choice." When her words bring a fresh bout of tears, she wipes them away for me. "We suffered more apart. Hey, look at me."

She follows my gaze until I look her in the eyes again. "We're meant to be together." Her smile is serene, and I know she's found peace now. They all have.

But it still hurts.

"I'll work on it." I can't guarantee that I'll ever stop feeling guilty about the sacrifices this war has demanded. "Promise."

"I'll take it." She chuckles and then loops her arm in mine. "Come on. Someone has been waiting for you." Callie turns me toward the mass of souls before us.

Creatures and beings of all kinds surround us. Woodland Fae bow their heads in respect as I pass. A treelike being, similar to Pan and the Librarians, touches my shoulder in reverence. All of them smiling and glad to see their Titan again.

The crowd parts, splitting down the middle. Before me, in a straight line, standing attentively, is a line of people. Women.

Callie urges me forward with her hand on my back. Sweeping her arm out as if presenting them to me, she says, "Your Generals."

"My Generals?"

Moving to stand in front of them, I look at the first person, and my spirit alights with joy as I recognize who is there.

Someone whose face is as familiar as my own, because it once was my face.

"Juliet!" I rush in to hug her, and she drops her formalities, embracing me with a chuckle.

"Goddess. It's good to have you back." She smiles sweetly, then steps back, letting me look at who is next.

"Danaë." I remember the hardship of that lifetime. Such torment, held in constant captivity. That was the lifetime of the Trojan War, when we lost Patroclus.

Next to her is an aura I would recognize anywhere. Rich burgundy, just like her hair, Cleopatra smiles widely, happy to see me. "Get over here and give me a hug."

Down the line I move. One woman to the next, each one a face that used to be mine. A body that served as a vessel, giving me a chance to try and end this curse and stop this war.

Movement at the line's end catches in the corner of my eye. Whoever stands at the end is peeking out, and when I look, they snap back out of my view.

With a curious smile, I skip the others and walk to the end. Tilting my head to see around them, my smile drops when my eyes land on the shy face at the end of the line.

With an aura the color of spun honey, the eyes of a young girl look back at me.

"Rhea." I can barely whisper her name; my name.

I just stare at her for a moment, unable to speak, seeing a younger form of myself standing before me. Her hands are folded in front of her, and she's picking at her fingers, her nervousness simmering inside her at my arrival.

It's not her demeanor that pulls at my heart but her youth.

She was so young.

Still a child, her life ended at only fourteen years old.

She should have still had warm summer nights to chase lightning bugs around a darkening field. The time to learn to drive, to be asked on a date. To have a life.

A life she would never get to live because it was ripped away from her violently. And her body became my vessel. From that moment on, hunted.

A tear rolls down my face as I look at her.

Nervously, she finally looks at me. Just a glance at first, before looking away quickly. I reach out and take her hand, holding it gently in mine.

She smiles sheepishly, finally looking me in the eye. "Did —" She pauses, her voice so gentle. "Did I make you proud?"

The final tether holding back the last of my composure crumbles with her quiet question. Tears rush out of my eyes, unable to hold them back any longer.

"Oh, Rhea." I pull her into a hug, and she grips me back. Her scared little form trembles, and I realize she is crying too. I guess souls can cry.

"You made me so proud." I hold her tightly, wanting to comfort her, to protect her. "I'm so proud of you." I stroke her hair, and even formed of light, it's as soft as you would expect it to be. I rest my cheek on the top of her head until she calms down, gently swaying back and forth to soothe her. "We did it. We survived."

Finally, pulling away, I look at her again. Holding her cheeks in my hands, she smiles. Her earlier anxiety is gone.

Young Rhea steps back into the line, and when Hermes approaches, she gives him a small wave, which he returns. I wrap my arm around his waist, and he kisses the top of my head.

"It's time."

I nod, knowing we need to get back to Gaea soon. Delaying will only give Loki more time to torment those who survive. More time to inflict torment and capture more minds.

Callie hands the younger form of myself a sort of shell, made of clear opalescent light. Young Rhea nods and smiles at her. Reaching down, she scoops some of the dark water into the shell. "The Waters of Remembrance."

I look to Hermes, surprised.

Working so hard to stay away from the water in the Labyrinth, this is the antithesis. Those waters made you forget. But these waters, "These waters will help me remember?"

"Yes, however it's not just your memories that are important." Callie explains. "This war started long before you, and the Void retains the memories of all souls within this water."

"This will let me see the memories of Chaos too, won't it?"

Callie nods. "My brother had the right idea." She gives Hermes a knowing look. "To get to the end, you have to go back to the beginning."

Young Rhea offers me the shell, and I take it with both hands. "Are you ready to go back to the beginning?"

The Age of Artemis

I sit among my siblings, feeling the joy of our gathering yet distracted by the curious absence of our eldest sister. The Circle of the Ancients has been our sacred gathering place since the time of the Titans began. The rising sun casts long, slender shadows across the ground, moving slowly like a natural sundial. The rays land on Artemis's throne, which is never vacant—except today.

Prometheus voices his growing impatience to start the celebration, while Oceanus advocates for patience. A cold unease settles over me. Artemis's absence is unusual, uncharacteristic of her.

"Shouldn't we wait for Artemis?" I ask, my voice tinged with concern that the others seem too festive to share. My siblings brush off my worries nonchalantly.

"Relax, Chaos."

"Does no one else find it odd?" I huff, looking at each of my siblings in their casual merriment.

"You act as if there is a threat." Prometheus dismisses me from his throne of volcanic rock, its surface rough and porous from once-flowing lava. "What harm can come to a Titan?" They jest, but the mirth does not reach my eyes. I feel a disturbance, a whisper in the cosmic winds that chills me to my core.

"Besides, the twins aren't here either." Oceanus slouches lazily in his large, blue-veined marble throne, as rich as the ocean he commands. "And what of Coeus? Do you also complain of his absence, brother?"

Unable to shake the dread tightening around my heart, I excuse myself and retreat to my realm. The air in the Void is thick with the echoes of souls, a constant murmur of life and death I navigate daily. But today, it feels oppressive, heavy with a foreboding I cannot ignore.

I delve deeper into the Void, seeking clarity from the silent whispers of the ancient departed. The Wellspring of Destinies trickles with the Waters of Remembrance. Gently cascading off one ledge and pooling in another, the waters empty into the great Sea of Oblivion, a shallow expanse of black waters serving as a conduit for the comings and goings of souls.

Reaching into the dark sky above, I take a pinch of stardust and sprinkle it with reverence into the top of the Wellspring. The stardust swirls with the gentle churn of the water, casting a pearlescent light, akin to the radiant glow of Avalon's great moon, as I beg a vision of my oldest sister's realm. In the second pool, the stardust fades, overtaken by rich green—the color of envy and gluttony. Then cascading into the final pool of the Wellspring, black.

It doesn't take long before the grim truth reveals itself—a ripple of disorder so profound that it could only mean one thing: an unnatural shift in the delicate balance of the realms.

Artemis is dead.

The knowledge hits me like a physical blow, staggering in

its brutality. Driven by a mix of duty and disbelief, I rush to her realm, Avalon, where the air should be alive with the essence of the wild, but now hangs heavy, tainted with death.

The scene that greets me is a nightmare made manifest. Artemis, the mighty huntress, lies slain, her body a testament to a violent, gruesome end. The ground around her is stained with her blood, the flora wilted and blackened by the corruption of her spilled death—a clear sign that her Titan powers were not just taken but ripped from her with savage force.

A wave of grief crashes over me, threatening to drown me in its depths. Memories of Artemis—her laughter, her strength, her unwavering presence—flood my mind, each one a fresh stab of pain. Who could have done this? What force dares to strike down a Titan with such brazen ferocity?

I fall to my knees beside her lifeless body, my hands trembling as they reach out to touch her cold, still form. A faint flicker within the residue of her blood swirls under the pearlescent moon of Avalon. It's barely there, a whisper of what was once a roar—the essence of Artemis's Titan power, the might of the great huntress.

Carefully, with a reverence that befits her and the power she wielded, I extract these remnants. It is a delicate task, preserving what little remains of her essence, an essence that must not fade into oblivion.

Once secured, I take it back to the Void, where it can be safeguarded against further desecration. Here, in my domain, it will be kept untouched, a fragment of a once-mighty Titan and a somber reminder of our vulnerability, no matter how powerful.

I hang my head in sorrow at the immense loss of my oldest sister, but there is no time to grieve—not yet. I must return to the council to bring the news of this tragedy. There are decisions to be made, answers to be sought, and justice to be pursued. The death of Artemis will not go unanswered, not while I draw breath.

100 Years Later

"It has been one hundred years, Chaos, and still, you persist with this hysteria?" Fenrir spears another piece of roasted boar as he dines alone at his grand table. The air is thick with the age and power of my eldest brother, who looks upon me with a mixture of skepticism and concern.

I need his support, but first, I must convince him of the gravity of the threat we face, so I work to remain calm. Patience will win today.

"The whispers from the Void grow louder and more ominous. They speak of a darkness rising, one that questions our rule and overthrowing the Titans."

"Chaos, we have heard your concerns before. You speak of shadows and whispers, but provide no proof. What makes you think this threat is real?"

"Because, brother, the souls do not lie. They are free from the ambitions that drive the living. And they speak of Artemis not in passing but as a harbinger of what is to come. If we ignore this, we do so at our peril."

Fenrir shifts, the ancient wood throne beneath him groaning slightly. "And you believe that someone is hunting Titans? That Artemis, the great huntress, was slain by such a hunter?"

"Yes," I assert, feeling the weight of the word. "Nothing less than a Titan can slay another, true. But what if there is something we have not yet perceived? We must consider all possibilities."

Fenrir considers this, his brow furrowing before taking another bite. "And what do you propose we do, Chaos?"

"Look for a hunter that is starving enough to consume a Titan. I have faith in you, most of all brother, to follow the scent of our sister's blood and find the god-killer who awaits at the end of that trail."

Fenrir stares at his empty plate, deep in thought. Raising a thick eyebrow, the eldest brother of the Titans has always been incredibly perceptive to his younger siblings. He knows I have more to ask. "And that is all?"

I take a deep breath, readying my request. "Give me a drop of your Titan essence. Let me keep it with what remains of Artemis's powers in the Void. It is a place no other can tread. If something were to happen to any of us, this essence would be a means to avenge and perhaps restore balance."

Fenrir sits silent for a long moment, the gears of contemplation turning behind his ancient eyes. As the seconds stretch on, doubt gnaws at my resolve. Do they all think me mad? My heart pounds in my chest, each beat echoing the rising panic. Finally, he nods slowly.

"I do not share your belief in these shadows, Chaos. But I trust in your dedication to our siblings." Relief and frustration wash over me in equal measure. Relief that he does not dismiss me outright, but frustration at his continued skepticism.

He extends his hand, and from it, a shimmering crimson bead of blood—his Titan essence, concentrated and powerful. "Take it then, safeguard it. Let us hope it is an exercise in caution rather than necessity."

"I hope to never need it, but I am grateful for your trust."

The Age of Erebus

While the dark realm of Elysium feels as natural to me as my own realm, the same cannot be said for the secluded chamber concealing our meeting. The confined space puts me on edge, and the writhing shadows feel all too nosy for my comfort. "The evidence is undeniable now, Themis; Fenrir was murdered, just as Artemis. There is a predator targeting the Titans."

Themis, always stern, now radiates outright hostility. Her glare is accusatory as she regards me with thinly veiled contempt. Erebus, meanwhile, maintains their usual detached demeanor, seemingly unfazed by the undercurrents of distrust swirling around us.

"Chaos, always the herald of doom, but always the first to find our fallen," Themis remarks sharply, her voice laced with suspicion. "Curious how you were the last to see Fenrir alive, isn't it?"

Frustration surges through me at her insinuations. "Are you implying that I am the god-killer, Themis? That I would turn against my own kind?" I ask, my voice steady despite the turmoil inside. "You know me, sister. You know my realm and my duties. Why would I seek the destruction of our own?"

Themis snorts, unmoved by my defense. "Blind faith in family is a dangerous folly, Chaos. Perhaps you seek to control more than just the souls of your hidden realm."

Before I can respond, Erebus, ever the voice of calm in our storms, interjects smoothly. "Or perhaps it is you, Themis, trying to cast suspicion elsewhere while hiding your own guilt. Anyone of us could be under scrutiny with such logic."

Themis's eyes flash with anger, but before she can retort,

Erebus turns to me and hands over a shimmering drop of their own essence. "Safeguard it as you have promised. If Themis is so certain of her innocence, she should have no objection to this precaution."

Themis's scoff is a sharp sound in the tense air, but she does not stop Erebus's gesture. Her silence in the face of their logic speaks volumes, her pride preventing her from acknowledging the wisdom in their words.

"Why deny him if you have nothing to hide?" Erebus adds, their gaze steady on Themis.

"Do not be so blind, sister. We face a danger unlike any before. Dismissing it will be our undoing." I say, meeting Themis's gaze directly. "We must stand united, despite the shadows that seek to divide us, for divided we are surely doomed."

Lady Justice holds my gaze with unwavering suspicion. Swallowing my contempt for her misplaced blame, I take a deep breath. "Themis, you believe me guilty, then lend your powers of Sonus to detect the whispers and loyalties that elude even the most vigilant among us. Uncover the god-killer and those loyal to the monster that is slaying the Titans. Your sense of justice and precision in hearing the truth are crucial now more than ever."

She remains silent for a moment, then nods, my plea doing nothing to convince her of my devotion to the Titans. "Very well, Chaos. I will lend my powers to this search. But remember, justice will be served, no matter where it leads—even if it leads to your doorstep."

Thousands of Years Later: Lapetus—The Lost Realm of the Mind Titan

The vast and infinite abyss stretches endlessly, a dark canvas upon which the stars painted their ancient light. After countless years of searching, navigating through the cosmos, I finally found the lost realm of Lapetus, where Coeus has secluded himself.

The realm of the great Mind Titan is unlike any other. A massive pyramid that Coeus constructed. This architectural marvel stands solemnly amidst the drifting cosmos, a monument to my brother's immense intellect and equally immense isolation.

I find Coeus atop the highest point of the pyramid, his faceless gaze cast out across the stars. He appears serene, but I can see the long solitude has taken its toll, twisting his thoughts into labyrinths as complex as the structure he inhabits.

"You've lost weight, brother." I look across the endless backdrop of swirling galaxies. Coeus's essence is the last I need to collect.

"I knew you'd be the one to eventually come," his voice devoid of warmth, floats across my mind like a leaf on the wind. His tone, once vibrant with the excitement of knowledge, now seems distant, unfocused.

"I have been searching for you for ages," I reply. "There is turmoil among the Titans. Artemis is slain, her essence stolen. Fenrir and Cronus too met the same fate. I fear a dark game is afoot, and it threatens us all."

Coeus has no face. The three sides of his stony head, each one as flat as the other but I see him in my mind. The face he wants me to envision him with against the stony facade of his head.

And across that face, he smiles. A strange, unsettling curve of his lips that does not reach his infinitely seeing black eyes. *"Ah, the games of gods. Why concern yourself with such trivialities, brother? In the grand scheme, what are a few fallen deities?"*

I frown, sensing the depth of his detachment. "Trivialities? Coeus, these are our siblings. Someone is hunting Titans. I do not expect you to help but I do need something from you."

He turns away, looking out into the cosmos again. *"Always so dramatic, Chaos. You see a conspiracy in every shadow, a game in every whisper. But suppose it is a game, I deduce the rules must be fair. One must not hoard the pieces but let them lay where they fall."*

From his thick brown robe, he extracts a vial. A drop of his shimmering Titan essence already extracted. "Coeus, what have you done?"

The rules must be fair.

"Are you saying you have dispersed your essence already, Coeus? That you've partaken in this madness?" Alarm races through me from his coded implications.

Coeus's chuckle drips into my mind, a sound that sends a shiver down my spine. *"Isn't life more interesting with a bit of uncertainty? Remember, brother, to keep the game fair."*

I stare at him, my mind racing to piece together his cryptic words. "Coeus, this is no game! If you have shared your power, you must tell me who you gave it to." I lunge for him, my hands reaching for the scratchy brown robe of the mages.

He simply shakes his head, the ghost of a smirk playing on his lips from the vision in my head as reality falls away from me.

"Always trying to control the chaos, aren't you?" His final

words are a whisper in my mind as I fall into the twists of his illusion.

Bending and moving through space, I emerge with dizzying stillness to the beaches of Hesperides, the vial of his power clutched in my hand.

The realm of Wind, usually serene, is now a storm-torn landscape, and before me lie the bodies of Aellai and Thuellai, the twin Titans of Wind, lifeless and devoid of their divine essence.

My heart sinks as I take in the sight of my fallen sisters, their once vibrant forms now cold and still. Aellai, with her laughter that could lift the darkest clouds, and Thuellai, whose whispers could calm the fiercest storms—both gone. How could this happen? The grief is a physical weight, pressing down on me, but beneath it, a burning fury ignites. Whoever did this will pay dearly.

Above, a massive cyclone tears through the realm. At its center, the monster who has devoured the powers of five Titans. I cannot see him within the swirling vortex, but I feel it the moment his dark eyes meet mine. I sense the wave of insatiable hunger, a compulsion almost, to consume my power thrumming out of him.

The rage boils within me, threatening to erupt. This abomination has taken so much already, and now it stands before me, ready to claim more. My mind races with thoughts of vengeance, strategies to bring this monster down, but amid the chaos, a cold clarity settles. I must be careful. I cannot let my emotions cloud my judgment. I am the guardian of our essences, and I will not let our sacrifices be in vain.

My anger at Coeus simmers as I watch the devastation. His game has escalated far beyond a mere contest of wits or will. It's a war against the very fabric of our existence, pitting Titan against Titan, realm against realm, until nothing but ruin remains.

As the wind howls and the sand stings my face, I clutch the vial tighter. This is no longer just about salvaging the remnants of Titan power or seeking retribution for isolated crimes.

A realization dawns on me, colder than the fiercest gale. Coeus, my brilliant yet twisted brother, has orchestrated this disorder. This war is not born of necessity or destiny but of his own perverse sense of entertainment. He has turned our lives into a lethal game, our deaths into mere pawns on his board.

The betrayal cuts deeper than any blade, and the weight of his actions crashes over me like a relentless tide. My resolve hardens, the fire of righteous anger burning brighter than ever.

I look into the eyes of the monster who has killed my family, the dark vortex of hunger and power that has consumed so many. In those eyes, I see not just a beast, but the manifestation of my brother's cruel intellect.

Coeus thinks himself untouchable, hiding behind his riddles and illusions, but he has underestimated the might of Death, the strength of my will. I must put an end to this senseless carnage. I cannot let Coeus's twisted intrigues destroy us. I will use every ounce of my power, every fragment of essence I have safeguarded, to ensure the survival of our kind, even if it means my own end.

With steely determination, I rise, the vial clutched in my hand a symbol of the hope and vengeance that drives me.

This is no longer a mere battle for survival. It is a war for the protection of life, for the preservation of all that the Titans stand for. My path is clear, and I will walk it without hesitation. For my fallen siblings, for the balance of the realms, and for the end of Coeus's cruel game, I know what must be done.

Remember, brother, to keep the game fair.

Coeus has created our demise.

I will create our savior.

The Sacrifice of Chaos

As I stand amidst the ethereal landscape of the Void, where the essence of departed souls whirl like dancing comets, I feel the weight of my responsibility. Here, in the cradle and resting place of souls, I am reminded of the sacred duty entrusted to me—the protection and guidance of souls along their cosmic journey. The power I wield over death and rebirth is not merely a tool of dominion but a cornerstone of existence itself.

My brother Coeus, lost to his own intellect and isolation, has crafted a monstrous game, one that birthed a god-killer—Loki. Under Coeus's twisted tutelage, Loki has become a force of unimaginable destruction, driven by an insatiable hunger for power and a dangerous obsession with ending the reign of Titans.

Loki poses a threat unlike any other.

With each Titan essence he consumes, he grows stronger, his capabilities expanding into realms that should never intersect. If Loki were to acquire the power of Death, the balance of life would shatter, allowing him to manipulate souls not just as a ruler but as a destroyer. Without souls, the cycles of life would end permanently.

I close my eyes, the voices of the myriad souls whispering through the Void, each a reminder of what is at stake. I cannot, I will not allow Loki to obtain this final piece of power.

Carrying the power of my siblings into the depths of the Void, the power of beings that shaped the cosmos pulse, immense and raw, within my hands.

Around me, the souls of the Void, silent witnesses to the eons of existence, gather and I find comfort in their presence.

As I look upon the thrumming power of my brothers and sisters, I offer a whispered prayer to the very essence of the Void itself.

"Hear the cries of the souls who find refuge within your depths. In this time of darkness, born from madness, grant us a savior. Let a force arise from within you, powerful and pure, to combat the shadows that threaten to engulf everything that is beautiful."

The air around me thickens as my words echo into the nothingness, the souls resonating with my plea, amplifying my prayer.

Understanding the gravity of what is required, this act will be my last, but it will be one of hope.

Slowly, with a solemnity that permeates the very air, I begin to extract the fullness of my essence. The pain is agonizing, each thread of my power pulled from the core of my being, but my resolve does not waver. My vision blurs with the intensity of the pain, and for a moment, I fear I might not have the strength to complete the task. But the thought of Loki, unchecked and unstoppable, drives me forward.

Tears of agony and determination streak down my face as I continue, each moment an eternity. The souls of the Void lend their comfort, understanding the necessity of my sacrifice.

"This is for you, Artemis. For all of us," I whisper through gritted teeth. As my essence ebbs away, I feel a profound sense of peace. I am not just ending; I am transforming, becoming a part of something greater. My final thought is a prayer—that my sacrifice will herald the dawn of a new guardian, one capable of standing against the darkness.

The moment fades into infinite timelessness as I drift away, my final moment of consciousness dissolves as the essence of Death becomes enshrined in the stars and the eternal watchfulness of the Void.

I remember the moment I came into consciousness. It was as if I didn't exist, and then one day, I did. As I hold this newborn soul in my hands, its aura golden amber like warm honey, I wonder if this little being will feel as confused as I did.

The vast empty expanse of the Void has been my home since the moment my eyes opened. It speaks to me in whispers, sharing the secrets of the realms and the souls living their experiences within them. The Void told me my name and showed me how to observe the lives of others through the stars of the cosmos. But it never answered the single burning question within me: what is my purpose?

As souls return to the Void at the end of their lives, I hold them in my hands. The memories of the beauty they experienced play in my mind. The laughter they shared or the feeling of warm summer rain on their faces—I see it all. I laugh and smile as their lives flash before me. Years, eternities, become the sum of several flashes of light, showcasing the best moments they enjoyed most.

These are things I will only savor from afar. The richness is muted, the enjoyment never my own. My solitary existence in this realm means always seeing the glow of the comet's tail after it has passed or feeling the fading warmth of the sun once it's dipped below the horizon. The emptiness that follows is a constant ache, a reminder of my isolation and the unanswered question of my purpose. The blazing fire of life is always in the palm of my hands but never within my reach.

I've never seen the birth of a new soul before. It's so young, so vulnerable, and it stirs something deep within me. For a fleeting moment, I feel a glimmer of purpose. Who else can protect such beauty as it prepares for the experiences of the realms? The thought fills me with both hope and despair as I accept my eternal loneliness.

Sometimes souls return with scuffs from their recent lives marring their brilliant shine, and I can't help but feel a pang of empathy. My aura ignites, a tremendous pulsing power within me, encasing the soul and cleansing the bruises. Yet, as I heal them, I can't ignore the growing emptiness within myself, the unfulfilled longing to be more than a healer, to share in the experiences that leave these marks. Each scuff I mend deepens my own invisible scars, reminders of the life I can never lead.

A war is raging in the realms, and these days, more souls return damaged than whole. Occasionally, a soul cannot be helped. The light within them fades, turning dark, and they disintegrate into fine particles of stardust, returning to the cosmos. The soul is gone forever.

But I have high hopes for this little soul in my hands, a hope that is both bright and bitter. As the others gather around me, we look upon this new being with a collective sense of anticipation. Yet, as they share in the joy of new beginnings, I feel the weight of my isolation even more acutely. Their hope is for a future filled with experiences and connections, while mine remains tethered to the silent vastness of the Void, forever longing for a purpose beyond watching and waiting.

A gasp of excitement escapes my mouth, echoing into the eternal darkness. The ball of light stretches and swirls as it comes into itself. "I think it's waking up." The souls around me exchange happy glances, and we hold our collective breath as the new soul takes shape.

Such a small beauty, with long honey hair, the soul looks at me with wide, curious eyes. "Well, hello there." Kneeling down, I tuck the fabrics of my stola around me. "I am Nyx." The soul is bashful with all these eyes looking upon it as it sees for the first time in its existence. "Would you like to take a look at your life, little one?"

The radiant little being jumps up on two unsteady feet and embraces my neck. "Yes, I would like that very much." Such a sweet little voice this gentle soul carries, and she pulls a smile from all gathered around her.

Taking my hand, we walk to the Wellspring. Unlike me, the souls are born knowing the purpose of their existence: to experience life. The Wellspring's eternal babbling waters trickle down the alternating basins. Eventually, they stream into the endless Sea of Oblivion, the shallow layer of water that covers the entirety of the Void.

Holding my palm to the eternally dark sky above, a shower of stardust falls into my hand, warm and golden yellow, just like the soul before me. Sprinkling the dust into the top of the pools, we watch earnestly as the fine particles of the cosmos show us the first life of this new soul.

"Look there, a beautiful and happy life is ahead for you." I interpret the flows of waters and the luminescent dust of old stars as it sways and curls with the gentle currents. "Long and full of love, your first life will be spent with many loving souls around you that will bid you farewell as you return to the Void."

Amid the turbulence raging within the realms of the living, I delight in this fresh soul having a fate so kind for her first life.

"When will my life be ready for me?"

"We never know, little Honey. Your thread will appear when the time is right and not a moment sooner." I smile, running my hand through her long hair. "But we will wait for it together."

The war of the realms concerns me. It has raged so long, and by the state of the souls as they return to the Void, it shows no signs of stopping. This conflict was a monstrous beast that existed before my consciousness, and I fear it may go on for eternity, forever harming the light within my souls, ripping them apart until only darkness remains.

Laying in the waters with my head resting upon the Wellspring, I watch the stars in the sky above. They aren't really stars but reflections of souls as they travel down the thread of their fate. Beneath the dark water and emanating from the Wellspring, the threads of fate are woven, providing a path for the souls' travel.

These are the souls that are experiencing life. Existing on the plane of the living realms, their journey makes their light shine and pulse. When the life reaches the end of its thread, the star departs from the sky, falling back to the Void and preparing to live again.

Above me, it's a beautiful kaleidoscope of brightly colored stars.

"You watch that one a lot." Honey's sweet voice startles me as the young soul joins me. She's not wrong. Often when I look to the stars, it's this one that I seek out first. Brilliant and blue, it seems to shine brighter than all the others. It calls to me, drawing my eye every time.

"It's very curious, don't you think?"

Honey lies down next to me, both of us looking at the sapphire star above.

"Watch how it jumps." I point at it with my finger, seeing the light shine brighter. I have come to know that this means the soul is about to find a new location in the sky. Just as I thought, the star disappears from the spot it just occupied, appearing in another. "There it is." I point again, always able to find the star quickly.

Honey giggles before asking me about the life that soul is living. It's a favorite way we pass the time. She points to a star above us, and I tell her of the happy things that life is experiencing. But my smile falters because the life of this soul is a difficult one.

A battle-worn warrior, this man has known war most of his life. War is never happy, though the spirit of this soul is strong, and he often finds amusement despite the dark conflicts around him.

"Well, he's very brave," I begin.

"Is he handsome?" Honey giggles.

"Very." I call the star to me, and it floats gently into my hand. The azure light shines brightly, showing us the face of the man. For a moment, I lose myself in the intensity of life that sparkles in his blue eyes. Clearing my throat, I remember Honey and continue to tell her about him.

"Do you know his name?"

"No, but watch this." I begin to hum a tune I sing when I'm alone, having tended to the souls and finally able to relax.

Like always, the star burns brighter in my hand. It jumps, disappearing from my palm, and Honey laughs. Standing up and spinning around, she searches the sky above until she finds it.

"There!"

Singing again, the star brightens and flashes to a new spot. She has a harder time finding it, and when I give her a hint, she points excitedly again. "Found it!"

Over and over, we watch the star jump as I sing. Other souls join us, everyone delighted as we watch Honey enjoy the game. The many spots the star lands indicate a new realm of the living.

We all ignore the dark spots in the sky, the places where billions of stars used to burn, now a desolate expanse of nothing, those realms destroyed and lost to the ether of the cosmos.

I've never seen another being move across the realms as this one does. A property that seems unique to this individual, and I always wonder if one day the star in my hands would be able to appear here.

Just as I'm about to tell Honey it's time to stop, the star's light gets bright, and brighter still. Lighting up the dark sky, the star blazes so hot it turns white, flickering and sparking, and it jumps across the sky erratically. Concern washes over me as I watch the peculiar behavior. Perhaps our game has caused the soul distress.

Alarmed, I call the star back to my hand and offer my calming lullaby. The surrounding souls back away, letting me soothe the star, but it doesn't seem to be working. Within my palm, it flickers as if in constant motion, moving too quickly to see its path. Cupping the delicate orb of light in my palms, I raise it to my chest, letting the calm beat of my heart act as a soothing balm for the star.

Faster and faster it blazes within my hand until it suddenly stops.

Ripples form within the dark water below me, and I sense a heaviness behind me. A presence, like another awareness, is here. Something I have never felt in the Void before, and my heart races within my chest. I seem to know what I will find even before I lift my eyes.

Steadying my breath, my gaze moves from the ripples in the water, slowly up the body of a man until I look into those burning blue eyes that have held my attention so many times.

He's here, standing on a plane that no other being but me has ever crossed.

Releasing the star in my hand to return to the sky above, he follows it before his gaze snaps back to me. A jolt runs through me as if every awareness I've ever had fires within me at once.

His breath is racing. His shoulders rise and fall as if he's just run a great distance. I look at the sword in his hands, then back to his eyes. He notices and holds out a hand in surrender. He moves slowly to put the sword behind his back, fixing it into a holster strapped across his shoulders.

"I–I heard singing." His voice is much deeper than I imagined, yet it feels perfectly familiar to me. "I had to find out who was singing." He just stares at me, as if the answers to all his questions are found in my face.

He hardly blinks, and it's almost as if he has forgotten how to speak entirely.

I have never been around one of the living before. Since my existence began, I have only resided with my souls and seen the experiences of the living through their memories and by watching the stars.

His presence scares me, but nothing about him makes me feel afraid. It is more the unfamiliarity of being around another, suddenly feeling the weight of his stare as he shares the space with me. In him, I sense the same pulsing and tremendous power that resides within me, and that sense of familiarity puts me at ease.

I have seen many ways the living greet each other, and I'm not certain which is correct, but there is one that I like the most.

Taking several slow and tentative steps toward him, my movement inspires him, and he meets me after a few careful strides of his own. Extending my hand, his touch meets mine, and the explosion of a thousand stars ignites within me. "I am Nyx."

Raising my hand to his mouth, his lips touch my knuckles, a gentle kiss left on my skin as his gaze never wavers from my eyes. "I am Hermes."

It's difficult to tell the passage of time here. It moves in a churn, flowing in all directions. Time is not such a straightforward concept within the Void as it exists in the realms of the living.

I think that is why Hermes likes coming here so much. He can take an endless break from the war of the realms and rest.

"I think he likes coming here for you," Honey says with a smirk as we watch the Wellspring show an old soul their next life.

"I would agree with the youngling, goddess," the older soul chimes in, siding with everyone's favorite youngling. In truth, Honey is our only youngling.

I cannot deny the excitement I feel as I watch the blue star of the Void sky flare to a powerful brilliance. It means Hermes is coming to visit, and my stomach flips on its end.

The flash of his aura bursts in the darkness, and my smile radiates just as brightly. But he holds something within his hand, his other shielding my view. He looks at me, a curious expression on his face of concentration but also amusement.

He takes careful steps as if the item he carries is very precious to him. "I want to show you something."

Intrigue pulls me to him like a tether, and I peek around his hands. "What is that?" The curious little item seems so delicate as he holds it gently in his large hands.

"It's a flower."

"Is it dangerous?"

Hermes's laugh is one of the most joyful sounds I have experienced, and I love watching his eyes brighten with enjoyment when he does it.

"Why is my question funny? You carry it as if it will erupt at any moment."

"It is not dangerous, just delicate. It's a dandelion, my sister's favorite flower."

"A dandelion," I repeat the name of the flower as I move to inspect it, trying to understand why Hermes carries it so carefully. It's like a sunburst of white threads perched atop the green stem. I cannot understand how it remains poised on such a small pedestal. It looks like a cloud has been captured, and Hermes is shielding it before it blows away.

"What do you do with it?"

"You make a wish."

"I have heard of a wish, but I've never seen one. What do they look like?"

"A wish can be anything you want to come true." Hermes hands the gentle flower to me, and I grasp the stem carefully between my fingers. "A wish is like a dream that you carry inside you, hoping it comes true one day."

"Then you make the wish out of this flower?"

"Not exactly. Some wishes never come true, but others may." Hermes stands next to me, his hand covering mine as he raises the flower higher. "When you blow on this flower, each seed will carry your thoughts and dreams into the breeze. And maybe the winds will bring your wish back to you."

He watches me as I look at the flower, his words tumbling around in my mind. So many things I would wish for, I'm not sure which I should send into the wind first. Holding the flower in my hand, smelling its gentle fragrance, I would wish to see more things like this.

But most of all, I wish Hermes would be the one to show them to me. This thought makes my cheeks burn as embarrassment rises within me. Forming an "o" with my mouth, I blow a gentle breath and watch as the tiny white spires catch and spiral upward.

They drift gracefully, carried by the gentle currents, the elegance of their flight filling me with a profound sense of wonder. I watch until the darkness of the Void takes them over.

"What did you wish for?" It's a simple question, but Hermes's tone and the intensity in his deep blue eyes make me feel like his next breath is bound to my answer. Without meaning to, I realize I've turned to face him, and our nearness makes my heart thunder in my chest. It's pounding so loudly, I'm afraid he'll hear it.

"I–wished to see all the flowers of all the realms," my gaze dances between his eyes. He's holding on to my words, as if begging me to say more. "with you."

I don't know what compelled me to reveal the last of my wish, but I wanted him to know. For so long I've wanted nothing more than to know the experiences of the living. But now, I want nothing more than to live those experiences with Hermes.

He steps closer to me, and looking down, he takes my hand in his. "I made a wish as well."

My heart stills, no longer galloping within me, now it waits with anticipation.

"I wished I could take you to see all the flowers of all the realms." Hermes tenderly strokes my cheek with two knuckles. The feeling of his gentle touch is such a contrast to the raging tempest it ignites within me.

"I have seen many moments like this through the memories of the souls." Seizing a moment of bravery, I raise my hands to his chest, feeling his taught muscles beneath his clothes. Under my palms, I feel his pounding heart, a mirror of my own. Hermes holds me within the safe harbor of his arms, his hands resting low on my back. "Is this the moment we are to kiss?"

A crooked smile sneaks onto Hermes's face, but it is quickly overtaken by a look of intense desire. "Would you like me to kiss you?" His breath against my lips is warm, so close as he leans toward me. Inch by inch, he moves so carefully as if I am an animal he is trying not to scare away.

"I would like that very much."

A s Hermes' lips touch mine, the Void falls away in gentle waves of silence, leaving just the two of us adrift in this single, elongated moment. My hands wander up his chest. Exploring his skin, I run my fingers through his soft dark hair at the nape of his neck. There's a tenderness in his kiss that catches me off guard, not just by its softness, but by the profound effect it has on me.

Why does it feel as if every nerve in my body is suddenly awake, electric with anticipation? The warmth of his lips against mine sends a ripple of sensations through me, stirring a cascade of emotions I hadn't anticipated. A part of me wants to draw back, to retreat into the familiar shell of my solitude, but a stronger part urges me to linger, to savor this sweet, new sensation.

My mind races with questions and doubts. Is this okay? Does he feel the same shiver of excitement, the same tumultuous thrill that's barreling through me? His hand, gentle on my cheek, seems to answer my unspoken worries, grounding me in the reality of the moment. It's okay. I'm okay.

As the kiss deepens, my thoughts begin to quiet. The growing awareness of every point of contact between us overshadows everything else. The Void, with its endless whispers and the constant rush of life and death, fades into a distant hum. All that matters now is the cocoon of Hermes' embrace that envelops me.

I feel vulnerable, yet there's a strength in this vulnerability, a courage found within the soft press of lips that murmur unspoken promises. It's as if every nerve in my body is suddenly awake, electric with anticipation, and I'm curious if this is what love feels like. The memories of souls carry this profound sentiment back with them most of all. Love.

We could have been here for seconds or centuries, and I wouldn't know the difference. All I know now is this moment —this kiss, this man.

As we finally part, a breathless laugh escapes me. It's a sound of surprise at my own daring, a release of the solitary tension that has built up inside me.

The smile across Hermes' face is one I want to memorize. The tenderness in his gaze that softens just for me is something I don't think I could ever bear parting with. He chuckles along with me. Lifting me by my waist and spinning me around before lowering me to the ground again.

My heart races, not with fear, but with joy and excitement for what might come. For the multitude of experiences that I may finally get to hold within my hands. And right now, I want to feel more of Hermes and have another taste of his lips.

Circling my arms around his neck, he holds me tightly around my waist. "I wish I could kiss you again." The molten heat that takes over his eyes steals my breath.

"That is a wish I want to make come true for the rest of forever."

"I know you worry about him, goddess, but your Hermes has always come back to you." My friends gather around me as I watch the Wellspring. It shows me Hermes and the realm of eternal sunlight where he and others are residing.

They are fleeing from the war that is consuming the realms, and while Hermes has told me of the battles, I know he tries to hold back the worst of it. Our time together is fleeting, and neither of us wants to spend it discussing death.

But the war of the living harms my souls. It impedes the life the Wellspring intends for them, like an invasive and carnivorous weed. I would be lying if I said it is only the souls under my care that concern me.

It is Hermes that I also worry about now. He is a brave warrior, faithful to fight alongside his mother and father. He and his sister are both formidable in combat. But the sooner this war can end, the sooner my souls can be free from harm, and the sooner Hermes will be safe.

I hum my gentle song. The one that somehow reaches his soul, and I watch the moment it wraps around him. The smile that spreads across his face is mirrored on my own. Within a moment, he has excused himself from his father, and the power he commands surrounds him.

I've come to learn that I can sense the thrum of his magic and know where his portal of blue starlight will open. I rush to it the second I feel it, and when it swirls to life, I jump into his arms.

His starving lips collide with mine. One hand fists my long raven hair, and the other holds me up, my legs circling his hips as I grasp his neck. We pull away, breathless, and he rests his forehead against mine. "Gods, I've missed you so much."

The happy moment of our reunion is ruptured by an enormous lightning crack across the Void sky. We look up at once, and horror freezes me as I watch the stars fall.

"No," I whisper, helpless to combat the devastation unfolding.

"What is happening?" Hermes keeps his hold around me, protective and strong, even though we both know there is no danger capable of reaching this realm.

Before I can answer, the souls begin arriving.

So many, I can't keep track of them as they hurl toward us, burning and singed. Their wails bombard us, and I'm overwhelmed with the sheer volume of stars passing us by, bouncing into the waters of the Void from every direction.

"Nyx, tell me what is happening."

"They're all dying." I sob, falling to my knees as a fading soul hits the dark waters right in front of us, coming to a stop at my feet. "No." I beg as the light is extinguished and the soul fades into stardust in my hands.

All around me, souls die. My tears choke me as I crawl to the next soul closest to me. My power surrounds it, healing the damage as my eyes dart to the next one.

Hermes takes my shoulders, kneeling to meet my eye. "What realm is this?" His eyes are frantic as he comes to understand. "A realm is being destroyed; do you know which?"

"So much fire." I whisper, large tears pooling in my eyes, holding back their retreat a moment before racing down my face.

"Ares." Hermes breathes the name as he looks to the sky above us. The region of the sky where the stars are falling becomes darker and darker with each passing second. He looks back at me, his gentle hand cupping my cheek as he winces at my pain. "What can I do?"

I don't know what can be done to stop the monster that is this ravaging war. I cannot see down the horizon on either end to know the start or the end of this conflict, but I feel the crack against my heart with each soul that dims forever.

A high-pitched ring resonates through the infinite abyss, gentle and beautiful. Within the Void sky, a yellow light like a burst of sun pulses. The wave of its light ripples outward.

"It's my father." Hermes watches the yellow wave of light, then looks to me. There is a war within him, ripping him in two pieces. He needs to go help, but he doesn't want to leave me.

I rush into his arms and kiss him with desperation. As the souls of a realm die and fall around us, I suddenly feel the very real fear that Hermes could leave and never return again. "Don't go down there." I plea, knowing he must.

"Nyx, my heart is breaking at the thought of leaving you like this." He holds my face with both his hands, kissing my forehead, my cheek, then my lips. "I know you're safe here, but I must go. More will die if I stay." While I know he is right, the words are like a stab to my stomach. "Nyx, look at me, please."

He takes my chin, gently lifting my gaze to his. "There is not a power strong enough that could take me from you." The sincerity of his declaration is evident in the intensity of his eyes, but I know he can't stay here. "But they need you." He looks around at the constant stream of falling stars among the rising dust of extinguished life. "I promise I'll come back for you."

I nod as tears fall from my face.

"Okay? I promise." Hermes kisses me and wipes the tears

from my eyes with his thumbs. "Tell me you believe me." He rests his forehead against mine, whispering his plea as the tug on his conscience pulls harder.

"I believe you." I take his face between my hands and hold his eyes before kissing him. "Go." Kiss. "I'll be here, waiting for you among the stars." Kiss. "Always."

Still holding onto my hand, he stands, not wanting to break our touch until the last moment. As soon as he lets go, the swirl of his portal engulfs him. My outstretched hand is so close I feel the warmth of Tartarus brush against me.

From my fingertips, a swirl of power emits from me. Something I have never encountered before. As if some power within me has awakened, and I want to call upon it again, but another bombardment of falling souls pulls my gaze with a snap.

The despair of their misery has become a haunting melody that echoes across the Void and demands my help. Standing, I raise my arms. Focusing my power and my connection to this realm, it pulses out of me.

Wave after wave of silver starlight rolls down my body and across the Void. Damaged souls are mended. The souls beyond my help are held within my embrace as the cosmos reclaims them, and I weep for each one.

Around me are beings of light, rocked by the sudden departure of so many souls. Clinging to each other in comfort, the reality of this war settles in and cements itself around my mind. The Void is my domain, and while I do not walk among the realms of the living, their strife affects my realm and the souls under my care as much as it does theirs.

No longer will I remain here and watch the destruction of another realm as souls become a star shower around me.

With determination set in my mind, I walk to the Wellspring. Palm raised to the Void sky, I receive an offering of stardust and cast it into the waters, demanding to know how I came to be. My purpose cannot be a fate of eternal loneliness in a land of infinite darkness. Not when there is so much wonder and light within my heart. Right now, that light is a burning cauldron of fire that heats more with each soul that falls from the sky.

This war existed before me, but it will end, with me.

The Wellspring answers my demand.

As the memories of Chaos fade to black, I open my eyes as if seeing for the first time. Looking at my hands, they look different but the same. It is as if I could always see every tiny particle of life that made up my flesh, but now I know why.

The power of twelve immense beings resides within me, and one of them just died.

Prometheus, Titan of Fire and guardian over the realm of Vulcan, was struck down. His realm, destroyed and all life that inhabited it, consumed.

Only two Titans remain to combat the evil devouring the realms. But this being, this entity has stolen the power of nine Titans. Even fighting together, they will be no match for him. The realms they safeguard—

The thought of absolute destruction halts in my mind before I can finish it.

Cold dread encases me as I realize it's only a matter of time before these final realms fall as well. And Hermes has just returned to one of them.

My eyes shoot to the sky above, and I find him in an instant.

The radiant blue beacon that glows clearer than all other

stars calls to me, and I want to go to him. I want to fight with him, and within my hands, pulsing beneath my flesh, is the only power strong enough to stop this devastation.

Chaos ensured his power over these delicate beings would never fall into the hands of the gluttonous monster that hunts the realms of the living. He prayed to the Void for a savior and ended his life so that mine may begin.

As thunder rolls across the Void sky above me, I am determined to leave this realm to join the fight of the living, just as Chaos intended. The souls that rest here in the infinite Void are mine to guard, but so are the ones experiencing their life. Housed within the bodies of the living, those souls need me too.

A second loud crack of lightning flashes above, and my heart breaks open with it.

Another realm is under attack, and now I know it's Tartarus, realm of Earth and the Titan Hyperion. The realm where Hermes is.

I hold my breath as a stream of stars begins falling from the dark sky above. Tartarus is fighting back, and the losses are much less than the star shower that fell from Vulcan just a moment ago.

I catch the falling souls with a blanket of my power, healing them as they return to the haven of darkness, but my gaze never wavers from the blue star that still shines in the sky.

As Hermes' power flares, my heart leaps with hope that the fight is over and he is returning, but disappointment swallows me when he jumps to another realm. The realm of Oceanus and the power of Water, Gaea.

His powers flash as he travels back and forth. A streak of fast-moving light that is teleporting between realms. Stars fall in a continuous stream from Tartarus, victims of the battle that is raging there.

Warriors are rallying against the monster, and if I can join them, we can put an end to this.

Looking at my hands, I pull the ribbons of power within me, thinking of Hermes and the swirling portal of his starlit power. Chaos also used this power, coming and going from many realms as he pleased, always returning to the Void anytime he wished. If he could leave, then so can I.

Within my mind, I see the black rolling smoke and feel the electric tingle of power come alive within me. Above, the stars are descending faster. More lives are coming to an end too soon, and the immortal that holds my heart in his hands is fighting in the very center of it all.

I watch the flashes of Hermes' power as he jumps from realm to realm. Faster he moves as more souls fall to the Void. Within me, my torment and determination build to an apex as swells of black mist seep out of me.

Silver lightning flashes within my power as I work to understand it, to form it into a doorway that will open at my command.

Another crack resonates above me, another wave of hurt and dying souls floods the Void. The light of Hermes' star is beginning to spark and flash, like a star on the verge of implosion.

My tears turn to anger as the darkness around me churns into a raging tempest.

Holding my hand out in front of me, I push everything I can into it, my mind set on Hermes.

Finally, the vortex forms, and lightning flashes around the

edges. The flare of Hermes' power grows, and I know he's nearing an end.

Of what, I don't know, or perhaps I'm too scared to admit.

But it's the final push of my desperation that breathes life into the portal. With a flash of silver starlight, shrouded in black mist, I feel the opening before me.

Keeping my eyes fixed on the churning portal of my power, I think of my destination, my home. Hermes.

Moving one foot after the other, I walk out of the realm where I have lived in solitary darkness for so many ages and step forward into a new realm.

I step forward, into my destiny.

I had often wondered what path a soul takes as it returns to the Void. Never did I imagine I would return as a soul myself. Never did I think I would die.

"Oh, our goddess, what happened to you?"

Seeing the Void through the eyes of a soul, it looks so different yet still the same. Just as before, one moment, I didn't exist, and the next, I did. But this is the painful opposite of my first awakening. For Hermes, for the friends I have made during my time on Gaea, one moment I existed, and the next, I didn't.

This enemy is a clever one, or perhaps I am too naive. Anger courses through me that we didn't discover the truth of the monster that devours Titans until it was far too late.

But as Chaos ensured the power of Death would never fall into Loki's hands, I did as well. As I lay upon the cyan-colored grass of Avalon, looking into the eyes of my weeping mate, I offered my sacrifice to safeguard the souls of my realm, of all the realms. I handed over my power as the life drained from my body.

As the realm of souls opened to welcome me back to the

Void, I left my mate behind with a promise that he would never be able to hear: *"I'll be here, waiting for you among the stars."*

Returning to the Void was as easy as opening my eyes after a long slumber, surrounded by the beautiful beings I am to protect, and I feel as though I have failed them.

"I missed you, goddess." Honey wraps her golden light around me.

Tears well up as I kneel before her, my voice trembling with the weight of our reunion. "I missed you too, sweet Honey." Her golden light envelops me, warming the cold void within my heart. I hold her tightly, feeling the delicate pulse of her essence against mine, a reminder of all I have lost and found again in this fragile moment.

"My new life is still not ready yet. I was worried you would miss it." Her innocence is so endearing, and I remind myself, she is the only new soul that has been born of the infinite cosmos in so many ages. As all these beings darken into nothing, one radiant beam of light has emerged, and her smile is enough to bring me back to my calling, to my purpose as the protector of souls.

Holding her hand, I bop her on the tip of her nose, and she lets loose a chuckle that I've so dearly missed hearing. "I wouldn't miss it for all the realms."

Walking to the Wellspring of Destinies, I swallow the torrents of grief that want to consume me as news spreads of my return and my souls gather. Peering into the waters, I beg a favor of the Void.

Show him to me.

The water within the Wellspring glimmers with the beautiful blue shine that matches Hermes' aura. His reflection comes into view, and grief weighs him down so heavily. I want to reach out and touch him, to comfort him so that he knows I am still here.

But as my finger touches the surface of the water, it ripples, distorting my view of him, and I pull it away. He sits atop the tall falls where we committed our fated bond, gazing up at a full moon. The breeze rustles his dark hair, and I pretend that it is me, running my fingers through his soft locks.

I hum the tune that called him to me and watch as he closes his eyes, lifting his face to the moonlight as a tear rolls down his cheek. He is beautiful, wrapped in the velvet cloak of night, but I have to look away as I fear my sorrow may cause me to stay here where I can watch him forever.

There is much work to be done so I can return to him.

Preparing the question I need to ask, I look at the souls around me, knowing the weight of my request will be a heavy one. The principle of a soul's existence is built around the fundamental of life, living out vast experiences, and I must ask one of them to forfeit that. A request I do not take lightly.

"A boundless terror plagues the last realm of the great Titans. Gaea is the final stronghold in a long and terrible war." I pause as more gather. The babbling waters of the Wellspring showcase my memories of the war that rages within that realm. "The Titan-slayer has consumed all the powers of the Titans, except Chaos'. You all know the sacrifice made to ensure the power of Death does not fall into his hands. A sacrifice I have been forced to repeat."

A wave of sadness washes over me as the last moments of my life are displayed for the souls of the Void. Clearing my throat, I draw strength from the faces around me and continue.

"But I must ask another sacrifice to be paid when the time

comes. I must ask for a life, but please know, I do not do so lightly."

"You may have mine, my goddess." The answer from a willing soul is immediate and brings warm tears to my eyes.

"You may have mine as well."

"Take my life, goddess."

All around me, the voices of souls rise up. Each of them willing to offer their opportunity to fulfill their calling and give it to me.

"Before you agree," I hold my hand up, and they quiet. "For the one who ties their life to mine, I have to warn that you do so at the risk of great peril. This decision will alter the destiny of that life, and there will be no certainty of what you will face."

My warning does nothing to thwart the volunteers, and while I am grateful to have so many, we must be selective if the plan is to work.

"We will watch the Wellspring when a life is ready, but not every thread can be shared by two souls. We must wait for the right one, and if the soul is willing, I will share it with you and offer my eternal gratitude."

Ages seem to pass before the souls rush to me, excitement thrumming through their translucent bodies of light. The Wellspring has provided a life, and it is perfect.

"How do you know which life is the right one, goddess?" Honey holds my hand as we walk the Sea of Oblivion, following the thread of filament as it glows in the dark water.

"See how the thread turns and bends, its color bright, the

fibers strong. And just there," I point with my finger, and young Honey follows with her curious eyes. "A knot in the thread. Along the journey, this soul will encounter a tremendous event. What kind, I do not know, but the soul can either end their journey there and return to the Void or persevere and continue their experience of life."

"And that is when you will take the life?"

"Yes, I will take the thread in that moment, and the remainder of that life will be mine. The soul will return and await another."

Eve approaches, the light of her soul thrumming along with the pulse of the thread. Her kind eyes hold me without a kernel of fear, ready to give the offering of her life for my cause.

"Are you sure about this?"

"Yes, my goddess," Eve says, her voice steady and unwavering. As she extends her hand, a warm smile spreads across her face, though her eyes glisten with unshed tears. "It would be my greatest honor to help you return to your true form and end this terrible war." Her hand in mine feels both fragile and resolute, a symbol of the immense sacrifice she is ready to make. "This is not just for you," she whispers, her voice breaking, "but for the fate of all souls." The weight of her words presses heavily on my heart, and I squeeze her hand, drawing strength from her courage.

Nodding, I grasp her wrist, feeling the pulse of her determination mirroring my own tumultuous emotions. "I am ready," Eve says, her firm nod conveying a certainty I desperately try to match.

As her words hang in the air, a wave of nervousness surges within me, the prospect of seeing my mate again intertwining with the fear of failure. My soul thrums against the walls of my being, a relentless reminder of the stakes we face.

The monster that hunts the Titans' power will detect the essence of my aura, in that I have no doubts. Created by the Void, I will forever carry the residue of power that was imbued within me during my creation. From the moment Eve closes her eyes and I open them, I will be hunted.

Holding my hand, Eve takes a steadying breath. Closing her eyes, she grabs the radiant filament. Her soul begins the journey, and she joins the stars above. The thread now rests within my hands as I carefully watch the course of her life.

As the ball of light moves along its path, overlapping with other souls on journeys of their own, she navigates the twists and turns of her life. She is nearing the knot in the thread; the moment of exchange is so near, and anticipation leaps in my throat.

Taking the knot in my hands, I close my eyes and feel the moment of her ascension. As if a great vacuum has opened, I'm pulled from the Void. The realm before me stretches and blurs as I race along the thread of this soul's life, ready to walk the rest of this path, defeating my enemy, and reuniting with my mate.

A thousand times we've done this, and a thousand times, we've failed. So many lives have been abandoned to this effort, and each time I return unsuccessful, the Void grows darker and darker for me.

While I have amassed an army of generals, who stand at the

Wellspring, inspecting each thread carefully, I cannot ignore the doubt that plagues me during these periods of wait.

Sometimes centuries pass in the realm of Gaea, and other times, millennia. But any length of time separated from my mate seems like an eternity. Every moment is another opportunity for the great hunter to devise new plans and prepare for my next arrival.

As I return from each life, I beg a favor of the Wellspring to see him. It was after my second death, during the life of Eve, when my hunter began using the waters of forgetting. Raining Lethe upon the realm, they forgot me.

Crying into the Wellsprings waters, I mourned the death of their memories. The work we put into preparing for our victory, would be lost, forgotten, along with our staggering defeat. And as I wept, the Void granted me a favor: The Waters of Remembrance.

A single drop rained upon my mate. His memories of our lifetime together, returned.

Since then, a thousand favors have been granted by the Void. After each death, amid the raining Lethe that poisons the memories of my loved ones, fragments of the recent lifetime we just shared return to them.

Looking upon my soul at the marks and scars that mar me, my sorrow plummets. My gaze wanders to the souls around me, damaged by the brutalities of these war-struck lives, we display the harsh reality of my absent powers. Without the power of the Titan within me, I cannot heal them when they return with the wounds of their life.

And I cannot heal myself either.

The wounds of my thousand trials come with me into each

life as I attempt to end this war, and I carry them like heavy chains.

Spending my time waiting, I always come back to the Void sky and watch the beaconing light of my mate. Commotion approaching to my side grows louder as several of my generals bicker in hushed tones.

"What is all the fuss about?"

Cleopatra and Eve exchange a cautionary glance while Persephone stands with her arms crossed. "I told them you aren't going to go for it."

"Go for what?"

"A life is ready." Cleo interjects.

"Wonderful." A thrill runs through me as only four centuries have passed since our last trial. "Who does it belong to?"

My shoulders sag, and the elation that just surged through me is blown out in an instant. Juliet steps out from behind the others with her hands on Honey's shoulders. The deep golden hue of her aura pulses, as it does for all souls when their next life is ready.

***

"Absolutely not." I nearly bark at Cleopatra and Eve's consideration. "She is a youngling, her soul brand new. We will not put her in such harm's way."

"Goddess," Joan interjects. Her voice always calm and one of logic. "I believe you should consider it."

"I will not put this on the shoulders of a child. You know yourself how difficult the journey is, and your knot was further along the thread than Honey's. Your soul, much older than hers." I release a huff of exasperation. "Three souls have not survived ascension and returned to stardust. Do you wish her to be another?"

"But I can do it, goddess." Honey practically stomps her feet, frustrated I'm not allowing her to give up the thread of her life as the others have.

Kneeling down, I hold her chin and make her look at me. "I believe you could do it, little one, but you should not have to. Look at your thread, Honey." The golden glow of the thread is brilliant, the brightest we've seen in a long time. "You'll have so much happiness and a wonderfully long experience. We have waited for this day since you arrived in the Void, and it's finally here."

She tries to look away from me as angry tears well in her eyes. "I'm so excited to watch your first journey, and I can't wait until you return to share all the amazing things your life will give you."

Taking her hand in mine, I turn back to my generals. "We'll wait for the next one."

Arguments and discussions create a dull roar around us as more of my generals gather for the conversation.

There is a tug on my arm that pulls my head to Honey as she reaches for the thread, her hand locked in mine. "I promise I will make you proud," Honey whispers, her voice a fragile string that weaves through the tumult of emotions that rush through me.

As her small hand reaches for the thread of her life, fear jolts through me. My aura surges around her, desperate to protect yet powerless to stop her sacrifice. The brilliant golden light of her essence merges with my own, a bittersweet convergence of her hope and my despair. Tears blur my vision as her final words echo in my mind.

"NO!" My voice bounces in an endless echo as my generals watch in shock. I stare at my empty hand, the one that just held the small soul safely here. Now, instead of her golden glow, I hold the thread of her life, entirely devoured by my own silver aura.

The shine of the light reflects on the Void sky above like a silver beacon blazing brightly for all to see. The essence of my power surrounded her as her soul was born into the body she will inhabit. She will be hunted the second she opens her eyes.

"We're so sorry, goddess." Cleo tries to soothe me, but I can't look at anything else but the tether of Honey's life. She has two parents, and they name her Rhea.

They are kind and gentle, just as the Wellspring showed us. She has a brother and loves him so. He is supposed to be with her when she ends her life as a very old woman.

The immortals detect my aura that encases her. Anticipation builds as the threads around her begin converging. I look ahead, beyond the knot, and see the threads of destiny change as our actions have altered the course of this life.

The glow of her light travels closer to the knot, and the moment of her ascension draws near as my anger rises. The green blazing aura of my hunter stalks ever closer to the silver shine that is now Honey.

The attack begins too soon: a car accident.

"Please," I whisper a plea to the realms to spare her as powerful immortals surround her, their powers invading her mind, drawing out the agony with mindless cruelty as they control the crashing car.

My hands shake, and my vision turns to static. My rage

billows out of me as the hunter arrives. It's his power that takes her life, extinguishing the lives of her mortal family with her.

The Void is filled with a plume of black mist so entirely that all I can see is the thread in my hand and the little silver bead of light traveling upon it. My eyes dart ahead, following the shifted threads that show fate's new path.

The line of another's life converges with this one, and together, the two threads travel on until they disappear into the darkness of my mist. The brilliant silver shimmer of this thread meets with the blazing sapphire light of my mate, and in the center of my soul, I know this is it.

This is the lifetime the hunt for my power ends.

I look back to my generals as they see the new course of destiny.

Cleopatra nods, her face set in stern determination. "We will be ready for your return, no matter the outcome."

"When I return," I look back to the thread as Honey approaches the knot. "be ready for war."

I f Chaos was my father, then darkness was my mother, and I was created from a prayer and a sacrifice in the womb of the Void. Now, standing in the abyss of souls, I gaze into the Wellspring. The Waters of Remembrance have healed every crevasse in my memory, restoring the fullness of my past lives to me and Hermes. The weight of a thousand deaths is heavy, and I take a moment to let it settle.

The journey to this moment has been filled with pain, loss, and immeasurable sacrifice. But as I look across the sea of souls, their lights blazing, I know what I'm fighting for.

Calypso stands with her mates, turning on tiptoe to kiss each of them. Scars stripe her back, gleaming brighter than the rest of her translucent form. I grimace, knowing the torment she endured, much of it by my side.

Facing me, she passes me a look of understanding. *"Don't blame yourself."*

"You can't tell me what to do," I jest, though sorrow coats my words.

Hermes stands next to me, my constant comfort across a thousand lives. We've waited so long for this moment, and now that it's here, I can't bring myself to take one more step.

"Everything changes after this moment," my voice shakes with rising nerves.

"No," Hermes strokes my cheek, taking his time as he searches my eyes. "Everything changed the second Honey started this life. You changed fate, determined to protect her and ensure her sacrifice wouldn't be in vain."

"She didn't deserve this."

"Neither did you." Hermes turns me to him, softening his voice as he rubs my arms. "She had a life with a family that loved her, just like you promised her. It's you who endured the hardships after the car crash. You had no one fighting for you."

Tears gather as my throat tightens.

"And look at you. You became the protector you needed ten years ago. You overcame every trial of your thousand lives because you refused to give up on what you were fighting for. It's them—the souls that rest in this realm of darkness." Hermes looks around, marveling at the stars above us. "You ordained this moment long ago, so let's live in it."

Nodding, I take a deep breath and release it.

Reaching into the bottom pool of the Wellspring, I find what I have been searching for. With my fingers around the handle, I close my eyes. The culmination of a thousand sacrifices has brought me here. As I lift the Caduceus from the black waters, I feel the weight of the powers within, ready to reunite with me. Taking it in both hands, I open my eyes, beholding the staff of Hermes for the first time in ages.

The winding snakes hold the powers of the Mind. The eternally burning flame dances with the soft current of the Void's wind, holding the power of Fire. And the wings of the phoenix represent Death. The Caduceus gleams with my ancient power, pulsating with the energies it has safeguarded through the ages.

As it rests in my hands, a surge of familiarity washes over me. My fingers wrap around the cool, metallic shaft, and a flood of emotions stirs within me. The staff vibrates gently, eager to return what has been withheld from me for so long.

With a deep, steadying breath, I close my eyes and open my heart to restore my immortality. A pulsating thrum echoes silently through the Void. The staff responds, its glyphs and symbols illuminating with a brilliant silver glow. The air thickens, heavy with power, as the moment suspends in time.

Slowly, I feel the essences of Mind, Fire, and Death stir from their confinement. They emerge like ethereal wisps, spiraling around the Caduceus and inching closer to me.

The soft current of the Void grows stronger as my powers caress my skin, blowing my hair and disturbing the stillness of the dark water at my feet. The wind rages as I feel the essence of my powers return to me.

The Caduceus vibrates and rattles my arms. The sensations are so intense that I grit my teeth and squint my eyes, holding on to the staff with every fiber of my being. The power of the Mind rakes its cold talons across my scalp, as the gentle hum of the realm's thoughts moves to the background of my consciousness.

Fire ignites within, engulfing my body in silver flames, lifting me into the air. The furnace of my resolve blazes to life as the dark cloak of Death surrounds me, its weight a comforting embrace restored within me.

The powers of the Titans, freely given, return to their rightful place within me. As my feet touch the ground again, I open my eyes with the fullness of my reclaimed powers. The realm around me is sharper, more vibrant, and beneath it all, there is a profound sense of peace. I am whole again, no longer fragmented, no longer vulnerable to the gluttonous ambitions of a monster.

I look across the souls that reside in my domain, central among them, Calypso. For so long they have carried the wounds of their lives, patiently waiting for the day their Titan returned to heal them.

Stepping to her, she meets me. My chosen sister, who entered the dread of battle with me countless times, who served as the guiding light when others were losing their way, stands with her hands in mine.

Leaning our foreheads together, the swell of Death surrounds us, a gentle embrace as the wounds of our lives heal. The stripes on her back gleam with yellow aura and then fade as my powers repair her soul. Hanging my head with shame, I keep my eyes closed, not wanting to see the thousands of scars on my own body.

Through closed eyes, the glare of my aura burns with intensity, warming me as the marks and scars of my battles heal. As the light subsides and I open my eyes, I meet the steadfast gaze of my friend. Steady now, just as she was in life, Callie stays with me through it.

"Don't ever be ashamed of the scars from your life." Her grip on my hands tightens as tears flow from my eyes. "Each one is a testament to a battle you fought and survived." A sob breaks loose from me and she wraps me in a hug. "Each one is part of what got you here today, and each one makes you beautiful."

I nod because Callie won't let go of me until I agree with

her. By the time I make it out of her arms, I'm laughing and wiping my tear-stained cheeks.

Hermes interjects, his soft smile and the rich navy blue of his eyes taking my breath away. "May I have a turn, Titaness of Death?"

I see the stain on his soul like a scorch mark over his heart. A man who survived a thousand heartbreaks stands before me, radiating with love. I'm trying hard not to cry again as I place a kiss over his heart and lay my hand on his chest.

He takes my chin between his thumb and forefinger, holding my gaze as my power gently swirls within him. The pulse of his blue aura brightens as I heal him, but I know I can do nothing for the memories of torment he'll carry forever. "You have made every second of my life matter."

With a soft kiss on the tip of my nose, he nods to the waiting crowd of souls. Facing the beautiful beams of light, I look across them as my aura surges away from me. So many of them brighten, the marks on their souls illuminating as my power heals them.

Achilles carried a gash along his chest that shines as it stitches back together, the lasting wound from ripping away his own heart to take his mate's life. And Patroclus, knowing his mates had to watch his mind torn apart, radiates with the aqua light of his soul that matched his sea-foam eyes.

Achilles wraps his strong arm around his mate. Patroclus leans up, their lips meeting. As their souls mend, they hold each other, only parting when Callie approaches so they can sweep her into their loving arms.

Hermes pulls me to him as we watch the souls of the Void heal. Laying my head on his chest, I take in the sad beauty of the many auras brightening, knowing so many had to carry the scars of their lives for long.

But happiness swells within me as I know they will never bear these pains again. With my powers restored, I can tend to them as they rest in the Void, waiting for their next life. And when we end this war and the realms see peace for the first time in ages, fewer souls will have to carry such wounds.

As I continue to look across the sea of souls, my eyes land on a familiar face and I gasp. "Hermes, it's Triton."

We greet him as an old friend, the somber nature of our last encounter a brief shadow on our happy reunion. In an instant, I'm flooded with emotions as I turn in circles, looking at the crowd of souls and eager to see more of our loved ones.

"Where are Athena and Teddy?" I stand on tiptoe, trying to see better when I remember I can use my power to find them. The swell of my aura curls around the dark water, searching for the people of our past that we lost in this battle.

I know Hermes would like to see his father again, and as my powers meander through the crowd, I'm curious why Apollo didn't greet us right away as Callie, Pat, and Achilles did.

Calypso sees me from across the crowd as I search. My hands raise, gesturing my confusion. Darkness settles over her like a storm cloud. My powers cannot find a trace of their presence, and my stomach plummets.

"They aren't here, Rhea," Triton answers the question I had not yet asked, and the murmuring crowd quiets.

I take mental inventory of who should be here, not understanding what is missing until I lock eyes with Patroclus.

It's as if his gaze alone gives me the answer. I cover my mouth with my hands in shock. Bile rises within me, and I put my hands on my knees, taking deep breaths to calm myself.

"He has them." The words choke out of me like a garbled mess. "Hermes, Loki has their souls somehow." I shake my head, not wanting to believe but knowing it's true.

Loki has obsessed over the power of Death ever since he saw Chaos on the shores of Hesperides. He became fanatical in his quest, locking a realm in an endless cycle of war and reincarnation. Through the ages, he figured out a way to keep souls from returning to the Void.

"How can you be sure they haven't met a dark fate in Elysium?" Hermes asks, somehow thinking that would be better than being trapped by this monster.

"Because everyone he killed is missing." I answer as Hermes looks around at those we love, thinking of the ends of their lives.

"Oh, my gods," Hermes whispers as understanding sinks in. "He was trying to capture Pat's soul that day on the battlefield of Troy. But Achilles took Pat's life before Loki could."

"Your father." A tear drops from my eye as I replay their deaths, thinking of the horrors Loki could be doing to their souls. "He made Ares kill Apollo, but it was Loki controlling everything."

And Teddy. So sweet, so innocent, just like Honey. Her young soul was so excited for life but unable to live it. My mind flashes to the gladiator pit the night I fought the Dark Mage. I couldn't free him in time, and the look on his face as he lay in the sand will haunt me forever.

This chilling realization sends a surge of fury through me.

The souls should cycle back to the Void to rest but have been ensnared, denied their rightful passage and purpose. Despite the sacrifice of Chaos and the endless battles to keep the power of Death from his hands, Loki has disrupted the sacred cycle of life and death.

The Void, usually calm, resonates with my anger.

This anger steels my resolve rather than blinds it. This is no longer a battle for retribution—it is a fight to restore the very order of the cosmos. With a deep, grounding breath, I channel my fury into action, calling my generals to my side.

Loki will find that in underestimating me, he has unleashed a force far greater than he anticipated. I am not just an immortal; I am a protector.

I am Goddess of the Twelve Realms and guardian of the Titans' powers.

I am the savior created in the womb of the Void.

I am Nyx, and Persephone. I am Honey and I am Teddy. I am Rhea.

I am the vengeance of the forgotten.

I am Death, and the moment of my retribution is at hand.

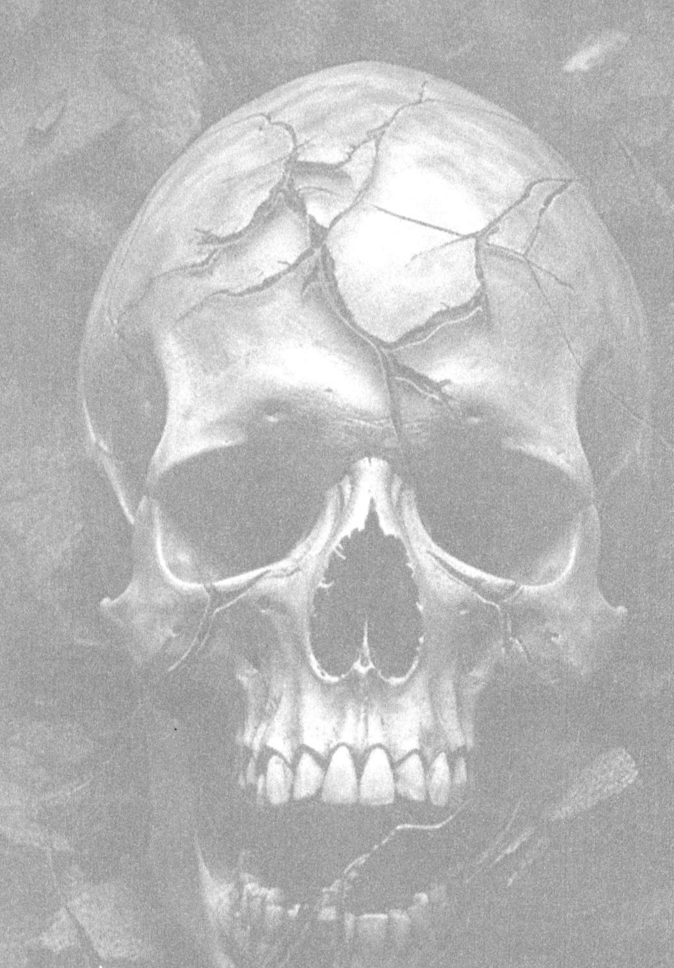

ACT III

PART 2:
VENGEANCE OF
THE FORGOTTEN GODDESS

The cool breeze of the Mediterranean surrounds me as I walk the Grecian shoreline. The waves lap gently at my feet, a soothing contrast to the storm of emotions within me. Today, with the scent of salt in the air and the timeless landscape stretching before me, I feel the full circle of destiny drawing to its close.

This is where it all started for Loki and me. When I conjured my first portal and took my first steps out of the Void, it was this beach that welcomed me. It was these waves that witnessed a hunter set eyes on his new prey. And this will be the battlefield where it all ends.

Gaea has been reduced to a desolate wasteland. Once sprawling cities are now rubble. Ancient ruins have been obliterated to dust, their historic and monumental foundations erased from the landscape.

Closing my eyes, I lift my face to the sky and soak in the warmth of the sun. The battles of a thousand lives stream through my memories. Each one, a lesson. Each one painful but necessary. Now, as the waves break against the shore, I feel a resonance with the relentless, cyclical nature of the sea—always returning, always enduring.

Loki has slithered through the eons of civilization, spreading his lies into the cracks and crevices of our lives. Slowly, he laced his marionettes around our necks like a snare, waiting for the right moment to pull them tight, strangling us with his deceptions.

He waited for me. At times, forcing my ascension. Abducting women by the thousands. Lining them up like sheep for slaughter. Looking into their eyes as they died, hoping to find me looking back at him with the next blink.

He crafted civilizations to treat their woman as property. Nothing more than cattle to be possessed, owned. Burned at the stake, erased from history, pitted against each other, the women of this realm have suffered most in his game, all to ensure we felt weaker. All to ensure we were docile, compliant.

He locked this realm in a vice of torment, patiently waiting for the day he could complete his collection. The day he would finally be able to claim his last trophy. With each defeat, with every setback, we planted the seeds needed for our victory.

We buried weapons in the sands of secret beaches, scattering the map to our salvation across the cosmos. With diligent patience and steadfast faith, we never lost sight of what we were fighting for.

Loki is a master composer of chaos, and my mind was his masterpiece.

But I was forged in the darkness of the Void, the Titan of Death's sacrifice woven into the fibers of my being, the powers of twelve, freely given. If chaos is what Loki wants, then chaos is what I will give him.

Pulling the currents of the realm to me, I feed the essence of my aura into them. Gathering above me in a vortex, I fill the funnel with rolling black mist and silver starlight. The static electricity of my combined powers snaps around me as lightning cracks and thunder rolls across the sky.

Like a bomb, my cloud of power drops to the ground, shooting out in all directions, blanketing the realm with my presence.

Filling every corner, each peak and valley and every dark cave, I send a calling card to my hunter, and I know he won't resist the temptation of my challenge. Teleporting to the plain above with the Grecian landscape to my left and the steadfast Mediterranean on my right, the great deceiver doesn't make me wait long.

Across the horizon, a wall of green fog billows slowly toward me. Flashes of emerald lightning zap within as the sky darkens by Loki's power. The fog lifts as Loki reveals himself and his army.

His eyes, a mirror to his soul, reveal no remorse—only the dark gleam of anticipation. With a cruel smirk playing upon his lips, he surveys the seemingly empty field where I stand alone. His arrogance fills the air, a tangible smog that clings to the salt breeze. He takes a few steps away from his army—a formidable legion of creatures twisted by his dark influence—materializing out of the shadows behind him.

"So dramatic." With my shields firmly in place, I use the element of Darkness, calling upon the shadows that remain from Loki's fog to reveal what secrets I know he will be hiding. Deception is his strongest weapon and I need to be ready for any trick he may attempt to pull.

"I thought our big showdown deserved an entrance."

Loki's army is formidable as I look across the plane at his

assembly: gods who wield the raw powers of the elements, their eyes alight with a lust for destruction; Shifters, a menagerie of claws and fangs ready to strike; and the dark beings from the shadowy depths of the Labyrinth, their forms barely contained by this reality, shadows twisted and writhing like smoke in the wind.

Among them, there is something else that I can't yet determine. Something Loki is heavily masking, likely waiting for the right moment to pull back his deceptive curtain.

With nothing but an open field around me, I've made it clear I'm alone, but Loki makes a dramatic show of searching the plain.

"Aw, what happened to your mate?" Loki's voice drips with false sympathy, his eyes glittering with cruel amusement.

I tighten my jaw, refusing to give him the satisfaction of a reaction. Inside, my heart pounds, but I keep my face impassive.

Loki spreads his powers across the realm, searching for signs of Hermes' presence. Sniffing the air as if detecting something on the wind, he pauses. "You return from the Labyrinth with a dead mate... and," Loki looks at me with displeasure, shaking his head in disbelief, "and you still have not recovered the last of your powers."

Jutting my chin out, I remain silent to his provocation and let him work out the truth I am weaving. I only need to stall a few more minutes and knowing the control Loki craves, I'll let him think he has it.

"What a total disappointment you have turned out to be. I had such high hopes when you managed to get so far." Loki scolds me like a father nagging a child.

"Well, I'm sorry to let you down." My voice wavers with

feigned emotion, tears pricking at my eyes. But beneath the surface, my mind is sharp, calculating.

"Why challenge me then? Your bond has been broken; you retain your weak mortal form. Are you just hoping I'll kill you and reset our little game back to the beginning?"

"I wouldn't be so quick to underestimate me, or my army." My voice is steady, but beneath it lies a current of defiance.

Loki scoffs, a dismissive sound. "What army? You can't fathom the legions I have at my disposal."

Behind me, the air shimmers and shifts, and my own army appears as I lift my Mirage—rows upon rows of immortals stand side by side. Librarians are dispersed among the Shifters and Elementals as all stand ready for the war of ages to begin.

Loki's eyes flick to Lucas on my left, then Medusa on my right. With a sinister smile, he evokes his power of Shifting, his form morphing into an exact copy of the Gorgon by my side.

Just as Kai is able to take on the form of others, so is Loki. But unlike Kai, Loki is able to mimic the movements of Medusa's braids using the power of Earth, delivering a very convincing spectacle.

"So good to see you again, *Deuce*." Loki mocks Hermes' endearing nickname. Within my tightly woven shields, I can sense the power of the Mind he is using to make his voice sound like hers. If my wards were not erected, we would hear her voice instead of Loki's.

I think of the memory Triton shared with me in the Underworld, just before I released him of this life. It was never Medusa that boarded his ship and surrounded him with green burning Soul-Fire. It was Loki.

It has always been Loki.

"Clever disguise." Medusa says unimpressed. "If I could

choose between looking like you or looking like me, I'd choose me too."

"It's come in handy many, many times." Loki turns his head, spitting on the grass and returning to his own form. The air crackles with the power of our imminent clash, the sea and sky poised to witness our battle.

As the tension on the battlefield rises to a near-palpable level, with each side ready to unleash their fury, Loki halts with a theatrical flair, his grin widening maliciously. "Wait," he calls out, his voice echoing strangely against the roar of the ocean waves. "Before we begin, Rhea, perhaps you'd like to see the full extent of my army."

With a sweeping gesture, Loki's figure blurs, and the air ripples as another illusion dissolves before us. Among the throngs of monstrous beings and dark creatures, I now see thousands of mortals—men, women, young, and old— standing listlessly among the immortal army of a tyrant. Their eyes are vacant, their postures rigid and unnaturally still.

My heart breaks looking at Loki's human puppets held up by invisible strings and it turns to blazing fury within me. This was the secret he was concealing though I'm sure he has more.

These are innocents, humans, ensnared by Loki as he dropped thousands of bombs on their cities. He opened a protective haven just like Hermes and I did. But he planned to use them as shields and tools in his cruel game. The sight of them, so vulnerable and exploited, sharpens my resolve while also tugging painfully at my conscience.

"Using mortals as pawns, Loki?" I call out, my voice ringing loud and clear over the battlefield. "Are you so threatened by me that you must hide behind the innocent?"

Loki laughs, a sound that chills the warm sea breeze.

"Threatened? No, dear Rhea. Strategic. Even if you are just a broken Titaness, you wouldn't unleash your powers against these helpless souls, would you? Even you wouldn't risk harming them to get to me."

The realm behind me trembles. Darkness takes over the sky as I flex my powers. Deep rolling thunder growls in the black clouds above us as silver lightning claps within. Reality ripples as the winds of the realm shift.

Loki's previous smugness wanes, giving way to a flicker of uncertainty as he registers the charge in the atmosphere.

"You're right Loki," My voice echoes with a power that momentarily stills the murmurs of both armies, "we should introduce the rest of our armies."

The horizon behind me is an endless plume of black smoke and white fire. The ground beneath our feet begins to shake and while my army remains steadfast, the army of my hunter shifts their eyes, hoping for early glimpses of the attack coming for them.

The currents whip around me, raising off the ground as my hair swirls within the churn that is building the oncoming storm. "My army arrives on the fiery winds of a vengeful Siren."

A portal rips open in the fabric of the air behind me as the fire and smoke race forward. From this swirling vortex of shadows, a torrent of lights bursts forth—countless orbs of radiant energy, each one a soul that had once walked the realms of the living, surge past me.

At the forefront of my army of souls are three particularly radiant spirits: Calypso, Achilles, and Patroclus. Their auras are woven together, glowing brighter through the bond of their souls. In life, they were warriors and lovers, their story intertwined by fate and torn apart by Loki. In death, their spirits have not waned but have been forged into something just as formidable.

Loki's face, usually so full of derision, falters as he takes in the sight of the glowing army, his eyes widening as he understands what the rushing sea of orbs are. I lower the shields I placed around my aura and let the fullness of my Titan powers pulse out of me.

A smile creeps across my face as I watch Loki realize my powers have been restored, that with the Void behind me and an army of souls before me, I wield the essence he has sought for so long.

"Death is here for you, hunter." I whisper my taunt into his mind, and his eyes flare with rage as I pierce his mental shields. The green centers brighten, burning with the anger of his jade fire. Releasing a guttural scream of deep-rooted malice, Loki charges his hands back, gathering his powers to lash out.

A wall of power blasts toward me and crashes against an equally powerful barrier of my elements as our armies charge toward each other.

To my right, Medusa conjures a rolling wave of earth that plows down the first line of Loki's army. Churning, their bodies are pulled under, consumed by the Gorgon's fury. To my left where the image of Lucas stood, a beautiful golden eagle takes flight. The caw that echoes across the plain commands the army of Shifters to attack.

As the clash of powers erupts across the battlefield, the scene transforms into a vivid spectacle of light and shadow. The air thrums with energy as my army of souls swoops gracefully among the ensnared mortals caught in Loki's vile plan.

Their radiant energy acts as a purifier, liberating the

mortals from the dark tendrils of Loki's mind control. The effect is immediate and visible: the mortals' eyes clear, their slack expressions gaining awareness and confusion, then horror as they take in the chaos around them.

As my shields push against Loki's, I summon my dark portals. Every mortal touched by one of my souls is teleported off the field of battle. Thousands of shimmering silver gateways get them out of harm's way, delivering them to the protected Wyoming territory of the Shifters.

As Loki's forces reel from the unexpected counterattack, his frustration becomes palpable. His strategy relied on using the mortals as shields, a cowardly tactic that is now crumbling before his eyes. The battlefield shifts when the last of the mortals is removed from the plane. Momentum surges as my forces press forward with renewed vigor.

The Shades rush forward under Loki's command, and Hecate steps into her element.

Cloaked in a swirling mantle of midnight, she absorbs the scant light around her. Raising her hands, the very air thickens. Darkness coalesces into tangible power at her fingertips. Hecate unleashes her mastery over the Dark, a torrent of inky blackness that flows like a river of night toward the advancing Shades.

Darkness meets darkness—Hecate's power enveloping the Shades, not with the intention to harm, but to reclaim. Her magic is ancient, as nuanced and deep as the Void itself, and it wraps around the Shades, nullifying their malice, calming their rage. It's a mesmerizing dance of control, a battle of wills where light does not necessarily mean good, and darkness does not imply evil.

The Shades are outmatched by a darkness that does not

destroy but transforms. Hecate's darkness is different—an almost maternal, enveloping presence that seeks to restore rather than obliterate. One by one, the Shades within her dark river slow, their forms becoming less defined, less menacing. The viciousness in their movements ebbs away, replaced by tranquility as they are absorbed back into the fold of night from which they came.

As Hecate's dark tendrils encircle the frenzied Shades, a moment of recognition flickers across her face—a flicker that turns to sorrow. Amid the mass of shadows, she spots Odysseus and Penelope. Two figures that inspired legends are now reduced to mere shadows twisted into nightmares.

The sadness in Hecate's eyes deepens as she extends her powers to envelop them, her gestures gentle, almost hesitant.

Hecate's dark river swirls around Odysseus and Penelope, seeping into their essence, subduing the chaos that grips their spectral forms. Her powers, a blend of control and compassion, attempt to ease their suffering as they are drawn back into the depths of the dark, away from the violence they were compelled to partake in.

As the battle between Loki and me intensifies, the very air around us thrums with the raw power of unleashed elements. My army of souls combat the darkness with Hecate and the Fire mages. Loki attempts to infiltrate my thoughts with whispers of doubt and confusion. He tries to ensnare me into an illusion that attempts to pull away my reality.

His eyes flash with the thrill of the battle. The flames of his green Soul-Fire strike me with tendrils of creeping darkness that lash out from the smoke and soot. He aims to overwhelm me physically and psychologically.

But the armor that protects me was tempered by one of the

strongest Flames to ever live and Achilles ensured it would resist Soul-Fire.

I fortify my mental shields, wrapping my consciousness in layers of impenetrable will. My mental barriers toss Loki's psychic intrusions aside like waves crashing against solid rock.

I summon the most vicious of winds from the most formidable seas, and it rushes to my call. Swirling around us in powerful gusts that counter the heat of Loki's fire, snuffing out flames and dispersing smoke. The silver starlight of my aura becomes projectiles and shields that devastate Loki's dark attacks.

His obscure tendrils attempt to snare me, to bind me in shadows and pull me into despair, but the starlight carries me just out of reach, my form blurring with my speed. The starlight, pure and piercing, slices through the darkness, each beam a blade that cuts not just through physical forms but through the fabric of Loki's darker magics.

Our battle becomes a storm of contrasting energies—his shadows and fire against my wind and starlight. We are like night and day clashing under the cosmos. Our power resonates across the battlefield, sending shockwaves through the ranks of both armies.

Medusa stumbles as she flips a large wolf-Shifter over her shoulder. The beast not traveling as far or fast, but it doesn't stop the long tendrils of her hair, wrapped around the Shifter's neck, to pull tight, dispatching the body and head.

"Do you two mind?" She screams across the fray. "I'm trying to work here."

As we continue to battle, I draw Loki away from our armies.

This fight, so long in the making, is more than a confrontation; it's a declaration. My powers, like the stars themselves, ancient and enduring, and I will not yield today. As Loki and I circle one another, the fate of the realm's souls hangs in the balance. I am ready. Ready to end this, to restore the balance of the Titans' powers as the realms intended.

The ground beneath my feet trembles, the vibrations growing stronger and more insistent. At first, I mistake the low rumble for thunder—a product of the war of gods and monsters raging around us—but the steady, rhythmic pounding suggests something else is approaching. Something huge.

Over the horizon, an enormous shape emerges, casting a vast shadow across the land. It's a colossal horse, as large as a giant, with eight thundering legs churning up the earth beneath it. This beast, forged from the soil itself, from the raw power of the Earth element, is a moving mass of dirt and stone, animated by Loki's dark will.

The horse's approach is like a living earthquake, its hooves pounding the ground with such force that immortals from both armies are caught under its relentless charge. Each stomp of the creature's giant feet means the loss of elemental life, trampled to death by the earthen beast. Loki has no regard for his own soldiers, killing them along with mine.

"We need to take this horse down!" Zara calls out in the minds of the Shifters.

"On it," Lexi answers.

Before there is time to form an attack, the ocean churns in an angry whirl. Beyond the cliffs, an enormous serpent rises with a terrifying hiss that echoes through the air. The snake's immense body is crafted from the roiling waters of the ocean, its scales shimmering with the deadly beauty of the deep sea, reflecting the chaos of the battlefield in its liquid form.

"That is all you, Medusa," Daphne calls out, sparing a quick glance at the beast before returning to the legions of fighters before her.

"Gee, thanks," Medusa answers. Clenching her fist, the dozen elementals she turned to porous rock explode. The stone projectiles, guided like bullets, hit her targets within Loki's army.

The giant serpent moves with horrifying grace, slithering onto the battlefield with the unstoppable force of a tidal wave. Immortals caught in its path are swept away or battered by the sheer mass of its watery body. Its mouth, a gaping maw of swirling currents, shoots jets of venomous water with enough force to pierce armor and flesh alike.

Medusa raises her own serpent—a coiling mass of earth and mud that hisses at its larger opponent. The two snakes circle each other, hissing and spitting venom before they strike. The troops nearby have time to flee, but others are caught within the slithering bodies of the monsters.

Lexi's eyes are fixed on the giant stallion that tramples our lines. Her panther's coat, as black as shadows under the moonlight, almost shines purple amid the flashes of elemental light as she races across the battlefield. With a powerful surge of her muscular legs, Lexi launches herself forward, her paws barely making a sound on the ground despite her speed. The earthen horse, massive and formidable, continues its rampage, unaware of the predator stalking it from behind. Lexi's approach is a blur of retribution driven by the cries of Shifters crushed by the stallion's granite hooves.

She leaps high into the air, her body coiling like a spring unleashed. She lands deftly on the back of the giant steed, her claws unsheathed. She races along its spine, her claws digging into the earthen flesh, securing her hold as she makes her way toward its massive neck.

The stallion realizes the threat too late and bucks wildly. Lexi clings on with the tenacity of a true predator, her body low and sleek against the convulsing form beneath her. Reaching the horse's neck, she repositions herself, her powerful jaws aiming for a critical point. With a calculated strike, she clamps down, her teeth sinking into what would be sinew and veins, had this beast been made of flesh and blood.

The lionesses of Zara's pack join Lexi, and the Shifters unify their assault. The stallion stumbles, its movements becoming erratic as it tries to shake off the Shifters working to bring it down. Lexi's relentless onslaught works: with a final, powerful twist and pull, she throws the massive creature off balance.

I turn the ground beneath the steed into a churning pit of mud that reaches up like hands from the grave, pulling the horse downward. Lexi leaps off the disappearing form of the stallion, landing gracefully on the battlefield. The lionesses follow their Alpha back into the battle as Lexi eyes her next target.

As the massive water serpent tightens its lethal embrace around my army, the sense of urgency mounts with every passing second. Hecate and Daphne fight back-to-back, facing off against Loki's encroaching forces. Their combined powers create a small bastion of resistance within the serpent's shadow. They are trapped within the snake's coiled body as it fights Medusa's serpent.

Hecate's dark magic sends out waves of shadow while Daphne, just as formidable a huntress as Artemis, summons arrows formed of her aura, her elemental power of emotions imbued within. Daphne's strike confuses and disorients their enemies before Hecate's darkness devours them.

"I can't hold it back," Medusa's serpent struggles against the Titans' serpent.

Loki's massive snake draws tighter around Hecate and Daphne, its jaws poised to deliver a crushing bite that would kill them both. The serpent raises its head, its enormous jaw expanding and preparing to devour them. The body of the snake ripples as it prepares to strike.

Before the beast can attack, I call upon my own behemoth. From the tumultuous sea beyond the cliffs, stirred by my command, emerge two colossal tentacles, slick and powerful, surging with the might of the ocean itself.

More tentacles emerge from the cliffs as the Kraken pulls its massive body up. Opening its large mouth, the Kraken's roar shakes Gaea to the core, the ground at our feet trembling to hold its might.

A direct challenge for the giant serpent, it snaps its jaws shut and turns its large head toward my sea monster. The snake strikes, aiming for the Kraken's head but lands in a confusing swirl of tentacles. There is a moment of intense struggle where the sea and the serpent battle, a clash of forces under Loki's and my titanic command.

The Kraken acts with swift decisiveness. Its enormous beak, hidden beneath the waves of its massive tentacles, clamps down on the serpent's head. With a gruesome finality, the Kraken severs the serpent's head. The body, now headless, writhes at the cliff's edge before falling like a waterfall, splashing onto the Grecian beach below.

"Enough of this toying around," Loki builds his power to an apex, a green thrum of his colliding elements becoming a ball within his hands. I build my own power to match his, and we release our attacks at once. As our elements race toward each other like two bombs on the verge of detonation, I form two long whips of starlight and lightning. Taking advantage of the blinding light of our powers, I snap the whips in a long arc and strike Loki twice. I slice through him, drawing a bead of red blood on his cheek as our powers ignite.

My shield was already erected, casting it as soon as I snapped my whips. Like a massive wall of my powers, it protects my army against the blast. Several fighters outside my reach jump into my portals and land within range of my defense.

The powers of Titans collide, and a deafening silence stretches around us before the blast erupts. Bearing down and pushing back, I hold the shield as Loki's powers collide with mine. My army drops to the ground, taking shelter, but my cover holds. Loki and his army are blasted back, tumbling hundreds of yards. He skids to a halt and raises his eyes in warning to me.

"I'll take the point for that round," I call out mockingly.

He thrives on control most of all. Control over the minds of those around him. Control over the twelve elements is his obsession. So, control is what I'll take from him. Then, I'll take the Titans' powers from him.

He stands as his army recovers behind him. Wiping the line

of blood with the back of his forearm, a sinister smile overtakes him as the veins under his skin turn black. The thunderous tremble of another stampede sounds from the horizon beyond him. My aura blankets the battleground, sensing a herd of eight-legged stallions.

A fresh wave of shifted wolves runs alongside them, flocks of harpies and furies fly together, and I feel the shadowy tendrils of darkness seeping up from the ground. He's calling more dark legions from the Labyrinth, refreshing his army to overwhelm mine that will soon tire and dwindle in numbers.

Well then... looks like it's time to call in my reinforcements.

Sending three taps down our bond, I signal Hermes as I lower my protective shield. I hold Medusa back with me as the rest of my forces charge forward. "Hermes says he has a surprise for us."

"Does he know we're fighting a battle?" she jests but still waits with me.

Loki's army responds, racing toward mine. The Shifters of both armies begin to outrun the Elementals and quickly become the front lines of our forces.

Loki and I keep our eyes locked on each other. I can sense what he is pulling out from the depths of the earth as he tries to mask the portals he's conjured from the Labyrinth.

Between the two lines of armies, a trench of shadows arises from the earth as Shades and Shadow Lurkers climb out of Loki's dark cloud. He planned for his dark battalion to surprise my Shifters, consuming them and leaving my elementals to fend off the rest of his army.

Keeping my eyes locked on him, I want to watch Loki's elation plummet as I release my counterattack. Two swirling portals of silver starlight open simultaneously in the sky above, one on each end of our lines of fighters, perfectly aligned with Loki's newly summoned dark soldiers.

From the first portal, gleaming with the brilliance of a deep blue sapphire, Hermes emerges in his dragon form. He is a vision of shimmering scales, his eyes alight with fierce determination. He commands the sky, his wings spread wide, casting blue light across the battlefield like reflections of the ocean under the sun.

From the second portal, a massive red dragon—Lucas— emerges with a roar that vibrates through the air and ground alike. His scales are like molten lava, glowing with an inner fire that illuminates the smoke-filled battlefield. Lucas, just as large and fierce as Hermes, joins his comrade in the sky, their movements synchronized as they prepare their assault.

Together, Hermes and Lucas swoop down over Loki's forces in a coordinated dance of destruction. With a deep, resonant roar, they unleash torrents of flame upon the soldiers made of darkness.

The shadows and specters conjured from the darkness beneath Gaea scream and hiss as the flames engulf them, their forms dissipating under the intense heat that purifies. The brilliance of the dragons' assault cuts through the battlefield, lighting up the faces of our warriors as they keep racing forward.

Loki witnesses the decimation of his new forces in shock. He believed Hermes was lost to the Labyrinth, our bond severed by death, rendering me weaker. But my mate is very much alive and incredibly pissed off.

Loki knew of Hermes' dragon, but he did not know about Lucas. Drawn out within my thick protective shield in Wyoming, Lucas' dragon manifested out of Loki's sight. His face contorts with rage and desperation, and a satisfied smile stretches across mine. The presence of these mighty dragons, especially Hermes, shakes the confidence he is trying to hold onto.

I can see it in his eyes. He's afraid the battle is slipping from his grasp, his strategies unraveled by the goddess he underestimated. But I need him to lose all sense of control. I need him to ooze with desperation and reveal the souls he has hidden from me. Only when I have recovered what belongs to me will I reclaim what Loki stole from the Titans.

Behind me, the Kraken prepares to defend us in case Loki decides to flank us. Its long tentacles stretch out on each side of my army. The tip of one slithering limb rests on the ground between Medusa and me.

"It's been a long time since I've seen the Kraken," she says, rubbing the smooth appendage as she admires the colossal beast. "He's a beauty."

"I thought it was a fitting tribute to honor our Goddess of War." I pat the tentacle, feeling the cool water that forms its body beneath my touch. "It's like having a piece of Athena with us today."

"It's perfect." She holds my gaze as we share a brief moment amid the turmoil of the battlefield. "She'd be proud of you."

I give her a thin-lipped smile as I hold back the rush of emotions that statement brings out in me. "She'd be proud of you too."

53 Rhea

The massive herd of Loki's stallions and wolves **clears the horizon, racing toward us.** A dozen large beasts, formed of rock and dirt, each with eight legs, would certainly trample my army—but it pays to befriend giants.

The swirl of Hermes' portal begins to churn as he builds the opening. *"You two should get a running start,"* Hermes' dragon voice growls in our minds as Medusa and I exchange confused glances.

Like a star exploding, Hermes' portal bursts open. The three cyclops, freed from the quarry of Tartarus and hungry for retribution, step forward. Their massive feet stomp the ground in unison, creating a tidal wave of earth that ripples toward Loki's troops. They bellow, sounding like three deep horns blasting a call to war.

After the giants, two-winged horses race through the air, their massive wings beating majestically against the blue sky. A gleaming white horse whinnies as it crosses the barrier.

"Perseus!" Medusa calls out happily, clapping her hands together once.

I gasp, seeing the other horse. Like night incarnate, the rich black wings of a beautiful Shadowmare beat against the wind, and a pair of starlight eyes search for me.

"Nocturna," I whisper before releasing a choked laugh. *"I thought you died."*

The language of shadows is odd and unspoken, but through the obscurity, I receive Nocturna's snarky response. *"Well, I didn't know you knew curse words either."*

Nocturna huffs, impatiently wanting me to mount her.

The tribespeople of Tartarus rush through the portal from the ground. The Sisyphus tribe rides tall Flamesteeds, setting long spears on fire off the horses' fiery hides. Alongside them, the women of the Danaide ride their Sphinxes. Above us, the Gorgons fly in on a herd of Pegasus. At their forefront, pulling a shocked gasp from Medusa, are her sisters.

They search for her on the ground and, finding her, pump their fists in the air, emitting a high-pitched series of yelps. Medusa returns the greeting, her eyes more alive than I've ever seen them. "Wanna race?"

"No," I chuckle. "I want to fly into battle with you."

Medusa smiles and holds her hand out, waiting for me to grasp it. "Well, then let's fucking go." Clasping her hand in mine, we both look above, finding our horses.

The Kraken's tentacle beside us unforms, becoming nothing more than a puddle of water under our feet. Reforming, it surges us upward toward our approaching steeds. We balance on one of the beast's giant arms, both of us excited to meet our horses in the air.

Perseus reaches Medusa first, and she deftly jumps onto his back, grabbing his pure white mane as his large pearlescent wings beat with strength and purpose. From the opposite direction, Nocturna approaches, and I mount her in the same way.

Our horses loop around in an arc, and we fly side-by-side toward Loki's army. A line of Gorgon warriors riding on the backs of their beautiful, winged horses join us. Euryale and Stheno fly next to their sister.

"Long time, no see," Medusa calls out over the wind to her sisters.

"When this war is over, I'm kicking your ass," Euryale calls back.

Medusa throws her head back, releasing a laugh. "You can try." Tucking her head and spurring her horse on, Perseus gallops on the wind. Nocturna and Perseus set the pace, and the rest of the herd flies with us.

The realm trembles again when the three giant cyclops stomp, releasing another seismic wave of their earthen power, which races beneath us. The giants set off in a run, their large central eyes fixed on the colossal horses.

Releasing my black mist, I darken the sky around us, my power becoming a curtain to conceal my allies. The army of souls is behind me, Elementals and Shifters below me, the tribes and giants of Tartarus riding by my side, and the mighty beating wings of two enormous dragons fix our rage on Loki and his forces.

An angry craze burns hot in Loki's eyes. He's practically buzzing with wrath as I pull on every thread of his carefully constructed battle plan. Loki sends waves of his power over the mind toward us, hoping to fashion his strings of control back around us, but Hermes and I shielded ourselves and our army's minds against him. Hermes' light of truth provides clarity to see through the illusions Loki tries to cast. My power creates an impenetrable forcefield for everyone fighting under my banner.

Loki's face turns red with anger as he blasts a thick wall of his green aura in front of his army, stopping their path forward. The large horses of conjured earth and the new battalions running with them still approach. I suppose he wants to send the herd of steeds through us first, but my army doesn't slow down. The two dragons at our side open their massive jaws. Heat glows from their bellies, traveling up the long columns of their throats as Hermes and Lucas prepare their dragon's fire.

Gathering the powers of the twelve realms within me, my aura shines like a collection of the galaxy's stars. Erupting out of me, a pulsating wave of every element surges toward Loki's defense, ready to slice through it like a hot knife through butter. Following me, the two Titans by my side breathe columns of red and blue flames, scorching Loki's protective shield.

Loki lets out a frustrated growl, his fists clenched as his body trembles in anger. "You think you will win this, but we are far from over." All around his army, more shadows seep up from the ground like vents of a smoking volcano as he summons more Shades and Shadow Lurkers. "I will drown you in darkness until you are nothing."

"You're not the only Titan of Darkness," I call back to him through our minds. He's trying to block me out, but his emotions are making him sloppy. *"You were consumed by darkness, but I was born from it. You would do well to remember that, hunter."*

The massive eight-legged horses are close enough, and Loki is nearing the point of explosion. I know he's holding on to something, waiting for his moment of desperation to release the last of his depravity. So, I push another domino over.

Behind Loki's army, the giant swirl of a shadow portal forms on the ground. A large arm emerges from it, grabbing the legs of a horse and pulling it inside. Another arm, then another, rises from the dark portal as the ten-armed giant of the Labyrinth climbs out.

Grabbing horses with the collection of arms on each side of his hulking frame, the cyclops holds the giants of Loki's creation by their necks or legs. Swinging them in a massive arc, his earthen power turns them to stone as he slams them to the ground. A cloud of dust billows in all directions, obscuring the view of the other two giants that we also freed from imprisonment.

As the mighty cyclopses climb out of the hole, dozens of large Doberman shadow dogs use their large bodies, running and jumping off them and soaring to the surface above. Larger than the shifted wolves of Loki's army, Cerberus and all his shadowed replicas go after them. Some of his forms split into two or three heads as they attack.

Seeing the disturbance, the winged creatures of Loki's army divert their paths. The harpies and furies arc in circles, readying to dive for the shadow dogs and giants attacking from the rear.

"Is this all you can raise against me, Loki?" I yell across the field. My powers make my voice carry for all to hear. Like a colony of bats shooting out of a murky cave, more of my masses rise from Cerberus' shadow portal.

The King of the Vampires is like a dark streak of power as Vladimir erupts from the crypt below Gaea, his legions of Vampires following him. Next to them, the fallen Archangels of Hel follow Michael as I add more winged soldiers to fight in the skies.

Long ago, the Archangels betrayed their Titan, slaying Theia, the cosmic dragon of Light, and readying her for Loki to consume. After he devoured her remaining essence, Loki betrayed the angels, locking them in the Labyrinth, holding them like prisoners until he wanted to use them.

Still, in death, they are bound to the Light of their realm, and even the loyalty of a traitor can be bought with a price. Hermes demanded they pay back the blood debt of the Titan they betrayed, and I offered to send them to Elysium, freeing them from their entrapment on Gaea. Getting revenge on the god that deceived them is just a bonus.

Loki's shield is holding but weakening. Hermes, Lucas, and I keep up our assault as the masses of Gaea and Tartarus' immortals race to his line. Reaching further within myself, I knit my powers into a tighter weave, strengthening my assault with the fibers of the Void that created me and the sacrifice of Chaos, who gave his life to ensure we could defeat the blight of Loki. Pulsing out of me in faster waves, brighter and with the combined resolve of the slain Titans, my aura streams out of me, concentrating in the center of the dragons' fire. My scream joins their roar.

Medusa spurs her Pegasus on faster, and the warriors around us follow her lead. "We're not stopping!" she calls out to our mass of allies, who join in the chorus of our charge.

The fractures in Loki's shield grow as he pushes more of himself to fortify it. A slow line of blood trickles from his nose as he pushes himself further.

"He's almost there," I speak into the minds of the generals leading my army of warriors.

"*Well, let's push him a little further then,*" Hermes growls into my mind. "*Hey Luke, want to go be annoying?*"

"*I mean, that's your area of expertise, so... lead the way.*"

W hen Loki's shield breaks, a fast-moving wave of Rhea's aura shoots across the realm. The forces we have amassed surge across the destroyed boundary with ages of pent-up anger and resentment for the god-killer who has decimated the balance of the realms, the murderer who has stolen so many lives and locked us in a recurring state of torment.

Even if he calls all the Shades and darkness from the Labyrinth, he's not winning today.

Our army is like a swarm, covering the battlefield and overwhelming him with relentless perseverance. He can't fight us all and conjure elemental giants while trying to take over our minds. He's falling back on all the tactics and ploys he's used over the ages. And we're ready for everything.

With the fullness of our memories restored by the Void's healing waters, we've crafted a plan. We've gathered allies willing to lay down their lives, and we're here to make sure Loki doesn't walk off the battlefield today. We just need the stolen souls.

The Gorgons position both their legs to one side of their horses, preparing for a running dismount. Perfectly tuned to the movements of their steeds, they race off their horses, which glide back into the air on their impressive wings. The warriors fight on the ground while the horses join the fight in the skies.

When Rhea's feet hit the ground, Cerberus is by her side. "Good boy," she says, patting him quickly as she launches into the battle.

"I thought I was your good boy," I tease her. The gravel of my voice rolls down her spine, and she adjusts her shoulders to clear herself of the sensation.

The corner of her mouth ticks up in amusement. *"Don't distract me."* With daggers in hand, she moves quickly, working her way to Loki.

"Gross," Medusa huffs as she takes the head of a petrified harpy.

"Speaking of good boys... Lucas," I say, pausing long enough to catch a wolf-shifter launching themselves at Medusa. I squeeze them in my large, clawed hand until their body bursts. *"So proud of your big dragon, all grown up."*

"If you don't shut up, I'm going to bite you." Rhea is keeping our telepathy open so the Elementals and Shifters can communicate as we fight.

"How do you know I'm not into that sort of thing?" I feel Rhea chuckle down our bond as she listens to my teasing.

"Rhea, would you be upset if I ate your mate?"

"I would," she grunts, driving her blades through a Shade. Her aura dispels the darkness, destroying the creature.

"Hermes, when you said, 'let's go be annoying'," Lucas huffs as he carries a massive eight-legged horse off the ground. With his large tail and crimson wings, he spins several times before flipping the beast to the ground, crumbling the earth giant into a pile of dirt and stone. *"I thought you meant Loki."*

"Yeah, let's go. Just like we practiced."

Loki calls out more water and land giants. Snakes and eight-legged horses keep flooding the battlefield, but between the Kraken, Lucas, and me, as well as the giants, they don't reach our army on the ground. The Vampires and Archangels in the skies with the flying horses are taking over the swarms of harpies and furies. The warriors on the ground are making headway in taking down Loki's army.

The souls take on the dark beings that rise from the shadows and port our injured warriors off the battlefield for healing. They return with fresh soldiers who jump into the fight.

Narrowing my eyes, I fly toward the man who has tormented my mate across the ages, and is responsible for the deaths of my family. It takes all my willpower to restrain my anger, and follow our plan.

Loki has never been a hand-to-hand fighter, so we'll kick his ass until he blows his gasket.

With my wings spread wide, I glide down, closer and closer so he knows I'm coming for him. He keeps his eyes locked on me as Lucas approaches from behind. At the last second, I shift quickly back to my human form, the momentum of my flight propelling me as my fist connects with his face.

He's turned around by the impact, just in time for Lucas to do the same. Wearing armor from the Gorgons, Lucas takes the blades fixed in holsters around his body, flinging them at Loki, who deflects them with shields conjured by the winds.

"Whoa!" Kai's voice rings out as she releases a dead harpy from the claws of her golden eagle. *"Did you go shopping on Tartarus, Lucas? That armor."*

The Gorgons' armor can withstand their mutation to

stone, reverting back to its form just as they do. Apparently, it works for Shifters too.

My whip snaps in the air, glowing blue with the power of my element. *"Yes, thank the goddess Lucas doesn't have to fight with his crown jewels out."*

This elicits a laugh from Medusa as she drives two petrified furies into the ground with her hands around their necks.

Lucas and I spar with Loki, neither of us letting up, keeping him in a constant state of defense.

"How do you tolerate him, Medusa?" Lucas gruffs as Loki flings one of the blades back at him with Flaying Wind. Lucas turns his shoulder just as the blade passes, narrowly missing being stabbed by his own weapon. Like lightning, Lucas catches the blade between his fingers and hurls it back at Loki.

"Ah, he'll grow on you," Medusa says, several of her braids dragging across her forehead, whipping the sweat from her brow. *"Besides, he makes coming to work more fun."*

"Time to get in here, Deuce," I tell her.

She begins to sprint, making her way over a wolf-shifter like she's sliding across the hood of a car. *"Give me a boost?"*

We've done this move a thousand times. As Lucas keeps Loki busy, Medusa runs in. Hooking our arms together, I use her momentum, adding my own to it, spinning her around as she kicks.

Loki is caught off guard when her boot connects with his chest, sending him flying back, but we don't ease up. We're going to back him into a corner. Then, like any caged animal, he'll lash out, and that is exactly where we want him.

Our assault is brutal, and he stays busy deflecting us. Medusa and I add our elements into the fight as Lucas keeps up the physical attacks. Loki's anger is becoming palpable, filling the atmosphere with his frustration.

"What? No witty banter while we kick your ass?" I taunt him but all he gives me is a sneer and grunt as he tries to take the three of us on.

Well, good fucking luck with that.

His back is to his army, partly because he doesn't care if they all die, but also because we're keeping him distracted while our forces decimate his.

"Bridget, you're up."

I've never seen a witch move like she does, but we're using it. She turns to smoke and feathers, becoming an obscure flock of crows that swarm around Loki. Dozens of small claws and beaks nip and scrape at him as Lucas lands a punch to Loki's stomach.

"Are you ready, baby?" I keep Rhea in my sights during the battle, wrapped in my Light so I know she's okay.

"Yeah, let's do it."

Medusa and I surround him from behind and capture him with our whips. The tendrils of Medusa's hair circle his neck, pulling tighter as she begins to push her power into him. Her sisters join in, kicking at Loki's knees and bringing him to the ground.

My whip of light captures his arms, pulling them behind his back.

He fights against the Gorgons' petrification; he tries to use his darkness to counter my light, but Bridget and Lucas keep on him. We're pulling at so many of his elements at once, all while he claws desperately at the Mind Shields Rhea is holding.

We turn him around and show his dwindling army to him. Loki glares defiantly, even in his bound state, his eyes flickering with the remnants of cunning and malice that have long defined him.

Rhea uses the wind to clear an aisle for herself, pushing his forces out of her way and striding with sure steps to her captured hunter. I've wrapped him in my Light, holding him with my bindings of power. Bridget's flock of obscurity and crows pulls away, and from their mass, she appears in front of us again. Lucas steps away as we make room for Loki's reckoning.

I grab him roughly by the hair and tilt his head up so he can see her, so he can take a good look at Death as the goddess of the realms extracts what she wants from him.

The edges of Rhea's honey eyes glow silver with the strength of the Titans' essence within her. The inky black mist that pours out of her as she walks reaches Loki first, filling his mouth and nose, crawling into his eyes and ears. Her powers invade him, taking away his senses.

For ten years, she was tormented with the haunting image of a small boy choking to death on her powers while a car spun out of control. It was a lie, but it broke her apart and beat her down along with the rest of Demeter's abuse. And Rhea is going to use it to break Loki, forcing him to reveal the souls he's harboring.

"You took things that don't belong to you," Rhea begins as Loki tremors.

Part of it is fear, that much I can see within his aura. But he's pushing back against us, trying to fight to get out of our hold as he suffocates on Rhea's power.

Medusa and her sisters keep asserting their earthen abilities into him, working to petrify his legs and shoulders. It's a battle of wills, a tug and pull of powers as his skin and clothes turn to rock, then dissolve and morph back.

"And I'm going to take them back," Rhea leans close, talking into his ear. "I'm going to steal from you what you have stolen from so many others."

I read the light within his aura. He's still pushing at our Minds, but Earth is the element he is calling now, abandoning all the others.

With a glance at Medusa and a nod, the Gorgons let him push their power out. There is a palpable shift in his demeanor —a tension that warns of a brewing storm. Hiding within the thrum of his aura, he concealed the attack of Light he was building. I nearly missed it.

A fraction of a second before he released his wave of Absolute Light, my realization traveled down our bond. Rhea dropped her assault and cast her own attack in defense. Rhea consumes his light within her darkness as the blast rushes out. Wrapping my aura around my mate and our allies, I port us just outside the radius and out of harm's way.

Rhea pushes back against Loki, her brow furrowed as she builds the obscurity. The second her darkness devours the light, a deafening crack echoes across the realm. The ground shakes violently, knocking the battlefield off their feet. Even the large giants have to steady themselves as the ground below us splits, a great chasm tearing through the battlefield, swallowing light and darkening our hope as it widens.

The vibrations grow stronger, more insistent—a foreboding rhythm that warns us to flee from what approaches. Regaining our footing, we stand, alert and tensed for what approaches. From within the endless crevasse, a deep, resonating growl rolls through the earth, its primal sound echoing up through the very soil we stand on. It's unlike any beast we have encountered today, or any of our past battles; it is deeper, filled with a hunger and ferocity that chills the air around us. The growl reverberates, not just a sound but a palpable wave of dread that washes over both armies.

I exchange a glance with Rhea, seeing in her eyes the same resolve mixed with uncertainty. Whatever Loki has unleashed now, it was kept hidden even deeper, reserved for a moment of desperation or as a final play in his twisted game. This is it. This is what we have been pushing him for.

The crack splits the armies, and we back away, taking inventory of wounds. I'm glad to see our fighters are withstanding Loki's army with few injuries that can be treated. There have been several deaths, but the number of losses is low compared to those in Loki's army who receive no mercy.

Lucas is next to me, still in human form as we watch. His Shifters are close by, remaining alert and ready to fight again. Kai and Zara stand with Cappa and the others. Bridget and Circe huddle with my mother and Hecate as Lexi prowls up next to them. Medusa and her sisters are by Rhea along with more of the tribes from Tartarus.

The ground begins to crack, fissures spreading like a web from a central point, a sign that the creature is burrowing its way to the surface. The anticipation is nearly as harrowing as the threat itself; each warrior grips their weapon tighter, their stances bracing against the unknown terror that approaches.

As the growling intensifies, a massive form starts to emerge from the largest of the fissures, and we get our first glimpse of Loki's creature of unimaginable size. "By the gods," my mother whispers behind me.

"Do you know what this is?" I ask her, tilting my head to the side but keeping my eyes on the monster.

"I thought it was only a myth, but there was one account in the library."

"The Typhon," Rhea says, looking at the monster with a stoic expression.

"Yes," my mother whispers back, her voice stolen by the shock of this moment. "A formidable monster, created for one reason."

"To defeat me," Rhea concludes.

As the ground beneath us trembles with the monstrous weight of the emerging beast, we draw a collective breath. The Typhon rises before us. It is a colossal entity, each part of its body seemingly larger and more menacing than the rest.

The head of a bull is perched upon broad shoulders that branch out into an array of snake bodies, each moving with a mind of its own. Hundreds of serpentine forms writhe and hiss, their scales glinting like polished armor under the scant light that shines behind the massive, bat-like wings.

Unfurling for what seems like ages, the monster's wings, dark and immense, stretch wide, casting a shadow that envelops the battlefield, plunging us into a darkness that feels almost tangible.

The legs of the beast, if they can be called that, are a mass of wriggling snake tails, each one undulating over the earth, crushing and constricting anything in their path. The creature's skin is a patchwork of scales and rough, armored plates, providing formidable natural armor. Horns and tusks jut out at menacing angles, and several sets of eyes, glowing with malevolence, seem to be looking everywhere at once.

The sight of such a beast would chill the heart of the

bravest warrior, and murmurs ripple through our ranks. Yet, standing here, facing this epitome of destruction, I feel a surge of determination rise within me.

This is why I have fought so long and hard, why we have all battled and sacrificed. If the Typhon is not stopped, the destruction it could unleash across this realm would be catastrophic.

The monster opens its mouth, and as the bull's head rises to the sky, so do the hundreds of serpents that protrude from the Typhon's neck and shoulders. The Typhon roars, a sound that shakes the very air. At first, it sounds like the wailing of a thousand voices all crying out at once, then deepens to a monstrous bellow.

Rhea's posture shifts ever so slightly—a tremor of disbelief that does not escape my notice. "What's wrong?" I ask, observing Rhea's gaze fixed on the Typhon, her expression one of deepening horror.

Her golden eyes meet mine, and within them, I see a tumult of emotions—confusion, sorrow, and anger. "Hermes," her voice barely above a whisper, yet carrying the weight of her realization. "The souls... The captured souls. They're... they're within the Typhon."

The revelation strikes like a bolt, and my eyes snap to the monster.

"This isn't just a beast; it's a cage—a living cage created by Loki."

I give myself seconds to be horrified over a single thought: my father's soul is trapped in the belly of this beast. Turning to my mate, I take her by the shoulders, facing her to me. "We're going to stick to the plan." Rhea can't pull her eyes away from the Typhon, away from the souls suffering inside. "Rhea, look at me."

Finally, she snaps out of the haze of disbelief and looks at me. Caressing her jaw with my hand, I pull her to me for a kiss. "We're sticking to the plan." I repeat, and she nods. "So, you take the big guy, and I'll take the little guy." I smirk.

"Are you sure about this?" Her worried eyes look me over.

"It's going to be fine." I give her a promise I'm not sure I can keep, but I'll fight for it with every molecule of my immortal being. I stand and help her to her feet, stealing one more kiss. "Lower the shields."

"I love you." Rhea takes my face between her hands, her touch desperate as I feel the mental shield of her power drift away from my mind. She places her hand over my heart where our bond thrums within us. "Remember, only this is real."

"Go get your souls back, little goddess, and if I get lost, come find me."

"I'll always find you." Tears bloom in her eyes before she blinks them away.

Rhea opens a portal, revealing the darkness of the Void within, and her army of souls returns to their realm. She doesn't want them near this beast until she can understand how Loki is trapping the souls. She doesn't want to risk harm coming to any more of them.

Rhea motions for the warriors to follow her as I turn to Lucas. "You ready?"

"As I'll ever be." He holds his fist out to me, and we bump knuckles before facing Loki.

"Let's go fight the Mind Mage on his battleground."

The air around us feels charged, electric as the shields fall away, and I become acutely aware of the mental warfare that has been playing out. The field is drenched in emotions and waves of confusion that aim to strike the mentality of the warriors—not with a physical assault, but a mental one.

The fact that Rhea is blocking all of this from impacting our fighters astounds me, and I have to lock away the moment of admiration I'm feeling for my mate. We need to keep our mental focus clear and sharp as we approach the Mind Mage who became a Titan-killer.

Lucas, standing beside me, gives a sharp nod. His expression hardens, the readiness in his eyes mirroring my own. We understand the risk Rhea has taken by removing these protections; it exposes us to direct mental attacks, but it also unchains our full potential to counterattack.

"You good?" I ask him, already feeling the undercurrents of Loki's psychic probes trying to seep into our thoughts.

"Yeah. It's time to end this," Lucas replies, his voice a mix of determination and a rage finely honed for this very confrontation.

"How gentlemanly of you," Loki calls out. "Letting your mate handle the big scary monster all alone?" I feel the cool touch of Loki's power as he tests Rhea's shields again. It's like ice sliding across my brain, and I resist the urge to shiver with repulsion.

"That just tells me you think so little of yourself, seeing the Typhon as the larger adversary."

"It's fitting of your stature," Lucas adds.

Loki's smirk wavers, a flicker of annoyance passing over his features. "I'll enjoy turning your mind to sludge while I force you to watch me dissect your little goddess." As Loki speaks, his body shifts into that of a massive green dragon.

Kicking off the surface of the earth, he takes to the skies. Lucas and I shift. Our wings beat in powerful, synchronized strokes, sending gusts of wind swirling below as we chase Loki.

He leads us higher, his winding body slicing through the clouds. His green scales occasionally catch the sunlight, flashing signals of his direction as he maneuvers with cunning, aiming to lose us in the upper reaches of the sky.

The moment he is going to pull us into an illusion is coming soon, and I prepare Lucas. The icy talon of Loki's power wraps around me, and I know he's going to drag the curtain of reality closed, locking us inside his deception.

As we reach the peak of our ascent, Loki suddenly folds his wings against his body, initiating a sharp dive towards the ocean below. He's fast, a green streak against the sky, and the currents of wind that swirl off his body are supposed to mask the illusion as it slips over us.

Without hesitation, Lucas and I fold our wings similarly, diving after him.

As we follow Loki's plunging dive through the air, the

atmosphere abruptly changes. The clear sky morphs into a roiling tempest, the winds escalating to hurricane force around us, threatening to slam our massive dragon forms off course. Below us, the ocean transforms into a monstrous whirlpool, its center roiling with chaotic energy.

I recognize this scene with a jolt of cold realization—it's not just any storm, but the very one from the darkest chapters of my own past. The swirling vortex of water below, the water monster Scylla snarling and thrashing in the waves, and the tall old ships struggling against the tempest with their large sails billowing in the violent wind.

Even though I wasn't there, I know what this moment is. Loki has pulled us into a vivid recreation of the night Calypso was lost at sea, the night that preceded her long captivity.

"Lucas!" I shout over the howling wind, my voice steady despite the chaos. "This is an illusion! A memory! Focus on the real enemy, not the phantoms!"

Lucas, recognizing the intensity in my voice, nods, his dragon eyes sharp and focusing on the surroundings. We stabilize our flight, adjusting to the unnatural wind patterns, but the swirling whirlpool below beckons us. Like the sweetest song from a siren's mouth, I feel the gravity of its melody wrap around me and tug me toward the surface.

Loki races downward, rocketing toward the water's surface far below. Turning his head, his gaze locks onto mine, a twisted satisfaction gleaming in his eyes. His voice, edged with a sinister weight, invades my mind.

"Hermes, do you think your sister's sufferings were by chance?" he taunts, his tone mockingly sympathetic. *"Every abduction, every ordeal she endured—I orchestrated them all.*

Each was a step to forge her, to mold her into something resilient, unbreakable."

The confession sends a wave of cold fury through me. We figured as much, but hearing Loki admit that Calypso's torment was merely a pawn in his cruel game enrages me.

"And why?" Loki continues, his voice rising with fervor. *"Because when the time came to strip her of what she held most dear—Achilles and Patroclus—I wanted her survival. I wanted her strong, not shattered. Strong enough to endure their loss and still remain by my side."*

His words are like venom, each syllable meant to wound, to provoke. *"Imagine it, Hermes. Your sister, the resilient Calypso, sitting at my feet, a princess in my new order once I consume Rhea's power over Death. What a sight that would be, don't you agree? Do you think the mighty Apollo would love seeing his daughter become my daughter?"*

The depth of his malice crystallizes within me an unyielding resolve. I feel the raw power of my dragon form surge, the energy crackling through my scales. This is no illusion. My anger and palpable hate for him are real.

Letting the raging column of fire rise from my throat, I blast him. Loki pulls out of his dive, and we follow, circling around to meet the god-killer from both sides.

As Loki's monologue reverberates through my ears, a disturbing suspicion begins to gnaw at the edges of my mind. His confidence, his taunting, it's all too orchestrated, too deliberate. Even as we circle him, supposedly high in the air, a flicker of confusion catches my attention—the way the air feels around us, the sound of the wind—it doesn't align with our perceived altitude.

In a flash of intuition, I realize the terrifying truth: Loki has enveloped us in another layer of illusion. We aren't soaring at great heights as we believed; instead, we're perilously close to the ocean's surface, being drawn into a deceptive dive that could have catastrophic results upon impact.

"Lucas!" I shout, my voice urgent over the rush of wind and the beating of our wings. "Pull up! It's another trick!"

Trusting my instincts, I forcefully spread my wings to their fullest span, straining against the momentum of our dive. The sudden resistance against the air slows my descent dramatically, a maneuver that requires every ounce of strength and control I possess.

But Lucas doesn't respond. He remains locked in a perilous dive, oblivious to the fast-approaching danger. It becomes painfully clear that Loki has ensnared him in a separate, potent illusion, tailor-made to exploit his deepest fears or distract him completely.

Powerless to intervene from my position, I can only watch in mounting horror as Lucas, still caught in the deceptive embrace of the illusion, plummets into the ocean. Below, the waters churn ominously around the massive, shadowy form of a water serpent—an extension of Loki's trap, lying in wait with its mouth gaping open.

The impact is devastating. Lucas, in his full dragon form, crashes into the water with such force that a colossal spray of seawater soars into the air. The serpent's jaws clamp shut with a sickening, resonant snap. The ocean around the beast swirls into a dark crimson swirl of Lucas's immortal blood.

A cry of rage and grief escapes me as I circle helplessly above the scene. The serpent, satisfied with its catch, slowly submerges, dragging Lucas's lifeless form beneath the waves. The water's surface calms, a stark contrast to the chaos of moments ago. The reality of the loss—the Shifters Titan—sinks in, leaving a void filled with cold fury and a sharp thirst for justice.

My grief is palpable, but it fuels a new, burning rage. No more illusions, no more tricks—we end this, now.

Turning back to Loki, who observes the aftermath of his illusion with smug satisfaction, my entire being hardens. *"Loki!"* I roar, my voice echoing across the waters, carrying the weight of every loss, every betrayal. *"This ends now!"*

With Lucas's tragic fall as a catalyst, my approach shifts. No longer am I just a participant in this battle; I am its arbiter. I dive toward Loki, fueled by a mixture of sorrow and wrath, my heart set not only on stopping him but on dismantling the very foundations of his power. Every wingbeat is a drumming of war, every breath a furnace of fury.

As I close the distance, the ocean spray and the cry of the winds merge into a symphony of battle. Today, Loki will answer for his crimes, and I will not rest until balance is restored, until the shadows he cast are purged by the light of justice.

I've gained on him, and the look of terror in his eyes is like nectar from the gods, fueling me with fresh resolve. Reaching his long tail, I capture it between my large teeth. The hard scales give way to my powerful jaws. I feel the rush of his blood and hear the shriek of his pain.

With a heavy tug and a targeted flap of my wings, I change the course of our flight and send Loki plummeting. Before he can fix his trajectory, I reach out with sharp taloned claws that dig into his body, holding him.

Opening my mouth wide, I roar as I bite down.

The sudden shift in scenery is as jarring as it is unexpected. One moment, I am a dragon, soaring through the air with rage and sorrow burning through my veins. The next, I am Hermes again—no longer scaled but flesh and blood, seated on a portico bathed in the warmth of a serene afternoon. The violent roiling of the ocean and the sounds of battle have vanished, replaced by the tranquil whisper of a gentle breeze and the distant call of birds.

Wasn't I just dreaming? A spectacular dream where I transformed into a mighty dragon, battling a great enemy. But the details of what we were fighting for and who I was fighting with drift away with the gentle wind rustling my hair.

My body tingles as if I can still feel the dragon's hide against my skin. My breath rushes out as if I just finished racing a marathon. My eyes struggle to focus in the brilliance of the sun, as if it's shining right next to me.

Rubbing my eyes, I hear the sound of clinking cutlery against a bronze plate as my awareness clears. I look next to me and realize it's not the brilliance of the sun but a gleaming aura I never thought I would feel again. Warm and reassuring, the unmistakable presence of my father encases me. I blink quickly, pushing away the remnants of my dream as I fixate on him.

Sitting beside me, eating breakfast, my father, Apollo, is the very image of calm and contemplation. He lifts a cup to his lips, the action steeped in normalcy. His appearance is exactly the same as I always remembered.

For a moment, I am frozen, caught between the realities of war and this sudden peace. My mind races to catch up with the events unfolding around me. He died so long ago, on Ares' blade. I watched him bleed out, his blue eyes, just like mine, dimming just before they closed.

But sitting here before me, he is real. Flesh and bone, with the energy of life flowing within him.

"Father..." I start, my voice tinged with confusion and disbelief. "How...?" My words trail off, unable to fully articulate the whirlwind of emotions and questions swirling within me.

"Son," my father's voice rings out around me like a bell. "It's been so long."

As I cast a final glance at Hermes, my heart tightens with a mixture of concern and unyielding faith. He's more than my fated mate; he's my guiding light in the darkness. A cunning warrior, his resilience has been tested through countless battles. Today, he faces Loki, whose deceptions know no bounds. Our shared glance is brief but filled with the promise of our love. I know he'll fight through every battle Loki wages against him.

Turning from Hermes, I steel myself for the monstrous Typhon that looms ahead.

The moment I set eyes on the monster, time seems to slow. The souls within sense me and reach out. I hear their wails of misery, suspended between the life that ended and their blocked ascension to the Void.

My blood turns ice cold when two forms step forward, peering down at me from the Typhon's great height. Even from the distance, I can pick out the yellow shining aura of the sun god and his faithful mate, a living volcano. Apollo and Ares stand together, their powerful yellow and orange auras swaying like a brilliant sun flare.

I feel the waves of torment they faced under Loki's depravity. He pulled apart Apollo's emotions as he controlled Ares' mind, making them hate each other with vicious words and then separating them. Apollo couldn't accept it. Something about it never felt right, and he went back for Ares again and again.

Finally tiring of the charade, Loki made them fight each other. Ares was always aware of what was happening, always able to hear and feel but never in control. As Apollo lay dying, Loki opened a link between them, wanting Apollo to know the truth of the torment his mate was enduring. Loki meant it as another form of torture, but Ares was granted a solitary gift. He used that moment to ensure Apollo knew the depths of his love. It was a weak message, but Apollo heard it, and that was all that mattered to Ares.

"My heart will forever be entwined with yours."

I wipe a tear from my cheek and move my hand to cover my mouth, trapping the gasp inside as the forms within the Typhon move. The golden glow of Athena's soul steps forward, and the small brown soul with her pulls a sob from my chest and brings me to my knees. Teddy.

A dark storm with rolling black clouds builds in the sky behind me as my sorrow turns to determination. Silver lightning streaks across the sky as I pour the torrents of my pain into it. Around us, the battle has died. Loki's forces have run, abandoning their oppressor at the first sight of the Typhon.

Our forces returned to the safety of the Wyoming territory to help the mortals pulled from the battlefield at the start of this war. Aside from my small circle of fighters, only the Cyclopes and the Kraken remain. These giants, dwarfed in the shadow of the Typhon, stand ready for our next battle.

Beside me, an assembly of goddesses, each a formidable warrior, ready their weapons and magic to face the Typhon with me. Their presence comforts me and brings unity to our shared purpose. Among them, Medusa prepares to mount Perseus. His wings flap gently, stirring the dirt at our feet, as ready as we are to face the impending storm.

Daphne stands with me, Hecate next to her. Circe, Naomi, and Lexi keep watch around us with Kai circling high above. Bridget and Zara are on my right with Euryale and Stheno by their side.

Mounting Nocturna, I feel the familiar surge of our connection as she works to steady me. Her powerful form resonates with quiet strength, her dark eyes reflecting the resolve that mirrors my own.

The Typhon is a towering mass of destruction with countless writhing heads and a roar that challenges the heavens. Its body, a grotesque collection of limbs and scales, houses the imprisoned souls—innocent lives caught in Loki's unnatural manipulations.

"We have to be careful," I call out to the line of goddesses flanking me. "Strike with precision. We cannot afford to be reckless. There is precious cargo inside that monster that we need to recover."

Medusa nods, her gaze steely, as she maneuvers Perseus alongside Nocturna. "Is she in there?" Medusa's eyes hold me with all the rage and anger of her resentment, accumulated over the eons. Her brutal separation from Athena, their bond ripped out of them, has left a scar on her soul.

I nod, confirming her fear. She clenches her jaw, working to reign back her focus to the moment before us.

High above, Kai circles the Typhon, assessing its movements, its weaknesses. The beast's eyes, wild with fury, track our every move, but there must be a method to our dance. We will be the tempest, weaving through the chaos it embodies until we find a way to bring the monster down.

As the battle unfolds, Medusa and her sisters strike first. Their gazes target the serpentine appendages that adorn the Typhon's neck and shoulders, solidifying the flesh into stone. The Cyclopes hurl massive boulders and land devastating blows that resonate like thunder across the battlefield.

Hecate enlists Circe and Bridget, and the three mistresses of dark elements combine their powers to manifest a dark monster of swirling shadow. A behemoth that mirrors the Typhon's size and form serves as a distraction. Their creature of darkness lunges forward, engaging the beast, its form shifting and swirling, a mass of shadow and malevolence that captivates the Typhon.

While Loki's champion contends with this new adversary, Daphne takes advantage of the distraction. Positioned with a clear vantage point, she nocks arrow after arrow, each tipped with a radiant energy that seeks the Typhon's multitude of eyes. Her aim is precise, each shot calculated to blind the mammoth, reducing its ability to counter our multifaceted assault effectively.

The Shifters attack the Typhon's massive body, working as a pack to maneuver around him and strike as one. Kai soars above the Typhon, diving at strategic moments to distract and harry the creature from above. Her sharp talons rake across the Typhon's eyes and softer tissues, drawing its attention upward while she deftly dodges the striking snakes that are not yet petrified by the work of the Gorgons.

Lexi, with the sleek agility of a deadly feline, maneuvers around the monsters massive limbs. She targets the tendons and softer underbelly, her attacks a blur of motion, aimed at weakening the beast's mobility. Her movements are a dance of death—graceful, silent, and deadly.

Naomi charges at the base of the Typhon in her large bear form. Her powerful strikes aim to destabilize the creature, her roars echoing Daphne's arrows and Kai's aerial assaults. Each swipe of her massive paws delivers a force capable of shaking the very earth.

As the Typhon writhes and roars under our relentless assault, I guide Nocturna through the skies, her powerful wings beating with a steady rhythm as we dodge the flying debris and flailing arms of the Typhon. The chaos below us is a blur of motion, but my focus remains fixed on freeing the trapped souls within the goliath's monstrous form.

I need to understand how Loki has contained them in the first place.

The battle's intensity doesn't waver, but amidst the cacophony, I am attuned to the Typhon's movements. My eyes scan for anything that might reveal the key to unlocking the prison of souls it harbors.

As the Typhon reels from another coordinated strike, it throws its massive head back in a primal roar, a sound that shakes the fractured earth around us. The monster's multiple heads begin to coil and align, converging into a singular, focused posture. The air around its massive body crackles with accumulating power, a visible aura of raw, dark energy building around its gaping mouth.

As I watch from atop Nocturna, a chill runs down my

spine. Recognizing the beast is preparing to attack, I shout, "Everyone, back!" My voice amplifies in the atmosphere, carrying over the din of combat.

Everyone quickly heeds the warning, pulling back with fervor. Their eyes are fixed on the Typhon as it completes its dreadful charge. With a thunderous roar that seems to shake the very core of Gaea, the Typhon unleashes its fury.

From its mouth, a torrent of destructive energy bursts forth—a searing beam of light and shadow mixed with elemental force. Within its chest, a glowing, undulating pulse steals my attention. The blast from the Typhon strikes the ground where my forces had just been, tearing through the earth and creating a massive trench as it dissipates into the distance.

"Try to get it to do that again!" I call out, steering Nocturna to a new vantage point.

"Are you kidding?" Medusa calls back.

"I think I saw something!"

With a reluctant grunt, the Gorgon steadies herself with a deep breath. "All right, ladies, let's kick this up a notch." Medusa organizes the goddess warriors fighting with us and turns to the giants. "Boys, do your worst."

The immortals push against the boundaries of their powers, targeting the monolithic beast. Pouring my aura over them, I add strength to their resolve and mental prowess. The essence of their elements resides within me, and as I fortify them, their powers swell.

The Typhon rears its head back again, exposing its neck. I see a long line, like a sealed incision, running down its sternum. Positioning Nocturna higher, I watch intently as the beast unleashes its second attack. Enraged, the beam of light and shadow is charged with static electricity, and bolts of lightning shoot to the ground, the dirt sizzling and smoking.

Within the beast, the elements collide as they rise out of its throat. And there, attached to the beast's heart, I see the silhouette of a familiar amulet.

"Medusa, it's an amulet!" I announce when the roar of the Typhon's blast ceases.

"Oh, by the gods. I got my fill of amulets in Egypt," Medusa huffs.

I chuckle, recalling my life as Cleopatra, a general under Medusa when she reigned as Pharaoh. Ten amulets caused quite a problem for the realm. "Well, you get to help me destroy one more."

Medusa and her sisters have petrified most of the snakes that protrude from the Typhon's neck. It's nearly blind with only a few eyes remaining but it's still standing. The hundreds of serpent tails that form its legs are a challenge. As several are severed, the remaining snakes reposition themselves to keep the Typhon from falling over.

"Okay, Nocturna, you're not going to like this but fly around and get me close." I work my feet onto the horse's back. Holding onto her midnight black mane, standing in a crouch, I prepare myself to jump. The daggers in my holsters won't be long enough to break through the sternum, so I conjure a sword of darkness and starlight.

"Work on the snake tails at the back of the legs only," I call out to the Gorgons and the Shifters, who pivot and get to work. "Can you make that shadow mirage larger?" I ask Hecate and the others, who push more darkness and shadow into their tall Typhon-like replica. "And get ready to punch. I need the Typhon to look up."

The giants drop their boulders and take a position behind the Typhon, ready to charge forward at the right moment. It will take all of us attacking at once to get this right.

Nocturna circles back and flies at the perfect angle for me to jump off. We've just got to get the timing right. The Typhon takes a large breath, readying another blast. "Now!" I call out.

Hecate, Circe, and Bridget push the dark being of their conjuring to form a fist and drive it upward. They strike the Typhon perfectly with such force that the wind created by the impact pushes against me as Nocturna flies around the front of the monster.

The beast tips its head backward, exposing the soft spot at the top of its chest. Pushing off Nocturna with my dark sword raised overhead, I grasp the hilt with both hands. Driving the sharp blade into the weak spot, I use my powers to pull myself down. My elemental blade cuts through the tough armor of the Typhon's scales and hide.

The pained scream of the Typhon travels the realm as I slice its chest open to reveal the heart of the monster. "Take him down!" I call out. My grip tightens on my blade as I prepare for the Typhon's collapse.

The giants charge at once, aiming for the back of the Typhon's legs. Most of the snake tails that form the legs have been decimated by the Shifters or turned to stone by the Gorgons. Hecate and the witches' dark monster takes a large step forward, and its massive hands push against the Typhon's chest as the giants ram into the beast's legs from behind.

Now turned to stone, the snakes' bodies crumble to dust, and the strike from both sides brings the beast down. Keeping a firm grip on the hilt of my sword, I ride the monster as it cuts its path downward. The impact draws up a cloud of dust that shoots outward for a mile in all directions. A sizable divot is embedded into the earth from the massive weight of the beast.

The immortals and giants around me celebrate their triumph in bringing the monster down, but the souls are still trapped, and the beast is still alive. The amulet fixed to its heart could be imbued with all manner of elemental power and spells of protection, or harm. Loki has found a way to use the amulet to control this monster and trap souls within it. There is no telling what else this amulet could contain.

I summon the Kraken and walk up the Typhon's chest toward its neck. As the beast takes a breath in, its mighty chest rises, and I lose my footing. Placing my hand on the protective scales, I'm nearly blinded by the rush of images and pleas from the beast to end its suffering. I see the prison where Loki confined the monster with huge chains, deep within the realm's interior. A toxin dripped from a carnivorous plant kept the beast suspended in a catatonic state. The moans and cries from the souls trapped inside the monster tormented him, constantly resonating through the hidden chamber of its imprisonment and driving it mad with hysteria.

The beast knows that destroying the amulet fixed to its heart will cause its death, and it's begging me to alleviate its suffering.

"Oh, my gods." I work to catch my breath as others climb atop the beast.

"Rhea, are you okay?" Daphne finds me on my knees with my hands on the Typhon's chest, tears streaming down my face.

"It's in pain," I choke on my sob because the agony flowing from the beast is overwhelming me. Daphne, a powerful Sensor, freezes as she takes in the waves of emotions.

"How terrible," she mutters.

We've blinded the beast with our attacks, so I send a message of our intent to the Typhon, hoping it understands me. I don't want to drag out the beast's death, but there is only one way we can kill it. I do my best to send a calming essence to the monster, hoping it will serve as a balm to help soothe what will happen next. The Kraken slithers its tentacles on each side of the long gash I created and pulls the Typhon's chest apart, revealing the large beating heart of the monster.

Just as I saw, a massive amulet in the shape of the revered dung beetle is fixed to the beast's heart with a web of darkness. Suspended is a sack of black magic that contains the trapped souls. The Typhon groans in pain but otherwise lays still.

I jump onto the amulet and pull my daggers. Forged of Stygian Iron by Hephaestus in the volcano of the Fire realm, the blades have the capability of siphoning the essence of any immortal power from any being. Monsters and immortals alike, none are immune to the alloys of the metals.

Driving my blades into the amulet, a jet of dark energy blasts out, reaching into the sky and clouding around me. The whistle of a loud wind grows stronger, and the darkness races out of the vessel. I hold my daggers steady against the rush of power. Squinting my eyes shut and turning my head away from the blast, I remain firm.

In an instant, the whistle stops when the last of the dark matter has been absorbed by my daggers. The body of the Typhon goes limp under me. While I'm pained for the monster and its suffering, my heart races with joy when the trapped souls surge out of their confinement.

All around me, the warriors who helped me free them laugh, others cry tears of happiness, and the orbs of light race around, happy to be free. Medusa's eyes move quickly from orb to orb, searching for the soul of her lost mate. I'm the only one able to discern them with any certainty, the others unable to view them as I do.

They've been trapped for ages, the ascension back to the Void unnaturally delayed. I have no idea what kind of damage that could do to the souls, so I open my portal and watch them return to the realm that is their sanctuary.

Putting my arm around Medusa's shoulder, I turn toward our fighters waiting on the ground below. "Come on. Let's go get the others."

Sliding off the body of the dead Typhon, we walk to the small circle where Hermes, Lucas, and Cappa are keeping an eye on Loki. Still bound in Hermes' powers, my captured hunter is still kneeling on the ground, lost in the depths of my Mirage. Lucas is no longer within the hallucination, but Hermes is.

"Did he kill you?" I ask Lucas with an understanding smile.

"Yeah, man. He drove me into a giant snake's mouth." He blinks and shakes his head as if trying to clear the image from his mind. "That was the most messed up thing I've ever done."

The other Shifters return to their human forms, and I walk up to my mate. All around us, it feels as if the realm is taking a collective sigh of relief, but I'm the lone immortal still holding my breath, terrified of what I may find when I try to retrieve my mate from the illusion.

Standing still with his eyes closed, Hermes is keeping Loki busy within his own mind. Placing my hand on his chest, I send three taps down our bond. Smiling when I feel his reply, the tension of a thousand deaths leaves my body.

Gently, I pull Hermes from my illusion, leaving Loki there by himself a little longer.

With a deep exhale, Hermes opens his beautiful blue eyes and looks down at me with a grin that widens to a smile. Wrapping his arms around me, he scans the field behind me, taking in the dead Typhon and our captured prisoner. "You, little goddess, are a genius."

Hermes

My lips can't find hers fast enough as my little goddess and I bask in the glow of our victory. We've reached the end of the longest journey, and while a path of healing and recovery lies ahead, we know that together, nothing can stand in our way. The bond between us, forged in the fires of adversity and sealed with our shared triumphs, is stronger than ever. Now we can look toward the future, hand in hand, ready to face whatever comes next, knowing that our love is our greatest strength.

Rhea pours her relief down our bond, saturating me with her worry that I would be hurt by Loki when she pulled us into her illusion. Filling him with her darkness, she took away all his senses for just a moment. She dipped him in a temporary void of obscurity and pushed him to move his final chess piece. When he summoned the Typhon, Loki thought he was calling out his victory, but in reality, he became a pawn in her game; he just didn't know it yet.

"You took things that don't belong to you, and I'm going to take them back," she told him. Loki thought she was talking about the Titans' powers he stole, but she wanted her souls.

"I'm going to steal from you what you have stolen from so

many others." Rhea wasn't referring to the power she was going to remove from him; she was talking about his freedom of thought.

She would strip him of control over his mind, the same way he stripped so many others. Those precious few seconds where Rhea filled him with clouds of darkness, she was locking him into a void of mirrors. Any illusion he cast would be reflected back to him.

When we parted ways for her to rescue her souls, she put Lucas and me in there with him. The illusions of a powerful Mind mage are hardly perceptible, and many immortals have lost themselves forever in a vault of their own mind.

This was the part of the plan Rhea was most concerned about, scared the illusions Loki would cast once inside would be damaging or harmful to us. But I never had a moment of doubt, knowing I was in the safe harbor of her power the whole time.

"You're sure you're okay?" she asks, searching my eyes with hers, still tense with worry.

I run my fingers through her silky hair, warmth filling me, knowing I get to do this for the rest of eternity. "There is nothing Loki could show me that would be worse than watching the light leave your eyes a thousand times." I hold her face between my hands and place a tender kiss on her forehead.

Loki thrashes around in his bindings, growling and spitting nonsense, still locked in the illusion. Medusa, Kai, and Bridget watch with blank faces as the greatest plague that has swept the twelve realms flails around with spit on his chin.

"So embarrassing," Kai shakes her head with her arms crossed over her chest.

"That's what I'm saying," Medusa chimes in. "Could never

be me. Honestly. You would never catch me acting a fool like this."

Rhea stands in front of me, and I wrap my arms around her, holding her close and sending my reassurance down our bond. She's still shaken from worry over me and Lucas while we played with Loki inside the illusion, but each second, she relaxes more. I catch my mother's eye and find her watching Rhea and me. Soft tears well in her eyes, and she wears a blissful smile.

"I'm so happy for you, son," she says.

Emotion grabs at my heart, but the moment is broken when Hecate passes between us with her hands on her hips. With a smile and a wink at my mother, she joins her sister.

"Well, I suppose we should get this over with," Hecate says, looking Loki over.

"We could leave him here a few centuries at least," Medusa jests.

Rhea takes my hand, and we face the man who has tormented her over a thousand lifetimes, destroyed our realm, and torn our loved ones away from us. Everything has led to this moment, and it feels almost surreal. A film of silver starlight coats Loki's skin like a veil. Touching her finger to his forehead, Rhea releases him from her illusion.

The world comes back into sharp focus for Loki in an instant. His green eyes widen with the abrupt clarity and the disorientation of being forcefully awakened from a deep dream. His gaze darts around, taking in the scene: the empty battlefield, the fallen Typhon, and most importantly, his own defeat. Rage builds in his face, veins bulging in his neck, his complexion turning purple.

YOU...!" He tries to lunge at Rhea but only topples over in

the dirt face-first before rolling to his side. Medusa and her sisters snicker quietly, their whispered conversation floating across the small crowd of warriors.

"So embarrassing."

"...Just making himself look even more pathetic."

Loki tries and fails to sit up. We leave him lying on his side, his hands bound behind his back and tied to his ankles. The thick ropes of my power wrapped around him so firmly, he could never break free.

Rhea takes a dagger from her thigh holster, spinning the blade on her palm before grasping it firmly. She studies him. "What's wrong? You don't like it when someone makes you see the world through the veil you've used to blind so many others?"

He presses his mouth shut firmly and glares at her.

"Well, too bad." She leans over, resting her hands on her knees and tilting her head to the side.

"So, what, you're going to kill me now?"

Shaking her head, she stands up straight. "No. I'm not going to perpetuate cycles of mindless cruelty. I won't become what you are, Loki." Looking to me, Rhea nods toward Loki.

With my power, I adjust his bindings, ensuring he's still firmly secured in the hold of my aura. Lucas and I stand him up and hold him still for Rhea to issue his justice.

"You don't deserve to take another breath, much less hold a drop of elemental power. But like I said, I'm no monster like you." Rhea takes the tip of her blade and gently runs it down the side of his face.

He tries to jerk away, but Lucas and I don't let him budge. "You..."

"Stop talking." Rhea pulls the air from his lungs, leaving

him gasping. "I'm going to allow you to retain your immortality. I'm taking every speck of power away from you and locking you in the very prison you created."

Rhea sticks the tip of her blade into his flesh, barely piercing his skin. He flinches and makes futile attempts to resist as the Stygian Iron devours the Titan essence within him. The runes of Rhea's blade allow her to control what she pulls out of her victim. Allowing him to keep his life is a courtesy he doesn't deserve, but making him live an immortal life, powerless and confined in the realm's center for all eternity, is a torture he has earned.

No longer a god, Loki has no ability to hide anything from Rhea. She scours his mind and finds the entrance to the prison of the Typhon. She learns every secret he ever kept. Her first goal is to lock her hunter away forever.

Teleporting to a remote island in the center of the ocean, Rhea disassembles the heavy wards that hid Loki's secret prison. Guiding our captive down the long rocky tunnel that leads to the realm's center, we find a fork in the pathway. Rhea probes the atmosphere with her powers and leads us down the tunnel on the right.

The tunnel opens into an enormous chamber. Heat from a river of magma makes the atmosphere ripple. Enormous chains that once restrained the Typhon are shrunk by Medusa's power of Earth and shackled around Loki's wrists and ankles.

Pulling a lever on the far side of the chamber, the chains are pulled tight. His arms are raised, his stance widened, and we step back, taking one last look at our tormentor. Standing forever in the shape of an X, Loki will remain here until the end of time, with nothing more than the flowing magma and his tormented thoughts for company.

I hope that as he watches the magma flow, it reminds him of my father and Ares—the brilliant flare of their yellow and orange auras surrounding him for all time.

"You'll remain here until the realm ceases to exist, and its fate will become yours."

With those parting words, Loki is secured within the chamber. Back at the entrance, Rhea calls upon her command of Earth and submerges the small island beneath the pounding waves of the ocean, forever burying her hunter within the center of the earth. The reign of a tyrant has ended, but the scars of his torment can't be buried away so easily and will take a long time to heal.

As the waters of the realm swallow the island, it marks the end of one era and the beginning of another—a period of rebuilding and healing. A period where we get to craft a future for ourselves; a future of peace.

E cstasy is the only word that comes to mind as the morning sun shines through the window of our tiny cabin. Proficient is the next that comes to mind as my mate is currently positioned with his head between my thighs. His wonderfully proficient tongue is bringing me quickly to my second orgasm of the morning, and absolute ecstasy courses through my body.

Hermes crawls up and pushes the sheet off his head. Smug satisfaction is painted on his face as he lays down next to me, and we instantly entangle ourselves around each other. My lips ache for him, and my tongue misses the taste of him. Thankfully, he's just as hungry for me as I am for him. Our mouths are like magnets, and we're pulled together. I pull a groan from him when I suck on his lip, savoring the taste of myself on him.

"You're a messy eater," I laugh, pulling away and wiping his face with a corner of the sheet.

"Don't make me go back for thirds, little goddess," he pulls me back into a possessive kiss as his hands roam my back, "because you are a meal I will never get tired of devouring."

I lay my head on the soft pillow, looking into his eyes. I stroke the short stubble on his face, and he moves a section of my hair back behind my ear. We just lay in the unhurried silence of the morning, enjoying being together the first morning of our freedom. The first real morning of our lives together.

From this day on, we finally have the chance to decide what we're going to do without the threat of death chasing us through each lifetime. No longer will we have to look over our shoulder for the shadow of a hunter or say goodbye, not knowing how long we will be separated by the stars.

Hermes' hand burns a slow path down my back. Rubbing my thigh, he pulls my leg over his hip, scooting us even closer. The breath I exhale becomes the one he inhales, and he only needs to tilt his head to reach my lips.

"You know what I was just thinking about?" His deep voice rumbles against me and strokes my desire.

"Hmm?"

"A long time ago, we made a wish among the stars." He pauses, his gaze moving to both of my eyes before he continues. "I think it's time we make that wish come true."

I bite my lip to hold back the silly little grin that is spreading across my face.

"Rhea Crenshaw, Goddess of the Twelve Realms, commander of my heart and greediest little goddess that has ever lived... Will you travel the realms with me so I can show you every flower of every realm?"

My heart swelling with a warmth that could light up even the darkest corners of the Void. His words, so earnest and filled with love, draw a laugh that is part joy, part disbelief at the prospect of finally commanding our own future.

Hermes takes my hand and places a tender kiss on my knuckles. Threading our fingers together, I savor the familiar roughness of his palms that have wielded both weapon and my heart.

I put his arm back around me and wrap my arms around him. "Yes, I will travel the realms with you." I pull him into a kiss, sweeping my tongue along his as he runs his hand up my neck, his fingers threading in my hair. "Forever." Kiss. "And ever." Kiss. "And ever."

"Good." Smirking triumphantly, he rolls onto his back, pulling me along with him. I straddle him, running my hands along the divots of his toned muscles as I grind against his impressively pierced erection. "Now show your good boy how much you love this cock." He thrusts along with me, my head rolling back in pleasure as his barbells glide along my clit. "Forever." Thrust. "And ever." Thrust. "And ever."

Saying goodbye is never easy, but these goodbyes are said with the promise of reunion. For so long, our farewells have been tinged with sorrow, knowing we may never see someone again. But today, as we look at the bands of immortals gathered on the Grecian beaches, we witness friends hugging with warm smiles and a look that says, "I'll see you again."

Lucas and Hermes finish their argument over which of them has the larger dragon. Lucas finally gives up with a massive roll of his eyes when Hermes says, "It's not the size of the dragon that counts, right, Luke? It's what you can do with it that really matters."

Kai smacks Cappa's arm when he fails to stifle his laugh, and Lucas glares at him as he makes his way over to me. With a big hug and thanks for everything, he pulls away, looking at me with the slightest hint of emotion in his hazel eyes. "No one deserves happiness more than you two." For all the bickering and teasing between him and Hermes, I'm glad for the friendship they have formed.

But after he hugs me, Lucas rubs the back of his neck, warring with himself as if holding back something.

"What?" I cross my arms over my chest.

"Let's just say, I also deserved the happiness of a mate," I already know where Lucas is going with this and a sly smile spreads across my face. "Can you tell me where The Morrigan hid her?" His tone turns serious as his eyes darken slightly. "Did she at least survive?"

His concern steals my humor as my smile is replaced with empathy. "She survived." I reassure him. Turning away, my mischievous smile returns. "But I'm not telling you where she is." I wink as I make my way over to Kai.

"Oh come on!" Lucas throws his hands up in exasperation.

"And ruin a good love story?" I call behind me. "Never."

After goodbyes from Kai, Zara, and Naomi, Lexi gives me a nod as she stands on the edges of the crowd with her mother. I return the gesture, a small understanding of respect passing between us.

Next to them, Flora has her arm through Zephyr's elbow, and the couple waves to me. A vial of the Waters of Remembrance healed Zephyr's memories. Though they have no recollection of anything that occurred in the Labyrinth, I'm actually thankful for that.

"You thought a flock of Furies could take me down?" Medusa jests at Hermes as they talk of her survival in the Labyrinth. "Frankly, I'm offended."

Hera bows her head to me, her beautiful red hair blowing

in the gentle breeze. The richness in her brown eyes is tinged with the lingering sadness of her captivity, a darkness that will likely remain with her forever.

Once Hera led Cappa and Zephyr safely to the Labyrinth's entrance, Cappa told her to wait there and promised we would be back for her. It's the first place Hecate, Daphne, and I went last night after we dealt with Loki.

There were so many immortals captured and falsely imprisoned by Loki over the ages inside the Labyrinth. The Life and Water Elementals worked all night to heal and restore those we freed, but Flora and I personally aided Hera as a thank you for her help.

Hecate didn't want to join the farewells today, so she gave her blessings this morning after breakfast and returned to dismantle the Labyrinth. It has become a living and breathing entity since Hecate constructed it and is not the form of Darkness that she practices.

Daphne gives Hermes a hug for the hundredth time, making him promise to send falcons regularly as we're on our travels.

The massive giants wait patiently as the pegasus and other winged beasts graze in the short grass. I feel a gentle tremor below my feet that steals my attention.

The realms are telling me it is time.

Making my way to Medusa, she stands with her sisters and the rest of the Gorgons. "So, what will you do?" I ask her, biting back my smile.

"Ah, I will probably go back to Tartarus. I don't know if there is anything left here for me." She looks across the waters of the Mediterranean with sorrow darkening her green eyes. "What about you two?"

"We'll just be like a dandelion seed on the wind and see where things take us."

She smiles and nods before giving me a hug.

Our allies from Tartarus make their way to the center of the field, Medusa at the front of them as she takes her place among her sisters again. I give Hermes the okay, and he opens his portal back to Tartarus.

It's like opening an oven door as the heat from the desert realm of sunlight flows out of the portal. The winds of Gaea and Tartarus mingle, swirling into an excited vortex as the ground tremors again.

This time others feel it, and I'm nearly bouncing with excitement as they glance around with worried expressions. Hermes gives me a curious look as he joins me, taking my hand.

"Just watch." I whisper, nodding toward Medusa, who looks across the trembling ground with concern.

"By the gods, what now?" She exclaims as the rushing winds of the realm push her through the portal. As soon as her feet touch the crimson sand of the desert, it captures her in a churning vortex.

"Medusa!" Her sisters exclaim at once, but I hold them back.

"It's okay. I promise." I try to reassure her sisters. Stentho watches, but Euryale is less convinced, and I have to hold her back by her arm.

The churn of the winds and sand completely consumes our view of Medusa, spinning faster and faster. The brilliant emerald burn of her aura gets brighter, and finally, we can see her shadowed silhouette.

The winds are spinning so fast, Medusa is suspended in the air within the funnel. Her back is bowed, and she seems frozen inside the swirl. Euryale tries to go for her again, but the light begins to dim. The vortex lowers her to the ground and dissipates.

Breathless, Medusa looks at her hands and arms with wide eyes before looking to me as if searching for confirmation. But it's the giants, knights of their realm, guardians of Tartarus that sense the power the realm has bestowed upon Medusa. Dropping to one knee with their fists on the ground, the giants bow in reverence to Medusa, Titan of Tartarus.

Her sisters gasp. Stentho claps her hands over her mouth as Euryale looks on with wide eyes. The tribespeople follow the giants and drop to one knee, all giving their respect to the return of their Titan.

"I–I don't understand." Medusa stammers, still reeling from the gift of the realm.

"The Titans were first created by the realms. How or why, no one knows, but Loki stole power that was not his to take. The realms are restoring that balance." I take her hands as I try to steady my nervousness for this next part. My eyes burn as I try to push back the tears that are rising. Taking a deep breath and swallowing hard, I meet her gaze again.

"I can't do anything to bring her back." Medusa flinches when I mention Athena, but she remains quiet and lets me continue. "I can't apologize for the way I suspected you, and I can't make up for ages of torment that you have unjustly endured."

"Rhea, you are not responsible for everything–" She interjects but stops when I hold my hand out.

"I can't heal the wounds of your past, but there is one wound I can help with, if you will allow me?"

Medusa holds my stare a moment before nodding her head.

I step back a few paces, and she takes a deep breath, not sure what to expect.

"This is going to sting a little." I warn her.

"Bring it on… I guess." She looks around with uncertainty. Swaying back and forth on her feet, she shakes her arms out by her sides.

Evoking the power of Death within me, I surround her with my aura. A blazing golden light erupts from her center, and she winces, dropping to the ground and clutching her chest.

Mating bonds are a contract between souls forged in the cosmos. Loki ripped it away from Athena and Medusa, forever scarring their souls. I can't bring people back from the dead, but I can mend the soul.

As the burning blaze recedes, Medusa pants heavily as tears flow from her face. "It's back," she chokes out through her sobs. "The mating bond, I–I feel it again."

I take her hands and help her stand. The wind around us becomes stronger, exciting the waves of the Mediterranean behind us.

"Like I said…I can't do anything to bring her back, but the realms are capable of more than we could ever understand."

A crack resounds in the atmosphere above as all eyes turn to the sky. A comet, golden and blazing with the intensity of a thousand suns, streaks across the sky. Its trail is a fiery spectacle, illuminating the heavens as it races to the ground, crashing into the sea before us.

From the impact, a massive vortex spirals downward, its waters swirling in a dance of chaotic beauty. A golden blaze shines in the center, glowing brighter as it rises to the surface.

We look on intently, but no one takes in the spectacle with

more awe than Medusa. Rising from the waters, the glow fades, and a collective gasp echoes around us. Medusa is breathlessly silent as she looks into the rich brown eyes of her mate.

Athena's emergence from the vortex is both majestic and serene, the waters of the ocean obeying her slightest gesture as they calm around her. Her long black hair billows with the wind as her white stola dances upon the surface of the water. Her eyes are locked on Medusa as she takes her first step forward.

The movement breaks Medusa from her trance, and she smiles. "My baby always makes an entrance." With sure strides, Medusa meets Athena at the shoreline.

The mates, separated by eons of torment, then separated by death, are reunited. Medusa lifts Athena by her waist, and the lovers release their joy as they spin. Returning her feet to the ground, Medusa pulls Athena to her. One arm holds her waist tightly, the other is threaded through her hair. Athena holds both sides of Medusa's face as they share a passionate kiss.

The pain of their absence melts with each caress of their lips. Athena has been reincarnated by the collective will and power of the realms and carries the mantle of the Water Titan. As I lean my head against Hermes' shoulder, watching these powerful transformations, I feel a surge of hope and wonder.

Athena, reborn with purpose and power, and Medusa, embracing her role with the steadfastness of the earth itself, symbolize a new beginning for all of us.

The realms have deemed them worthy to bear the responsibility of Titan, and I know they will work together to repair the damage done to both realms. As the realms declare more worthy to carry the title of Titan, we will soon see a day when all the realms thrive again.

As the sea calms and the last of the comet's light fades from the sky, I take Hermes' hand in mine. Together, we turn towards the horizon, ready to explore the wonders of the realms, to witness the growth and beauty that will flourish under this new future.

It is with bittersweet farewells that we leave Gaea, the realm where my greatest battle was a hard-won victory but also the realm where I found family and loyalty. Where I found myself and my purpose.

As we step into a portal, I have no idea what waits for us, but this I know for certain: I will weather all storms, find the strength to overcome, and above all, I will not just survive, I will live.

The End

EPILOGUE

"**Hey, baby, just slow down. Take a deep breath.**" Hermes grabs my shoulders and inhales deeply, then slowly releases it. I follow him, doing the same as I try to calm my nerves.

"I just don't want to be late." I shake my hands, trying to make my fingers stop tingling.

He takes my hands and kisses them. "You look amazing, and we'll be right on time. Okay?"

I nod, fixing my hair over my shoulder as he opens his portal, and we walk hand in hand to the Void. The second the portal closes, Honey's arms are wrapped around my waist.

"I knew you would come," she exclaims.

"I wouldn't miss this for all the realms." I squeeze her back as Callie chuckles.

"She has been bouncing all over the place since the thread lit up." Callie wraps her arms around Pat as he and Achilles arrive, giving Hermes a nod.

"Hey there, kiddo." Apollo gives me a big hug.

"Why do you always say hi to her first? I'm your son," Hermes teases.

"She's sweeter than you are," Ares answers for his mate, giving me a peck on the cheek. "Let's get this party started. What do you say, little one?" he asks Honey.

"I'll race you!" Teddy says with a giggle, already turning around and dashing to the Wellspring.

The entire Void claims Honey as their own, and it's no surprise Ares and Apollo do as well. There have still been no new souls born since Honey, but I have hope that one day we'll see the arrival of fresh souls. There were so many lost to the cosmos during the Titans' war, and balance will one day be restored.

But until then, today is a day for celebration. The Wellspring is thrumming with a beautiful golden light, the color of warm honey, and our favorite little soul is thrumming along with it.

Honey's next life is ready, and we're all gathered around to send her off. She looks at the glowing thread and takes my hand, giving me a nervous squeeze.

"Hey," I kneel next to her with a soft smile. "There is nothing to be nervous about. Do you want me to tell you about your life?"

She thinks for a moment, then shakes her head no. "I want to be surprised."

"Okay, are you ready?"

With a brave smile, she nods and faces her new life, giving me one more look.

"I'll be here, waiting for you among the stars."

And with that, the brave little soul who sacrificed her first life for me gets a shot at a new one. As she grabs hold of the thread and the waters of the Void send her on her journey, we all look to the dark sky above, finding the new gold-shim-mering star that brightens the Void sky.

Hermes puts his hand on my shoulder, and I cover his with mine. "Will she have a good life?" he asks.

With a nod and a smile, I look at him with watery eyes. "She will. She'll have a wonderful, perfect life."

Acknowledgements

Well... I did it. I finished the story that has lived in my mind for over a decade.

Over ten years ago, I woke up from a bizarre dream and thought, "That would be a really cool ending to a book." It was such an unusual dream for me because I never remember them. If I hold on to any details of a dream, they slip away from me like a scarf caught in the wind. Within an hour of waking up, it's totally gone.

But not this time. This time, it was different. I remembered it so vividly, it was like a movie playing in my imagination for days. As I kept thinking it over, I wanted to know what the beginning of the story was. What was the catalyst that led to this epic scene that was playing out in my mind?

The only thing I could do was go back to the beginning of the story... so eventually, I could get to that epic ending. And it's finally here.

This story came together with elements of my past, set to the tune of ancient Greece. It's a story of healing from repressed trauma and the multitude of emotions that arise as you uncover the layers of pain you have survived.

At some point in my past, I sealed myself off to those

emotions. I denied myself permission to feel them because my survival depended on it. As I wrote this series, I gave myself permission to feel the abundance of emotions along with Rhea.

As the pages of my books filled with my story, there were only two words that gave me pause. Two little words that I had to process before I typed them: The end.

It's been a long road getting here. A journey I never thought I would take, and now that the story is done, I couldn't bring myself to type those two little words.

It felt so finite. As if the moment my fingers ran over the keyboard, this world would cease to exist. The characters would float away on the wind like the details of my dreams, and I wasn't ready to say goodbye to them yet.

But I realized, this world, these characters, and this adventure will live eternally within my heart, forever a piece of me. They will thrive within the pages of these books, always ready for new readers to take them on an amazing journey. And just as ready to welcome you back any time you need them.

I am a storyteller. I have a multitude of worlds, brimming with formidable characters, and overflowing with excitement. While this story has come to its conclusion, for me... this is not the end.

This... is just the beginning.

Thank you so much for reading, and I hope something within this story entertained you and made you laugh. Perhaps you shed a tear or called out in frustration, but ultimately, I hope that when you close this cover, it made you smile. And just know that Rhea and Hermes, Achilles, Patroclus, and Calypso... yes... even Atlas... will always be here waiting for you.

Until our next adventure,

Rebekah Sinclair
Writes

To stay informed on my upcoming releases, book signing events, and more, visit my website and sign up for my newsletter.

www.rebekahsinclairwrites.com

If you'd like to chat with other readers, join the Rebekah Sinclair Writes discord!

When a traitor queen faces trial on the misting isle of Avalon, the dark fae find themselves in need of a new ruler.

Look for more adventures with Orion, the Morrigan and Hypnos in the next dark fantasy series from Rebekah Sinclair.

RETURN TO AVALON

2025